The Poe Letters

JOHN MAY

John May is also the author of *Poe & Fanny*
Algonquin Books of Chapel Hill, 2004.

The Poe Letters

:: :: ::

A Novel

JOHN MAY

The Poe Letters

Bonaventure Books
ISBN 978–0692311561

Cover art by Kimber Lynn
Cover photographs, clockwise surrounding Poe from upper left:
Stella Lewis, Sarah Helen Whitman, Edward E. Gayle, Elmira
Shelton, Jane Locke, Nancy Richmond, Sarah Helen Whitman
engaged in a séance, Susan Talley Weiss, Marie Louise Shew,
and Kate, Grace, and Sarah (Burkhead) Gayle.

For Alice Murdoch Brown May

Introduction

::

I dislike introductions. I confess that I seldom read them and survive guilt-free. Just as fervently, I dislike writers prefacing a reading of their work with the phrase: *"What you need to know is . . ."* Something arcane in the word "need" puts me off. I don't like to be told what to think; I prefer to get to the story and form my own opinion. Yet here I am writing an introduction, suggesting that there is something I *wish* you to know in advance. Forgive me. I do it solely for the purpose of illuminating what follows—what might otherwise appear a hodgepodge—and to describe the means by which the material came into my hands. I beg your indulgence.

By way of a personal introduction, I need say only that I am a middle-aged professor of American literature with a concentration in poetry and—by dint of our university's heritage—a more particular concentration in the female American poets of the nineteenth century. I teach at a public university wherein I am considered something of a Poe scholar. This said, I hasten to add that I pale beside the likes of a host of more renowned Poe scholars, living and dead. What can I say? I like Poe; I'm little more than a fan. At any rate, my familiarity with the man was sufficient to qualify me a few years ago to be chosen by my dean and by our special collections librarian to be the recipient of a gift to our university of a collection of letters and papers. That the special collections librarian herself did not elect to make the effort, speaks to the lack of regard with which the gift was anticipated. Suffice it to say, an elderly alumna who had graduated nearly eighty years earlier when our university was exclusively female was cleaning out her attic. That, at any rate, was the perception. I was told only that the papers had something to do with Poe and was dispatched to a small town in the extreme southeastern corner of our state, a three-hour drive from campus. Furthermore, I was instructed to accept the gift with enthusiasm befitting the possibility of a sizable gift of cash that might follow at the woman's death. For a public university in these times of budget cuts, funds are in short supply; whereas—far more often than not—old papers are a storage problem. Such gifts are often accepted with the proviso that the university reserves the right to sell, trade, or discard anything it deems of little value to its core collections.

I wormed my way to Whiteville, North Carolina, on a cloudless July morning when the thermometer was expected to reach triple digits. I say "wormed" because Whiteville is not accessible by any artery approaching a super highway. A town of five thousand, it is located in what is called Carolina Bay country. Somewhat inland—thirty miles from the coast—its population has remained more or less the same for over fifty years. With a too-heavy reliance on textiles and tobacco, job opportunities have declined for many years running; therefore, Whiteville's best and brightest have long migrated away, a trend that will doubtless continue.

Carolina bays are boggy depressions—in some cases, shallow lakes—oval in shape with a southeast/northwest orientation that scientists believe were formed by a prehistoric meteor shower, though there is some disagreement on this point which, in the interest of brevity, I will omit. Whiteville proper sits on a rise, more or less surrounded by swamp. The soil is wet and sandy, suitable for agriculture if not too low, and the climate is semitropical. Succulents do well; in fact, vegetation is riotous, as is, so I learned, mildew and rot.

My appointment was with Miss Kate Gayle, a tiny woman in her mid-nineties, never married, a former elementary schoolteacher, born in the very house in which she still lived at 600 Pinkney Street, now 1102 Pinckney Street. I mention this, because the details of how this misspelling occurred consumed the first twenty minutes of our conversation, a subject of apparent distress to Miss Kate. (I wondered if she had worried that I would fail to find the house due to the error.) Pinkney, it seemed, was still very much dead and buried in the local cemetery, as Kate would prove to me after lunch, the correct spelling of his name apparent on the gravestone to anyone with a primary school education with the exception of certain careless members of the town bureaucracy who had added the "c" when new green street signs were erected some years earlier.

Kate was no more than five feet tall and could not have weighed ninety pounds, but, despite this and her advanced age, she was quite spry. She wore glasses much too large for her delicate little face, but I thought her wispy gray hair was rather fashionably cut. We began with lunch in the dining room—breast of chicken, squash, freshly picked butter peas, and a salad of tomatoes and cucumbers served by a young African American girl who was overly solicitous to Miss Kate and who seemed so amused by her eccentricities that I judged she'd been engaged for the occasion of my visit. Due to Kate's poor eyesight and the light of the chandelier being somewhat dim, the maid was instructed to drag a floor lamp from one corner of the room to the head of the table where Kate sat, and then to remove the shade. Once this was done and for reasons I could not fathom, Kate had the maid draw the curtains, shutting out daylight, which seemed much brighter than the light cast by the dusty, naked, sixty-watt bulb of the floor lamp. Amid this eerie, ocher light, I lunched while Kate forked butter peas around her plate and grilled me on my qualifications for receiving the gift of letters and papers that constituted her bequest. I found myself defending my qualifications, employing all the rigor with which I had defended my dissertation fifteen years earlier. Kate was nothing if not an exacting schoolmarm.

After lunch I was instructed to bring my suitcase up to the front guest room, this despite my protestations of putting her out. In truth I would have been happier at the Holiday Inn, but Kate would not be denied. I resigned myself to a foregone happy-hour and an early-to-bed, wondering as I did what pay-back might be extracted from the dean and special collections librarian for having sent me on this errand.

We then drove out into the country, north of town, to the Whiteville cemetery, which was old and beautiful and shaded by tall pines. Though it was stifling hot—not a breath of a breeze—the serenity of the place made me think I could be quite happy buried there. Following Kate's instruction, I pulled the car off the pavement, and we got out to follow a preplanned tour of grave sites that included Kate's sister, Sarah, her mother, Pinkney (in order to prove the irksome misspelling), and assorted relatives and local notables.

We then returned to 600 Pinkney Street, a house built in 1888 and purchased by her father in 1896, to which he added a second story and where Kate was born. I half expected to be shown the collection of letters and papers that evening, but by then I'd come to accept that Kate had a plan from which she would not stray, and that all would be revealed in time. Truthfully, I was intrigued, but more for the sake of my growing fascination with this woman and her family than for any hope of the collection being noteworthy. I was—I admit—having fun.

Supper had been planned for the porch, but Kate changed her mind due to the heat and the late afternoon sun beating down on that corner of the porch where her outdoor table was situated. With kind apologies, she instructed the maid to move place settings to the dining room, which was cooled by a window air-conditioning unit, then she led me into the parlor. I sat on a tufted, Victorian settee in the front bay window, as Kate brought out a stack of photograph albums. I correctly suspected that her plan for the evening was to put faces to the graves we'd visited. She sat down beside me, and for nearly an hour, I was introduced to everyone. It was as if, by virtue of the gift about to be entrusted to me, I should meet with the approval of generations of Gayles.

The maid came to the parlor door to announce supper. Kate stood, straightened, and, looking at the maid, gave some rather lengthy instruction to which I paid no heed. Instead, I became lost in my own thoughts, staring into space, I suppose, feeling a bit disgusted with myself for my petty preconceptions. When I looked up, Kate was staring at me with a strained look on her face. What had she inferred from my expression? I smiled, followed her into the dining room, and tried, during supper, to cover over what had happened by being excessively chatty, but I perceived a change in Kate's manner. Her earlier enthusiasm had disappeared. I tried to engage her, but the only concern to which she admitted was that the roast was overdone and that she should have supervised the cooking rather than go on about the past. I protested, but to no avail. Kate was hurt. My protestations fell flat. She put the best face on dessert and coffee and excused herself to bed.

I went out on the porch for a smoke and cursed myself and the dean and special collections librarian and the whole university system for our collective disrespect. I resolved that the following day I would be enthusiastic and gushing in my response to whatever Kate presented.

I came down for breakfast at half past seven and found Kate cutting up fruit in the kitchen. My offer to help was refused. Instead she pointed to a pot of coffee and suggested I pour myself a cup and take it onto the porch until breakfast was ready. When called twenty minutes later, I entered the dining room to find the plates served, Kate in her chair, and in the middle of the table, a faded blue-and-white gingham pillowcase filled with something—I guessed the letters. Kate passed me a basket of hot biscuits and suggested I help myself to butter and preserves. I smiled. "What's in the pillowcase, Miss Kate?"

"Old letters," she said. "I make the preserves myself. I want you to try them. There are three varieties. Though I never had a family, I learned to cook and have always been considered a fine one."

I knew better than to hurry the process, but as soon as the breakfast dishes were carried to the kitchen and the table cleared and wiped clean, Kate picked up one end of the pillowcase and let the letters spill out. It seemed there were hundreds of them tied in bundles of varying sizes with faded red grosgrain ribbon. Kate did a bit of sorting, placing the bundles side-by-side, then handed me one of the larger ones and suggested I untie the ribbon and examine the letter on top. It was addressed to Cadet Captain Edward E. Gayle at the United States Military Academy, West Point, New York, and postdated March 1876. On the back of the envelope, above a broken red wax seal was a name and return address in ink gone brown with age and written in the finest, tiniest handwriting I'd ever seen. I studied it, thinking as I did that a magnifying glass might come in handy, but just as that thought entered my mind, the name on the envelop registered as did also the city, Providence, Rhode Island. I shot Kate a glance.

"Sarah Helen Whitman!"

Perceiving my recognition, Kate could not contain a smile that failed to conceal her glee—this, despite all her apparent resolve to remain calm and nonchalant.

"Helen Whitman was . . ." I said, hesitating, almost disbelieving what I was seeing—"She was a very important poet, and not only that, she was at one time engaged to Edgar Allan Poe. They would have married had she not called it off the day before the wedding."

"Yes, I know that," Kate said, matter-of-factly.

"Miss Kate!"

I turned back to the letters. In all there must have been twenty from Helen Whitman, all addressed to Edward Gayle. "What's the connection? I don't understand." In my head I did the math—Poe died in 1849; I knew that. Helen Whitman had been older than he. How long after that could she have lived?

"It's a long story," Kate said, "but it's all there. You'll see. My father, Edward Edgerly Gayle graduated from West Point in 1876. He was only four-feet-eight-inches tall—the shortest man *ever* to attend the academy. What's more, he taught there during the 1890s—artillery, literature, and wrestling. He was decorated for service in the Indian Wars *and* the Spanish American War. He retired from the army in 1909 and died in 1918 while on a trip to Washington on a matter relating to his pension. He is buried in Arlington National Cemetery. Due to the fact that there was a war on, it proved easier for us girls to travel to Washington for his funeral than for his remains to return home. All the letters you see were addressed to him."

Kate told me this with great pride. She had the upper hand now. Perhaps she had concluded from my expression the night before that I had been bored or disrespectful, but now the tables were turned. She had my undivided attention and wished to savor it.

"The letters concern Poe," she continued, "—all of them. All that you see. All written by women who personally knew him. The only exceptions are those written by my mother, but as you will learn, she knew as much about Poe as anyone."

I listened as Kate explained her father's lifelong fascination with Poe, how he might have, at one time, planned to spend his retirement years writing a biography of Poe, but the work had never materialized for reasons she could only guess. She thought her mother's death might have had something to do with it. Not only were there letters, she explained, there were also journals and narratives, many of them, all related to Poe. She rose, went to the sideboard and returned with a stack of papers and composition books. She took the chair beside me, and we leafed through the material, including photographs of her father at various stages of his military career. He was quite handsome, stern in appearance, clean-shaven in his cadet pictures, though he wore a mustache in later years. There were photographs taken out west, in Havana, the Philippines, at West Point.

Then Kate jumped ahead, explaining that in later years she and her two sisters—elderly now—lunched together every Wednesday at the Acme Drug Store on the courthouse square in downtown Whiteville. The sisters were often joined by children, grandchildren, and even great grandchildren for a sandwich, French fries, and an orangeade. It became such a time-honored tradition that Mr. Andrews who owned Acme Drugs reserved a large round table near the back of the store just for them. On rare occasions the Gayle sisters talked about their father, and on even rarer occasions, about his hobby—his correspondence—the letters tied and stored in neat bundles in the blue-and-white gingham pillowcase in one of the colonel's trunks stored in the attic of the house Kate had inherited on Pinkney Street. By way of explanation, they described to their progeny the colonel's love of detective stories and his long idle hours while stationed on the frontier or in Cuba or the Philippines with time on his hands when his letters were the thing that brought him greatest joy. They wondered aloud about how one thing had led to another, how his first correspondent had introduced another Poe acquaintance who introduced another and another until at one point their father was corresponding with ten or more at the same time, and how the exchange of letters had often forged close friendships, though face-to-face contact was rare and in most cases never occurred at all. Curiously, all his correspondents were women, and they had died off, one-by-one—the last just a year before the colonel's own death.

The sisters opined that their father's intention might have been to spend his retirement years writing a book, but for some reason he had never done so. Kate's sister, Grace, was of the opinion that other biographers had "stolen a march on him" in military parlance—George Woodberry, for example, had published an exhaustive, two-volume biography of Poe just a few years before their father retired—but Kate didn't hold with this opinion. Her other sister, Sarah, who had been head librarian of the Whiteville Public Library for almost as many years as Kate taught public school would often remark that the letters should be donated to a university library, maybe Chapel Hill, but Sarah was always careful in saying this, because the letters now rightly belonged to Kate along with the rest of Colonel Gayle's things, and Sarah, being an older sister, was reluctant to tell Kate what to do. After all, though no one used the phrase, Kate was an "old maid school-teacher" with nothing but a big house and small pension while Sarah and Grace had respectable husbands with good practices.

Their father's things had not been touched in years, though earlier Kate had given some to her nephews when they were young—uniforms, medals, swords, and souvenirs from all the places Colonel Gayle had been. And he had been so short that his uniforms fit eight- and nine-year-olds perfectly. It was a shame not to let them play with them, but now it seemed like all those things had disappeared, and Kate had been determined to save the rest. What for, she didn't rightly know. She had been certain there was treasure there, though she had once seen derision on the face of one of Grace's grown sons when the subject of the letters came up at a Sunday family gathering in the late 1950s. Kate never forgot that, and for a while resigned herself to the fact that it was partially true, that the letters were nothing special, just old letters. And thus they remained, nearly forgotten, right where they had been since her father died—sorted and tied with ribbon, hidden away for nearly a century now in a camphor-wood chest that the colonel had brought back from the Philippines—those bundles of letters that the Gayle sisters always referred to as "The Poe Letters."

Once in a while a gift comes—unexpected—from someone unexpected, even someone previously unknown. In the manner just described, I became the recipient of a unique and remarkable gift that contains a precious piece of information—a tidbit charged with the power to alter long-held perceptions. For most people, such a thing would be of little import, but for a man whose life has been the subject of more scrutiny than any American writer ever, it is precious beyond measure.

The Gayle bequest is hereafter presented in three forms. First are letters, those I deemed most informative and those significant in revealing how Edward Gayle went about collecting the material. Also included are letters that shed light on his motivation, the process he followed, and perhaps also and most important, the reason he abandoned the project. It must be understood that the only letters extant are those he received. Only one of the many letters he wrote to his Poe correspondents survives. In all cases the letters are numbered just as they were by Colonel Gayle.

Second, there are journal entries, identified as such, included because they reveal the colonel's inner thoughts regarding the information gathered. Sadly, these are few in number. Last—and the bulk of what follows—are short individual narratives written by Colonel Gayle. His method was to rearrange information into a chronological telling of each correspondent's story. The journals and narratives were written in composition books and on loose pages, on every kind of paper imaginable, from ruled notepaper to the backs of muster rolls, issues of equipment, and military orders. They contain innumerable inserts, additions, and glosses that wander off in every direction and waste no scrap of writing space.

Thus informed, I leave you to the story and to your own opinion.

John May
July 2004

March 1865

Late on a sunny, blustery Thursday afternoon a party of three mounted cavalry gallops east along a muddy, rutted, post road. Nearing a cross-roads two miles north of the village of Whiteville, North Carolina, and in view of a two-story frame farmhouse, the soldiers slow their horses to a walk and approach the front stoop. Though faded and worn and splattered with mud, the men's uniforms are unmistakably Union blue, and the lead rider, a captain, wears the gold-braided insignia of his rank on his shoulders. A sword rattles against his side; a pistol is strapped to his belt, its dark-stained wooden butt protruding from the holster. His eyes are ocean-blue, his long hair, yellow and fine as corn silk.

As the soldiers approach, twenty-eight-year-old Mary Jane Gayle steps from the house onto the porch. She wears a calico dress of a faded green pattern, unbuttoned at the neck, and pulled tight at her waist by a sash. Her sleeves are rolled to above her elbows, and her dark brown hair is pulled back and pinned, exposing her ears and neck. Beside her stands her son, Edward, who turned eleven the week before and is as tall as she, or, more accurately, as short. And clinging to Mary Jane's skirts is her three-year-old daughter, Dixie. The Gayle farm is too poor to be called a plantation, but a single Negro slave, plow harness in one hand, appears at a corner of the house just as the soldiers reign in their horses. The captain smiles, swaggers in his saddle, removes his hat, and runs his fingers through blond hair, sweeping it from his face. He could not be more than twenty. "Pardon, ma'am," he says, his voice cheerful as a choirboy, "would you be so kind as to let us water our horses?"

"If you're aiming to burn us out, you can go to the devil." Mary Jane says, her words straight as her gaze, defiance showing on her lips, but there is fear in her brown eyes. Her hands wring tight the dishcloth she's just dampened to cover a loaf of salt-rising bread. She hadn't expected Union soldiers, having been assured that the army of William Tecumseh Sherman would pass far to the west—no closer than Laurinburg, she'd been told by those who reckoned the state capital in Raleigh was Sherman's destination. But here they are, and maybe Sherman's dreaded bummers are close at hand, aiming to steal anything of value then burn the house. She decides their goal must be Wilmington instead of Raleigh. Whiteville's in for it, she thinks, the same devastation that trailed through Georgia and South Carolina—a forty-mile-wide swath of terror—looted bare and burned to the ground. From her husband's letters describing the siege of Richmond, Mary Jane has learned something about war, though it has never touched these parts except for taking their men. With her hand, she shields her eyes from the late afternoon sun and searches the western horizon for black smoke rising over Chadbourn, six miles distant, but the evening sky is clear. She turns back to the captain, the cocksure rascal smug in his faded blues.

He smiles again, broader this time, showing white teeth like he's about to burst out laughing. Is he thinking she's a pretty little thing or is he thinking she's sure a lot of spitfire to be wrapped in so small a package? She can't be five feet tall, and he notices that her skirts don't quite hide her bare feet. And does the sight of bare toes make him wonder what a shame it is, those kids and that Negro, watching from the corner of the house? Might be fun, teasing her a bit; she might even come around, especially if she fears infantry is coming, and, of course, he won't let on otherwise.

But not today. The afternoon is getting on, and the captain has strict orders. "Won't be no fires lit," he says. "Not here. Uncle Billy's orders."

Mary Jane studies the captain, searching his features for the truth. Then she studies the faces of the other two. There she sees a disheartening resolve—wild stares like the most sinful kind of starving and a surliness that betrays their captain's put-on manners. Like it or not, she'll have to put her hope in him, and that thought seems to turn her stomach.

"If 'Uncle Billy' is who I think he is," she says, "he's the devil incarnate, and he can slither back down into that snake pit where he came from." Mary Jane watches her words hit the mark, but they fail to wipe the grin off the arrogant captain's face. Then she lets go her breath and turns to her son. "Lead 'em round to the trough, Eddy. I'll be watching," and she nudges him forward, her hand pressing the small of his back.

Eddy Gayle, unnerved by his mother's tone, steps off the stoop and heads around the side of the house. He too is barefooted, and his too-short dungarees are held up by suspenders over one of his father's white shirts. The soldiers follow, and the Negro stands motionless, his back flush against the clapboards, his expression impenetrable—the artifice of lifelong practice. At the trough the soldiers dismount, pull the reigns over their horses' heads, and lead them to drink, slaking their own thirst with cupped hands and filling their canteens. Eddy stands by, watching.

"What's down that road, boy?" the captain asks, nodding south and taking a reading on the sun's position.

Eddy hesitates, his breath shallow, trying to imagine what it must look like, a whole town up in flames. He won't be the one to say what's down that road.

The captain pulls a map from his saddlebags and studies it. "Whiteville. Right? 'Bout a mile or two?" Eddy says nothing. "That means Clarkton's that-a-way; right Eddy?" The captain points north then turns back to the boy. Why did he use Eddy's given name? That's just like a scheming Yankee. Eddy clenches his teeth, determined to say nothing. He's no rat. The captain chuckles. "You ain't telling, are you?"

"I smell bread," one of the other soldiers says, a corporal. "Hot bread and butter sure would be a nice change, wouldn't it, Jim? And a pitcher of milk? There's a milk cow in the barnyard and chickens in the coop. Ain't that just a homely sight? When's the last time you had fried chicken and fresh baked bread? We could camp right here tonight. I'd kill for a home-cooked meal."

The captain seems to consider the idea, maybe thinking of supper in the dining room with Eddy's mama, and he wonders what her name might be. He has a bottle of fine brandy in his saddlebags. He could promise to guard the house, though no Yankee bummers are coming to require protection. Then he shakes the idea from his head—she'll never come around, and he doesn't need to wonder why his army is so hated by all these husbandless women. He pulls his horse's head from the trough and lifts his boot to the stirrup. "There's daylight left. We better get a move on."

The soldiers mount up and turn to go, but the captain pulls his horse to the side and turns back toward Eddy. "Tell you what, boy; I'll make you a deal. I'll tell you something you want to know if you tell me something I want to know. I'll even go first. Fair enough?"

Eddy stares, noncommittal.

"Uncle Billy's army ain't coming this way. Understand? I'm the last bluecoat you're going to see for the rest of this war. You tell that to your mama and anybody else you want to tell it to. In return, I need to know if I'm right about Whiteville being down that road. I ain't aiming to go to Whiteville; I ain't aiming to hurt anybody. Just riding through; that's all. Now tell me straight, Eddy. I trust you; you kept your mouth shut like a good soldier. It's a fair trade. How 'bout it?" The captain turns to make sure the others are out of earshot, then he adds, "Your mama's lucky I'm the bluecoat she said those things to. Anybody else would've made her life a living hell."

Eddy's mind works as he stares at this Yankee captain. What if they'd camped the night? His mama's scared. No telling what she might do. She's got a loaded pistol hanging on a nail, hidden up inside the chifforobe in her bedroom, and she knows how to use it too. No doubt she went to get it as soon as he stepped off the porch. She might just kill one of them and get herself killed or something worse. Eddy can't take his eyes off the captain's horse. He's never seen a horse so magnificent as the captain's mount with its fine lines, the white blaze down its nose and four white socks, well-fed and curried by the looks of him, a horse for a greater man than this captain. Probably stole it off some Georgia plantation. But for some reason the captain doesn't seem like the kind of man who would take advantage of a woman, like so many reports of Sherman's march had told. And there's the gilt-edged sword and soiled, fringe-trimmed white sash, the royal blue, battle-worn uniform with gold braid and brass buttons—he's fine, this swaggering captain, but also charitable it seems. Or is that just his deviousness, sugar-coated Yankee charm thin as piecrust? Eddy can't help but admire him, though, envy him even, and just then it *does* seem like a fair trade. Folks in Whiteville might even be grateful, so he nods his head but says nothing.

The captain smiles again and turns in his saddle to face the boy squarely. "You can also tell that pretty mama of yours that this war's 'bout over. Her Johnny'll be coming home soon if he's still alive; home in time to plant, I'd bet. When'd you last hear from him?"

"About a month ago," Eddy blurts, following a protective instinct to signal to the captain that there *was* a man of the house, a man still very much alive.

"With a wife like her, he must be one brave Johnny. What's her name, Eddy?"

"That ain't none of your business."

The captain chuckles again, looks toward the back porch as if hoping to see Mary Jane one more time, then he squares in the saddle, spurs his horse, and canters out of the yard.

HELEN WHITMAN

::

(ITEM 1: *Sarah Helen Whitman to Edward Edgerly Gayle*)

...

March 2, 1876
Benefit Street
Providence, Rhode Island

Dear Cadet Captain Gayle,

If you have read his complete works, you should be aware that Edgar Poe wrote two poems entitled "To Helen." The first, addressed to Helen of Troy, was inspired by the death of his boyhood friend's mother, Helen Stanard [*sic*: Jane Stith Stanard, d. April 28, 1824] to whom he was exceedingly devoted. Written while still in his passionate youth, it is, I think, one of his most perfect compositions. Long ago I committed it to memory and each time I resort to those lines, my spirit is transported in the most magical way as if to an ethereal rhapsody of wonder, and I am thereby able to rise above the mundane cares that infest daily life. It is the soul of genius that such a transfiguration can be effected in a mere fifteen lines. As you correctly deduced, Edgar's second "To Helen" was addressed to me, as are other of his poems. They remain my greatest treasures.

As for Dr. Griswold's memoir of EAP [Rufus Wilmot Griswold, 1815–1857], it is the inky essence of injustice. Never in the history of mankind did outrage so unfairly debase a human life. The error of which you write regarding Griswold's charge that EAP was dismissed dishonorably from West Point is well-known to me. I am now and have been for some years in correspondence with a man from England, John Henry Ingram, who is preparing a new biography of EAP that will hopefully repair the damage Griswold wrought. Another biography by an American, William F. Gill, is due later this year, but, though its tone will be sympathetic, I fear for its quality and accuracy and regret that my name will be associated with it. Yet another memoir by a man unknown to me, a Mr. Didier of Baltimore, is, so I understand, also in press or about to be. That the life of EAP is now the subject of such widespread interest is not only a testament to his literary accomplishments, but also to the long-held belief among his friends that justice has not been served as regards his character. My fear is that an accurate account has been too long in coming—nearly thirty years.

Some years ago I, myself, tried to correct the matter with the little volume that is enclosed and that I must insist that you return when finished. Alas, I am a poet, not an historian. My small effort proved to have little effect in rectifying Griswold's crime, and crime it was.

Whenever presented, as in this case, with questions regarding Griswold's memoir, it has inevitably been my response to refute at once the most irresponsible and heinous of his accusations against EAP, lest they remain in the mind of the reader who, for reasons of propriety, refrains from questioning the matter. In referring to EAP's relationship with his foster father's second wife, Louisa Allan [Louisa Gabriella Patterson Allan, 1800?–1881], Griswold states that they quarreled, then he goes on to say that "a different story, scarcely suitable for repetition here, was told by the friends of the other party" (i.e., Louisa Allan). Surely you read it; I pray you read it with skepticism. Referring to this "different story" in a footnote, he claims that it "throws a dark shade upon the quarrel and a very ugly light upon Poe's character . . . that sins heteroclital and such as want name or precedent . . . &c."

Would that these words were not seared in memory. Their implication is unmistakable: a charge that EAP was guilty of sins against nature with his foster father's new young wife. Forgive my bluntness, Captain Gayle, but the charge is monstrous and absent of foundation, a fiction of Griswold's sordid imagination and evidence of his envy for a man who possessed genius the like of which Griswold could only lust. Of this there is proof, as you shall see when Ingram's biography is published. Forgive me if I appear to belabor the point, but you impress me as sincere in your interest and appreciation of EAP, and I only wish for your impressions to be free of the cloud of an unreliable and vicious defamation.

As for your evidence relating to EAP's departure from West Point, I am certain that Mr. Ingram will appreciate any new intelligence on the matter, though he has, as I have said, some better knowledge of that event. Please furnish me, therefore, with any details in your possession, and I will forward them immediately.

Yours most sincerely,
Sarah Helen Whitman

:: THE HOUSE AT 76 BENEFIT STREET IS PAINTED BARN RED, a color that appears to Helen Whitman when she thinks of the number seven. The house is large, three stories, shaded by elms that line the street in this, an old and still fashionable section of Providence. The shutters, trim, and narrow porch on the south side of the house are a darker reddish-brown. In back the land slopes away, running downhill, accommodating a root cellar and basement beneath the house with a door to the garden, which in warmer months is filled with flowers— mignonette, heliotrope, tea roses. Beyond the garden, at the bottom of the lot, is a little-used outbuilding overgrown with ivy and sumac. Inside is a stall and wood crib smelling damp and earthy. No horse is stabled here.

The main house has a small front parlor, cluttered with ponderous, dark-stained furniture, including a maroon tufted-velvet settee that stands on four claw-footed feet against the front window. Over the mantle, facing the settee, hangs an oval portrait of Helen painted eight years earlier by a local artist, a man of modest skill and a close friend of the family. In the portrait Helen wears a white dress, cut low and off her shoulders, and covering her head is a white organdy veil like a wedding veil. Though her eyes are youthful and intense, the tempersome set of her mouth is anything but that of a bride. In fact, Helen was sixty-six when the portrait was painted, and the artist's flattering attempt to make her appear thirty years younger was a failure bordering on farce. She would like to replace it with something else—a mirror, a landscape, anything—but she worries that its removal would hurt her artist friend's feelings.

Sitting at her desk, Helen reads over her letter to Cadet Captain Gayle, curious to know if her response is sufficiently courteous without sounding enthusiastic. She doubts that there is much more with regard to the West Point matter than is already known, and, after all, is it really important? She has become so weary of correspondence relating to Edgar Allan Poe that she resists encouraging yet another self-appointed Poe defender, eager to bond together in some sort of preservation society. Satisfied with the tone of her letter, she reaches for the sealing wax.

The shutters outside her window knock against the house with the force of a March wind. It is cold and overcast; she cannot go out and finds this irritating. She longs for spring. Or is the true source of her irritation John Ingram's last troublesome letter of which Cadet Captain Gayle has unwittingly reminded her? She has been so put out with Ingram that she has not responded, thinking for the past week that she might cease all correspondence on the subject of Poe. She picks up the little bell that sits on her desk and shakes it furiously, ringing for Charlotte. (Oh, don't take it out on her!)

"Mum?" Charlotte asks, calling from the hall where she has been on her knees washing the Persian rug where the cat, Cato, spit up earlier.

"More coals, Charlotte," Helen says without turning to face her. "I'm freezing to death." And with that she drops a dollop of red wax onto the envelope and imprints it with her seal. Where is the book, she wonders, wondering also why she bothers even answering this soldier's letter? There are no truths to tell. Truth is mere phantasm. Or is this the weary perspective of a seventy-three-year-old woman who should have been dead years ago and cannot get warm to save her life. Charlotte finishes adding coals to the fire. Helen hears her brushing the black dust from her fingertips and senses her curtsying before leaving the room. Helen decides she must write Ingram; it may be that corresponding with him is the very thing that is keeping her alive. But if this is the case, would it not be all the more reason to stop? There are times she aches for the grave, ready to start over and live a new life, and if that is not what happens, so be it. She would not have had doubts two years earlier, so certain had she always been of a life that follows, not to be confused with an afterlife—that superstitious myth. Come ahead, she thinks. Let her feel the final, fatal jolt in her chest, fall from her chair, and expire before the fire. At least she'll go feeling the warmth of fresh coals.

She can hear Charlotte scrubbing again. Cato refuses to throw up anywhere else. It must be a Persian preference. Helen no longer brags that Cato's name was in part inspired by Edgar's tabby, Catterina, but then she no longer brags at all. Or did she brag in this letter to Cadet Captain Gayle? Mentioning the second "To Helen" might be construed as bragging, and now she regrets having done it. But he asked, did he not?

She could have said more: Sarah Helen Whitman nee Powell, born Providence, January 19, 1803 (six years to the day, incidentally, before Edgar was born in Boston), mother lamentably deceased, father best not mentioned, husband deceased though not lamentably, sister lamentably deranged, financially comfortable though, lamentably, not wealthy. "Six years to the day"—she returns to that notion suddenly. That means that she was precisely six years older than Edgar on the day he composed "To Helen" and on the day he proposed marriage to her and on the day their banns were published *and* on the day, two days before Christmas, 1848, that the whole thing was called off because Edgar broke his promise. True, Griswold's charge that the police were called to subdue him is a vicious lie, but little comfort that. Now, as Helen feels the bitterness of being the subject of gossip, she wonders why she has spent twenty-five years defending the man. Is it that her vanity refuses to admit that he was only after her money and that he never intended to keep his promise not to imbibe? That's it in a cockleshell. Men had called her beautiful; men had called her brilliant. But Edgar wanted the money. Now even vanity has betrayed her. She can no longer bear to view herself in a mirror, seeing only knots and wrinkles, particularly when her teeth are out, and, when they are in, they pinch her gums such that it is painful to chew. Gritting her teeth is a distant, almost pleasurable, memory.

I'll have a cup of tea, she decides. "Charlotte, I'll have a cup of tea." And when it comes, she will have Charlotte pull the doors to, so she can take out her teeth. She reaches for a clean sheet of stationary, reminding herself to find a copy of her book to post with her letter to the soldier. And where is Ingram's last letter? Ah. She opens the envelope. "*My dear Providence*," he begins. The first time he used that greeting, Helen thought it so clever. Now she sees it as manipulative, flattering deference for the purpose of milking her memory, and she stood still for it. Suddenly she imagines a man's fingers squeezing pendulous udders and finds the image erotic. She imagines being naked on hands and knees then shudders at the thought. Why does she have such thoughts at her age; they arise unwanted, still they come. Would Edgar's fingers have given pleasure? Did he even want to touch her? She takes a deep breath, exhales, and forces her attention to Ingram's letter. She reads, skimming down to the paragraph she found so irritating,

> Do you not think there must be some mistake about Annie Richmond having ever visited Fordham, as you have described? Who could have given you the information? Nothing one gets about Poe seems to be reliable. Sometimes I fancy that he never lived & sometimes, I think there must have been two Poes!

Helen begins,

> Yours of Feb. 14 just received. Something in its tone pains me more than I can express. Are there then two Ingrams as well as "two Poes"?

Why would Annie Richmond lie and why would Ingram doubt Helen after all this time? They have corresponded for over three years, and in that time she has entrusted almost every scintilla of information she possesses—almost all, but by no means all. There remain guarded morsels that will never see the light of day. Helen has furnished names and addresses; she must have written him a hundred letters; she has provided advice, corrected errors, pointed directions, and now he questions her accuracy. It is so like men to be mindless of the past and act impulsively. It's as if they suffer memory loss when quite convenient. Edgar was guilty of the same, and now Helen has tiptoed around that with Ingram. This recalls to mind an afternoon in December when the police were *not* called in to subdue Edgar as she has insisted Ingram emphasize.

Charlotte returns with tea, and Helen clears a space on the desk for the tray. "Pull the doors to," she says as Charlotte leaves, and when Helen hears them come together, she reaches in her mouth and extracts the dentures, wishing now that she had thought to ask Charlotte to bring a glass of water also. Instead she wraps them in the napkin, pours herself a cup of tea, and, pausing before her letter to Ingram, she returns her thoughts to that December morning.

Helen can still evoke the sense of betrayal she felt that afternoon twenty-eight years ago. Or was it betrayal? Somehow the word feels harsh, but "disappointment" feels too lenient. (Oh, well, suffice it to say, nearer the former than the latter.) Helen closes her eyes and summons the players—Edgar, her mother, and, of course, Pabodie—she'll never forgive Pabodie and was not in the least saddened when he killed himself six years ago. It had been William Pabodie who spread the rumors about the police. He denied it, but Helen is certain. Anyway, they were in this very room. Helen's sister, Anna, due to her indelicate condition, ruled the household, but on that afternoon she remained upstairs in her bedroom, confused and frightened. Pabodie and her mother argued with Edgar who refused to admit drinking a glass of wine with his breakfast that morning at the hotel. All morning Helen had suspected nothing, and later, when she and Edgar went for a carriage ride to the Athenaeum, a friend, a man of unimpeachable honesty, slipped Helen a note testifying to have witnessed the early-morning libation—the second time in as many days that Edgar had broken his promise. As they drove back home, Helen's heartbeat raced; the news might just do her in, she feared. For most of her adult life she has suffered a weak heart; her threshold for anything approaching conflict is almost nonexistent. Once at home, within the bosom of her family and the protection of Pabodie, she confronted Edgar. When he denied it, Helen lay down on the sofa and let the others take over. She soaked her handkerchief in ether, closed her eyes, and inhaled the fumes. The din, loud at first, faded with her consciousness, as if she were covering her ears with her hands. She became pleasantly lightheaded. Pabodie seemed positively gleeful at the prospect of the dissolution of her engagement to Edgar; for years he had been relentless in his pursuit of her, but she would never have married him. At one point during the evening she remembers Edgar kneeling beside her. "Say you love me, Helen," he asked. "I love you," she had said without hesitation, and the hubbub resumed. That's all she remembers. When she came to, the room was dark. Edgar was gone, and she never saw him again.

"Say you love me, Helen.—Say you love me, Helen.—Say you love me, Helen." Those were his last words. Now the memory is a sort of irresistible self-torture in which she wallows as if wiping dust from an urn of ashes on the mantle. Somehow it restores her equanimity and ennobles the work of the last twenty-five years.

She turns to face his photograph that sits on a small gilt easel in the corner cupboard. As if he were standing there, she addresses him, thinking the words without speaking them: You don't deserve this. (Though he stares at her from out of the photograph, she imagines him looking away.) Don't turn away like you did that afternoon, pretending to be hurt when in fact you were getting what you wanted. You brought it on yourself. You betrayed me; you know it, and see what I'm doing for you? I am turning the tide for you. I am putting Wilmot Griswold in his place. Don't think for a minute that what I'm doing is self-serving. And it's not because I love you; I no longer do, not in *that* way. Perhaps I did then; I don't recall. I do it for one reason and one reason only—Griswold. No one deserves what he did to you. He has been dead for nineteen years, nineteen years come August, but were he still alive, I would ask him why. I never did that. In the end I so despised him that I refused to even answer his letters. But in the years that have passed that question has come to the fore. Why did he do it to you, Edgar? What was between the two of you? It has become the supreme mystery of your life. I knew he loved Fanny too, but that doesn't explain it. It could not have been jealousy alone that caused him to treat you the way he did, after all, by then Fanny was dead and gone too. There is something more, and I want to know. I demand to know. Ingram has asked repeatedly. Gill is not clever enough to ask; his biography will be a sham. Those who knew you have always wondered, and now others too—this soldier who longs to respect you. For twenty-four years your friends have felt only indignation for what Griswold did, but that emotion has exhausted us. We are left with only curiosity. Would you tell me? I haven't held a séance in two years, but I haven't lost my powers. Lately that idea has been so much on my mind that I think I must act on it. I will summon you here to the very room where you betrayed me. It should not be difficult. You would not dare resist. Otherwise I will tell Ingram other things, things you do not want me telling him. You know what I'm talking about.

Helen turns back to her desk and looks out the window through the red leaves of the nandina that almost totally obstructs the view. With Edgar's image still in mind, she pictures Griswold—young, tall, receding hairline, deeply furrowed brow, and inquiring eyes, a Puritan minister's close-cropped beard, handsome mouth, exceptionally handsome full lips. It was well that he did not garnish his finest feature with a mustache. As fellow writers invariably did, she had liked him well enough at first when he had come to Providence that summer before she met Edgar, but probing the surface of the man revealed disturbing signs, so she had kept her distance. That he had nothing but disdain for women was evident. She saw him only twice more, and only briefly, once in the home of Alice Carey in New York City shortly before he died. On that occasion he had refused to even acknowledge her presence in the room, knowing by then how she despised him. And there was his strange marriage to the Charleston Jewess, unconsummated due to some mysterious deformity. Or was it her being fifteen years his senior? Though the woman allegedly possessed the unnamed deformity, it was Griswold doing the alleging while the defenseless woman was a thousand miles away. He had played the victim, and everyone bought it. His ceremonious treatment of women was patronizing; it masked his bias and discomfort in their presence, a sure and all-too-common sign of superiority. So infuriating. You, Edgar, were not like that at all; a lover of women, you. Too great a lover. Not surprising, therefore, that the two of you did not see eye-to-eye, so why make a pact with a man you disliked who disliked you? Why entrust your legacy to such a man—you consigned your gift to the world to a man who hated you? How could you be so irresponsible? And Fanny followed suit; both of you like lambs to the slaughter. He crucified you then saw to it she was forgotten, utterly forgotten. Why?

Helen had been told that when Griswold was found by Alice Carey, green as a ghost, stiff as a nail, smelling rotten, that his head was propped against the headboard of his bed, staring wide-eyed at the portraits of Edgar and Fanny hanging on the opposite wall, those two portraits Fanny's husband had painted. Griswold had been dead for three days. Why were the portraits there? Of all places. In his bedroom! Helen could understand Fanny's portrait hanging there, but why Edgar's? And what did Griswold see at the instant he died that appeared to frighten him? Edgar, the time has come to tell all.

(ITEM 2: *Whitman*)

...

March 18, 1876
76 Benefit Street
Providence, Rhode Island

Dearest Captain Gayle,

I must be candid, Captain. The first half of your letter of March 10th wearied me so that I could hardly bear to read it. That must seem to you the nadir of ingratitude in light of your kind words regarding my book about EAP. Your response is obviously heartfelt and generous, and I am grateful.

When at last I read that your classmates call you a "sawed-off jerk-water," I laughed out loud. I don't know the term, "jerkwater," and can't imagine its origin. Tell me please. I imagine it is used derisively; I know how schoolboys can be brutal to one another. I hope it is used with affection also. How did West Point admit you if you are so short? Do they not have rules about such things? I would think the uniforms alone would pose a problem; must yours be tailored?

You are a genuinely inquisitive, perceptive, and personable young man, and you must forgive my impatience as that of an old woman, foolish enough to become the self-appointed defender of Edgar Allan Poe. By so doing, I invited a veritable deluge of inquiry from those who decided I was the oracle to be consulted. I am weary of it; sometimes I rue the day that I published that little volume. Keep it; it is yours. I resign my commission; I wish to pass that torch to a new generation. You may bear it henceforth and thereby provide me a more restful dotage.

It is now I who jest, Captain (about my dotage that is). Something tells me that a sense of humor was not wasted on you. I do not laugh often, Captain Gayle, so, for that favor I am indebted to you. The last half of your letter cheered me more than I can say. What a feat of detective work you have done! Your conclusion regarding EAP's departure from West Point is entirely plausible, and I am convinced that at last we know the truth. If only Griswold had done the spadework you have done, but I think he wrote what he wanted the world to believe. You must be correct in saying that EAP took the only path open to him. Like other cadets, he could not survive on army pay alone and needed assistance from home which was not forthcoming. Hence the debts he incurred and could not pay. Since permission for withdrawal was withheld by an unloving foster father, he had no choice but to put himself in the way of dismissal. The academy understood and sympathized, hence their leniency regarding his separation. To be fair, it seems that as with other misfortunes of his youth, his foster father must bear a share of the responsibility.

All this explains a certain story of youthful high jinks that I have heard and that has always puzzled me—perhaps you have heard it—regarding a certain state of undress during inspection. If you have not, I cannot provide the details, as they would make me blush, and I do not know you well enough. Suffice it to say that EAP did what he had to do to extricate himself from the academy. I am having my secretary, Charlotte Ayers, copy that portion of your letter pertaining to the incident, and it will soon be on its way to England. You have done yeoman's service, and I congratulate and thank you.

As for the questions you pose in the first half of your letter regarding my book: the unnamed portrait referred to on page 20 was of Frances Osgood, a great poet and dear friend who spent much time here in Providence where her brother lived and where his family resides today. Fanny was a native of Boston and is buried in Mount Auburn Cemetery in Cambridge. She lived in NYC during the 1840s when EAP worked there, and for a time they were close friends. That is all you need to know regarding the two of them. Later, after EAP left NYC, Griswold befriended Fanny. At this time her husband, a portrait artist and foolish man, left her to seek his fortune in the gold mines of California. During that time Griswold's attentions came to mean much to Fanny, since she had recently also lost her youngest daughter, was raising two older daughters by herself, and had, sadly, come down with the consumption. In a word, she was vulnerable. I cannot deny that Griswold was very handsome and also charming, but his manner was purposeful and his attentions invariably carried a price. I believe he fell in love with Fanny and resented her great and undying regard for EAP. This may explain his animosity toward Edgar, hence his slanderous memoir, but I think not fully.

EAP was, indeed, the sensitive person I described in my book. Yes, doubtless, his work revealed his inner self, and he did indeed struggle with the awful mystery of death. This set him apart from the other poets of his age who wrote to be well-received, or to preach to "the rabble," or to make a comfortable living. In saying this I don't deny that EAP too wanted to make a living by his pen, but he abhorred moralizing and could never write for the marketplace; he could only write from his soul. This explains both his genius and his downfall.

I was saddened by your story—the loss of so many brothers and sisters and of your father's untimely death, and I could not help but wonder if your family had been touched by the war. Probably so. The South has suffered terribly. You have my sympathy. It is the province of the young to put death out of their mind as you say you have done. Believe me, when you approach my age, death will rear its wretched head in the most implacable and infuriating ways. For example, I cannot get warm to save my life, and sometimes I wonder if Satan is trying to lure me with his warming flames. I joke again, of course; I do not believe in the devil, but the things I do believe—I do believe would shock a young, Southern soldier, so I will say no more. I admire your resolve to read EAP's "Eureka," but I shudder to think of its effect on you, if, indeed, you can make heads or tails of it. Please let me know; I am all ears.

I have not answered all your questions. Perhaps later I will write regarding the "detective stories," as you called them. They are important, and, though I did not mention them by name in my book, I did have them in mind when I made a certain point, but more of that later. My hand is tired, and it's almost time to begin supper. As for the portion you quoted that appeared at the end of the book—that certain aspects of EAP's life would "appall the boldest heart"—I was in no way agreeing with Griswold. Please do not put me on the same side of any issue with such a perfidious man; you would pain me to the core. That said, there are certain things that cannot be denied. Let that be enough for now.

Yours,
Helen

(ITEM 4: *Whitman*)

...

April 12, 1876
Providence, Rhode Island

Dear Captain Gayle,

You may *not* use my name in any correspondence to Louisa Allan. To my knowledge she does not even know that I exist, and I only learned recently (from Ingram) that she still lives. But at any rate, I am told she is bitter and has remained silent on the subject of EAP for many years. Who knows what the source of Griswold's claim was?—he stated "a friend of the family," and I would be surprised (amazed, in fact) if that individual remained a "friend" long after Griswold's memoir was published. She is most likely and understandably distrustful of any inquiry. I seriously doubt that she would answer your letter, much less agree to see you, but, of course, you may do as you wish. In any event, however, do *not* mention my name. I refuse to be a cause of further distress to the lady.

As for one of your questions: EAP and Mrs. Osgood were close friends, nothing more. Being both poets, they had much in common, and EAP published many of her poems in the *Broadway Journal*. He had great respect for her work, and the poems he addressed to her were poems of admiration and friendship; they should not be construed otherwise. Mrs. Osgood was also devoted to EAP's wife, Virginia, and to Virginia's mother, Mrs. Clemm, and she was a frequent visitor in their home in Greenwich Village.

Regarding your other questions, you have correctly deduced that I am weary to the bone of answering questions about EAP. If you require answers, you might address your questions to Louise Houghton [Marie Louise Shew Houghton, 1821?–1877]. "Louie," as EAP called her, resides on Long Island and, insofar as Griswold is concerned, knows as much or more than I. She nursed Virginia during her final illness—and she also knew Griswold well. Though I don't know her personally, I know that she is considerably younger than I and, therefore, undoubtedly, more energetic. I obtained her mailing address from John Ingram and will have my secretary insert it below.

Thank you, Helen Whitman

(ITEM 5: *Whitman*)

...

April 20, 1876
Providence

Dear Captain Gayle,

I confess to feeling dreadful for the curt tone of my last letter. Please don't think me a shrew, Captain—"soon to be 'demoted' as you joke, to 2nd Lieutenant." Suffice it to say, I have good days and bad days and woe be to he who is addressed on the latter.

I read your letter of March 25 again several days later, sensing that I had omitted something, which indeed I had, and on second reading was thoroughly captivated by stories of your home and upbringing. By the way, you must tell me what "yearling camp" is—I presume nothing to do with horses. For my part, now that I know full-well of your persistence, I am not at all surprised to learn how you overcame the (shall I say "shortcoming"?) of being the shortest man at West Point. If I may be so bold, Captain Gayle, you have a way of inveigling others so as to become oddly indispensable, and I admit to being annoyed with myself for having risked cutting short our correspondence. I hope you will write again, but please, I can abide no further questions about EAP.

It was horribly rude of me, in my letter of April 12th, not to acknowledge your wish to pay a visit. We do not have overnight guests in our home, Captain. I am elderly and my sister is not well; I'm afraid Charlotte has her hands full. Instead, be my guest for a night's stay at the City Hotel which is old but clean and nearby. We would enjoy having you for supper on the evening of your arrival, and you can resume your journey the next morning by ferry to NYC. Are you quite certain that Providence is on your way home? It seems rather out of the way to me; nonetheless, you are welcome, as I expect I shall be well entertained by you. Please inform me of the date.

A most promising idea has occurred to me. Since your journey home from Providence will necessarily require you to travel through NYC, I have a particular favor to ask which may require you to spend a night or more in that city. Would this be possible and not too costly for you? By way of your investigative work at West Point, you have proven yourself a very capable sleuth; therefore, I have a challenge for you that would prove invaluable were you to succeed. For years John Ingram and I have been trying to find a woman named Mary Star or Starr [Mary Starr Jennings, 1816–1887] who was a lifelong friend of the Poes and, according to Louise Houghton, an early love of EAP. She is married, but we are unable to uncover her married name. Her husband was a haberdasher in New York City, but the family lived in Jersey City. Mrs. Houghton cannot remember her married name; she believes that it was a common name beginning with the letter "J" but was not Jones. These are all the clues we have. Mary Star was with Mrs. Houghton at Fordham the morning of Virginia Poe's death. We believe that the information she can provide would be invaluable. Solve this riddle for us Captain and you will be doing this great effort on behalf of EAP another inestimable service.

Truly your friend,
Helen

(ITEM 8: *Whitman*)

...

May 10, 1876
Providence

Dear Captain Gayle,

Your letters bring such cheer. In short time you have become my most pleasurable correspondent, as I find only enjoyment in your letters and none of the chore of so much of my other correspondence, particularly from Ingram who is relentless and insatiable in his demands for information—for facts. I ask you, is a life nothing more than a catalogue of verifiable facts? How antiseptic the approach! But enough of that.

I must tell you something about me, Captain—Eddy—may I please call you Eddy? I wish to do something that you may find a bit unnerving, but that you may also find helpful in learning things you wish to know about "you-know-who," as you called our mutual friend in your last letter. (Henceforth, shall we refer to him as YKW—"You-Know-Who"? Yes, we must.) In short, I am a Spiritualist and have for many years been a medium. Do you know what I mean? I warrant you don't have mediums in the Carolinas, or if you do, as like as not they go by a different name, and I wonder what it might be? Mine is a God-given gift that has both burdened and enriched my life, and, though I would not trade it for the world, I would not wish it on another living soul.

How shall I explain, my dear Eddy? There are spirits all about us, the spirits of those who have come before and who have moved on by way of what we call death, but death is not an end; it is, rather, a gateway, if you will, to a new life. Perhaps Wordsworth said it best:

> Our birth is but a sleep and a forgetting:
> The Soul that rises with us, our life's Star,
> Hath had elsewhere its setting,
> And cometh from afar.

In other words, a soul's journey long exceeds a mere lifetime. We need have no fear of death; indeed, I welcome it even now as I feel it drawing nigh. And it is joyous to me to know with such certainty that I shall soon be shed this spent human shell. Oh, the wonders I shall soon meet!—family, loves, friends of my youth. They are there waiting, and this I know, not by faith, not by hope, but by virtue of my gift, for I have heard them speak. And with them I shall begin a new life.

I do not know if you are a religious man. If so, you must be unsettled by what I say, for I speak not of Heaven in the biblical sense, though I suspect that the Heaven we are taught, or something very near to it, is evidenced by the spirit-lives. But I cannot say for sure. By my gift, I do not claim wisdom or knowledge of things hereafter. Rather I am like a Spirit Telegraph; I have the gift to connect the living with those who have gone beyond.

Are you a brave man, Captain Eddy? I wonder. Your coming presents me with an opportunity. You are young; your hopes are high; your curiosity is boundless; your trust is pure. In short you possess those qualities that the spirits prize most highly and find most welcoming.

I shall hold a séance the night of your visit. There! You are forewarned. In one of your letters you wonder at the cause of Griswold's resentment toward YKW. I believe that in answer to your query, I provided reasons, but in truth, I have never believed that I knew the most basic, the most primal answer to that question, and before I die, I must know. This is the answer we shall seek the night of your visit. I have my own reasons for wanting to know; they have to do with my afterlife; I do not wish to leave this life without first knowing; and that is all I shall say by way of explanation. In short, my reasons are personal and private. Perhaps you are shocked by all of this, perhaps humored, no doubt skeptical, since many equate Spiritualism with quackery. It is not; I assure you. Perhaps you now wish you had never invited yourself to "Providence!" But your impulses are not happenstance. Don't you see?—"Eddy"—you even share the same nickname with YKW, and what does it mean? Maelström. Is there a more apt metaphor for his life?—"Descent into the Maelström."

You were destined to come; you were chosen. Why? I do not know—but it is a certainty that you were meant to come and come you must.

Yours, eagerly,
Helen

The Spirit Telegraph! What had I gotten myself into? It seemed that in Helen's mind I had taken on a whole new identity. Did she think me the reincarnation of "you-know-who?" It did seem a coincidence that we shared the same odd spelling of a nickname, but I don't attach much significance to coincidence, never have. News of Helen being a conjurer—or whatever such folks are properly called—was a surprise to be sure, and I seriously considered some excuse to cancel my trip to Providence. Truth is, Providence was far out of my way. But on the other hand, I thought a séance might be an interesting new experience or, at the very least, good sport. I'm a sucker for good sport. So I caught the train to Boston, then another to Providence, and registered at the City Hotel by mid-afternoon. I washed up, put on my dress uniform, and walked the short distance to Helen's house—the Power house, so the hotel manager called it, since it had belonged to Helen's mother.

I was greeted at the door by Helen's secretary, Charlotte Ayers. Immediately upon seeing Miss Ayers, I decided that the evening would be considerably more pleasurable than I had expected. I guessed she was in her late teens, tall, erect, and proper as you please. Not a hair on her golden head out of place, she was comely and fresh-scented as a gardenia, though she seemed more than a little undone at meeting a man who stood little more than eye level with her you-know-whats.

"Mrs. Whitman is resting," she explained as she ushered me into the parlor, avoiding eye contact as if embarrassed by having to look down at a grown-up man.

Needless to say, I look up to almost everyone; I've done it all my life and hardly notice except when someone is as ill-at-ease as Miss Ayers.

"Mrs. Whitman wanted to be informed of your arrival," she continued, "so I'll just do that, then get you some tea. Would you like tea?" she asked as if thinking I may not yet be old enough.

"Nothing in this wide world could make me happier, Miss Ayers," I said in an exaggerated Southern accent, trying to put her at ease, and she departed rather gleefully, leaving me to occupy myself with looking about the room. The first thing I noticed was Helen's portrait, and I studied it, judging that it must have been done years ago—I didn't know precisely how old she was but surely in her late sixties or seventies. Beneath the portrait on the mantel, a handsome brass clock ticked a metronome. Otherwise the house was quiet. In a curio cabinet in one corner of the room I found two daguerreotypes of Poe and studied them as well. They appeared to have been done at about the same time, and Poe's expression is similar in each—intelligent, inscrutable, not pleasant, not unpleasant, but in both he looked haggard as if he hadn't slept well the night before or—perish the thought—as if he'd had a touch too much tanglefoot. In front of the portraits was a gold thimble which I judged to be significant and perhaps in some way related to Poe. Just then Miss Ayers reappeared with a sterling silver tea service and news that Mrs. Whitman was on her way down. Almost simultaneously that very lady entered the parlor wearing the most disarming smile imaginable. One would have thought I was Paris and she, Helen of Troy.

"Captain Gayle. Oh what joy! Welcome to Providence. Please sit," and she motioned me to a chair in front of the curio cabinet and beside the maroon settee where she indicated she would sit in order to pour from the service Miss Ayers had placed on the tea table.

Helen's manner put me at ease. Any qualms I might have had evaporated, though I was just then heartedly glad I was staying at the hotel and not under Helen's roof, this only because it occurred to me just then that I would have to put forth my best manners so long as I was there. Putting forth good manners is not alien to me, but having just finished four years of the most rigorous discipline imaginable, I was chomping at the bit for a spell of at-ease.

Helen began with questions and smiled at my accent such that I thought she would burst out laughing. Noticing my reaction, she insisted to be charmed by the way I spoke—like music, she said, claiming she could never tire of such melodious speech. So I talked over tea, telling her stories of life at West Point. I even told, in the most delicate terms I could muster, the story that Helen had referred to in one of her letters about a certain "state of undress." I explained, demonstrating on my own uniform and standing at attention for her, that at inspection, the three most scrutinized parts of a uniform are the sash, the belt buckle, and the boots. The former must be spotlessly white and the latter two, shined to perfection. The story goes that in his efforts to be expelled, Poe arrived for inspection one morning with a spotlessly white sash, glittering belt buckle, highly glossed boots, and wearing not another stitch. Through her face powder, I swear I perceived a blush on Helen's face; she covered her mouth to hide her embarrassment, then we both laughed out loud.

After a half-hour of such talk, during a pause, our teacups being drained, Helen became earnest, and I sensed what was coming. Up to that time there had been no mention of the séance that had been promised and I hoped against hope that it had been dropped from the evening's agenda.

"I have invited another guest for dinner, Captain," she said.

"It's lieutenant now, ma'am," I said, "but call me Eddy if you like."

She smiled and I figured I'd asked for it, mentioning that nickname. It had popped out without thinking. She stared at me thoughtfully, like she was searching for words.

"Have you ever heard of synesthesia?"

"No, ma'am," I said and found myself folding my hands awkwardly together like I was about to say a prayer. I wondered if the word might be something akin to anesthesia.

Helen cleared her throat, lifted her chin, and looked up toward the ceiling as if to clear her mind. "Synesthesia is a phenomena by which certain things—letters or numbers, for example—stimulate sensations unrelated to the symbol itself." She dropped her gaze to look at me, measuring my response. She'd lost me, but didn't seem to grasp that fact. "Take numbers, for instance. I see the numerical symbol and understand it, of course, because I learned it in school, but simultaneously I see a particular color. Odd numbers are always warmer than even numbers. Three is lemon-yellow, four is royal blue, five is orange and hot like a setting sun, six is the color of clover, seven is blood-red, eight is a grayish-green like the underside of a holly-leaf, and on-and-on. And it's not just numbers and letters, Eddy, but also abstract concepts, people, animals. Everything evokes colors or smells or degrees of sharpness or loudness, even degrees of what might be termed fidelity or even fear—all seemingly unrelated to the object itself, but I think they are not unrelated. It's difficult to explain. I learned at an early age that others did not see things the way I do, and I felt odd and singular until I came to see my extra vision, if I may call it that, as a special gift. These associative perceptions became the pith and marrow of my poetry. And in time I learned that they endowed me with an even more astonishing sensitivity." Helen paused, and I was certain she'd come to that moment when she would reveal the dreaded thing. "Do you understand what I'm saying?"

"I suppose I do, ma'am," I said. "I'm pretty good at math, myself, but I confess that all I see are numbers."

Helen smiled politely, and I wondered if she thought me a total hayseed.

"Eddy," she said with excessive compassion in her voice and staring intently at me, "I possess the capability of communicating with spirits. In time I learned from other spiritualists, attended scores of séances, and, you might say, perfected my craft, if such it may be called, and I think it may be. I believe my sister, Anna, also has the gift, but in her case, sadly, it was crippling, and I don't mean physically."

She paused again, looking away, far away, and for a moment I was keenly aware of the clock ticking. I sensed the mood changing even as I listened; something was not the way she imagined it, and I guessed it was me.

"This must seem strange to you, Lieutenant Gayle. I don't think I can bear to call you Eddy. Forgive me," and she laughed nervously and turned back to me. "Not for anything you've done. I can see you are a fine man. Perhaps I was mistaken, and I'm suddenly very tired. I should rest before supper. Perhaps you'd like to go back to the hotel and rest as well. Shall we say six-thirty? And, oh yes, Walter Brown is going to join us for supper. Walter is a dear friend, and I thought you might enjoy the company of another man. He's older than you, but still a young man. He painted my portrait."

With this the two of us glanced up at the portrait over the mantel.

Then Helen extended her hand to be helped up from the settee. She walked me to the front hall and bade me goodbye.

I walked back to the hotel feeling like I'd failed an examination. I decided Helen regretted my coming. For one thing, I was too short. Griswold's memoir reports that Poe was of medium height, and judging from the daguerreotypes in Helen's parlor, he was a man of serious mien. As for me, I can't keep a lopsided grin off my face to save my life. Poe was said to be a brilliant conversationalist; whereas, I can't resist a bawdy story like the one I told Helen about Poe showing up for inspection naked as a jaybird. Edgar Allan Poe and I were about as alike as a hayride and hay fever, and, though I hated to let Helen down, on the positive side I hoped she might change her mind about the séance.

But the minute I arrived back at Helen's at 6:30, I knew I was in for it. As soon as Miss Ayers opened the door, I could see Helen standing at the entrance to the parlor giving directions to someone within. The parlor had been rearranged. Gone was Helen's portrait and in its place a God-awful painting of a Raven plucking out the strings of a harp with its beak. Gone was the tea table, and the doors of the curio cabinet were opened, and things had been removed. The chair that I had sat in that afternoon had been moved to the far end of the room, the curtains were drawn, and fresh, unlit candles had been placed all about the room.

"Lieutenant Gayle is here," Helen announced as if my arrival was just the thing she'd been waiting for. "Please come in and meet Walter Brown. Walter, Lieutenant Edward Gayle."

As I passed from the hall into the parlor, I noticed a woman sitting in the dark in the dining room just opposite the parlor. She sat with her back to the door so that I couldn't see her face, and she did not turn to look, nor did Helen acknowledge her presence. It was as if she wasn't there. I guessed her to be Anna, the sister Helen had referred to that afternoon, and I assumed she would join us when the time came. I judged Walter Brown to be in his late thirties or thereabouts. He was a good foot taller than I, light brown hair that was starting to thin, and his manner was shy, even a bit effeminate. Yep, I reckoned right off, he's the artist all right. Walter seemed as disconcerted by my size as was Miss Ayers earlier. Generally I say nothing, but sometimes I'll say something like, "Didn't know a dwarf was coming for supper, didja'?" But it seemed this was not the time for levity; there being a séance afoot, and Walter seemed as undone by that prospect as by my sawed-off stature.

"Come in, everyone," Helen said; "Charlotte you too."

Everyone moved to take seats, Miss Ayers and Walter Brown to the settee. I moved to the chair where I'd sat earlier in the day that had been moved to the end of the room, but Helen stopped me, motioning me to another chair, one from the dining room brought into the parlor for the occasion and placed just beside the fireplace. Just then a smug, coal-gray Persian cat sauntered into the room. It caught Helen's eye and, as if sensing it was not welcomed, tunneled up under the claw-footed settee.

"Charlotte, take Cato and close him in the kitchen," Helen barked, and there followed a desperate attempt by Miss Ayers to fetch the cat from under the settee. He refused to be coaxed. I rose from my chair with intentions of coming to her aid, but Helen sharply motioned me back, indicating with her raised hand her confidence in Miss Ayers to master the task. On hands and knees, pleading impatiently with Cato, Miss Ayers presented me with her backside, the soles of her shoes, her white stockings clear up to the backs of her knees, and layer upon layer of eyelet petticoat—the most enticing sight I'd seen in a month of Sundays. For modesty's sake, I tried to turn away, and my gaze landed on Helen who stared stern-jawed, not in the least amused. I bit my lip for fear of laughing out loud. Poor Miss Ayers, in near panic, was exposing herself, and, though I could not bear to look, I could not bear not to. It must be remembered that—one—I was twenty-two years old and, despite my size, in possession of a full-grown share of manly appetites, and—two—I had not seen a single, eligible girl for over a year with the lone exception of my little sister, and—three—Miss Ayers possessed a stature and beauty that a man standing four-foot-eight could only dream of. The last thing I wanted was to take advantage of her frenzied efforts to fulfill Mrs. Whitman's commands, but there, not three feet before my eyes, were her petticoats and her shapely, bestockinged calves. What was I to do?

Finally Cato, still beneath the settee, nipped at Miss Ayers when she tried to pull him out by the nape of his neck, and she recoiled in pain, squeezing a droplet of blood from a bite on her thumb so precious that it took all the discipline I could muster not to fall on my knees to console her and give the cat *what for* with the business end of my boot. I held myself in check, resolved that later I would somehow express my deepest sympathy for her plight and the difficulty with which I had restrained myself. Unfortunately the opportunity never arose. I desperately hoped, however, that the message was conveyed by my sympathetic expression after Miss Ayers had flushed Cato out from under the settee with the poker, followed him in hot pursuit, closed him (presumably in the kitchen), and returned to her seat beside Walter Brown. During this entire episode not one word was spoken. Furthermore, I briefly fancied that my expression of sympathy was gratefully accepted, but then I decided that Miss Ayers's nervous smile was merely concealing her embarrassment. She had failed to grasp the chivalry I intended, and never in my life had I so hated my size and the shyness that naturally attended it. I cursed myself.

Helen appeared oblivious to all. She stood, walked to the doors, and pulled them to, leaving her sister—if, indeed, that's who she was—sitting across the hall in almost total darkness in the dining room. Helen then moved to her chair at the far end of the room in front of the desk, and it was then I noticed a pedestal table sitting beside it, draped with an ornately embroidered cloth of dark blue velvet on top of which sat a book, a piece of white stationery, the two daguerreotypes of Poe, the gold thimble, a long-necked vase like something from ancient Greece, a teaspoon, and small purple vial. Folded beside these items was a transparent black veil. Helen then pointed to one of the gaslights, prompting Miss Ayers to rise again, walk to the mantel, fetch a box of sulfur matches, and begin lighting the candles that had been placed about the room, on side tables, the mantel, and even inside the fireplace, which had earlier been swept clean, its grate removed.

I had realized, of course—even as Miss Ayers doused the gaslights—that the séance was about to begin and supper would come after. Had I thought about it, I might have guessed that a full stomach was not conducive to conjuring the spirits, or I would have eaten at the hotel beforehand. My last meal had been between trains in Boston, and I was hungry enough to eat a caisson mule. With supper in mind I looked over the coffee table at Walter Brown, but the grave expression on Walter's face was enough to subdue the heartiest appetite. I assumed this was not his first séance, for he was in puredee horror of it.

With the gaslights doused, the candles lit, and everyone in their place, Helen carefully donned a pair of white gloves, preparing, I supposed, to begin tapping out messages on the spirit telegraph. For the first time I took particular note of her attire. She wore a purple velvet dress with long sleeves and a full skirt edged at the hem with rows of elaborate tatting and squares of white velvet, and almost totally covering her dress was a black velvet cape with pale violet rosette clasps embroidered in rows down the front. The woman was dressed to kill! Hanging by a white ribbon around her neck was her fan, which she now began to toy with gloved fingers. Presumably for my benefit, she began with an orientation: "Much has been made of the séance that is false and sensational," she said, "—the hocus-pocus of gypsies and charlatans whose purpose is monetary gain. The rappings and tappings of visiting spirits that have been reported are pure balderdash and serve only to denigrate and adulterate a truth—that the spirits of those who have departed this dimension dwell in another. I don't pretend to understand. The world of which I speak is mysterious and far beyond the comprehension of mortals like us who lack the power to perceive the boundless possibilities of the universe. I ask you only to be receptive, to refrain from judging, to remain humble, and to accept that potential is infinite."

With this said, Helen took the purple vial, poured a teaspoon of lemony-colored liquid, and sipped it down. Then she took the piece of stationery from the pedestal table, and, since her end of the room was in almost total darkness, held it so that it received the candlelight from the mantel.

"Here is written," she announced, "Edgar Poe's poem 'To Helen.'" With this she began reading or reciting; I couldn't be certain which. I imagined she must know the words by heart. It was the "To Helen" addressed to her, and being a long poem and somewhat convoluted to a muddled brain like mine, my thoughts began to wander—first back to Miss Ayers's petticoats, but knowing that was an improper frame of mind, I considered what was at hand. Why was Helen reading this particular poem? Then it came to me. She was inviting the spirit of Edgar Allan Poe. Well, I'll be switched!

For the life of me, I couldn't "be receptive," hard as I tried. I'm as humble as the next guy, but I was certain I failed in all other respects and felt right guilty about it. I couldn't stop myself from imagining that Mr. Poe's spirit might swoop right down the chimney, his way lit by the candles in the fireplace. Just as I was thinking my normally jocular nature might just queer the whole deal, Helen suddenly raised a knotty, begloved finger as if she had read my thoughts and wished to banish me from the parlor. She was, however, merely emphasizing certain key lines of the poem which she all but shouted: "And thou, a ghost, amid the entombing trees / Didst glide away. Only thine eyes remained. / They would not go—*they never yet have gone.*"

Her message was clear as reveille. If the spirit of Edgar Poe was out there somewhere, wandering in the night, he must know by now that he was being summoned, but, unfortunately, not for supper.

When the recitation ended, Helen instructed us to close our eyes, though I couldn't resist a peek now and again. I spied her take the black veil and drape it over her head so that I could no longer see her features clearly, then she lifted the piece of stationery on which Poe's poem was written and held it to her forehead. From then on, it seemed she spoke only to the spirit world. "We have come with compassion in our hearts. We seek the spirit of Edgar Allan Poe. Though the book beside me contains a memoir that is contemptible to thee, it is here for a reason that is just and in no way threatening, for there is no hostility here, only love. And here amongst us for the first time is a young soldier who loves thee also. He comes of his own volition from great distance, because thy words have touched his soul. We have come together like rays of light to form a beacon, a lighthouse that guides ships in the night to safe harbor. We come with a question for which we seek an answer. We ask it for thy sake, for there are other men who love thee also and who wish to tell thy story. I know thee understands. So now we will clear our minds, relax our bodies, and give ourselves over, as we search for thy presence—ten, nine, eight, seven, six—purple, ocher, teal, red, clover, orange, royal . . ."

Now I dared not peek. The ticking of the clock and Helen's soft repetition of numbers and colors was hypnotic. In short time I felt drowsy and perhaps lost track of time, but being new to this, my mind moved to and fro, from repose to vigilance to repose again. Then, breaking the silence, the parlor door creaked open with a soft but unmistakable sound. Coming fully alert, my eyes closed tightly, I decided that one of the two doors could not remain completely closed, perhaps because of some small defect in the jamb. I marveled to think that of all the stirring noises that an old house makes as it expands and contracts, it was too, *too* coincidental that the first such sound should be an opening door. Was I right or was it a spirit or did Helen's sister have something to do with it? I felt my heartbeat race, but then all was quiet again, save the ticking of the clock. Again, as if mesmerized by a metronome, I lost track of time and gradually began to feel a pleasantness like wind or rushing water, then weightlessness followed after more minutes, then mild dizziness as if the blood were rushing to my head. Following this I was so overcome by a sense of vertigo that I had to open my eyes to steady myself. In front of me on the floor I perceived the poem, which must have fallen from Helen's hand. Perhaps the weight of holding up her arm had been too much, and when she dropped it to her lap, the stationery had fluttered to the floor. Crouched atop the poem was Cato.

I looked up to see Miss Ayers staring wide-eyed at the cat, a look of horror in her eyes. I decided the spell was broken, and hoping to get her frightened and unnerving gaze off of the cat, I rather timidly cleared my throat. With this Walter Brown opened his eyes also, and after puzzled glances at each other, the three of us returned our attention to Cato and waited patiently for Helen to come to. As for Cato, he didn't move a muscle, his gaze fixed on his mistress who seemed to be sound asleep, her head tilted to one side, still hidden by the veil. Was it laudanum she had taken, I wondered? That could put her out for quite a spell! But, needless to say, no one stirred.

Quietly, I took out my watch and looked at the time—half past seven. A few seconds later Helen's hands tightened reflexively. She bowed her head for a moment, massaging her forehead with her fingers, then sat up straight and removed her veil. The vision of Cato gave her a start, and noticing this, Cato stretched his forepaws, raised his haunches, tearing and crumpling the stationery. Then with deliberation he swept the poem behind him with his hind paws as if covering his stool with dirt. The action was unmistakably—how shall I say—excremental. Once finished he moved in among Helen's skirts, rubbing his nose and cheeks against her leg. Stiffly she tolerated this familiarity for a few seconds, then, with her jaw set firmly, she nudged Cato away with her foot. He turned casually and retreated to curl just at my feet where he lifted a hind leg and commenced licking himself.

"What time is it?" Helen asked, clearly undone. I told her and reached down to pick up the torn piece of stationery, thinking it must be offensive now. "Don't touch it," Helen commanded. I pulled back, and Helen seemed to consider the time for a instant, then she turned to Miss Ayers. "Did I not tell you to shut him in the kitchen?"

"I did, mum. He couldn't have gotten out unless Miss Power let him out."

"I did *not* let him out," came a gravelly voice from the hall. Miss Power must have been standing just outside the parlor door, which had cracked open just enough to allow Cato to enter.

I had already concluded that Miss Power was Helen's sister and, remembering what Helen had said about her earlier—that she too had the gift, but that in her case it had been crippling—I wondered if perhaps the cook could have done it. But I smelled nothing resembling supper and decided there must not be a cook.

At Helen's signal, Miss Ayers went to the doors and parted them to reveal a stern, heavyset woman with thick gray hair flowing almost to her waist. She was dressed in pitch black from head to toe, and her defiant eyes were fixed on Helen. "Nor did I open the parlor door," she said, "but someone did, and someone let Cato out of the kitchen. Wasn't me. I sat right where you told me to, not looking, not budging from my chair, just as I said I would. I warned you not to do this, sister. But you couldn't resist, could you? You know better than to not heed my advice, but now you'll have to live with it, won't you. It's your own fault."

With this, Miss Power turned and climbed the stairs. I could hear her ponderous steps until they ceased and a door slammed shut.

Helen composed herself, closed her eyes for a time, then opened them again. "Does anyone have anything to say?" she asked as if hoping no one would. She seemed unable to take her eyes off Cato who continued to lick himself just beyond the toe of my boot.

"I had a dream," Miss Ayers blurted, seeming to be eager to please Helen. "Or a vision. I can't say which it was. We were having supper in an eatery—you, Miss Power, and me. I didn't know the place. We were sitting near the back, and we'd just finished eating. Up near the front there were several men dressed in black coats, but we hadn't noticed them before. I didn't recognize them, but I could see they were gambling. I could tell, because I could see coins on the table that were black like their coats—all black. You noticed them too and became alarmed, so we hurried to leave, but you had to pay the bill first, and when you fetched the money from your purse, it was also black. I could see the coins in your hand—we both stared at them—Lady Liberty, the stars around her crown—all black. That's all I remember."

Helen seemed disturbed by what Miss Ayers reported. She considered it for a moment then rather reluctantly turned to Walter Brown as if hoping he would provide something a little less disquieting. He spoke for the first time since greeting me an hour earlier. "I do believe," he said, "that I dreamed without sleeping. It was most unusual. I was with you on a city street, but not here in Providence. It might have been New York or Boston perhaps. It was daylight, sunny and bright. Warm. You wore a black dress and bonnet; I sensed you were in mourning for someone. I was standing beside and a little behind you, so I could not see your face, but I knew it was you. You were holding your purse in your left hand, an umbrella in your right, and you were talking to a man, a distinguished looking middle-aged man. He wore no hat; his hair was receding; and he wore a beard but no mustache. He was smiling at you, but my impression is that he was trying to placate you, that his smile wasn't genuine. I think he might have been a minister, but I can't be sure of that. I couldn't hear what was said, but you seemed to be pleading with him."

"I know of the incident you speak," Helen intoned, animated now. "I recognized the vision immediately. It was the day I encountered Griswold on Broadway. Your description of him is flawless. He had no mustache, but he did have a beard and receding hairline. It's him, no doubt. He had been a minister in his youth and still preached on occasion. I had gone to New York to pay my respects to Fanny who was dying, hence my being in mourning. That was in May 1850. Fanny would be dead within a week. I saw Griswold on the street and stopped him. I'd heard he was writing a memoir of Edgar to be published in the collected works he was to bring out the following year. I was asking him to be kind to Edgar. I knew they disliked each other, but he promised he would. Of course, he broke that promise. This is significant, Walter."

"But I haven't told you all, Helen," Walter Brown insisted. "Somehow—I cannot tell you how—but when he walked away I realized that he was not wearing a minister's gown. He was wearing a dress. A lady's black dress. But that makes no sense."

Helen's eyes grew large, and I felt the hair on the back of my head begin to prickle. Suddenly Helen clutched her breast, and all of us jumped from our seats to go to her. She took quick, shallow breaths and looked at me imploringly, taking my hand. Between breaths she gasped, trying to speak, staring intently at me.

"Black money," she gasped. "I know what you think. Blackmail. Don't try to make sense of it. You don't know enough. Would to God we hadn't asked." She looked down at the floor. "The poem."

I fetched the torn stationery from where it still lay on the floor and brought it to her. She took it from me and crumpled it into a ball, then handed it to Miss Ayers.

"Burn it," she said. Then, coughing, almost choking. "Take me up."

With her arm around her, supporting her, Miss Ayers led Helen away, but at the door to the parlor, they paused and Helen turned back to me.

"Say nothing of this, Captain."

When she was gone, I turned to Walter Brown who shook his head with grave determination. "She's too old for this. I tried to tell her. She's been planning it ever since she got your letter. It's too dangerous. With a heart as weak as hers, she'll kill herself." He let go a sigh. "Well, I suppose dinner's off. Doesn't matter; I've lost my appetite anyway. Can I walk you back to your hotel?"

I thanked him but declined, and Walter seemed relieved. At the street, we shook hands; he went left, I went right. Just short of my hotel, I found a tavern, low-beamed ceiling, laughter, smell of smoke and humanity, and I couldn't resist. I'd had enough of the spirit-world for one night. I went in and ordered a glass of claret and a pipe. I'm not much of a drinker, but I needed one just then, and I do enjoy the occasional smoke. The effects of both were never more gratifying. After a second glass, my appetite returned, but I learned that the cook had gone home; it was too late for supper. Never mind, I thought. In the morning I'll have fried eggs, sunny-side up, toast, butter, honey, and a couple of pork chops. And two mornings from tomorrow, I could not resist thinking, I'll be home and breakfast will include ham-and-grits and red-eye gravy.

As I lay awake in a strange bed in a strange city, I wondered if I'd ever make heads or tails of the strange happenings I'd witnessed that night—a black cat seeming to defecate on Helen's poem, Miss Ayers's vision of men gambling with black coins, and Walter Brown's dream of a minister wearing a woman's dress, a man Helen Whitman seemed certain was Rufus Wilmot Griswold—the very man who had ruined Poe's reputation. But nothing seemed to tie these things together with the one possible exception of that word Helen had uttered— "blackmail." That was a clue for sure, and she saw it before I did. But she was right about me not knowing enough. And it occurred to me that she might never tell me enough, that hereafter her lips might be sealed on the whole affair. It even occurred to me that I might never again hear from Sarah Helen Whitman.

Time proved me wrong. It wasn't long before I learned that the gold thimble had belonged to Virginia Poe and that Helen had arranged for both daguerreotypes of "You-Know-Who." They had been made in December 1848, right there in Providence in the same studio at different times with Helen looking on and doubtless paying the bill. But though Helen and I would correspond right up until her death two years later, she never explained what the message or messages meant. She made it quite clear that she wished to speak no further on the subject of Edgar Allan Poe. Nevertheless, she knew or she came very close to knowing the answer to our question about Poe and Griswold. I became certain of that, but I concluded that those answers were, as she had said in one of her earlier letters, personal and private. And little did I know then that it would take another twenty years to piece together the whole story. But when I finally did, I realized that Helen had indeed summoned the spirit of Edgar Poe that night in Providence. There is simply no other explanation.

I put this out of my mind by welcoming instead a vision of the comely Miss Charlotte Bartlett Ayers.

April 25, 1876
Moldavia
Richmond, Virginia

Dear Cadet Gayle,

In response to your letter of May 5th I regret that I cannot receive you on your upcoming trip through Richmond, and I trust you will accept my apology for that and also my congratulations on the occasion of your graduation from West Point and on your commission as a 2nd Lieutenant in the Artillery. I wish you good fortune and safe keeping in your military service.

I glean from your enthusiasm—which indeed I share—your keen appreciation of the literary works of the late Edgar Poe. Believe me when I say that I wish with all my heart that his life had been as happy as are esteemed his tales and poems. The world should celebrate the brilliance of his pen and, out of respect for the dead, permit his sorrows and failings, of which, sadly, there were many, to fade from memory. Please understand that I impute such failings not to any misappropriation of God-given talents on his part, but quite the contrary, to the "slings and arrows" of misfortune of which the poor man suffered much for mere want of human understanding. Among the great men of letters throughout history and the world, is it not remarkable that literary success should be so often paired with personal failure, not necessarily of the monetary kind, but, for diverse reasons, in the interactions of such men with other human beings, including their own families? Such was the case with Mr. Poe, but having myself come, by virtue of experience gained in a long lifetime, to understand the singularities of such temperaments as his, I hasten to add that I hold him in as high regard as anyone upon the face of this earth.

Of my own personal contact with Mr. Poe, we met on only two brief occasions, the first following shortly after my marriage to his father, the late John Allan, and the second during my husband's final illness a few years later. Needless to say, such fleeting contact provided me with little in the way of insight into the man's character, but that fact has not forestalled Mr. Poe's memorialists from speculation regarding our relationship, and I can assure you that, though much has been written, not a scrap can lay claim to any resemblance of an accurate and true portrayal of the facts, and I hope that you can understand that, in light of the persistence of such erroneous and distorted accounts, I made it my policy years ago to speak no further on the subject, hence my regret in denying your request. Please forgive me and please understand also that I would not have replied to your letter at all were it not for the sincerity of your manner and interest.

I might add that there are many people living in Richmond who were acquainted with Edgar Poe; therefore, since your hope is to meet some such person, I suggest that you inquire at the office of the *Southern Literary Messenger* as I am quite certain they can supply you with names and addresses.

Cordially,

Louisa Allan

2

MARY STARR

::

(ITEM 9: *Mary Starr Jennings*)

...

August 1, 1876
Jersey City, New Jersey

Dear Lieutenant Gayle,

I have your letter of the 19th. Thank you. My husband told me the details of your conversation with him—that you are assisting a Mrs. Whitman who is in turn assisting a writer from England who has undertaken a memoir of Edgar Poe. Though I confess to being the person you seek, I do not believe I have anything to offer in the way of information. I was a casual friend of the Poes—my parents were neighbors of his aunt, Mrs. Clemm, in Baltimore for the brief time we lived there during the 1830s. At that time Edgar was living with his aunt who, as you may know, became also his mother-in-law after he married his cousin, Virginia. This was long before he became famous. I did visit the Poes in Fordham during Virginia's final illness, three short visits, if I correctly recall. My husband and I, being sympathetic with their plight during that tragic time, took small gifts of food and clothing for the family, but on those visits I had little intercourse with Edgar. I can only say that, at heart, Edgar Poe was a shy and gentle person, considerate of others, and very polite. He was devoted to his wife and mother-in-law, and I have never seen anyone so devastated by the death of a loved one as he was by the untimely death of his dear, sweet Virginia whom I had known as a young girl and for whom I grieved as well.

Please understand that I have been a wife and mother of five children and that I know nothing of interest as regards Edgar's life or literary accomplishments. I am quite certain that I would prove of no value to the writer of the memoir being undertaken and for personal reasons would prefer not to be consulted on the matter. Be so kind as to *not* forward my address to the English gentleman.

I thank you again for your letter and interest.

Most sincerely,

Mary Jennings

:: MY MOTHER THOUGHT I WAS A PRIZE, and she wasn't talking about my dowry. Financially my father always struggled. The reason we moved from Philadelphia to Baltimore was that my father needed work. The prize I possessed, to hear my mother tell it, was my beauty. I was tall—too tall—a head taller than my girlfriends, but mother said my height made me stunning. And I had red hair—"auburn," as she constantly corrected me, "auburn," as befit an Irish lass—but rather than curl, as was the fashion, it frizzed uncontrollably. What ruined my looks were freckles. It wasn't that they were so dark or so plentiful, it was that in addition to freckles on my cheeks and forehead, I also had freckles on my lips. I would stare at them in the mirror, counting them. They seemed so unnatural, and I wondered if a man would want to kiss a girl with freckles on her lips.

In the summer of 1832 my family moved to Baltimore into a wood-framed duplex on Essex Street with a porch divided in two by a balustrade. The Newmans lived on the other side, and they had a daughter my age, Mary Newman, and we became friends. My mother's cousin, James Devereaux, had a seed store in the old town, and he had persuaded my father to move from Philadelphia, promising work. My father was an engraver, but as it turned out, he could find no such work in Baltimore, so he worked as a carpenter. During our first year there, I was enrolled in school, thanks to my uncle James, but as my father's prospects were not good, he had already started talking about returning to Philadelphia by the time I met Edgar Poe.

Edgar had moved from Richmond a year earlier to live with his aunt, Mrs. Clemm, and her nine-year-old daughter, Virginia, on the second floor of a house on Wilks Street. I knew him as Eddy, and from my bedroom window I could see the back of the house where he lived, and one night in the autumn of our first year in Baltimore, I saw him working at the table in their kitchen. He was writing by candlelight, and, noticing me staring, he smiled and gave a little wave. This happened two or three times. Then one evening he waved his handkerchief out the window to get my attention, and when I opened my window to acknowledge him, he threw me a kiss. I found this audacious, but I confess I was flattered by it. A few evenings later Mary Newman and I were sitting on our porch steps when Eddy came walking home from work. He turned to speak.

"Two Marys," he said. "And I have the pleasure at last of meeting you both."

Mary turned to look at me, afraid to speak to him, because we had not yet been properly introduced. "How did you know our names?" I asked.

"My cousin told me," he said. "She's told me everything about you, Mary Starr. You see? I even know your last name. My cousin's a regular little tattletale."

I couldn't help but smile. I had met his cousin, Virginia, but she had little knowledge of me, and I couldn't imagine what she might have told him. He was fibbing as well as flirting.

He stared at me, waiting for me to say more, but I was determined to disappoint him, so I turned back to Mary Newman. He didn't go away. Rather, he continued to stare, not looking at Mary, but at me. When I finally returned his gaze, he smiled at me as if he'd won some contest, then he walked on home.

He began writing letters to me, having Virginia deliver them. Painfully shy, she had just turned nine; I was seventeen, and I think she was in awe of me. She had dark eyes like Eddy's, and her black hair was pure silk compared to my red frizz. I would walk out onto the front porch when she came, make her sit on the steps with me, and I'd brush her hair as I read his letter, usually an invitation to meet him at the bridge and walk with him. Knowing Virginia wanted to return with a response, I initially gave equivocal answers, but by the end of September, acceding to her pleas, I agreed to meet him. That's how it began.

Eddy was twenty-two, and knowing my parents would disapprove of our age difference, I was afraid to let him court me properly, but I would meet him at the bridge at the edge of town. As often as not he would be carrying a book of poetry, and we would leave the road, climb a fence, and follow a path up a hill from which we could sit and look back toward Baltimore. There he would read to me while I watched him. In evening light his dark eyes were violet; I was paralyzed by them. He had an intensity that was almost frightening; my girlfriends were scared to death of him. I suspect now that it was the sound of his voice and a tenderness and passion in his recitations that I had never heard in a man's voice before, and I was young and impressionable. I let him kiss me. I suppose I was excited by the fact that he would want to kiss a girl with freckles on her lips, so I let him as often as he liked, but only when we were away from town where no one could see. When we were not together he wrote me letters, beautiful letters, delivered by Virginia, and his interest in me became an open secret, though no one suspected that he had kissed me. It was after one of those kisses that he first said he loved me, and I knew at once that I loved him too.

It wasn't until our second summer in Baltimore that Eddy mentioned marriage. My father had become even more adamant about moving back to Philadelphia, and the idea of leaving Eddy depressed me, so I suppose I took him seriously even though his proposal was pure impulse. One July evening we left the house for a walk. It was still daylight. Just beyond the bridge was the Presbyterian manse, a little gray stone house sitting all by itself at the edge of woods.

"Come, Mary," he said, "let's get married. The minister can marry us in his parlor."

I laughed when he said this, and my laughing hurt his feelings. It was as if I had spurned his proposal. I was just eighteen and couldn't marry without my parent's consent, and, though Eddy had hinted at marriage before, I had never thought it might be something we would do so soon. What's more, Eddy had no job and no money to support a wife. He took my hand to pull me toward the manse, and, realizing he was serious, I broke free and ran home.

Not long after that night, he showed me a letter from his foster father, Mr. Allan. The letter said that if Eddy married me, Mr. Allan would cut him off without a shilling. At first I felt sorry for us both, but one evening, waiting for him to come for a visit, I began to wonder what Eddy had told his father about me and my family. When he didn't come, I became angry thinking about it, and when it grew dark, I gave up and left the front steps where I usually waited for him. As it was a hot night, Mary Newman's bedroom window was open, and she yelled down to me that I must be heartbroken since Mr. Poe had jilted me. This upset me even more, so I went into the parlor and sat in the chair in front of the window, looking out, my head cupped in my hands and my elbows resting on the windowsill. At about ten o'clock my mother called me to bed.

"I'm coming," I yelled to her, but I didn't go. Instead I started crying, and just then Eddy appeared. He climbed up onto the porch and, seeing me through the opened window, he sat down outside and leaned his head against the shutter. He told me that he had met some friends from West Point and that they had gone to Barnum's Hotel for supper. He bragged that they had sipped champagne, and I guessed he was tipsy. Ours was a large family; I had four brothers and a sister, and my parents were very religious. Spirits were strictly forbidden in our house, so I was wary of him.

"What did you tell your father about me?" I asked.

In the dark Eddy could not see that I had been crying, and he laughed at my question. "Come out on the porch, and I'll tell you," he said.

I knew by this that he wanted to kiss me, and I suspected he was tipsy enough to try it, though it was much too dangerous. I suspected also that Mary Newman would be watching us, and if she saw us kiss, the whole neighborhood would know. But I wanted an answer to my question, and, deciding I could fend him off if it came to that, I went back outside to talk to him. Eddy had always been respectful; he had never taken advantage of me, never made me do anything against my will. We sat down on the steps together.

A nearly full moon had just risen above the roof of the house across the street, and I gazed up at it, not wanting Eddy to see that I'd been crying. "What did you tell your father about me?" I asked again, whispering now.

Again he said nothing, but he tried to put his arm around my shoulder. I brushed him off.

"Did you tell him we are poor?" I asked. "My father is an engraver, not a carpenter, but that's all the work he can find. Did you tell your father that my father is a carpenter? Is that why he threatened you?"

"Mary," he said, "why are you going on about this? You know how I hate my father."

His manner was careless, his words slurred, and I decided he was drunk. I jumped up and ran around the house through the alley to the back door. My mother was in the kitchen, and not wanting her to see that I was upset, I hurried past her to the stairs. "Mary," she called after, "what's the matter with you?"

I heard the back door open again, and I knew that Eddy had followed me. I froze on the staircase, certain that my mother would see that he was drunk and knowing that she would be upset. "I want to talk to your daughter," he demanded. "Tell her to come down or I'm going after her. I have a right."

"No you do not," my mother said emphatically. "Leave my house, Mr. Poe."

"I have a right, I tell you," he said. "Mary is now my wife in the sight of heaven."

Just then I saw my brother, Tom, at the top of the stairs, his eyes flashing. He was older than I, almost as old as Eddy, and as big as our father.

"Get out of this house, Mr. Poe." My mother's voice came from the kitchen. "Go home and go to bed."

Tom descended the stairs, glaring at me, but thankfully I heard the back door slam and knew that Eddy had left.

Later that night after I had gone to bed, sleeping with my sister Emily on the bed in the garret, Tom came into our room and sat on my bedside. "You are not going to marry that man, Mary," he said. "I would rather see you in your grave than that man's wife. He can't support himself, let alone you."

"That's a horrible thing to say," I said and started crying, but Tom's resolve was unaffected by my tears, and I lashed out at him. "I would sooner live poor with him than in a palace with any other man."

He left me at once when he heard these words, and I knew that something would happen. He would go to my parents, and they would decide to move back to Philadelphia, and I would never see Eddy again. My father would never interfere unless my mother and Tom made him, and they would.

The next day my mother made me return Eddy's letters with a note saying I could not see him again and that he was not to come to our house. I delivered the letters to Mrs. Clemm, knowing Eddy would not be home. He was working day labor jobs then, and I had seen him leave for work that morning. That evening Virginia delivered a letter from him. She stood at the front door, her head bowed, her little hands shaking. I think she had come to adore me, knowing how her cousin loved me. My mother answered the door and called for me to come down. I suppose she wanted me to be the one to refuse the letter, as that would convey the message she wished Eddy to understand.

I knelt down so that my eyes and Virginia's were at the same level, and I grabbed her hands but did not take the letter. "I can't take it, Virginia," I said. "I'm sorry."

Her eyes looked down at the letter, and I could see her grief. I think she wanted us to be married, and I had come to love her as a little sister. I looked up at my mother to see if she saw the heart she was breaking, and she did. She was sympathetic but also resolute.

Again the next night he wrote, and sometime during the night he left the letter on our doorstep. My mother found it and made me read it to her. It was unkind and blaming and unforgiving, and it was soon after this that Eddy published a poem, "To Mary S——," in the *Saturday Visiter* in which he chastised me publically. I realized then that he could not bear the thought that I might love my parents or my brothers and sister also, or even love them at all. He demanded too much. At just that time my grandmother arrived for a visit, and my mother told her all about Mr. Poe barging into the kitchen drunk, demanding to see me, and claiming that I was his wife in the sight of heaven. My grandmother was shocked and assumed the worst, just as my mother had done, and she showed the letter to her nephew, my mother's cousin, Uncle James, and without my knowledge, he wrote Eddy a threatening letter. When my uncle saw the poem in the newspaper, he was even more irate. His letter had enraged Eddy, and one day soon after, Eddy showed up at Uncle James's seed store with a length of cowhide and started whipping him. My uncle had two sons who worked in the store with their father. They came to his rescue and threw Eddy out, tearing his coat up the back all the way to the collar. Somehow Eddy got away still holding the cowhide, and he marched straight to our house on Essex Street followed by a ragtag bunch of men and boys, itching to see a fight. Standing in the doorway, Eddy asked to see my father. I was upstairs but heard the commotion and was half way down the stairs when my mother caught me and refused to let me go farther. Eddy told my father what he had done, throwing my uncle's letter on the floor. When he saw me, he glared at me then threw the cowhide on the floor also.

"There," he said. "I make you a present of it."

Before two weeks were up, we had moved back to Philadelphia.

I thought I would never get over the heartbreak. I was sick for a while, couldn't eat, and lost weight. My parents were convinced that I had been seduced, that I might even be pregnant. When my father became convinced that I was not, he gave thanks to God there at the supper table; he thanked God for delivering me from the clutches of Satan.

I did not return to school after that; I helped my mother instead. That was a hard year for us. The country was in a depression, and there was little money. I had three younger brothers: Henry, named for my father, was eleven, then Ray, six, and the youngest, Cord, who was only four. My older brother, Tom, and my father had difficulty finding work. Mother made all our clothes, and I had to begin helping out. I took over much of the cooking and cleaning. My mother and father were patient with me. It was as if I'd survived some deathly illness. Though I was sad, I could not forgive Eddy for what he had done to my uncle. He did not write, and I gave up hope of ever seeing him again.

I loved my father—Henry Starr—more than any man I've ever known. He was a big, gentle man. I am tall and big boned like him. Though he was big and strong, I never heard him raise his voice; I never saw him strike man or animal, but no doubt the happiest day of his life was the day he realized I had escaped the spell of Edgar Poe. He never blamed me; he rejoiced for me; he wished only for my happiness. How could I disappoint him? So a few years later I met and married Will Jennings. I now think mostly I did it to make my father happy, pretending all the while that I loved the man. Thus convinced, my father went to his grave and for that I have never regretted my marriage.

Mr. Jennings was always conservatively dressed and immaculate in his dark suit as befit a haberdasher. He was a proper and admirable man. When we were courting, in the presence of my parents, he arched his back and stood erect—too erect. His posture amused my family. I was twenty-three when we married; he was two years older. I hadn't known him long, and I never felt for him the dizzy, trembling helplessness that I had felt in the presence of Edgar Poe. I wonder now that as a young woman I had thought falling in love was like losing my virginity, that I had but one chance at it—and, since I had fallen in love before Mr. Jennings entered my life, I had forfeited that prize.

My mother's coaxing proved persuasive. "You could do a lot worse, Mary," she had said as if his proposal was only one of many.

I knew what she really meant—that I could have done a lot worse and nearly did. It wasn't true. I hadn't almost married Edgar Poe despite what he said to her—that I was his wife in the sight of heaven. It was so like him to exaggerate in that way, especially when he was upset. Everything was life or death to Eddy, but my mother didn't know that. She feared that he had seduced me, which was not true. It had not been physical love that Eddy wanted—demanded—so much as adoration, and he could accept nothing less. Had he wanted, he could have seduced me, and I would have been helpless to deny him, but that was not his way. So, for what it was worth, Mr. Jennings married a virgin.

In the presence of our children and even our friends, I always referred to my husband as Mr. Jennings. Only in our bedroom or when I was angry did I call him Will. Had he ever said, "Darling, you must call me Will," I would have done so, but he never did in all the years we were married. He rather liked the respectful distance and never once did I resent it. He called me Mary; he was proud of me. Isn't it funny that years later at Fordham, in the Poe cottage, I called Edgar Poe, Eddy, and my own husband, Mr. Jennings? No one seemed to notice except me. It was as if Eddy, being a friend of my youth, should naturally be called by his nickname, and by doing this, I was also making a polite distinction, placing my husband above Eddy in a way that Mr. Jennings would have preferred. He looked down his nose at the Poes, and it wasn't only their poverty, it was also Eddy's intemperance—his wild intemperance. So far as Mr. Jennings was concerned, the Poes were my charity case, and it was only thus that he tolerated them. I let him think it; I suppose I thought it too.

Following our marriage we moved to New York City where my husband had a tailor shop, but after I gave birth to our first child, Emily, named for my sister, Mr. Jennings bought a house in Jersey City. Once Emily came I knew for certain that I no longer loved Edgar Poe.

Will was scrupulous in all things, and I accepted that. Now I look back on that year in Baltimore as a reckless time. While all my girlfriends were merely flirting with the other boys our age, I was being courted by a man nearly six years older, a man who had broken with his family, a man who had served in the army, had spent his youth in England, a man who drank whiskey, never attended church, and held strong opinions about things. It had been daring of me to fall for such a man, and I was the talk of my friends. I was the one kissing a man while other girls my age considered themselves daredevil if they held hands with those few boys bold enough to take a girl's hand. I was shocked to think that I had nearly eloped with someone wild enough to attack a man of fifty with a cowhide. I paled thinking about it and took comfort in being the dutiful wife of a man who kept regular hours, who abstained from spirits and tobacco, who never swore an oath, who attended church every Sunday, and who never spent a shilling frivolously. In a way he had saved me, and there were times when I would have kissed the ground he walked on for that act of salvation. I would dwell on these thoughts while I did some mundane chore that was keeping our home decent and good, chores like sweeping out the ashes or washing the floors. Once, for an entire week, I agonized over whether to ask Mr. Jennings if I might buy some New England rum with which to wash my hair. My auburn hair was the feature he most praised, and I wanted it to shine for him. In the end I could not do it; it was too much to ask. He considered bathing more than once a week excessive, and no doubt he would have considered New England rum thriftless vanity even though it was for him that I would have done it.

It was the pain of childbirth that cured me of such timidity. I abided sex as a wife's duty, but I could never quite give myself over to it. Edgar Poe had ruined desire; it had ceased to be a natural impulse, something to succumb to. I tried not to think about those kisses on the hill outside Baltimore. Those kisses had become something sinful, something to repress or court violence—a cowhiding. And I could not help but imagine Will Jennings's horror were Edgar Poe to enter his haberdashery wielding a rawhide whip. How could I have ever loved such a man?

But, as I said, childbirth changed me. Childbirth was more brutal than a cowhiding, and I thought about that during labor—oh, but for a cowhiding instead. But the result of such trauma was not my family's wrath and anguish as had been the case in Baltimore. The result was a precious child, a daughter—red hair like mine—a full head of it, more blond than red, but with that tinge of color that made me know it would turn red. I named her for my sister, Emily Starr Jennings. And the joy of Emily nursing at my breast was more pleasurable than any man could ever be. It was as if my penance had ended. I felt freer than I had ever felt before. I indulged myself and my daughter. The two of us would overrule Mr. Jennings. To my astonishment, he gave in, and I grew even bolder. As he watched me nurse Emily, Will Jennings decided he wanted a son, a boy to keep his name alive and take over his business. He talked about it constantly as Emily grew, as I dabbed my sore nipples with quince-seed oil and tried to regain my former figure, and I smiled at him—yes, I was thinking, I will bear you a son, but first, be a dear and buy me some New England rum so I can wash my hair and our daughter's hair. And he did.

The following summer, the summer of 1838, Emily and I took the train to Philadelphia to visit my family. One day as I was walking along the street with my cousin, having left Emily with my sister and mother, we met the Poes—Eddy, Mrs. Clemm, and Virginia.

Eddy was overjoyed to see me, and to my astonishment he introduced Virginia to my cousin as his wife. I could not believe my ears. I had always thought of them as brother and sister, and Virginia was no older than I had been when I first met Edgar. "We're on our way home," he said, "and you must come with us for a visit."

We agreed, and they led the way to Seventh Street, to an unfinished red brick house where the Poes occupied three finished rooms in back, three rooms that were wax clean. As we strolled along, I walked between Virginia and her mother, and Eddy followed behind conversing with my cousin. She knew nothing of my narrow escape in Baltimore—my parents had kept that quiet as had the Devereaux, maintaining a veil of silence for fear of ruining my reputation. Mrs. Clemm talked nonstop, but I could not take my eyes off Virginia, wondering if she had tamed her cousin's wildness. Still shy, still pale and thin, a girl dressed like a woman, with a woman's figure but the demeanor of a schoolgirl. How could she possibly bear his passion, I wondered? I was more curious than jealous, but I was jealous also and aware of it and hated feeling it.

Once we were in the parlor, tea having been served, Eddy asked me to sing. I agreed immediately to the surprise of my cousin. I no longer sang except to my child, but singing was something all girls learned to do. It is remarkable to think about it now, that singing had been something required of a young girl. We still sing, of course, after supper on the porch, mostly in the summertime when it's too hot to stay inside after supper, but everyone sings in unison now. Back then girls were expected to sing and play the piano or the harp. A good singing voice was the sign of good breeding, and the poor girl who could not carry a tune would need more than beauty to catch a man. Money would do it, but a fine singing voice was good as gold. I sang "Come Rest in This Bosom," knowing it was Eddy's favorite, and his eager eyes let me know that he too remembered those kisses in Baltimore. We had a delightful afternoon with the Poes, and Eddy walked my cousin and me back to her house as suppertime approached. I waited there until he was gone before returning to my parent's house, knowing how upset my mother would be were she to see Edgar Poe even after all those years. I told her, of course, that same night after supper as we washed the dishes; I told her with the equanimity and dispassion of the contented wife of a haberdasher and mother of a five-month-old child.

"But you don't still think of him, do you?" my mother asked.

"Oh, mother, of course not," I said as I wiped dry a plate and stacked it on the shelf with the others, and I didn't still think of him. Truly I didn't.

But I was proud of his success as a writer. He was not well known then, but he was making his way, and that modicum of success seemed to legitimize what was viewed as my teenage recklessness, made it more respectable now. Perhaps there had been something of substance in Edgar Poe, not just a hotheaded, spoiled, disinherited son of a Southern planter. He had redeemed himself from that cowhiding of my uncle, and I felt less guilt for my heedlessness. But it was truly a matter of little consequence.

I bore Will Jennings not one son, but four—four healthy boys. I did my duty. I spent the first twelve years of our marriage either pregnant or nursing. It's a wonder I didn't go on bearing children until I died giving birth. We lived in Jersey City, and Will took the ferry daily to New York. He became distracted by his business, forever cursing the dry goods stores that sold ready-made clothing, condemning their shoddy quality and the impatience of his dwindling clientele to wait for a suit to be made. "A man needs a tailor, not a clerk," he complained, "someone who knows the difference between worsted and kersey." I listened, sympathized, and wished for gaslight and running water. And I would turn away from him in bed, sometimes pretending to say my prayers, but when I did pray, as often as not, it was that the children would sleep through the night. Give me a night's rest—just this night.

On a Friday afternoon in late June of 1842, I was returning home from the market with my sister who was visiting—I had fish in my basket, wrapped in newspaper—and I was pregnant at the time with our second son. Our first had been named Henry for my father; this one would be named William Thomas Jennings, Jr. As we approached the house, I spied Edgar Poe standing on the porch. He had been waiting for my return, and I wondered why the cook had not invited him into the parlor until, on hearing him speak and seeing him open the door for me with a flourish of his top hat, I realized he'd been drinking. Feeling uneasy and glad that Emily was visiting from Philadelphia so that I was not alone, I invited him into the parlor. I took my shopping basket back to the kitchen, and asked the cook to brew some strong tea, then I returned to the parlor where Emily was listening with a bemused expression to Eddy's animated tale of his odyssey to find me. It seemed he had been to see Mr. Jennings to find out where we lived, but after taking the ferry he forgot the address and had to return to New York again, but could not find my husband, so he returned on the ferry to Jersey City, asking other passengers onboard if they knew where I lived. A deck hand had finally told him.

"I would have gone through hell to find you, Mary," he declared.

Emily and I cut our eyes at one another, biting our lips to keep from laughing. Eddy was not himself, but nor was he in any way threatening. He was most polite, and I invited him into the dining room for tea, since the children were playing in the parlor, my daughter looking after the baby.

"So you have married that haberdasher," he said as we entered the dining room. "Do you really love him, Mary? Did you marry him for love?"

My daughter and son had followed us into the dining room, and I had to shoo them back to the parlor. "That's none of your business, Mr. Poe," I said, pretending to be indignant. "That's between my husband and me."

"You don't love him," he insisted. "You *do* love me; you know you do."

My sister and I sat on the opposite side of the dining room table from Eddy. The cook brought out the tea service, and I poured. I ignored his talk of love, distracting him with questions about Mrs. Clemm and Virginia. They were still in Philadelphia, he explained, but he had resigned as editor of *Graham's Magazine*, having been promised a position in the Philadelphia Custom House, but as such a position was beginning to look doubtful, he was in New York seeking new employment. As he said this, he seemed to grow tired, and he dropped his eyes to the mahogany table and began wiping it with his hand in a circular motion as if he were polishing it. I knew he had been with *Graham's*, as I had always subscribed and read his articles and stories. I told him I had recently read "The Oval Portrait" that had appeared in the April issue and that I thought it a wonderful story. This seemed to make him sad, and I looked at my sister who returned my look, both of us sensing something wrong.

"Virginia had an accident in January," he said, looking up at me. "She was singing and burst a blood vessel."

"Is she all right?" I asked, drawing an immediate connection between Virginia and the dying maiden of the oval portrait in his story.

He said nothing for a few moments. As it was getting late in the afternoon, the cook began setting the table for supper. She placed a dish of radishes at the end of the table within Eddy's reach. He took a knife and began chopping the radishes.

"The doctor says she has bronchitis," he said as he chopped, and his chopping became more agitated and soon pieces of radish were littering that end of the dining room table.

"Eddy! Stop," I said reaching across the table and staying his hand. My use of his nickname brought him back to his senses, and he looked up at me almost in fright. "You mustn't do that," I continued, becoming worried that he might get out of hand. "I'm afraid it's time for you to go. We must prepare for supper. Come I'll walk you to the door."

He regained his composure. Perhaps the tea had sobered him a bit. I half expected to see Mr. Jennings home early, knowing that Eddy had gone to Will's office in order to find me. Eddy left. He walked away, dejected and aimless. My husband did arrive soon after. He told us that people on the ferry were talking about Eddy's asking for me and that he suspected Eddy had been drinking when he came to his shop just before lunch. We sat down for supper, my son in the high chair next to me, my sister sitting across from me with my daughter, her namesake, who was four and a half.

There were questions in Mr. Jennings's eyes as he stared at me while serving the plates at the head of the table. With my sister there, knowing the whole story, I became furious with Edgar Poe for putting me in such straits. My son sensed my irritation and started crying. "For heaven's sake, Will," I snapped, "I didn't ask him to come. I don't know what he wanted. His wife is ill. He was upset."

Will eyed me still as I took Henry from the high chair and sat him on my lap, wiping his mouth and trying to console him.

Why had Eddy come, I wondered? Perhaps Virginia was more ill than he let on. Did she have the consumption? I suppose I thought that because she had always seemed so frail and sickly, as those are who are taken by what some call the white plague. Was she dying? Had Eddy's story in *Graham's* been inspired by Virginia's illness and was it an indication of its seriousness?

I had told Mr. Jennings only that I had known Edgar Poe in Baltimore and that he had been a beau of sorts. I laughed it off as puppy love. My sister eyed me now, saying nothing and no doubt wondering what else I would say and would I dare tell Will about Eddy cowhiding Uncle James. I shifted my baby to my other knee and tried to interest him in a spoonful of mashed peas. Will sat patiently waiting as Henry's sobs were choked back by the clover-smelling paste that he gummed. I smiled at him, and he smiled back, his little mouth full of green muck. Both Emilys laughed at this, but Mr. Jennings was not amused.

As I spooned another mouthful into Henry, I cut Mr. Jennings a glance to judge his mood, feeling rather disgusted by the whole affair, and I decided not to spare him. I had borne his son. I had done my duty, and I would not be undone—I would not take the blame for something I had no hand in.

"If you knew he was intoxicated," I asked, "why did you give him our address? Did you think I wanted him here in such a state? And did you think to come warn me? No. You went about your business, leaving Emily and me to deal with the mess—a mess, Will, that you didn't have the decency to deal with yourself. Thankfully Mr. Poe is a decent man; he would not harm a fly despite his being distraught over his wife's illness and wanting only the sympathy of an old friend. If you're upset, it's your own fault."

With this I turned away from him, wiped my brow with the back of my hand, and shoveled another spoonful of green paste down Henry's throat. It's a wonder he didn't choke, but he sensed my resolve and chewed, big-eyed and obedient, as fast as his poor little jaws would work.

Will threw down his napkin and left the table, going out onto the porch.

My sister and I helped the cook wash the dishes, put the children to bed, and an hour and a half later joined him there. Emily said not a word during all these chores, but stared, smiling at me as if I had run Mr. Jennings through with a poker.

As we rocked on the porch and before a word was spoken, I started humming "Come, Rest in This Bosom," and in unison my sister and I started singing the words.

> Come, rest in this bosom, my own stricken deer!
> Tho' the herd have fled from thee, thy home is still here;
> Here still is the smile, that no cloud can o'ercast,
> And the heart and the hand all thy own to the last!
> I knew not, I ask not, if guilt's in that heart,
> I but know that I love thee, whatever thou art.

I don't know if Emily remembered that it was Eddy's favorite song, but I guessed she did, for she continued to smile at me with the same admiration that my Baltimore girlfriends had smiled at me, suspecting that I had been kissed while they were merely holding hands.

So undone was Will by this display that he left the porch and climbed the stairs to our bedroom. As our singing had run him away, we fell silent. Emily was nearly five years younger than I. The events in Baltimore had left her baffled and frightened, and she asked about them now. "Did he make love to you, Mary?" she whispered.

"What do you mean, love?" I asked, both of us knowing it was Edgar Poe under discussion.

"You know," she said, staring at me.

"Do you mean, did he take my clothes off?" I said, looking away.

"Did he?"

"No," I said emphatically, and I stood up and walked to the rail of the porch, turned and leaned against it, facing her. "I let him kiss me; that's all. Had he wanted to touch me, I would have let him. I don't think I knew how to resist him, but I don't think he knew how to touch me either. He was not so experienced as everyone thought, or perhaps he didn't want to touch me, or I don't know—something stopped him. We sat on that hill in the grass. It would have been so easy for him to push me down, raise my skirts, and climb on top of me. But he didn't. I almost wanted him to, but I don't think he knew how." I laughed thinking this. "Isn't that funny that he only kissed me and everyone assumed I was pregnant? It's all because of what he said to mother that night—about me being his wife in the sight of heaven. It wasn't sex that inspired that comment, it was poetry. He read too much Byron."

My sister stared at me. She said nothing. It was dark, but I could not see her face clearly, and I sensed she wanted more.

"I dream of lying naked in that grass," I said. "I wasted my youth."

"Don't be silly," she said. "You have two beautiful children—healthy children—and another on the way."

I laughed at the consolation she offered and wanted to ask her, in the intimacy of the truths we were sharing, if she would marry only for love. I didn't ask; I didn't want to spoil her dreams or imply that she might do as I had done—sacrifice passion for practicality. I turned, put my hands on the rail, and stared up at the night sky above the trees and the roofs of the houses across the street. The upstairs windows were open, and I wondered if Will could hear us. I wanted to ask Emily if she thought it possible that a woman could fall in love more than once in her lifetime. I asked myself that question instead and wondered if that explained the riddle of Edgar Poe's strange odyssey to Jersey City.

Had he married Virginia for much the same reason that I had married Will Jennings? Had he been as horrified by his cowhiding of my uncle as I? And in his remorse, in the shock of realization that he had spun out of control, had he married his cousin in a vain attempt to preserve some stability, some hold to family, motivated by desperate fear that without family, life breaks free of its orbit—defies gravity, wanders unrestrained? Is that our choice? And must we choose it at such a tender age without the wisdom of experience? Is life so exacting as to give us no second chance if we get it wrong the first time?

"I'm not in love with Edgar Poe," I blurted, "if that's what you're thinking."

There! I put it to rest—that question in her mind—and I wasn't in the least in love with Edgar Poe. That time had passed. And its passing made me realized suddenly that love was not necessarily forever. Therefore, it must be possible to fall in love more than once in a lifetime, and I cannot describe the gush of hope that flowed from this revelation. In strictly practical terms I don't know what I thought it meant. I only know that I was grateful to Eddy for having arrived drunk on our doorstep that day. It was as if I had been saved again, and I laughed at the notion that first there was Will Jennings—and I could almost hear him snoring in the bed upstairs—and now there was this new, unexpected savior, Edgar Poe, and I imagined him staggering down Broadway, reeling from lamppost to stoop, sleeping in some alleyway, and I hoped he was safe.

"Do you think he will make it home safely?" I asked, concerned for him suddenly.

"Do you care?" she asked.

"Of course I care," I said turning back to her. "Do you think I'm so heartless? I don't love him, but there was a time I did, and no one has ever loved me like he did. You don't understand him; no one understood him. I have never known a man with such passion. How many men would ride back and forth on the ferry all afternoon searching for someone they hadn't seen for years?"

"Oh, come, Mary," she said. "Don't be so dramatic. You saw him in Philadelphia not four years ago."

I *was* being dramatic but what of it? I turned back to the sky and watched the breeze blow the black leaves of the poplars. The hope I had earlier felt had evaporated as suddenly as it came. Yes, perhaps a woman can fall in love more than once in her lifetime, but I was not free to fall in love. Mr. Jennings snored upstairs, and the sonorous rhythm of that unheard noise was like the links of a chain, and his heavy exhales, deep sighs of capitulation.

"Let's go to bed," I said, and I turned toward the door.

"Mary, wait," Emily said, and she rose from her chair to go in with me, but there was something more she wished to say. "One night back in Baltimore, I was going to bed. I was about to take off my chemise and put on my nightgown. The shade was not pulled, but the room was dark, and I assumed no one could see. Then I saw him at his window staring at me. In the dark, I guess, he thought I was you, and I froze for what seemed like the longest time, standing beside the bed, nearly undressed. When he realized it was me, he turned away. I could tell he was ashamed. Afterward, I wondered if maybe you let him watch you undress, pretending that he wasn't looking. I didn't hate you for it. I was fourteen; I had some of those feelings too, but I did think you were evil. I guess I thought the worst like our parents did. Forgive me?"

Tears came to both our eyes, and we embraced, me granting her forgiveness as if granting also forgiveness to my father who was dead, and my mother and Tom who lived still and whose forgiveness in return I felt at that same instant.

When I pulled away from Emily, I laughed my tears away. "Oh," I said, "if I still had the body I had then, I think I would willingly show it to the world, freckles and all." And with our arms around each other we climbed the stairs to bed.

Mrs. Clemm was now a woman in her fifties. She had dark hair and wore black from boot to bonnet. I had met her in Baltimore, though only once did I go into the Poes' house, as my parents didn't think it proper. She had been happy that Eddy had a girlfriend, I think, and she appreciated my attentions to Virginia. As soon as I saw her on the front stoop of our house in Jersey City, I knew something must be dreadfully wrong. It was four or five days since Eddy's visit. My sister had returned to Philadelphia, and that morning as he usually did, Will had gone into New York City for work.

"Oh, Mary, Mary," Mrs. Clemm said when I answered the door, "Mrs. Jennings, I mean. Eddy's missing. I've come all the way from

Philadelphia to find him. He's been gone ten days, and we've not heard a word. It's not like Eddy not to write, and I'm certain something awful has happened. I found out at Wiley & Putnam that he had gone on a drinking spree with Mr. Wallace, and Mr. Wallace told me Eddy had gone off to find Mr. Jennings to learn where you lived. I've just come from your husband's shop. He told me Eddy visited you."

"Yes, Mr. Clemm, he did," I said. "But as Mr. Jennings surely told you, Eddy only stayed for tea. He was not here longer than an hour. Want you come in and sit, and let's think about what we should do? I'm certain he's all right."

On the contrary I wasn't certain at all, and I remembered my image of him sleeping in some alleyway. Perhaps he'd wondered into Five Points, and there was no telling what could befall him there.

Mrs. Clemm came inside, lugging her carpetbag. She took off her bonnet under which she wore a white widow's cap. I offered her some lemonade, but she refused, asking for water instead, and I went to fetch it. When I returned to the parlor, she was staring down at the carpet, lost in worried thought. I could see that she was scared, and I blamed myself for letting him wander off in such a state. It was unthinking of me.

"Did he say anything, Mary, about where he was going? And was he on one of his sprees?"

"I'm afraid he was, Mrs. Clemm," I said, "but he said nothing about where he was going, only that he was looking for work. I should not have let him leave. I feel horrible."

"No one in New York saw him again after he came over here," she said. "I went to all the places he said he was going. He was planning to return to Philadelphia on the day he came to see you. That was last Friday, wasn't it?"

I thought back. Yes it had been Friday, and my sister had returned to Philadelphia on Sunday. "You don't think he could still be in Jersey City, do you?"

"I don't know what else to think," Mrs. Clemm said. "If he had gone back to New York, it's likely one of his friends would have seen him, but I don't know all his friends."

"Let's go to the constable," I said. It was early afternoon. The children were down for their naps, and I would have the cook look in on them until we returned. I invited Mrs. Clemm to stay with us, and we took her bag up to the guest room, then she and I walked to the police station and explained everything. They had no knowledge of him, and a quick check of their records turned up nothing. Mrs. Clemm blanched when the constable told her that he had no one in jail by the name of Edgar Poe. I couldn't tell if she was disappointed or relieved. I gave him a detailed physical description with Mrs. Clemm adding bits of information.

"He bites his nails," she said. "Down to the quick."

I described his mustache, the suit he was wearing, his shoes and top hat. I told them he'd been drinking and about his strange trip over on the ferry.

"Well, at least he won't have frozen to death," the constable said smiling. "We'll do a check of all the taverns and the hospital, and I'll go round to have a chat with the ferryman. Maybe, if he made such a fuss coming over, they saw him return. If he's in Jersey City, we'll find him, Misses, likely as not he'll turn up before nightfall."

We returned to my house to wait. Mrs. Clemm sat in the parlor, on the edge of one of the chairs, tense with anticipation, her breathing coming fast as if she expected news at any moment. She told me Virginia was distraught, that she had to put her to bed and left her in the care of a neighbor, and she seemed as worried about Virginia as her son-in-law. I busied myself with the children and preparations for supper, leaving Mrs. Clemm to wait by herself in the parlor.

They found him the next day on the outskirts of Jersey City wandering in the woods, half out of his mind. I suppose he'd been there all weekend. I went with him and Mrs. Clemm to the ferry to see them off, gave Mrs. Clemm some money, and promised to write. He would be okay, she promised, once she got him home.

I did write, and from time to time received a note from Mrs. Clemm, asking for money as often as not. I would send a dollar or two—that was as generous as I could afford to be.

A few years later the Poes moved to New York where Eddy published his "Raven" and became quite famous, though unfortunately no less impoverished. Ultimately we moved back into New York City, and I once visited Mrs. Clemm and Virginia when they lived on Amity Street in Greenwich Village, but Eddy was away. I did not see him again until they had left the city and moved to Fordham. Mrs. Clemm wrote from there to say they were in the sorest need and that Virginia was quite ill. I judged from her words that Virginia was dying. That was in the summer of 1846, and in some of the New York papers, hateful things were being said about Eddy. He had become embroiled in some lawsuit. I couldn't believe all that I read and resolved to do what I could.

That night I announced my plan to Will—to take some old clothes and food. I asked him to help me. I wanted a suit of clothes for Eddy and whatever else he could spare from his shop that might be helpful, and I told him that I wanted to give them ten dollars and that I wanted him to go with me, as I was apprehensive about taking the train by myself all the way to Fordham. Reluctantly he agreed, sensing my resolve and reminding me that he was not a rich man, that his business suffered from the new department stores that were springing up. He mentioned Stewart's new store and others, retelling complaints I had heard ad nauseam. I reminded him how frugal I was and that I didn't ask for much, but insisted that I could not live with myself in good conscience if I failed to make this effort. He agreed to go, and I praised him for being a fine, Christian man, but my flattery failed to ease his misgivings.

As I said this at the supper table, my daughter, Emily, who was nine now, sensing the tension, stared big-eyed at me, and I wondered if she remembered that day four years earlier when Eddy had appeared at our door crazed with whiskey, saying he would have gone through hell to find Mary Starr. Was Emily making a connection that would someday lead to questions—mama, who was that man? I smiled at her, sitting across the dining room table as if to say, someday I will tell you everything, someday when you, too, have come to know all the vagaries of love and passion and disappointment and when you have learned how the love of children can wash all that away—then I will tell you. She was going to be tall like me and my father. I loved all my children equally, but Emily, my oldest and only girl, seemed to have been born with an old soul. It was as if she knew everything before I told her, indeed, before she was ever old enough to know, she seemed to understand. And I could see in her eyes then that she approved. Her big, brown eyes gave me heart, gave me confidence and courage; I knew then I was doing the right thing.

The Poes lived in a cottage that stood all by itself on a grassy hill not a distant walk through woods from the Harlem River and the Harlem train trestle that crossed the river from Manhattan. The word cottage was overly generous. It was worse than humble, overgrown with vines, too rustic for decent folk, yet it was spotlessly clean and prim, almost charming. It had a porch bordered by a weedless flower bed and beyond were two spreading cherry trees that shaded a yard filled with clover and dandelions that ran to a split rail fence enclosing a pasture where the Poe's landlord's sheep and cattle grazed.

They were delighted at our coming. Will and I toted bags of old clothes, baked goods that the cook and I had made, cheeses, a tin of coffee and one of tea, dried herbs that Mrs. Clemm had requested in her letter, jars of preserves and marmalade, and a special green tomato relish and pork jelly that were our cook's specialties. It was all we could carry, but it wasn't enough despite Mrs. Clemm's protestations about what a feast they would have.

It was clear to me that if Virginia survived to winter, her suffering would be severe. She slept in one of the two small bedrooms in the loft. I went up with Mrs. Clemm to see her, and she insisted on coming down to thank Mr. Jennings, though she was not up to it. She lay on a straw mattress in a room that was stifling hot with one narrow window that did not open to let in fresh air. Though I insisted to no avail that the effort was unnecessary, that Mr. Jennings would be happy to come up, she made her way down the narrow staircase with Mrs. Clemm leading the way and me following after to help Virginia down. She was too weak to make it by herself.

Eddy and Will stood on the porch in polite conversation. What in the world were they talking about, I wondered? Having nothing in common, the two men might have been discussing the weather, or perhaps, judging from the authoritative look on Will's face, he might have been decrying the unnecessary changes in fashion that were slowly eroding his business. I had come to ignore this litany of complaints, not realizing that I should have taken them more seriously, for our fortunes continued to dwindle, but at the time I was oblivious to all that. I only thought to rescue Eddy from Will's tirade, and, thankfully, Virginia's appearance brought their conversation to an end.

Mrs. Clemm led Virginia to a chair in the parlor, and Eddy brought Mr. Jennings inside. Virginia thanked him, and with more effort than she had the strength for, she chatted with us for a while. Mrs. Clemm served tea with the bread and marmalade we had brought. I insisted after tea that we must leave, fearful that our visit was overtaxing Virginia, and Will was relieved to be away.

Eddy walked us to the station. As we made our way there, he told us that he too had been ill during the spring and early summer, that he had been unable to write, but that he felt better now thanks to country air and the generosity of neighbors. He seemed rather more cheerful than I would have expected, judging from Virginia's condition, and he thanked us profusely, asking us to return soon, and he promised a gift, seeming to apologize for the absence of one then. He pumped Mr. Jennings hand with more force than necessary as if that gesture made up for his not knowing what to say in response to Will's business troubles. We left, Eddy waving at us from the platform, following as our train pulled away from the station. I carry that memory of him still—proud, erect, smiling as if all were well. I don't think I ever saw him smile again.

My old clothes were too big for Virginia and too small and unsuitable for Mrs. Clemm. I had done what I could. No reference had been made to Eddy's wild trip to Jersey City, and I wondered if he had any recollection of it. Had Mrs. Clemm told him? Perhaps he only knew of my visit to Amity Street, and the rest had been forgotten, erased like bad memories, things best left unmentioned like the cowhiding of Uncle James. Perhaps Edgar Poe had too many such unremembered events in his life. Perhaps he believed that he was not part of those events—like spying on my sister in her chemise, like things he trusted were forgiven and forgotten by those who truly loved him, and I accepted that, being one who had loved him. I realized on the train back to New York that for him I had boundless forgiveness—the love of my youth—that all things done in youthful love are infinitely forgivable. I would always love the memory of loving Edgar Poe; no amount of controversy, not intemperance, not lack of faith in God, not error or madness could change that.

Edgar Poe was a different man when he smiled. His likenesses never did him justice. Facsimiles of the daguerreotypes taken of him are ghastly in my opinion and failed to capture his warmth. I have always preferred the engraving taken from the portrait by Mr. Osgood. Perhaps that one is my preference because, when I knew Eddy in Baltimore, he wore no mustache, and in the engraving also there is the hint of a smile on his face. After Baltimore I never saw him without a mustache, and his mustache concealed the playfulness that had captivated me when I was seventeen.

When I saw him last, all of that had disappeared—his smile and the exuberance in his eyes. Instead his face was timeworn. There were always deep circles under his eyes betraying worry and perhaps dissipation as well. Loui Shew, whom I came to know in the final days of Virginia's illness, insisted that he was ill even when he seemed at his best. She maintained that he suffered from a lesion on his brain, that this was the cause of his susceptibility to spirits, that even the mildest drugs left him disoriented, half out of his mind. She had little hope for him.

In the late fall of that same year I read an article about the Poes in the *Home Journal*, an article by N. P. Willis. While I was heartened to learn from it that Virginia still lived, I suspected that her suffering must be wretched. I had not been back to Fordham; I had not been as attentive as I should have been. Though I had written once to Mrs. Clemm after our first visit, I had no response, and my mother had died the previous winter, and my brother, Ray, had come to live with us, and I now had four children, three of which were boys. That meant five males living in my house, each, regardless of their age, as demanding as the others.

I gathered what I could on short notice—an old woolen nightgown, wool socks. My daughter, Emily, helped, offering her cast-offs which I decided might not be too small for Virginia, and I praised her for her generosity. Again I saw those worried questions in her eyes, and I told her what I judged was appropriate for a nine-year-old to know. Emily had read "The Raven," and her precocious mind drew the same conclusions I had drawn, that this poet friend of my youth had been inspired to write about the death he envisioned, and I saw in Emily's sad eyes the same distress I felt myself. As we went through drawers and cupboards, she would hold up an object and say, "Mama, we could give them this." I do think she would have donated the counterpane off her bed, and I hugged her, she sensing mortality perhaps for the first time in her young life. I think of that afternoon as we rushed around, searching through the cellar and the attic for anything that might be useful as a measure of her goodness. Like Virginia Poe, she would be denied a long life. Of all the lives lost to me, Emily's is the one I can never bear. That night—it was early December, I think—the boys all tucked in and a coal fire in the grate—I read to her a poem of Eddy's that I sensed had been written with me in mind—not the one "To Mary S——," as I had not saved that one, but one from his book, one entitled "To Mary."

> Beloved! Thy memory is to me
> Like some enchanted far-off isle,
> In some tumultuous sea—
> Some ocean throbbing far and free
> With storms—but where, meanwhile,
> Serenest skies continually
> Just o'er that one bright island smile.

"Mama!" Emily exclaimed when I finished, her brown eyes big with amazement that I might be the beloved of the poem.

I smiled, hoping as I did that someday some boy would write her a poem, some lucky little boy that her fancy favored, a small treasure with simple rhymes to light a lifetime. That moment is one of my fondest memories of my daughter.

Mr. Willis had been right. The Poes lacked the bare necessities, and my meager offerings were scant indeed. It was on this visit that I first met Loui Shew. She had arrived earlier that day with a feather mattress and counterpane and had ordered Virginia's bed to be brought down from the loft and placed in a little room off the parlor, nearer the fireplace. It was being set up when I arrived. As I watched, I noticed something I had not noticed on my earlier trip. Over the door of the parlor was a bracket on which stood the plaster cast of a bird. I suppose it was a raven, but it might have been a parrot. I later learned that it was intended to be a raven, that it had been a gift to Eddy from a sculptor friend in New York, a woman as I recall.

Eddy had enlisted the help of a neighbor's boy with getting the bed frame down from the loft, and after preparations were complete, Eddy and Mrs. Clemm went back up to fetch Virginia. I merely watched as Loui coached the neighbor's boy in making a wood fire, and soon the little bedroom was warm as toast. Eddy appeared at the bottom of the stairs with Virginia in his arms and carried her to the newly made bed. She was so pitiful; she could not have weighed eighty pounds, but when she saw me, she smiled a big smile, and we embraced, me trying to hold back tears. She had turned twenty-four just that previous August.

Loui went about her work, assigning chores to each of us with the authority of her profession, authority that was a great comfort. She was a godsend. She banished Eddy and the neighbor's boy from the cottage, sending them for more firewood, instructing them to stack it on the porch where it would stay dry. It was not so cold, and the day was sunny, a good day for outside chores, still Virginia seemed to suffer with chills. Loui gave her a sponge bath, then dressed her in the nightgown I had brought and the pair of woolen socks. I assisted Mrs. Clemm in the kitchen with preparing an herb tea and a poultice that Loui had brought ingredients for, and soon the house smelled of camphor. Later she used the poultice in massaging Virginia's chest and back, and she coaxed her to drink a glass of red wine. She had brought several bottles for this purpose and cautioned Mrs. Clemm to see that they remained hidden from Eddy.

We remained the better part of the day thus occupied, and late that afternoon Loui and I rode back to New York on the train. She had no hope for Virginia, of course, but was determined to ease her suffering. She explained to me that she had only met the Poes the week before, that she had been urged to visit them by a New York friend, Mary Gove, a writer and acquaintance of Eddy's. Loui was divorced, as I recall, and had two children; she was several years younger than I. Very certain of herself, she explained that her father had been a country doctor and that she had learned her medicine from him. She talked incessantly; she seemed preoccupied by Eddy's illness, though he had seemed to me to be well that day. Eddy and I had hardly said a word to each other, as he was anxious to do Loui's bidding, so appreciative was he to have someone of her ability.

I returned again in early January and spent the day helping Mrs. Clemm wash bed linens, hanging them to dry in the parlor as Virginia lay in bed, so weak she could hardly lift her head. It was her coughing that made her so weak and gave her so much pain. She was exhausted by it, her body horribly wasted. Mrs. Clemm explained that she could hardly speak or swallow, that she had taken no solid food for days. Despite the cold, Eddy stayed away. He walked over to the palisades and stared at the river, so he told me as he walked me back to the train station. Virginia's dying was agonizing for him and for Mrs. Clemm, and I hoped it would end soon.

Again I took the train to Fordham on Friday, the 29th of January, and immediately upon seeing Virginia, I knew it was only a matter of a day or two, perhaps even hours. She was sitting in an armchair as Mrs. Clemm changed her bed linen, a thing she was now having to do every day, and Virginia's breathing came more easily when she was propped upright. I sat beside her and held her hand. Eddy sat on the other side of her, rubbing her other hand to keep it warm. She smiled at me so kindly, her head against the headrest, she lacking the strength to lift it. She took my hand and placed it in Eddy's. "Mary," she said, "be a friend to Eddy, and don't forsake him. He always loved you, didn't you, Eddy."

She did not look at him when she said this; she stared at me. Eddy was weeping uncontrollably; I could feel his hand shaking, and surely Virginia knew that he was crying. I felt tears come into my eyes too, and I promised her. This seemed to content her, and she closed her eyes.

When Eddy put her back to bed, he rubbed her feet to keep them warm, and Mrs. Clemm rubbed her hands. The Poes' cat, Catterina, jumped up on the bed and nestled close to Virginia, providing even more warmth. I decided to stay the night, sitting up all night with Eddy and Mrs. Clemm and trying to keep Virginia as warm and comfortable as possible. Twice Mrs. Clemm and I persuaded Eddy to go upstairs and get some rest, but he was back down again before twenty minutes were up to tend the fire. I think he was determined to be by her side when she died. It seemed Virginia's pain had subsided somewhat, and she grew more peaceful.

She died just after eight o'clock the next morning.

Eddy and Mrs. Clemm sat by her bedside, still rubbing her hands and arms. I went to the kitchen to prepare something for them to eat, if and when the time came. Eddy had written to Loui the day before, asking her to come that day. When I heard her footsteps on the porch, Eddy let out a cry and went to her, sobbing uncontrollably. Mrs. Clemm stayed by the bedside. She had pulled the sheet up as if preparing to cover Virginia's face, but couldn't bring herself to do it. Loui took over. She ushered Eddy and Mrs. Clemm out of the bedroom and into the kitchen, instructing them to eat something and then go upstairs to rest while she made the preparations. Arrangements had already been made; the Poes' landlord, Mr. Valentine, generously provided a coffin and offered a place in his own family's vault in the graveyard of the Old Dutch Reformed Church nearby. I served a breakfast of hot bread, ham, and fried potatoes. Eddy and Mrs. Clemm picked at their food in silence then went upstairs as Loui had ordered them to do, promising not to come back down until she called for them. During breakfast Loui had gone for a neighbor to send the necessary messages then she returned.

After cleaning the breakfast things, I peeked in on Loui in the little bedroom off the parlor. She had her watercolors out and was painting a portrait of Virginia. She told me that Eddy had begged her for a likeness of Virginia. I watched her work, standing in the doorway to the parlor, then she made me come and sit beside the bed. As she glanced at me from time to time, I imagined she was putting Virginia's head and face on my shoulders. She did not rush, and she seemed to be quite a fine artist. The house was quiet and peaceful. I could hear birds singing outside and also the bleating of the sheep. Inside there was only the occasional sputtering of the log fire.

"Help me, Mary. People will start arriving soon," Loui said, putting her pallet of paints away and placing her portrait on the mantle to dry.

First we stripped the bed, then put on a bedspread. From her bag Loui took out a linen dress, and she and I removed Virginia's nightgown. We bathed her, put on her chemise, her shoes and stockings, and the new dress. Then we smoothed out the spread beneath Virginia and crossed her arms over her chest. Loui had fixed her hair before painting her portrait, and in a few minutes she was dressed out and ready. We stepped away from the bed to observe her as one might observe a table setting in preparation for a dinner party. At once the black and orange tabby, Catterina, leapt up onto the bed and began pawing Virginia's stomach as if trying to awaken her. Before Loui could lift the cat off the corpse, she had curled herself next to Virginia, and we left her there where she stayed for the remainder of the day, her head resting on her paws, eying curious neighbors and well-wishers. Loui called upstairs to Eddy and Mrs. Clemm to come back down. When Mrs. Clemm arrived at the bottom of the stairs, she nearly fainted. Loui and I led her to the chair at the head of Virginia's bed, and I knelt down beside her as she stared at her daughter, weeping and babbling about how thrilled she was that Virginia would be buried in fine linen. Eddy did not come down until the parlor was crowded with neighbors who had come to pay their respects.

There were gifts, mostly of food, and I remained in the kitchen for most of the afternoon, arranging plates of food for the guests, brewing coffee and tea, and trying to keep the tiny room as neat as possible. At four o'clock, Loui peeked her head in the door and said it was time to go. I turned over my duty to a neighbor's wife who was willing to take charge, and Loui and I walked to the station to return to New York.

The funeral was on Tuesday at two o'clock. I met Loui at City Hall for a special horsecar that left at ten that morning and would return at four that afternoon. I was introduced to Mr. Willis and his partner, General Morris, Ann Stephens, Mary Gove, and others. It was a bitter cold day, and I decided to stay at the cottage and not go to the cemetery. Loui had tried to hide Eddy's gray military coat. She did not want him to wear it, thinking it too old and worn and the color inappropriate, but he wore it anyway. I had seen that coat covering Virginia like a blanket; I even think Eddy owned it when I knew him in Baltimore fifteen years earlier. While they were all at church, I straightened the cottage and kept the fire going.

Before leaving that afternoon, I remember embracing Eddy, but few words were said, and I cannot now remember what they were. The cottage was filled with neighbors and those who had come out from New York. Many were waiting to express condolences in that awful awkwardness that inhabits such moments. Like the gray military coat that Eddy wore against Loui's wishes, he bore up with the somber respectfulness that convention required when in fact he was inconsolable. It was not a time for words of a personal nature. I assumed that I would see him again. I never did.

I have always remembered Virginia's dying wish that I not forsake him, and in my heart I never have. My fifth child, Zachary Taylor Jennings was born a year later, and raising four boys seemed to consume the years that followed. Of course I was in no position to defend Eddy against the condemnation that naturally followed such a death as his. Because of all I had heard from Loui Shew about his mental state, I suppose I was not surprised. It was as if I had known all along that he would not grow old. Now he seems like someone rash, too thoughtless and careless of himself and often of others for some purpose beyond my comprehension and no doubt beyond prudence, but I sense in these qualities a certain vision and purpose that I can't help but admire. I am no judge of his accomplishments, but he has been dead for thirty years now, yet my children and grandchildren brag to their friends that Edgar Allan Poe was once in love with me. Imagine that! That brush with celebrity has become a source of pride to them, and I am moved by this to conclude that he was misjudged, that his rashness, his passion were like that particular lump of coal that for no apparent reason burns brighter and faster than all the others.

When my daughter, Emily, was to be married in 1858, I wrote to Mrs. Clemm, inviting her to the wedding. She was living with the family of an attorney in Alexandria, Virginia, doing their sewing and tending to their children. Regretting that she could not come, she wrote back to say that she wished to make a gift to Emily of Virginia's gold thimble. I would have treasured such a gift, but Mrs. Clemm asked that I pay her ten dollars for it. As we had many other expenses at the time, I could not afford to buy it.

I have outlived three of my five children and all of my siblings with the possible exception of my youngest brother, Cord. He was fifteen years younger than I, only eight when I married Will Jennings and left Philadelphia for New York. Because he still seems such a boy to me, I think of him often—his father dead when he was ten; his mother dead when he was sixteen—so young that perhaps he never came to feel the gravitational pull of family. Perhaps he is out west somewhere. Sometimes at night I gaze at a particular star and imagine that at that same instant Cord is gazing at that same star. He might have gone north in search of gold. Or perhaps even now he is on some sailing ship, standing watch, rounding Cape Horn. What I would give to see him! More likely he is in some nameless grave of which there are so many in Gettysburg and Manassas and those other battlefields, for no one in our family heard from him after the war.

I have never believed that I had anything important to add to what has been written about Edgar Poe. As you can glean from what I've written, my relationship with him had little significance. The poem he wrote to me, "To Mary," is of no great consequence except that it is reminiscent of another, more important one, "To Helen." I have always believed that his poem to me was a draft of that greater one. So, it seems, his gift to me became a gift to someone else. It doesn't matter. I have told you what I know. I have often wondered if Edgar Poe was the love of my life, but his fame keeps getting in the way of an honest answer to that question. I can't be sure, but that is not to say that I did not care deeply for him and his family. I did indeed. And when I die, though he will not be foremost in my thoughts, I have no doubt but that I will find him among those lurking there.

(ITEM 53: *Mary Starr Jennings*)
...

September 9, 1885
Philadelphia

Dearest Captain Gayle,

It was kind of you to write. Thank you for your generous expression of sympathy.

I hope you are well. I have most certainly not forgotten you as your note suggests; in fact, there have been times when I have deeply regretted that our exchange of letters seemed to languish—how many years ago? I understand, of course, that a soldier's life is busy and fraught with danger. You have more important things to occupy your time.

I decided to sell the house and move to Philadelphia to live with my sister, Emily. Mr. Jennings had been ill for some time, and I had planned this move when he was gone, since neither of my surviving sons had made their home nearby. There was little holding me there. Your letter took six weeks to find me, and I apologize for my additional delay in responding. I did delay for a reason that gives me considerable discomfort. My nephew, Augustus, raised an objection to my corresponding with you. I told him about you a few months ago when he revealed his plan to write an article about my relationship with Edgar Poe. He surprised me with this news and informed me that he had already arranged publication of his article in *Scribner's Magazine*. He is very enthusiastic about it, and, though I am considerably less enthusiastic, I want to let him do it if it makes him happy. I tried to convince him that you were initially seeking answers to questions I could not provide—that, though I told you much about Edgar, our correspondence had devolved into a purely personal exchange, but I regret to say that he is suspicious of your motives. Captain Gayle, admittedly he is young and headstrong, but I adore him so. I could never deny him.

When Augustus began interviewing me about my relationship with Edgar, I realized, suddenly, that I had confided in you things I would never reveal to him or to any member of my family or, in fact, to anyone else in the world. It, therefore, amazed and embarrassed me that I had done so with you. I wonder now how it happened that I so easily told you those things. On reflection I think I was touched by things you revealed to me, things of a personal nature—your loneliness, your fear that you might never find someone who would love you, your sympathy for the horrible plight of the Sioux, and the resulting uncertainty regarding your chosen career—all those things and more. In return I found it so easy, and, if I may say, appropriate to confide in you. Certainly I did so without thinking that there might be consequences. It occurs to me now that having lost my daughter shortly before receiving your first letter, I was vulnerable and wanted someone to talk to—a proper stranger, if you will. You and I had no mutual friends; I felt certain we would never meet. Most of all, I trusted your sincerity. Though I am embarrassed to say it (and I would not, but for our considerable age difference), you were like a lover in this respect. I never had a lover, but perhaps I came to think of you as someone I had loved, someone else called Eddy. In this way I found it easy to tell you the most intimate things. Writing letters to you was not unlike making entries into a dairy. It was almost as if you were not real.

Now your letter comes, and I see that you are very real indeed, and I am unhinged by it. Even worse, I can't quite explain how it happened. If I burdened you, please forgive me.

This said, I confess that I trust you utterly, and, though I never asked you to keep the things I told you confidential, I do so now. *Please*, Captain Gayle. I think of us as sharing friends. But you must understand, it was only when Augustus suggested that my experiences might be of interest to the public that it occurred to me that you could conceivably share that notion. Needless to say, I would appear a gullible fool. I sincerely hope this is not the case, for it would hurt me and my family were some of the things I told to you to be published in a magazine or book. I always felt that you were my friend, though unknown to me, and I, your friend. May I be reassured of your confidence?

Instinct tells me that you are appalled at my alarm. Such is my respect for you. I am certain this is the case, and so I will ask—for a second time in this letter—that you forgive me. And, furthermore, I will ask that you send me news—news of you, my dear friend, for I have missed you and your warm letters. Don't be a stranger. Please do an aging widow the favor of gracing her with one of your long, chatty letters full of your incomparable homespun. I eagerly anticipate it . . . even as I enclose my deep affection for you,

Mary Jennings

· · ·

· · ·

· · ·

(ITEM 10: *Whitman*)

· · ·

January 2, 1877
Providence

Dear Lieutenant Gayle,

What absolute bliss to hear from you. I understand perfectly your delay in writing. What an adventure you have had! Needless to say, with no forwarding address, I had no way to write to you, though I much wanted to. I so terribly wanted to see you the morning you left Providence, but so exhausted was I by the events of the evening before that by the time Charlotte and I arrived at your hotel, you'd left to catch the ferry.

As for the happenings of that evening, it may be that a spirit or spirits appeared and spoke to us. One can never be certain. And please understand, my dear Eddy, that the manifest matter of such meetings is often metaphorical and must be subjected to interpretation. In this way messages conveyed by the spirits are not unlike dreams, the significance of which can take years to ascertain, if, indeed, they can ever be. Don't concern yourself; I am confident that we uncovered nothing momentous. Allow me instead to apologize for the evening. My sister was right, the séance was ill-conceived, and we proved such poor hosts as to not provide supper for our guests, though we had, of course, planned and prepared to do just that—the roast was in the oven ready for carving. Please accept my apology and not hold it against your friend Helen that she was so ill-mannered. Yes, of course, we heard the news of General Custer and the dreadful massacre of his army. Had I any notion that you might be out west, I would have worried myself sick for fear you might be in the thick of it. Thank heavens that you had not yet arrived at Fort Russell. My thoughts are with you as are my hopes that you will keep safe and out of harm's way. Your description of Wyoming is fascinating and, as always, punctuated with your matchless humor—"cold enough to freeze the chiggers off a polar bear"—really, Lieutenant! Your habit of "firing off sallies," as you put it, so amuses me that I pray that in the future you will "spare no ammunition" on me.

As for Gill's biography, I understand it is delayed until the fall, but I will get you a copy and forward it then. As I think I told you, I have little faith that it will prove a worthy account. Perhaps it will slake your seemingly bottomless thirst for knowledge of EAP, but read it knowing that it lacks the scope and accuracy of Ingram's work-in-progress.

When you write to Mrs. Houghton next, please give her my regards. Mrs. Nichols address is Aldwyn Tower, Malvern, England. She was, indeed, as was I, a close friend of Fanny Osgood. I doubt she can shed more light on the subject. She introduced Mrs. Houghton (then Mrs. Shew) to the Poes that summer before Virginia Poe died of consumption, but probably Mrs. Houghton told you that. So far as I know Mrs. Nichols was always kindly disposed to EAP. John Ingram has been in contact with her; therefore, whatever she has to offer on the subject will be available with publication of his book.

Please write again soon, and tell me more about the Sioux, their appearance, customs, religion, crafts and art (if such they have), how they survive the brutal winters that you describe without starving to death in their tepees, &c. And give me news of Crazy Horse. Is he as awful as the papers report? Has he been captured? Will the war resume come spring? Everything. I wish to know everything.

Devotedly,

Helen

3

LOUI SHEW

::

(ITEM 7: *Marie Louise Shew Houghton*)
...

May 10, 1876
The Chestnuts
Whitestone
Long Island

Dear Cadet Captain Gayle,

Forgive my delay in responding. I am a country doctor with more patients than I have time to care for. Your letter arrived just as one of them was in failing health, and I remained at her home day and night for nearly a week. My daughter, Dora, brought your [*several words illegible*] my patient, but, alas, it was hopeless, and we bury her tomorrow, may God give her rest, for surely she suffered mightily.

I hope Mrs. Whitman is not ill, but your letter leads me to believe that she may be. I know she is advanced in years (though I am no spring chicken myself). Mrs. Whitman and I have never met nor corresponded, but we have known of each other since before Edgar died. She learned of my whereabouts—how? I do not know—and forwarded my address to John H. Ingram of London, England, with whom I have been in correspondence for the last year or so and with whom I have entrusted many of my valuable keepsakes relating to Edgar. I have no idea when his book will come out. My impression is that it is not yet written; therefore, I sympathize with the fact that, as you say in your letter, your "curiosity outruns your patience." (I might caution you about curiosity and the cat, but I reckon you know that story.)

As for Griswold, I hardly know where to begin. Mrs. Whitman was right in what she said to you about Griswold and his memoir. It was, to be blunt, a pack of slants and lies. (And him claiming to be a Doctor of Divinity.) As to what motivated him to do such a thing, the simple answer is that he hated Edgar. A harder question is why? I suspect it had something to do with debts and with Fanny Osgood and with the unkind things that Edgar said about Griswold's books. It may also have something to do with the unkind things that Edgar had to say about Longfellow's poems. Frankly, Edgar disliked Griswold as much as Griswold disliked him, but the real crime was that Mrs. Clemm (I suppose you know that she was Edgar's mother-in-law) gave Griswold the right to be Edgar's executor. The poor woman spent the rest of her life regretting that mistake, but Griswold's memoir blackened the name of Edgar Poe in the eyes of the world, and what was done was done. Mrs. Clemm had no one to blame but herself. I tried to talk sense into her, but she never listened to me. If she had, Edgar might be alive today, and that's the God's honest truth. She was an obstinate woman if ever He made one. But in my honest opinion, there was something else between Griswold and Edgar, something they wouldn't speak of, something that may have been buried with Griswold when he died which must have been twenty years ago now.

As for Louisa Allan, it is a miracle that she responded to your letter. To my knowledge she has not talked to a soul about Edgar for forty years. But regarding Louisa Allan I can tell you this much (which is in and of itself proof enough that Griswold was false): two days before she died, Virginia Poe (Edgar's wife and also his first cousin—did you know that?—she was twenty-five years old when she died—she and I were exactly the same age) she called Edgar and me to her bedside and asked for her portfolio which Edgar fetched. Inside she found a letter that Edgar had received from Louisa Allan after his foster father died (whose name was John Allan). Virginia handed the letter to Edgar who glanced at the first few lines, shook his head, and handed it to me to read. He couldn't bear to read it again. The letter was apologetic. Mrs. Allan confessed that she had been to blame for the rupture between Edgar and John Allan out of jealousy, and she begged him to return to Richmond after her year of mourning ended, saying she would provide for him. Edgar had refused. I can tell you that scar never healed so long as he lived, but Mrs. Allan wrote again, begging him to forgive her and to agree to her assistance. He refused again. Virginia had saved Mrs. Allan's two letters, so, as she told me two days before she died, the world would know the truth. "Promise me, Eddy," Virginia said, "here in the presence of Loui that you will preserve these letters and not burn them." I turned to him. His mouth showed the bitterness he still felt for that episode in his life, even after all those years. Nevertheless he promised. Being so near her end, he could not deny his "Sissy" (that was his pet name for her). He never denied her anything that was in his power to give. So I became witness to a solemn oath. But Mrs. Clemm later told me that she burned those letters along with hundreds of others (now is that not a crying shame?), so the proof is gone, but I saw them with my own eyes.

I ask you, Mr. Gayle, would Louisa Allan have done such a thing if Eddy were guilty of the crimes against her that Griswold claimed? No, indeed.

I know for a fact that John H. Ingram has tried without success to communicate with Louisa Allan, that she has refused to even answer his letters which explains my utter amazement that she would write to you. Since your letter must have softened her heart and resolve to remain silent, I beg you to write to her again, asking her to acknowledge that she wrote those two letters to Edgar after John Allan died and forward a copy of her response to John H. Ingram, #12 Wolsey Road, Mildway Park, London, England. You would be doing the memory of Edgar Allan Poe a great service. I have told Mr. Ingram about Louisa Allan's letters to Edgar, but he replied that without "corroboration"— his word—he could not credit it. I'm at a loss to explain why; sometimes I think the man doesn't believe a word I say, but I'd best hold my tongue on that subject. I know my writing is plain. My father adored me; he even spoiled me, but he saw no reason to pay for a daughter's education, and I left school when I was thirteen.

I must stop now, as Dora is waiting for me to go into town, and I won't have another chance to get to the post office until Monday week.

Yours truly,

M. Louise Houghton

P.S. Do you know of Mary Gove? If memory serves, her name is now Mary Nickolls [*sic*: Mary Gove Nichols, 1810–1884]. She is a fine person—a woman doctor like me—and we were good friends when she first moved to New York City, which was in December of 1845—I remember the date because it was just before I left Joel Shew, my first husband. Mary lived in our boarding house, and she knew Edgar well, but more to the point, she was closest friends with Fanny Osgood. Mrs. Osgood is long dead, of course, but, if there was ever anyone who knew why Griswold hated Poe and vice versa, it was Fanny. You may want to contact Mary Gove, as she may be able to answer your question better than I. All I can tell you is that she is still alive and lives somewhere in England (she moved there when the war broke out). I know this because John H. Ingram told me. Dora's calling again, so I have to close.

(ITEM 11: *Houghton*)
...

Jan. 3, 1877
Whitestone,
Long Island

Dear Lieutenant Gayle,

Your letter arrived just before Christmas, but what with all the festivities and my patients I have not had time to respond. Sometimes I think people suffer more during holidays than at other times. It seems like maladies get worse in the midst of merrymaking, and my patients require even more attention than usual. Two weeks from today I will celebrate my 55th birthday, and I'm thinking maybe I'm too old to carry so many burdens.

I know what you mean about cold winters. During the war my children and I moved north to live in the country near the Canadian border, and there we stayed for ten years, seldom seeing a magazine or newspaper and enduring winters that must have been as brutal as what you describe in Wyoming. We were not fleeing the war. We were hiding from my second husband, Roland Houghton, and for good reason. But that's another story.

I am glad to hear Mrs. Whitman is in good health. I have her address somewhere and will try to find time to write to her.

Of your questions about Griswold and Edgar, I don't know why I said that about there being something more. It's just an impression I had, not from Edgar but from Griswold. He had a bitterness toward Edgar that just seemed too deep to be explained away by debts or bad notices or Fanny Osgood or all these things put together. I never—in the two years that I knew Edgar—heard him say a word about Griswold, good or bad. Griswold died penniless and alone—did you know that? And with Edgar's and Fanny's portraits hanging on his bedroom wall. After what he did to Edgar, is that not the strangest thing? He had been married twice, and his second marriage was a strange one. And after that he all but proposed to Miss Alice Cary before they ever met. He persuaded her to move to New York from out west somewhere (Cincinnati, I think), but when she arrived, he must have changed his mind. That man was a riddle.

You tell me that you have a "clue" as to what was between them, but that is all you say. How can I comment if you don't tell me what the clue is?

As for Fanny Osgood, I never heard Edgar talk about her either. I did not meet Edgar until after all that was over, so I don't know what happened. All I can tell you is that no one talked about the two of them. It was like a forbidden subject. Did you ever write to Mrs. Nickolls? You had best ask her about this, not me. All I know is hearsay, and, though you tell me that you aren't writing a book, you will pardon me for saying that it sure seems like it—if not a book then maybe a magazine article. I won't be a source of gossip.

I have not heard from John H. Ingram for six months. I suppose he has gotten all the information out of me that he wants. Or maybe he is getting his book ready. I don't know. It's too bad that Mrs. Allan did not respond to your letter, since all she had to say was that she *did* write those two letters offering to provide for Edgar. That would have cleared him of the charge Griswold made. Anyway, I thank you for trying.

Yours,

Loui

P.S. I told John H. Ingram, so I may as well tell you. There are other people who could tell you about Griswold and Edgar, but it seems every one of them, including me, come down on one side or the other with the possible exception of Mrs. Oakes-Smith [Elizabeth Oakes Smith, 1806–1893]. Dunn English [Thomas Dunn English, 1819–1902] is still alive too, but he and Edgar had a bad quarrel that ended up in a lawsuit (which Edgar won), so I expect he would come down on the side of Griswold. Mr. Lowell [James Russell Lowell, 1819–1891] and Mr. Longfellow [Henry Wadsworth Longfellow, 1807–1882], the poets, are two more, but I know for a fact that Longfellow read Griswold's memoir before it was ever published, and he gave it his approval, so you need not ask them if you want a straight answer. In my opinion, Mrs. Whitman is the truest source.

Loui

Someone else who can tell you about Edgar—if she is still alive—is Mary Star [*sic*]. I remember her so well. She was at Fordham with me the morning Virginia died, and she helped me paint the watercolor I did of Virginia that Edgar begged me to paint. She was married, and I cannot remember her married name. It was a common name like Jones or something. But I don't think it was Jones. Her husband was a tailor in New York City, and I think she lived in Hoboken or maybe it was Jersey City. I told John H. Ingram about her, but I don't know if he ever found her or even tried. She had known Edgar since he was a young man. They had been sweethearts before Edgar married Virginia, and both he and Virginia were devoted to her as she was to them. I will never forget Mary Star [*sic*]; she was truly a dear person and the prettiest thing—tall, red hair, a beauty if there ever was one. If you can find her, please send me her address, since I would cherish hearing from her after all these years—30 to be exact—I remember because the day of Virginia's funeral was the last time I saw her, and that was 30 years ago this very month.

Loui

:: YOU MUST FORGIVE LOUI. SHE RAMBLES. Her mind is so filled with details that she cannot follow a train of thought to save her life. It's part of her charm. She writes fast, talks fast, to the point of breathlessness, piling digression upon digression to the point that she is left with no idea where the train originated. Perhaps this is attributable to her busy life, for she cannot refuse a request and ends up so over-committed that three people could not fulfill her obligations. Her portrait reveals a small, attractive young woman, but it can only fail in portraying her impetuous spirit, her brash defiance, and her virtuous and disarming honesty. What you see with Loui is what you get. John Ingram found her contradictory and frustratingly repetitive and concluded she was unreliable. Had he not lacked patience with her, he might have come to realize that she was his most willing, accurate, and dependable source.

Loui Shew painted Virginia's portrait on a Saturday morning. It was the next to the last day of January, a sunny but bitter cold day. She had come out early on the Harlem train from New York City, having received a pleading letter from Edgar the day before in which he confessed that Virginia was failing fast. He promised to be calm. When he heard Loui's steps on the porch, he rushed out to meet her, calling her name in such a grieving voice that she knew Virginia was dead. "Loui!" he cried, "we've lost her."

He was in wrinkled shirt sleeves, no collar, his vest unbuttoned. His dark hair was unkempt, curling as it always did; his face, crestfallen. Loui had always felt that Edgar's small mouth was the only defect in his looks; it inevitably betrayed his insecurity and vulnerability. Now his downturned mouth showed such sorrow that he was pathetic to behold.

He led Loui inside, through the parlor and into the little bedroom at the bottom of the staircase where Mrs. Clemm was sitting at her daughter's bedside. Mary Starr Jennings was there too, in the kitchen; she had been there all the night before. Edgar and Loui stood at the foot of the bed watching Mrs. Clemm stare at her daughter, sobbing and moaning. She had folded Virginia's arms across her chest, pulled the comforter up, and brushed her hair, laying her out properly. Virginia's eyes were closed, her suffering, still evident in her face. She was skin and bones.

"She said not a word this morning," Edgar said. "She was too weak. We sat with her all night. Just at sunrise, Muddy tried to get her to drink some water out of a teaspoon, but she couldn't even swallow. She just stared—first at me, then at Muddy—as if she were frightened or needed to say something before she left." He took a deep breath, sucking back sobs. "And then she just closed her eyes. Oh, Loui, she was just a little girl."

The bedroom smelled of the camphor Loui had prescribed for easing Virginia's coughs, but from the kitchen she could smell coffee and freshly baked bread.

"First things first," Loui said. "Go and eat something, both of you. It's time to come away, and you have to keep up your strength. Sissy's in a better place. Her pain is gone, and her coughing too. She's content now."

Loui turned Edgar toward the kitchen and nudged him away, then reached down and clasped Mrs. Clemm's shoulders, urging her up. Though reluctant, she obeyed. Loui pulled the bedroom door to and followed them through the parlor. "Will you paint her, Loui?" Edgar asked as they entered the kitchen. "You promised."

Mary Starr poured coffee into teacups, and slices of ham were frying in an iron skillet on the black stove. Edgar and Mrs. Clemm took seats at the green kitchen table.

"I will paint her if you promise to go upstairs and get some rest after breakfast. You, too, Mrs. Clemm. And don't come back down until I call you." Loui didn't want them about while she and Mary prepared the body and got the house ready for guests. While they breakfasted she put on her coat and hat and left the cottage on an errand to alert the pastor of the church where Virginia's funeral was to be held, knowing he would send the necessary messages and spread the word.

When she returned, Mary was alone downstairs, the breakfast things washed and put away. Loui got out her watercolors, and the two of them returned to the bedroom where Virginia lay. Loui went right to work, propping Virginia up on the pillows. She was not an accomplished portrait artist. Most of her paintings were landscapes, but she had done portraits of members of her family, including her three children. She sat in Mrs. Clemm's chair and studied her lifeless subject. Loui's usual method was to look for the shapes of the colors she saw rather than focus on the contours of the face. Then she would trace those shapes with pencil until they formed the face she was after. She had learned not to be surprised by the colors she found, so often unexpected, but there they were. On a cloudless, sunny day, though the sky is blue, the artist finds a full palette of colors there—red, yellow, purple—and a blue sky doesn't look real without them.

As she studied Virginia's face, searching for colors, the cat, Catterina, jumped up on the bed, curled next to Virginia, and stared at Loui. She was not a great lover of cats, but the first time she ever saw Virginia, she was lying on her bed under that awful gray military overcoat of Edgar's, freezing cold, poor thing, with that cat lying on her chest doing service as a warming blanket. That was when Loui first met the Poes. Mary Gove had begged her to accompany her to Fordham—they need your help, so she had said. A comforter was the first thing Loui provided—and that off her own bed.

It seemed to Loui that Catterina had more sense than many people she knew. The cat seemed to realize that she and Loui were there for the same useful purpose; they were colleagues. So Catterina had taken to Loui right off. No sooner did Loui arrive, but Catterina presented herself to her hands, looking Loui in the eye like she wished to know how best to help. So Loui always spoke to Catterina like she might speak to a servant "Now, you lie down here," Loui would say, patting a spot on the bedspread close to Virginia. The cat was a great comfort; her presence always took Virginia's mind off the pain. Though Loui sometimes worried that Catterina's presence aggravated Virginia's cough, she decided that the soothing effect of her devotion outweighed any harm, and ever since she has encouraged her shut-in patients to keep pets in the house and found this advice beneficial in alleviating their suffering.

Edgar was devoted to Catterina; he would get up in the middle of the night to let her in or out. She was a big, short-haired, orange and black tabby with a mottled face and inquiring, intelligent eyes that seemed liquid when caught by the light in a certain way. But Loui also found her frightening, as if possessed or clairvoyant. She has never since been at ease with the notion that animals don't have souls, even arguing with friends on the subject to the point that she thinks they might call into question her sanity.

One day that previous summer Catterina had caught a bird, a bobolink, and brought it into the house. Virginia told Loui the story. Edgar decided to keep it, and while it was trapped in the loft, he knocked together a crude cage. He caught the bird by throwing his overcoat over it, put it in the cage, and kept it there for a month, thinking it would become tame which it never did. Mrs. Clemm, Virginia, and Loui raised such a fuss that he finally let it go. They all watched it fly straight to the trough for a drink of water, then disappear into the woods where it belonged.

Now Loui wishes she had included Catterina in her portrait of Virginia, but at the time she had in mind a bust only, head and shoulders, so she looked beyond Catterina to Virginia, searching for color. There was green in Virginia's cheeks, a dull, lifeless green the color of lichen. And around her eyes Loui perceived violet like a winter sky after the sun has set. Her lips were gray as ash; her hair, jet black. These were deathly colors; they could not portray life, so she asked Mary Starr to open the curtain, hoping sunlight might bring warmer colors, but it did not help. Finally she asked Mary to sit beside the bed, and using her as a model, Loui painted the shape of Virginia's eyes, nose, and mouth using the living colors she saw in the face of Mary Starr. She worked fast, as one must with water colors, interrupted only when Mary rose to go add wood to the fireplace in the parlor. They did not speak, both of them lost in their task for an hour or more. The house was quiet. As she painted, Loui thought of how inadequate she was for the task.

She hadn't wanted to be an artist; she had wanted to be a doctor like her father. She had learned from him by being an extra pair of hands at the bedsides of his patients. Her mother wouldn't have it. She held that a well-bred girl was one who cultivated whatever talents she possessed so long as they were ladylike. It was for this reason that Loui studied art instead of medicine, though she much preferred her father's profession. His black leather satchel held greater treasure than her jars of paints.

She is not a very good artist, but such as she is, her kinship with the writer has always been apparent to her. Loui believes they share a common ancestor and that even today they do similar work. This notion stems from a belief that, at its awakening, the earth was well peopled. For thousands of years people must have been penetrating every corner of the earth, spreading like her watercolors wicked into the fibers of her tablet. This awakening, as she calls it, occurred with the invention of pictures. Whether they were etched in stone or painted on the walls of caves, those pictures were the first written words. At some point in the ancient past, artist and writer were one and the same. Loui can imagine the face of that primitive creature who lifted his head from the fire, gazed in wonder at a picture on the cave wall, and uttered the first ever grunt of sound that married spoken and written word. What a miracle that was.

Every fledgling artist has imagined that their work will earn them immortality. Loui had such girlish fantasies, but those notions faded before she was twenty. Now that she is well beyond middle age, though at fifty-seven she doesn't consider herself old—and she has long since given up painting pictures—comes a letter from London, England, wanting to know about her portrait of Virginia Poe. A picture is worth a thousand words, so it's said, and this idea of artist and writer is much on her mind now as she thinks about that portrait. She hadn't thought of it for years; she would have guessed that it was long lost. Others can remember Virginia Poe with words—black hair, big brown eyes, pale complexion, tall, thin, high cheekbones, soft chin—but Loui alone painted her. Edgar had no likeness of her, no silhouette, no daguerreotype. He had begged Loui to paint her before she died, but it proved impossible. Virginia was too weak; she could not sit up for long stretches of time, and she didn't want it done—a fading bit of vanity perhaps. "I was pretty once, Loui," she had said when Loui suggested she sit for it, "but no more. Put away your paints."

Since Loui could not paint her in life, she painted her in death. Though they were almost exactly the same age, Virginia seemed much younger. She had been her mother's patient for years, an invalid most of that time. Loui has come to believe that serious illness with its great dependence on others has a regressive effect, and such was the case with Virginia. She was an innocent child.

Today Loui makes her living, as she has for many years, by nursing the shut-in. Just now she has a sick neighbor, and for two months she has not slept three nights out of six. She is weary and sleepy as are most doctors, and there are people in Whitestone who would sooner call her than the real doctor. Loui has seen many-a-doctor do more harm than good for lack of common sense and practical experience of which she has an abundance. Healing is an art, not a science, and if medical schools would come to understand this, lives could be saved. Loui's own son, Henry, was betrothed to one she loved as dearly as if the girl were her own daughter, only Loui could not attend to her illness because of the snow that blocked the northern roads. Though the girl was seen to by a real doctor with a diploma and a license to practice, on the day she died she told her own mother that had Loui reached her in time she would have lived.

As a young girl Loui had been considered pretty and something of a flirt, which she was. Her father always assumed she would care for him in his old age, and she did. He was not a rich man, but he provided well for his family. When Loui married Joel Shew who was also a doctor, her father was pleased and proud. He supported Loui's husband's schemes, though they turned out to be misguided and self-serving. When Joel Shew started a journal to promote the water cure, Loui was with him heart and soul, but when his attention—and the subject of his articles—turned to colonization, she lost interest. His notions of his own importance swelled, and Loui became disenchanted with the man. She grew to detest him in fact. He was small, rather plump and growing bald, but his looks were not what repelled her. His self-esteem depended too much on her father's generosity, and in time Joel resented Loui and her father. It was as if her father's savings were Joel's by right of his marriage to Loui, and so he demanded rather than asked.

Colonization was the term applied to sending Negroes back to Africa. Joel pleaded the cause as if he were doing those people a favor, acceding to their wishes to return to their native land. To hear him, one would have thought he cared deeply for the Negro, but that wasn't his motive at all. He wanted to be rid of them, and he had no sympathy for the fact that most of them had no knowledge of their African roots. And how could Loui, a woman, understand such things? Or so he said. Those matters were somehow too weighty for a woman's brain. Loui had borne him three children in four years—indeed at one point she was nursing all three. Finally she dismissed Joel, told him to leave the house and not come back. He was pompous, indignant, abusive, and even violent, but the house belonged to her father. She refused to yield, demanded a divorce, and got it. All that happened during the summer and fall before she met Edgar Poe. She cannot remember which year it was—her memory doesn't work by numbers the way some peoples' do—and she is so wearied by sorrows that the outlines are faint as to dates and persons. It was the year before Virginia Poe died. What year would that be?

At noon on the Saturday Virginia died, the sexton came with the wagon bearing the coffin. As he and Edgar carried Virginia back out to the wagon, Catterina bolted out the door and disappeared. By mid-afternoon the cottage was crowded with neighbors, but Edgar lingered on the porch, calling for Catterina. Finally, late that night, he and Loui, with candles in their hands, went searching and found her sitting on the stack of firewood in the shed. Edgar brought her in by the fire, stroked her, and became quite melancholy, no doubt thinking that earlier that morning she had provided a bit of warmth and softness for Virginia's final moments.

The funeral was held on Monday which was a cold, raw day, so cold that Mary Starr decided not to leave the cottage to walk to the church. Loui had paid for Virginia's coffin and grave clothes, and Mary's husband furnished Edgar's mourning suit. Despite this he wore his gray, military overcoat even though Loui had hidden it, thinking it not proper for a funeral, but he had no other overcoat. Mary Gove helped Loui arrange the flowers and sprinkle the parlor with cologne, and after the funeral the little room was overflowing with the well-wishers who had come out from New York. N. P. Willis was there and Mr. Stoddard and General Morris, Willis's partner at the *Home Journal*. That was the last time Loui saw Mary Starr. She wishes now she could remember her married name, but she cannot. Her husband ran a haberdashery in the city, and perhaps he's still listed in the city directory. She was a real beauty, Mary Starr, though somewhat cold and aloof.

Almost as soon as Virginia died, Loui became Edgar's nurse. During that spring she spent as many nights at the Fordham cottage as she did in her own house in New York City, and this, despite having three toddlers—Henry, Alma, and Frank—all craving attention. Edgar sank into deep depression, became physically ill, and Loui soon realized that both his heart and brain were diseased. Often he ran a fever which brought on delirium in which he raved, out of his head. Loui would take his pulse continually, fearing for his life, and inevitably it beat ten regular beats then paused. It was what doctors call an "intermit." He reacted severely to the mildest sedatives, and such medicines had to be administered with care and constant observation. She was quite open with him about his condition, and one day when he was himself, he begged her to write down whatever he said when he was out of his head. This she did, though much of what he said was nonsensical. One morning after a feverish night during which Mrs. Clemm and Loui took turns sitting up with him, he came to his senses, sat up in bed, and picked at the breakfast Mrs. Clemm had fixed for him. Loui read to him the notes she'd made during the night, his nonsensical ravings.

"I know what I was talking about, Loui," he said, becoming lost in reflective thought. "That was when I was in France, in Havre de Grace, seeking passage back to America. I was delirious then too. I had been wounded in a duel in Paris with a swordsman more skillful than I. Do you see this scar?" With this he opened his nightshirt to expose his left shoulder whereupon Loui saw the scar, two inches long, just beneath his collarbone. "For thirteen weeks I lingered between life and death. A Scottish lady of noble birth learned of my suffering, and she came daily to nurse me and hired a nurse to stay with me at night. The Scottish lady had the most beautiful blue eyes I ever saw. They were like the sea at sunrise, clear and with a depth that seemed endless, and she had long dark lashes. She came every morning, often with her brother. One morning when I was nearly recovered, I presented her with a poem that I had written for her during the night. It was entitled 'Holy Eyes.' Though she appeared to appreciate it, when she realized that I was a writer, she became alarmed and begged me not to reveal her name to anyone, since she had come to France to rescue her brother who had become profligate and had squandered much of their family's fortune by gambling. The next morning she did not come, and the night nurse told me she had sailed to Scotland with her brother. I never saw her again, and I have never revealed her name to anyone except Virginia. Did I speak it in my ravings?"

Loui assured him he had not, and he seemed relieved which made her know that the story must be true. This pattern repeated itself time and again, and during that spring she came to know many things about Edgar Poe. She believes she knows more about him than any person alive. In February of that year, just two weeks after Virginia died, he presented her with a valentine poem, "To M.L.S——." Loui still has the original somewhere. In that poem he called her an angel:

And think that these weak lines are written by him—
By him who, as he pens them, thrills to think
His spirit is communing with an angel's.

It was sweet, and Loui was thrilled when Willis published it in the *Home Journal* later that spring.

It's a shame that all her chattels are so scattered, but she divided up many of her valuables when she lost interest in life, because her new husband belittled her constantly. Perhaps another poem by Edgar, a lost poem addressed to Loui and entitled "The Beloved Physician," is in the trunk that her son, Henry, took with him to Colorado. He was robbed in the mines there, but he assured her in a letter that the trunk was safe with friends in Denver. Henry was no rhymer, but as a boy, he loved poetry, and one of their closets is filled with little rolls of poetry clippings that he collected. At one time they used the rolls to light fires. Henry will be back in May, and they will try to find the poem Edgar wrote to her, of which she will speak of at length later.

Being unable to write that spring after Virginia died, Edgar had no money coming in. In addition to her nursing, therefore, Loui also became the Poes' provider. There was no one else. Mary Gove might have helped, but all the money she earned from her medical practice went to legal expenses associated with her divorce. Mary Starr seemed to disappear as soon as Virginia died. A woman named Stella Lewis was willing to help, but her help came with a selfish and painful condition that Edgar could not abide. Sooner than endure her presence, he would escape to the woods or the grounds of the Catholic school in the vicinity, leaving Loui and Mrs. Clemm to deal with Mrs. Lewis. On regular occasions Loui made the rounds of the publishers on Edgar's behalf to the point that they hated to see her coming. Once she raised a subscription of sixty dollars from the gentlemen at the Union Club. She had General Winfield Scott to thank for that. He donated five dollars, saying to the others assembled that he wished it could be five hundred. He said Poe possessed noble and generous traits and that true-hearted Americans ought to take care of their poets as well as their soldiers. Loui mentions this, because General Scott's generosity proves the lie that Wilmot Griswold told. He claimed that Edgar left West Point in disgrace, but if that were true, would General Scott have been so disposed to speak well of him and to give in such a generous manner? Loui thinks not.

When the weather warmed, Edgar and Loui spent long hours sitting on the porch, and as summer approached, he was even strong enough for walks in the woods. On several occasions they walked as far as the Harlem River. As they did, he told her many things about his youth. Often he talked about his school friend's mother who had been like a second mother to him, and in time he told Loui that she was as dear to him as that lady. The pencil notes Loui made during his dictations and delirium ran many, many pages, but she burned them last summer. She had kept them for years thinking one of her children would write something about her life, but she gave up on all that. Now, it seems, people all over the world want to know these things. Yesterday she found forty leaves of that journal in a vase. How they escaped the flames she cannot say, but the pages refer to two gifts that Virginia gave Loui two days before she died—a little jewel case that had belonged to Edgar's mother and a picture of Edgar that she took from under her pillow and kissed before giving to Loui. She showed Loui other things from her workbox, among them a miniature of Edgar's mother, Eliza, who was quite beautiful and wore her curls low on her forehead which was broad and intellectual like Edgar's. There was also a bundle of Eliza Poe's letters written in a round hand and two sketches of her, one in watercolor with Boston Harbor in the background and dated 1808. On the back was this inscription: "For my little son Edgar who should ever love Boston, the place of his birth and where his mother found her best and most sympathetic friends." As Loui studied the watercolor, Edgar explained that his father had not abandoned his mother, but that he had gone in search of employment since she was ill. That was the same day Virginia showed Loui the two letters from Louisa Allan, the letters that Mrs. Clemm burned.

As Mrs. Clemm later told Loui, when she was breaking up housekeeping at the cottage at Fordham, she built a bonfire on the lawn in front of the porch and fed those flames with bundle after bundle of letters and papers for no better reason than that she "couldn't carry everything." Better she had burned her furniture. She burned a packet of Loui's letters to Edgar, burned them without opening them, so she said. She could have at least returned them to Loui. And then she had the gall to blame Griswold for ruining her son-in-law's reputation when all along she was just as much to blame and blind to her own culpability. Loui prays that her soul rests in peace, but she has little sympathy for her.

On more than one occasion Edgar talked about his brother, William Henry, who was long dead. He had been a dashing cavalier, a poet, and the secretary to some foreign dignitary after which he had read law somewhere in Europe, but his tastes were somehow too wild for society, and he had died at a young age. Edgar always spoke of him with affection, but warned Loui to never mention his brother in the presence of Mrs. Clemm, as there had been bad feelings between the two of them that he wouldn't talk about. The brothers had been together in Europe, Loui gathered, at which time Edgar lived in Paris where he had written a novel, a "yellow-cover novel," so he called it, that he would never put his own name to. He sold it for francs equal to one hundred dollars. It was entitled *The Life of an Artist at Home and Abroad*, published anonymously, and thereafter attributed to Eugène Sue. Edgar claimed that he still had the manuscript, though he would not let Loui see it and vowed to destroy it before he died. "It's commonplace, Loui," he said with contempt in his voice. "I would hate myself if people thought I was capable of nothing more than a dime novel full of bad grammar and cheap profanity."

Though Loui begged him to revise and publish it for the money he so desperately needed, he refused, spurning and laughing at her suggestion.

He had also sold a poem while in Paris that was later credited to George Sand, a poem entitled "Humanity." None of these works appeared in Griswold's collection of Edgar's writing, nor did "The Beloved Physician," a poem he wrote to Loui a few months after Virginia died, a poem that the world would misunderstand. It went too far in his expression of affection, and Loui had to suppress it. She paid him twenty-five dollars for it—five dollars more than he had been offered—and it never saw the light of day. She has it somewhere, perhaps among her things at Pierrepont Manor where her family spent the war years and where Lida is buried, her son's fiancée. Loui has china, pictures, and furniture stored there too, including Henry's old desk that Lida gave him, all in Henry's third floor room where he nailed up a raven over the door nearly twenty years ago. Loui warrants it's still there and plans to go up there this summer—it is three hundred miles away, near the Canadian border—and she will try to find the lost poem.

When asked if Poe ever proposed marriage to her after Virginia died, she wondered if that question arose because of another valentine poem that was published, the one "To Marie Louise." Her answer was no, he never did, but at one time she worried that such might be his intentions. She suspects he sensed, however, that she would have refused him. Not once in her life did she think of him as someone she might come to love in *that* way. She is not in the least drawn to weak men, and he was one of the weakest she ever met. Other women were much enamored of his sensitivity and passion, but Loui could not ignore his frailty, and she never gave him sympathy. Not because his frailty was put on; it was not. Her interest in him was that of a doctor for an ill friend, a friend of whom she was quite fond, a friend who had much to offer this world. But she was not blinded by his genius as were other women. She can understand why some might think "To Marie Louise" was a love poem.

> Ah, Marie Louise!
> In deep humility
> I own that now
> All pride—all thought of power—
> All hope of fame—
> All wish for Heaven—is merged forevermore
> Beneath the palpitating tide of passion
> Heaped o'er my soul by thee.

She laughs, reading those lines now. How stupid of Griswold to leave it out; he did it to spite her. But Edgar Poe *could* write such a poem to a mere friend. It was a kind of projection, you see. Everyday life was somehow too mundane for him; he had to intensify it in some way, so friendship became love, solitude became despair, distraction became madness, illness became death. Women who failed to understand this about him mistakenly thought he was making love to them. He could not accept the ordinary. He could not be a yellow-cover novelist, a mere hack writer. It was for this reason that he could never write a poem on demand. Such requests had the opposite effect; in fact, they brought on sterility. He was a slave to inspiration, as in the case of his poem, "The Bells," but that came later.

Loui has no doubt but that Edgar came close to death that spring after Virginia died. The onset of fever inevitably elevated his pulse, and having become aware of the intermit, as she has said, she naturally endeavored to lower his fever. It was then she discovered that tonics and sedatives produced delirium—those ravings that she has described. She suspected he had a lesion on one side of his brain, a diagnosis later confirmed by the great Dr. Valentine Mott. The lesion meant that only half his brain was in proper working order. This condition, commonly known as brain fever, when combined with the irregular heartbeat, meant that medicines must be administered with extreme caution. When his pulse exceeded eighty beats per minute, she gave him a mild sedative after which he talked nonstop until both his fever and his heart rate diminished.

Drawing on her knowledge of the water cure, she made him bathe regularly, in cold water to help alleviate fever, and she altered his diet, much to Mrs. Clemm's chagrin. Loui insisted Mrs. Clemm bake wheat bread, using Hosford's yeast so as to restore phosphates to the brain, and she restricted his diet of meat to fish, clams, and oysters which supply brain power. She would not let him sit near the iron stove and made him keep a soapstone at his feet. He was allowed to drink lots of pure water, but no tea, coffee, or alcohol. By such care he began to recover his strength, the fevers subsided, and he began to write again.

It was during this time—in April or May—that he composed "The Beloved Physician," the poem addressed to Loui. As she said, it has never been published. She is certain that she has the manuscript somewhere among her scattered papers. Griswold suppressed it out of animosity toward her, as will be explained. The poem consisted of nine verses after Edgar cut it down for publication. It describes a nurse—Loui—holding her watch and taking his pulse, and each verse ends with the refrain, "The pulse beats ten and intermits. / God guide the soul that ne'er forgets." And she recalls two lines that she especially loves, "The soft head bows, the sweet eyes close / The large heart yields to sweet repose." One can imagine how perfectly he polished it, but as she said, she could not let him publish it, since she had become engaged to a man who held very old-fashioned notions about marriage and women. The marriage cost Loui her individuality, and she rues the day she met Roland Houghton, saying that she wept for three years, forgetting all she ever knew, and the day she declared her emancipation from him was the proudest day of her life.

The watch with which she took Edgar's pulse she gave to Griswold after Edgar died along with a diamond bracelet worth five hundred dollars as surety that he would not defame Edgar's name. He did it anyway. Wilmot Griswold was a snake in the grass—evil and vicious—yet he called himself a man of God. He sold his soul to the devil in order to elevate his own fame by blackening the name of Edgar Poe. She believes it was spite and jealousy, pure and simple, an injustice of the highest order. She trusts that he burns in hell. She told Mrs. Clemm that he could not be trusted, but Mrs. Clemm resorted to him anyway, giving him priceless manuscripts. Mr. Willis did justice to Edgar— Loui knew Willis, and not like the world knew Willis—she knew him personally, and he was a fine man. He is gone now too. He knew Edgar as well as any man alive, though there were many women who knew him better. Willis's memoir alone would have sufficed, but no, Griswold demanded the last word, and he poisoned Edgar's memory up to and including this day.

As anyone with a rudimentary understanding of human physiology would know, a man with a weak heart and brain disease would have little tolerance for strong spirits. Add to these physical ailments, the stress of being orphaned at a tender age, of being abandoned by one's foster family, of being unjustly condemned by the press, of abject poverty, of malnourishment, and of the long and ultimately fatal illness of a beloved wife, and one has the ingredients for a susceptible temperament. Such was the case with Edgar Poe. He neither sought nor enjoyed alcoholic spirits and did not partake of them except by the persistent persuasion of others and this, out of a natural desire to be accepted, but one sip brought on delirium and insanity. He could not sleep after taking stimulants; he could only rave uncontrollably. Self-esteem and self-reliance ran riot to the exclusion of prudence or caution. The only time Loui ever knew of Edgar being intoxicated was after dining with Griswold in an eating house. Her uncle, the honorable Hiram Barney, the great attorney of the firm Barney, Butler &

Parsons, had to carry him back to Fordham in Loui's little coupé, and always after that Edgar was grateful to her uncle and always asked to be remembered to him. She asks, is this the reaction of someone who was drunk or someone who was ill? But Griswold, out of jealousy of Edgar's genius, could not resist giving emphasis to his irrational behavior while he diminished Edgar's many more noble traits. He could not be generous and understanding in his memoir; such was not his nature.

Edgar was much recovered by summer, and Loui stopped going to Fordham, having trained Mrs. Clemm in his care and feeding, but such women as she have little respect for the knowledge and judgment of their own sex. Loui fears she ignored her advice. On occasion in June or July, Edgar came into the city, and he often stayed over, spending the night at Loui's house on Bond Street in Greenwich Village. In her house she had a music room with a harp and piano. The room faced south, and in the mornings sunlight flooded through the bay windows. She played and sang a little and enjoyed entertaining friends who could also play. The room was carpeted in blue, the upholstery was red and crimson. There was a music stand and a guitar with a blue ribbon and antique jars decorated the piano and mantle. On summer nights when she had guests, she often set up a little supper table in the bay, as it was so pleasant there with the windows open to let in the breeze. Edgar loved that room. There was a large painting over the piano of a cavalier that he especially loved for its softness and beauty, and also a portrait of Raphael that he considered a masterpiece worthy of a palace or church.

One evening as Loui was setting up the table, Edgar came into the room with pen and paper in his hand. It was still light outside. Loui had not yet lit the lamps, and a light breeze filled lace curtains which billowed into the room. Edgar collapsed in the Queen Anne chair next to the piano, tired from a day of making the rounds of the magazines. His cheeks were sunken and hollow, and his eyes, puffy from lack of sleep the night before. He had the look of gloom and defeat which he often affected to make others feel sorry for him. One would have thought he had fainted away by the way he slouched in that chair. Thinking he would have to stay the night, Loui couldn't help but feel somewhat irritated by his behavior.

"I'm drained, Loui," he said. "I have to write a poem, but can't. I don't have the energy for it."

As soon as the words were out of his mouth, the bell started clanging in the Bleecker Street Presbyterian Church steeple a block away. It clanged sharp and fast, then it was joined by other bells tolling in the distance, an indication that there was a fire somewhere in the city. Edgar closed his eyes, shook his head, and pressed his fingertips to his forehead as if in agony.

"I can't stand the sound of bells tonight," he said. "Close the windows!"

Loui took the pen and paper out of his hand, placed them on the little round table that stood beside the Queen Anne chair, and wrote, "'The Bells' by E. A. Poe." Then she handed it back to him. He looked at it, sneered, and went limp again, ignoring her prompting. She took the paper back and wrote out a line beneath his name, trying to imitate his style—"The bells, the little silver bells"—and again handed it back to him. This time he eyed her, amused by her efforts, she guessed. To humor her he wrote out a second line, then he started to hand the paper back, but, by virtue of an impulse, he took it back and wrote more.

Loui returned to the task of laying out the napkins and silverware. Still the bells continued their ringing. When she noticed him stop again, she walked over to see what he had written. He had completed a stanza, but the poem wanted more, so she wrote—"The bells, the heavy iron bells"—and again he took the cue. By the time supper was served, in a jovial mood now, he pronounced the poem finished and professed to be exceedingly pleased with it. He called it "Loui's poem" and said she was a genius. Later he added more stanzas and changed it altogether, bragging that it was even longer than "The Raven," but he always maintained to Loui that "The Bells" was her poem, not his. Loui jokes of being a "lunkhead" when it comes to poetry; she doesn't like painful poems such as Edgar wrote. She admits that, though she has a copy of his *Tales* published by Wiley & Putnam, she's never read a one of them.

That night he slept twelve hours and so soundly that, though Loui took up his wrist to take his pulse, she did not rouse him. He had the same irregular heartbeat as she has said—ten regular beats and then a pause. It is well known that employing the mind in creative ways is a great tonic. Edgar was happiest when in the act of creating, and Loui attributes that healthful night's sleep to his writing "The Bells." But too often he talked himself out of writing rather than forcing himself to do it. He was so susceptible to distraction and the influence of others. He had little self-discipline, a failing that contributed to his downfall. The next morning Loui took him to see Dr. Mott.

"His heart is diseased, Loui," Dr. Mott told her in confidence after his examination. "He will not live long, and how long depends on the storms or sunshine in his life."

When they arrived back at Loui's house, she sat him down in the music room and lectured him. She told him frankly what Dr. Mott had said, that nothing could save him but a prudent life. She advised him to find a new wife, adding that he had no hope of surviving without the sympathetic care of a strong woman, and she confessed that she was not that person. Edgar was twelve years older than Loui, and, as has been said, she was not attracted to him. Mary Starr was married, and anyway their affection for one another appeared to have waned; Edgar seemed to harbor some slight resentment toward her. Had Mary Gove any money, she would have been suitable, but she was as penniless as he, and she gave Loui no indication of interest in him in that special way. Loui professes to not be a scheming woman, but she urged him to marry as soon as possible, saying she would find the right woman for him if he could not. Disrespectful as this may seem, considering the fact that Virginia had been dead a mere six months, Loui resolved to get on with the search.

He stayed with Loui through that weekend, and on Saturday night he invited Mrs. Osgood to join them for a midnight service at the Twentieth Street Free Church to hear the great Dr. Mulhenberg. Though Edgar did not like structured forms of worship, he sang the psalms in a fine tenor voice to Loui's and Fanny's sopranos, holding the book with them. The subject of the sermon was Jesus's suffering, and often Dr. Mulhenberg repeated the phrase, "He was a man of sorrows and acquainted with grief." Edgar became much agitated hearing this, and half way through the sermon he left, saying he would meet them outside after the service. Loui worried about him, but he reappeared during the final hymn, "Jesus, Savior of My Soul," and sang again, never once having to look at the hymnal. In the carriage going home, he seemed much inspired and spoke highly of Dr. Mulhenberg.

Impressed that Loui had persuaded Edgar to attend church, Mrs. Osgood confided in her when they dropped her at her house, "Edgar will do anything you ask of him, Loui. He says he can refuse you nothing."

At this time Mrs. Osgood's husband was away painting portraits, and Loui knew the uncertain state of their marriage. Mary Gove had told her some things about the rumors that had gone the rounds about Edgar and Fanny, and Loui began to wonder if she might be someone he might marry. She was a fine candidate—beautiful, wealthy, and strong-willed—so, during breakfast on Sunday morning, Loui suggested that he propose.

"Don't you think her husband might object?" he said, laughing out loud.

She stared at him from across the breakfast table, their eyes locked as he sipped his tea. Something in his words made Loui suspect that the idea was not so preposterous. "From what I hear," she said, "he may not."

"You don't understand, Loui. And it's best that you don't."

And so the idea was dismissed or so she thought.

Loui has had two letters from Mary Gove, Mrs. Nichols now. She was sorry to hear about Mary's cataract operation. It's a shame she didn't know to use vegetable alternatives as well as vegetable food. At any rate, Mary told her that, in fact, Edgar did propose to Fanny. It was in August or September of that same year. Fanny was staying with her sister's family in Albany when Edgar appeared quite unexpectedly. In their parlor he dropped to one knee and begged her to marry him. She refused him, pleading with him to get up, and he left the house much embarrassed, so she said. His timing had been bad. Her youngest child was gravely ill and would die a month later. Loui didn't know at the time, but Mary Gove believed that Fanny was already suffering from the consumption that would ultimately take her life.

In the late fall of that year Loui began to be courted by Roland Houghton who would become her second husband. She decided it best to keep a discreet distance from Edgar for reasons that she said— the poems mainly. Mr. Houghton was a minister. He held Edgar in low esteem and frowned upon their friendship. Loui says she should never have let him rule her thus, for she had reason to believe that Edgar was not taking care of himself. She had even heard that he had given in to bouts of drinking again. He had also become somewhat too cloying and needy, so she backed away. She now thinks that her doing so might have cost him years of life, and she grieves to think that might be the case. At any rate, she saw little of him for the next year and a half. She had occasional letters, mostly lamenting his misfortunes, but she continued to refuse him sympathy.

In the spring of his last year, she had a pleading letter from Mrs. Clemm saying Edgar was in a bad way and desperately needed her help. Loui went out to Fordham to find a man she hardly recognized. He seemed to have aged years. She could tell from his eyes alone that he had abandoned all her advice. Though she said nothing, she blamed Mrs. Clemm, for she knew Edgar lacked the self-discipline or energy or desire to care for himself. He had given up on life. Loui did what she could, and on the train back to New York, decided she could do no more. She had her own concerns now and could no longer take on his.

She returned to Fordham for the last time in June of 1849—she *can* remember that date. Isn't it funny that of the few dates she can remember—her birthday, her children's birthdays—another is the year Edgar died, 1849. She persuaded Dr. Mulhenberg to accompany her, since she had decided that Edgar was beyond her help. Only God could help him now. Once inside the cottage Mrs. Clemm turned them toward the kitchen to acknowledge the presence of Stella Lewis who sat on a chair in front of the cupboard, plump as a partridge, dressed in burgundy satin, and looking like an overstuffed Broadway tart. On Loui's earlier visits, Edgar had complained of Mrs. Lewis's unwanted presence and how he hid from her in the woods until Mrs. Clemm came to fetch him, making him return to the cottage and be polite. Mrs. Lewis's real name was Sarah, not Stella as she pretended; she pretended to be a lot of things she wasn't. Her gifts to the Poes were bribes for favorable puffing of her poems, a cozy arrangement she had with Mrs. Clemm, but Edgar was mortified by her and her poems. She was a meddlesome woman. Loui knows for a fact that years later she intercepted and read a letter Loui wrote to Mrs. Clemm.

On that day in June Edgar's excuse for refusing to see Mrs. Lewis was the sore throat which Loui had learned of in a letter from him the day before. As a remedy, she had brought him a guava. Mrs. Clemm led them upstairs where they found him in bed, petting Catterina who lay beside him. Loui introduced him to Dr. Mulhenberg, and Edgar cut his eyes to her suspiciously as if he perceived her intentions. The room was stifling hot. She told Edgar about the guava she'd brought, then went straight to the point. "I came to say goodbye, Edgar. I'm engaged to be married, and we're moving to Hartford. You must remember all I've told you and heed my words. There's nothing I can do for you that you can't do yourself. Dr. Mulhenberg has kindly agreed to look in on you from time to time. I will send you my address as soon as I'm settled. Good-bye."

She leaned down to kiss him. The hurt look on his face brought tears to her eyes, but she was firm in her resolve. She gave Catterina a parting caress and hugged Mrs. Clemm, calling her "dear Muddy" and begging her to take care of him, then turned toward the stairs.

"Loui," he said as she left, "can it be that you are deserting your friend and patient?"

She refused to turn back. On the stairs she heard Dr. Mulhenberg trying to divert Edgar's attention away from her leaving, and she kept on, turning at the entrance to the parlor for one last look—the neat straw matting on the floor, the two pine tables that Edgar had made and covered with green baize, the window curtains of snow white muslin, the hanging shelf with his little collection of books. At the front door she nodded to Stella Lewis still sitting in the kitchen, an angry look on her chubby face. The young hussy would have to wait her turn. On the train back to New York, Loui cried like a baby, certain she would never see him again.

She had a pleading letter from him in August in which he spoke of disaster "following fast and following faster," quoting a line from "The Raven." She still carries that letter in her memorandum book. It is a painful reminder of how she abandoned him. She has grieved over it so often that it is worn and faded. She cannot part with it. He asked, "I hold you in my esteem in all solemnity beside the friend of my boyhood, the mother of my school fellow, of whom I told you. Are you to vanish like her from my forlorn and lost soul?"

She did vanish. She lost years. Had she known the troubles that would plague her in the time to come, she would have done many things differently. She told herself that she was bound to hurt Edgar's feelings, but after he died she deeply regretted leaving him like that. She will never forgive herself, and it was because of her remorse that she acceded to Mrs. Clemm's appeal for help in persuading Griswold to be generous toward Edgar in the biography he intended as a preface to the collection of Edgar's works that he was compiling. The harm had already been done. Mrs. Clemm maintained that it had been Edgar's wish that Wilmot Griswold should be his literary executor, but Loui doesn't believe that for a second. Edgar disliked and distrusted Griswold. She believes it was Mrs. Clemm's doing, that Griswold made her promises of money and that the arrangement was her idea, a greedy impulse. When Loui first learned of Griswold's intentions to write a biography of Edgar, she was more than sympathetic with Mrs. Clemm. She knew Griswold would be cruel, so she took her side and guarded her interests even in the face of Mrs. Clemm's eccentricities and desperation. Loui supposes it was desperation that drove her into the hands of Wilmot Griswold. It proved not only her undoing but also her torment. She later wrote to Loui to say that after Griswold's biography, she never smiled again. But it was her own fault—dire need is blind to the intent of betrayal.

A year or so after Edgar died, Loui went to see Griswold. At the time he was already organizing Edgar's manuscripts and trying to raise the necessary funds for the publication of the complete works. There was some muddle having to do with Edgar's trunk which had been lost in Baltimore but had been recovered by his cousin, Neilson Poe, but Edgar's sister, Rosalie, had laid claim to the trunk to the indignation of Mrs. Clemm who sued Rosalie with the help of Stella Lewis's husband, an attorney who lived in Brooklyn. Griswold claimed that he wished only to aid Mrs. Clemm, that once he recovered the publishing costs, most of the money would go to her. By necessity the work would run several volumes, and he revealed his plans to preface it with short memoirs, saying he would be writing one of them. Loui gave him her watch and diamond bracelet to help pay for publication on the condition that he leave out anything unkind or unpleasant, and Griswold promised, but from that day he avoided Loui, refusing even to answer her letters. She met him in Broadway one morning in a crowd, and he brushed her off by saying that Longfellow had given his approval and that the matter was closed.

"Approval for what?" she asked.

"To the biography which I have written," he said. "And Mrs. Clemm is reconciled."

Loui assumed he meant by this that unkind and unpleasant things *had* been written, so she explained her diagnosis of Edgar's physical maladies, hoping Griswold might see them as mitigating, but he sneered at her claim of brain disease. She decided he would be obstinate, so she told him with as much sarcasm as she could muster that he must be a lawyer, not a preacher. She asked to know the expense of the whole project, thinking she would underwrite it herself and be rid of Griswold. He named the amount, and she asked for a month in which to raise the funds, but her new husband threw a wet blanket over it and refused to stand with her. Loui was still young and lacked the courage and self-confidence to battle for what was right. She has never been so disheartened as when she saw what Griswold wrote. It was so unnecessary. Edgar was dead; there was nothing to be gained by treating him in such a cruel manner except that revenge were the motive.

Since Mrs. Clemm could no longer afford to rent the cottage at Fordham, she accepted Loui's invitation for an extended stay. On the very day she packed up, having not given Catterina a thought all day, she went back into the cottage for the last load of boxes and found the cat dead in a corner of the loft. She had never been as partial to Catterina as Edgar and Virginia, so Loui decided it fitting that the cat's life should end there where her mistress had died. Knowing Mrs. Clemm, Loui did not bother to ask if Catterina had been given a decent burial. Mrs. Clemm was not the sort to make a fuss over something like a cat.

Under Loui's roof, the two did not get on well. Mrs. Clemm was forever criticizing her, lecturing her on her childish simplicity or her ignorance of the latest fashions. At the end of two months she left and went to Lowell to live with Annie Richmond, one of the women Edgar had attached himself to after Virginia died. In time Loui's correspondence with Mrs. Clemm diminished. Later she had a letter from Annie Richmond who spoke bitterly of Mrs. Clemm, calling her treacherous and cruel. It seems Mrs. Clemm left a trail of burned bridges. Loui heard from her occasionally, but she never saw her again.

When the war came, her family left New York and went north to live at Pierrepont Manor. She had married Roland Houghton and bore him two children, Dora and Mary, but, thankfully, he did not follow them north. Why, after Joel Shew, Loui married a man with such conventional ideas about a wife's role, she cannot say. It was not dire need in her case, rather it was, by her own admission, dire stupidity. And like Mrs. Clemm, she has only herself to blame.

Loui later learned that Mrs. Clemm redeemed Loui's watch and that she looked for her in New York to return it. As for the bracelet, Griswold only got three hundred dollars for it, far below its value. Dr. Houghton, to whom Loui was still married at the time, demanded that Griswold either return it or provide just payment, but Roland Houghton was only thinking of how five hundred dollars would put him right. He didn't make the demand out of consideration for Loui or indignation for the injustice to Edgar. Just like her first husband, he was more interested in Loui's money than in her and her happiness. He and Griswold were cut out of the same bolt of cloth. Though they both professed to be men of God, they were interested only in their own station and comfort. To her husband Loui was his servant, and her desire to ease the suffering of others was nothing more to him than a nagging bother. He was a hypocrite who cared little for his fellow man, and this was not lost on his children who now care nothing for him. His portrait hangs alongside Loui's, and at Christmastime when Dora and Mary decorate her portrait and everything else in the house with sprigs of holly and mistletoe, they do not decorate his. When Loui asked Dora why, her daughter said, "we remember him in our cold hands, our weary feet, our daily sufferings and deprivations." Loui thought to defend him, but for what purpose?

As she has said, she is not fond of Edgar's poems and tales, though she understands that "The Raven" is a great wonder to scholars and lovers of literature. Life brings enough of sadness; she doesn't care to read about it. She believes she is cursed (and blessed) with a small brain. Cursed because she never became a person of great intellect, blessed because to sustain a large brain requires twice the nourishment. Edgar Poe had a large brain, and that was his curse. When by poverty or carelessness, he failed to adhere to a proper diet, he would go out of his head, raving mad, which many took for drunkenness when in fact it was disease, and, though Loui made this clear to him, and though she took him to Dr. Mott who concurred with her diagnosis, Edgar refused to heed her advice. As is said, you can lead a horse to water, &c, &c.

Sometimes Loui thinks Edgar liked her for her very indifference to his work. She was a rest for his spirit. With the exception of Virginia and Mrs. Clemm and perhaps Mary Starr, she was the only person he knew who did not seek some personal gain from his genius. Loui's daughter, Dora, looked for Edgar's books in the public library and in several private libraries in Whitestone and also in Flushing, but she could not find even one. That is a great shame, and Loui blames Wilmot Griswold. She wishes for someone to right this wrong, and for this reason speaks freely of what she knows about Edgar Poe. His was a failed and darkened spirit, and, though he possessed the brain of a genius and a generous heart, both were diseased, but that through no fault of his. His enemies still persist, Dunn English lives, and friends of Griswold keep the slanders circulating. English is a scoundrel, not to be trusted, and now he's running for the U.S. Congress. Imagine that!

Loui reports that a man named Jones—a bushy-headed rascal she called him—who claimed to be lame and unable to get out of his carriage, called at her gate recently and sent his driver to her door to inquire if she had any poems or manuscripts by Edgar Poe that had not been published. He wanted Loui to bring them out to his carriage so he could sell them to some greedy publisher. There are many such villains about, but Loui will give them nothing. She wishes only that someone do Edgar the justice he so rightly deserved and give his troubled soul some peace.

(ITEM 14: *Marie Louise Shew Houghton*)

…

April 6, 1877
The Chestnuts
Whitestone,
Long Island

Dear Lieutenant Gayle,

Just a note to say that in the future you should send your letters to Box 72, Whitestone, Queens County, Long Island. We will be giving up the

Flushing box after the first of May, and this summer we will be moving back into the city, as the time has come for Dora and Mary to find husbands. There are few suitable candidates out here in the country.

Yours,
Loui

(ITEM 21: *Dora Houghton*)

...

November 6, 1877
Greenwich Street, #5
New York City

Dear Mr. Gayle,

It grieves me to report that mother died in September. The doctor said it was the influenza, though mother insisted he was mistaken and that she had the pneumonia. I think she was right, because my sister and I nursed her without ever a day of sickness ourselves. We did everything she instructed us to do, but it wasn't enough I am sad to say.

One thing she told me was that when Henry comes back from Colorado to see if his trunk contains the poem she told you about, "The Beloved Physician" and to copy it out for you to have. But Henry's never come, and I don't know when he will. He couldn't make it home in time for mama's funeral, of course, and with her gone he just might not come back at all. Though he is my step-brother, he's much older than I, and we are not that close, so there's not really anything here for him to come back to except two teenage girls who might be more trouble than we are worth.

If it is possible I will try to get the poem for you, because mama was wanting you to have it so it wouldn't be lost forever as she feared might be the case if Henry were to sell it to somebody, him needing the money. If you will write to me from time to time to let me know your mailing address, I'll see that you get a copy if Henry ever comes back east.

Cordially,
Dora Houghton

June 12, 1877
76 Benefit Street
Providence, Rhode Island

Dearest Eddy,

I am writing you a short note today, having read in your letter just received that you have leave coming, that after nine months in the "wilds of Wyoming," it is your hope to spend your leave in "civilized and pleasant company," and that you are of an age and position now to consider marriage. My age has earned me license to be so bold as to suggest that you visit us here in Providence. We would be pleasant company and thrilled to have you, and I'm told we are civilized, though who can say?

But in all seriousness and by way of an inducement, let me recall to your mind my secretary, Charlotte Ayers. She is intelligent, attractive, of an appropriate age, and I can assure you that no human being I have ever known possesses her like in devotion and kindness, not to mention pleasantness. Furthermore, I can assure you that she is kindly disposed to you, though I'm quite certain she'd be mortified knowing I said so; therefore, you *must* not quote me. She has often spoken admiringly of you since your visit last summer. If it is pleasant and welcoming company you seek, Eddy, you will find it here, and I would be an extra—and I assure you, discreet—beneficiary of your entertaining presence. Of course you will plan to spend time in North Carolina with your mother and your sister and her family, but please consider also a day or more with us here in Providence.

Hoping for an affirmative response,
I remain yours, most sincerely,
Helen

August 28, 1877
76 Benefit Street
Providence, Rhode Island

My Dear Lieutenant Gayle,

What pleasure I take in hearing from you, sir. You surprised me when you asked permission to write. I gave it gladly, of course, not daring to hope for a letter so soon.

Your visit was most welcomed but much too brief. Mrs. Whitman had, of course, prepared me for your visit. Quite naturally I assumed it was for the purpose of discussing with her the subject of your mutual interest. To my surprise that subject was barely touched upon, and I was flattered and honored to be included in the evening's activities which is not always the case when Mrs. Whitman entertains, though she rarely does these days. Normally on such evenings my role is helping in the kitchen and serving dinner, a role I cherish, as would anyone for the likes of Mrs. Whitman. It occurred to me, therefore, when she insisted on brewing the coffee herself that your visit might have included seeing me. I cannot adequately express, Lieutenant Gayle, the thrill I felt that such might be the case. As you left, when you asked if you might write to me, I became certain that such was, indeed, the case, and I wished at that moment with all my heart that you were staying longer than one single evening. You will come again, won't you?

Yes, of course, I remember the night we met. I remember it fondly in that it marks the moment I first saw you, but in all other respects it was a night one might wish to forget. I know that you and Mrs. Whitman have corresponded, though I do not know the full nature of that correspondence. Quite frequently she has me copy her letters, if she wishes to keep a copy for her records, but that has never occurred in the case of her correspondence with you. You bring her much pleasure, and I had decided that she wished to keep you to herself. I wondered if she had discussed the events of that night with you, though from the tone of your letter, I assume she never did. I am not surprised, Lieutenant Gayle, for she has forbidden me to speak of that night.

I confess to not understanding the significance of what happened, only that in her mind it was dreadful. She remained mostly bedridden for more than a week afterward, eating little and refusing to see the doctor. We began to fear for her life. Mrs. Whitman's sister, Miss Power, has special needs. In so many ways the household revolves around her, and there are no servants. Mrs. Whitman could easily afford a serving girl or cook, but in the time that I have been her secretary, she has insisted on doing most chores herself, often seeming to wait on Miss Power hand and foot. You can imagine the strain on me after that night with Mrs. Whitman incapacitated and Miss Power distraught over her condition. I admit that I am somewhat afraid of Miss Power. One never knows when she might appear or where or what she might do or say. She can be very disconcerting and unruly. While Mrs. Whitman was bedridden, our next door neighbor came to lend a hand; otherwise, I could not have managed.

Mrs. Whitman seemed to me to be in a state of shock. Then one morning I arrived to find her dressed and sitting in the wing chair in her bedroom, waiting for me. "Get rid of the cat," she blurted the instant she saw me. That was all. I was confused. I wasn't sure what she meant for me to do, and she grew agitated. "I'm not coming down until the cat is gone, Charlotte. Go get rid of it now. I don't care what you do with it, so long as I never lay eyes on it again. Come tell me when the deed is done. Now go."

I have never been fond of cats and disliked Cato in particular. I believe to this day that the feeling was mutual. There was something uncanny about that cat; I had believed this long before the night of your visit. I took Cato to my mother's. What else could I do? I was afraid to leave Mrs. Whitman alone for long. Our house is only a few blocks away, but by the time I arrived, my hands and arms were bleeding from Cato's scratches. I explained to my mother what had happened. "Has she gone mad?" my mother exclaimed, referring to Mrs. Whitman, while I washed my cuts. "You cannot let the cat out," I told her, "or he'll return to Benefit Street."

"What am I to do?" she asked. "I don't know, Mother; Mrs. Whitman said get rid of it."

To this day I don't know what became of Cato. Mother told me only that she confined him in a basket and took him to the constable. I hate to think that Cato was killed because of what happened the night of your visit, but I suspect that was the case. Even though I did not like him, I cannot tell you how this has troubled me—I can't bear to harm a living thing. The remorse I feel is horrible. I returned to Mrs. Whitman, told her the cat was gone, and she came downstairs for breakfast. Cato has not been mentioned since. You mustn't tell Mrs. Whitman any of this. She would be upset with me if she knew that I had told you, but nor can I bring myself to refuse answering your questions or, at least, those I feel at liberty to answer.

Regarding the visions or dreams or whatever they were, one can't help but speculate on their meaning. I copy every letter that Mrs. Whitman writes to John Ingram, so I have learned much about Edgar Allan Poe, but I'm certain my notions of what happened are naive, and I don't dare speak them.

It is still very cold here. I long for spring as you must also, being in Montana or soon to be, that is. Please write to me and tell me of your visit to your family. I hope you found your mother and sister well. You told me that you grew up in the swamps of eastern North Carolina, but I decided you didn't mean literally in the swamps, but nearby. You were teasing me, were you not? I must tell you, Lieutenant Gayle that I don't take teasing well. I think it must be the nature of your sunny and generous personality to joke and tease, and I find your sense of humor refreshing and enjoyable, but I beg you not to tease me. Is yours the Dismal Swamp? A frightful name that! I have always found it mysterious and alluring. Please tell me more. I long to know more about you.

As for me, there is little more to say beyond what I told you on your visit. I've told you of my love for drawing. I am not skilled and being self-taught, I would be too embarrassed to show you my work, but I confess that I draw whenever time permits. I would like to paint but have never attempted it, though I would give anything for training in that medium. Another thing I love is to read, a pastime that has instilled in me a strong desire to see more of the world. Alas, I have been no farther than Boston; I have never even seen New York City, though it's only a day's ferry ride. In light of our exchange of letters, I fervently wish to learn more about the South—a place, I confess with some trepidation, that I have always thought of as wild and ungovernable, but also exotic, tropical, and enchanting. Forgive me this simpleminded and uneducated impression. Surely I am mistaken, and it is my sincerest hope that you will do me the honor of enlightening me on the subject.

Henceforth, address your letters to me at 18 Hope Street, Providence, Rhode Island, my mother's house.

With fondest feelings, I am

Charlotte Bartlett Ayers

(ITEM 23: *Whitman*)

...

November 21, 1877
76 Benefit Street
Providence, Rhode Island

My Dear Eddy,

I sympathize with your preparations for another cold winter. I am resolved that this one will be my last. My dematerialization is near at hand. Make no protest please. I will be seventy-five in January, and enough is enough. Surely you know I have no fear of death.

I am saddened by notice of Loui Shew Houghton's passing. How old was she, Eddy? I am somewhat surprised, as it's my recollection that she was much younger than I, and I inferred from all Ingram said about her that she was in quite good health. I will write to her daughters immediately. Does it not appear that the breed of us who knew EAP are fast becoming extinct? I am further resolved that I will not live to see Ingram's biography, and am reconciled that it is for the best. At one time I thought that effort was the thing keeping me in this world, but, of course, that was not true in the least. I continue to write poetry. It is my sole surviving pleasure, and, if there is anything holding me here, it is that. I believe you have come to know the joy of writing, Eddy. You so often tell me what great pleasure you take in your correspondence. Someday you will write about your experiences, perhaps even about our acquaintance, and you will then know the pure enjoyment of putting thought to paper.

Now for an answer to another of your interminable questions, only this one will be my pleasure. Where, I wonder, did you learn the name Stella Lewis [*sic*: Sarah Anna Lewis, 1824–1880]? Was it Loui? I think it must have been. I recall Ingram speaking of Mrs. Lewis in reference to his correspondence with Loui. Am I correct that both Loui and Mrs. Lewis were visitors to the Poe cottage after Virginia died? As I recall Mrs. Lewis's husband was a wealthy Brooklyn attorney, and he paid handsomely and shamelessly for favorable reviews of her atrocious poems. To understand, my dear boy, you need to know something about the publishing world. It is a nasty business. Writers should never be editors and vice versa, for this is nothing less than an invitation to the proverbial fox to revel in the hen house. In my youth I wrote reviews of other writers' work until I learned, to my cost, that if I said something flattering or unflattering, my own work was, in turn, flattered or condemned. But it doesn't end there. Publishers lobby, make promises, provide discounts for flattering reviews in order to assist in selling their stocks. The system is rotten to the core. But only in the gravest cases does money actually change hands, and Mrs. Lewis's poems, if by such label they may be dignified, were a grave case indeed.

It was no accident that the Lewises preyed on EAP at the very time he was most vulnerable. They were infamous in their scheming. He had lost his wife; he was deathly ill; and he had no means of support. Still, he abhorred Stella Lewis's presence and considered her poetry an abomination. Mrs. Clemm, however, being naive and desperate, encouraged the arrangement and berated her son-in-law until he relented. I cannot condemn him for it, because I know how it grieved him, how it went against his every professional principle, and how he loathed himself for the favor.

Since, to his credit, John Ingram believes that no stone should go unturned, he communicated with Mrs. Lewis who is now divorced and living in England. And since I have come to understand that you are of like-mind, I will have Charlotte enclose herewith Mrs. Lewis's last known address. The task will provide Charlotte with the opportunity of slipping a note of her own inside this envelope, as I feel certain she will do. Deal with Mrs. Lewis at your peril.

Penned with my deepest devotion,
Helen

4

STELLA LEWIS

::

(ITEM 24: *Sarah Anna Lewis*)
...

February 4, 1878
8 Bedford Place
Russell Square, London

My Dear Lt. Gayle,

Forgive my confounding your assertion that few survive who were personally acquainted with Edgar Poe. Though I have lived in England for some years, I keep abreast of events in America and would be well-informed of so cataclysmic and obliging an event as the collective demise of Ralph Waldo Emerson [1803–1882], Louis Godey [1804–1878], George Rex Graham [1813–1894], Henry Wadsworth Longfellow, Richard Henry Dana [1815–1882], Richard Henry Stoddard [1825–1903], Evert Duyckinck [1816–1878], James Russell Lowell, and assorted others of the publishing profession—rogues all—who not only knew Poe but wasted considerable, albeit fruitless, ink condeming him. You mention Griswold. I assure you he was only singing soprano in a chorus of base malcontents— many of whom, lamentably, survive to this day.

You need not trouble them, however, for an answer to your question regarding Edgar and Griswold, since, as with the women you have consulted, *no* answer shall be forthcoming. Does it surprise you to learn that those with whom you have communicated already, though they know the answer, withheld it from you? I assume they pleaded ignorance; I assure you they are *not*. I could name a dozen other men and women who know the answer also. Nor will they tell you. The answer is no secret among the initiate, but for reasons that are complicated, a conspiracy of silence has been universally observed for nearly thirty years now, even among conspirators who are otherwise sworn enemies. It is a most unlikely compact, as I think back on it. Truly remarkable.

You tell me, Lieutenant, that your interest in Edgar Poe is a hobby, but the question you ask is not a hobbyist's sort of inquiry. Take my word for it. I accept without suspicion what you say about yourself; therefore, I shall warn you that you are playing with fire, and in so saying I tell you more than is prudent, so in return I ask that you not quote me in the event your motives are less innocent than you profess.

This said, I wish to tell you, in all sincerity that Edgar was dear to me as I am certain I was to him—that despite what others might claim. I was not popular with the New York literary crowd, in part because I remained constant to my friendship with Edgar when others chose to distance themselves from him for reasons somewhat related to the above-mentioned conspiracy. My husband was an attorney and represented Edgar in a lawsuit against what could, without exaggeration, be labeled the New York Publishing Establishment. In winning the case for Edgar, he became something of a pariah in their estimation, so naturally I was tainted with the same brush. Now, years later, many of those same people have chosen to defend Edgar, his genius having become manifest, yet, though my husband and I are divorced, I remain an outcast in that society, a thing—unfair though it may be—I accept. I accept it, comforted in the knowledge that when his "fair-weather" friends chose to cast him out, I never once abandoned him. I was his *only* New York friend who remained constant to the end of his life, and my devotion meant much to him. How many nights when he, Mrs. Clemm, my husband, and I were playing whist in our parlor in Brooklyn, did he breast his cards, peer across the table at me—bone-weary, his eyes tearing—and lament, "Stella, I shudder to think what would have become of us but for you." He knew I would have done for him anything within my power, and it was for this reason that he addressed me affectionately in his poem. I *do not* refer to "Annabel Lee." That one was *not* addressed to me, though Mrs. Clemm insisted that it was and claimed it publically. She was flattering me for her own increasingly greedy self-interest, but I *do not fault her*; she was also increasingly desperate, particularly after Edgar died. I am not so naive as people think. Yet those same people have claimed that I believed Mrs. Clemm. I do not. Unquestionably, Virginia was the inspiration for "Annabel Lee"—she was the love of his life. Furthermore, and despite what is further rumored, I was never in love with him, and he was never in love with me or anyone else—before or *after* Virginia died. Edgar and I were friends—admirers and fellow-artists. That is all. Is this so difficult to believe?

In your letter you mention John Ingram. I met with him on one occasion and have corresponded with him, telling him freely—and as truthfully as I know how—my recollections regarding Edgar, even confiding in him things that happened after Edgar's death—one incident, in particular, of an exceedingly bizarre nature and quite possibly related to the conspiracy referred to at the beginning of this letter. That incident involved a writer named Lizzy Ellet [Elizabeth Freeze Lummis Ellet, 1818–1877]. I mention this because she is the *only* person I can think so perfidious and reckless as to provide the answer to your question, for she is the *only* person who had an ax to grind with both Edgar *and* Griswold. All others fall in one camp or the other, myself included. Unfortunately for you, Lizzy died last June (may her nosy soul burn in hell). Had you gotten to her in time, it may not have been necessary for you to write to me. I am tempted, therefore, to ask what you would pay for the answer to your question, but, since I don't need the money, don't trouble yourself with an offer. Are you truly a hobbyist? Yea or nay, if in time—if you please me greatly—and if I live long enough, I might just provide a clue or two. Are you a patient man, Lieutenant Gayle? A reply would be welcomed, not to mention, courteous, but that's entirely up to you.

Warmly, Sarah "Estella" Lewis

:: THEY ARE NOT INFREQUENT, THESE LETTERS addressed to "Mrs. Sarah *or* Mrs. Estella Lewis." The postman studies them, wondering perhaps if there are two of her—perhaps widowed wives of brothers, for he has never seen a man in the house. No doubt he has decided that the sisters-in-law forged a closeness over years of marriage to the Misters Lewis such that the sentiments of their correspondents contain no intimacy unsuitable for both pairs of eyes. The postman is a stooped little man with a gray mustache, liquid bloodshot eyes, and a garrulous disposition. He wears his postman's hat too far back on his head for propriety. Stella has seen in those veined eyes the question, "Are you the Mrs. Sarah or the Mrs. Estella?" She could tell him easily enough, for she knows at any given moment who she is. If, for example, she has just scribbled a note for the cook to carry to the grocer with her order for a five-pound roast and one pound each of Stilton and Dutch cheese and requested that he weigh them this time without his thumb pressing down on the scale, she is Sarah. If, on the other hand, she were to open a letter in the presence of the postman and read far enough to perceive questions regarding Edgar Poe, she would at once and without premeditation revert to Estella.

There is, of course, but one Mrs. Lewis and there was, thankfully, but one Mr. Lewis. Stella does not, however, reveal this to the postman. She lets him think whatever he likes, preferring not to explain, knowing that, if she did, the gossips on his route would rate her somewhere between profoundly eccentric and positively potty.

She cannot bridle a question, however: which of Edgar's friends put this soldier in touch with her and how did they know where to find her in England? Was it Mary Gove or Loui Shew—that pair of quacks allied against her? Are they alive? By now Stella would have expected that the icy water they prescribe for their patients would have turned them both into frozen prunes. Perhaps by now also this soldier has already perceived the bitterness and jealousy epidemic among Edgar's women friends in the wake of his death and of Griswold's nefarious memoir. Lieutenant Gayle is stirring a stew spoiled years ago by too many cooks. He will find it thankless just as Stella did. Seeing the futility of it, she chose to distance herself from those of like-mind who endeavored to mend the matter. Could it be that the passing time has rendered possible what was then impossible? Stella doubts it.

She was at first somewhat hesitant to respond, owing to the preconceived notions that she suspected Lieutenant Gayle might have formed about her. Sarah *or* Estella, she is *not* who he thinks. But the night before she received his first letter, Edgar Poe appeared to her in a dream.

"I have much to tell you," were the words she heard, though he never opened his mouth to speak. His expression was calm, kindly, almost smiling. The top and bottom two buttons of his black vest were buttoned, his right hand inserted between them in the way he often held it there when he recited.

In the usual disjointed murkiness of dreams, the rest is indistinct, but his message was undeniable—he was heralding the arrival of a letter and urging Stella to respond. She is one who heeds such messages. For the lieutenant's part, he may accept it as Edgar's consent for whatever his purpose might be. Were Stella to reveal her dream, she would caution him not to take it lightly. Some of Edgar's friends—and she's thinking particularly of Mrs. Whitman for whom she has great respect—were in contact with the supernatural. They would tell stranger things than this, and it seems the lieutenant is already aware of this. Don't dismiss them, Stella would caution, as the delusions of a harebrained woman. Accept them without judgment, hear them out, and Edgar will have been well-served. Still, Stella is on her guard, wondering if the man's motives are honorable.

In her second letter she reveals the riddle of her name, lest he also think her potty. Sarah was the name given her upon her birth, but at a still very young age she decided the name unsuitable. Sarah was not her, for she was quite extraordinary, and Sarah was altogether too ordinary a name. So she chose Stella, and her girlfriends nicknamed her "Stellie." It was child's play. When she was seven, she changed it to Blanche, and insisted that her family address her by that name. They humored her, despite her older sister's vociferous annoyance. She can recall her father looking up from his newspaper during breakfast and saying to her sister, "Your sister can be whoever she wants."

His tone was not indulgent; it was indifferent. Stella remembers staring at him after he said this, watching him return to his reading, pick up his cup, and sip his coffee. Then her focus moved beyond him, through the breakfast room windows, to the bay and the reflection of cold sunlight on water. She felt abandoned. He wanted them to hush. He didn't care who she was so long as she kept quiet.

She ultimately had other names. At ten she was Constance; at fifteen, Laura, but her classmates at Mrs. Willard's in Troy insisted on calling her "Laurie" which irked her. Petrarch would never have addressed his Laura by a nickname. So she professed to her classmates that her real name was Estella. She published her first poem under that name and soon realized that she was stuck with it. It wasn't that she disliked it but that she had painted herself into a corner. She had grown accustomed to changing not only her name, but also her personality, the way she spoke and acted, her favorite authors, her heroes and heroines, even her religion—always carefully thought out. She read what Emerson wrote about consistency and hobgoblins, and she embraced those words as a validation. She was not being fickle as others claimed. She could be whomever she wanted—whenever, wherever, and for as long as she liked.

Soon after arriving at Mrs. Willard's school, Stella realized that she had essentially become homeless. By then both her parents and her sister were dead; she was an orphan. She and Edgar Poe had that in common; it was one of the things that drew them together. Unless you have been an orphan, you cannot know the horrible certainty of isolation. Her childhood had been a series of tragedies. Her father, John Robinson, died in Cuba of malaria when Stella was seven. He spent half the year there looking after his plantations. Her mother— how shall she describe her? Her mother was confined to her bed after Stella's birth, looked after by a servant who slept in the room with her. As she found Stella's presence tiresome, Stella was only permitted into her mother's bedroom for an hour in the late afternoons before her mother's supper tray was brought up. Stella played beside her mother's bed as her mother watched in a silent, languid lassitude, her head propped on pillows, her nurse ready to intervene at the slightest provocation. A doctor came once a week, and when Stella's father was at home, the two of them held long, closed-door conversations in her father's study. She remembers sitting on the stairs, listening, her face pressed between the bannister posts. "Put her away," she thought she heard the doctor say. Or did he say, "Give her *her* way"? They lived near Baltimore where there existed a certain hospital for people like Stella's mother, Baltimore's equivalent of London's Bedlam. Stella's fairy tale mind carried her there. She saw her mother chained to the stones of her cell, serpent hair like Medusa, her gown soiled and torn, her ravage showing in her limp and lifeless limbs. That is the image Stella has of her mother. She conjured all manner of reasons for her mother's madness, but above all, it was the thing that prevented her loving Stella in the way mothers are supposed to love their daughters. Stella did not blame her. She loved her for what her girlish brain decided her mother would have been but could not be. She loves her still, though she died when Stella was nine.

There was a rumor about her father, one regarding his uncertain pedigree, the thing to which Stella came to attribute her mother's madness. Was he of English and Spanish descent as he claimed? He was Cuban by birth; his family had lived there for generations. He spoke flawless English; he had been educated in England. Nevertheless, as a child, Stella heard whispered the word, "Creole," regarding her father, and she came to understand its implication. It was the reason that her parents failed to gain entry into a certain Baltimore society. Her mother had been born in St. Kitts of English parents; she was, therefore, Kittitian—a title Stella loved; it sounding so classical and regal. Her mother's father had owned sugar plantations in the Leeward Islands; therefore she grew up thinking herself quite the blue blood. Did she—Stella's mother—later hear whispered the word "Creole" and go mad with the horror of having wed a man with African blood coursing through his veins? And were Stella's full lips and figure the result of this also? Did their family have a dark, shameful secret? Her own buried response was divided. On the one hand she relished the exotic mystery she had inherited as an explanation of why she felt so singular. On the other hand, she clung to a juvenile notion that she might be a lost child, a changeling.

The answer was buried with her parents. Her father, mother, and sister all died within a period of two years, and Stella became the ward of her father's younger brother. Nine years old and alone, she sailed to Cuba. Her uncle, whom she had never met and who had always been called Jacob by her parents, went by the name, Santiago, in Havana, and he considered himself quite the gallant. A bachelor, Santiago had a house two blocks west of the Catedral de San Cristóbal in Old Havana, white plaster and shutters of Cuban blue, a color that is not quite aquamarine, not quite cerulean. Santiago's day began at noon with a visit from his banker or tailor or barber. Once dressed he went out for lunch at two, that was followed by a promenade along the Malecón with his cavalier friends, an afternoon of flirting with the prostitutes who strutted their charms, handing out pasteboard calling cards as enticements for the night ahead. Following a late supper, he and his foppish cronies rode out to one of the opulent brothels in Marimar to drink and fornicate until sunup. Santiago was not about to allow a nine-year-old brat to cramp his hidalgo lifestyle, so he exiled Stella along with a governess, employed with overmuch haste, to her father's plantation in Viñales in the far west of Cuba near Piñar del Rios, a quaint village of shaded streets lined with weeping tropical pines. There on a tobacco plantation she lived for five years, neglected by a governess who spoke little English and a procession of ruthless and hard-drinking overseers, hired from among the flotsam of itinerants who moved from island to island, usually fleeing some heinous atrocity. In the beginning her only companions were the children of slaves, and she hated her uncle and resented her parents for abandoning her to a world in which she was friendless and unable to speak the language.

On Sundays she and her governess were driven into Piñar del Rios to attend Mass. One of the priests, Father Esteban, was young and handsome. He spoke the purest Castilian Spanish, enunciating his words with such precision that Stella came to understand them. Deciding she wanted him as a teacher, she insisted on being allowed to attend confession. There she confessed to the fictions of her imagination, things she'd heard whispered, outrageous sins she was too young to have committed or even understand. Her confessions achieved the desired end, however—regular visits from the Holy Father. Father Esteban was shy, and to Stella's immense joy, he spoke English well. They sat on the veranda and talked for hours on every subject imaginable. He saw through her scheming, perceived her loneliness, and become her friend if not officially her teacher. He advised her on what to read which not only included religious studies but also poetry and, of course, *Don Quixote*. Emboldened by his attentions, Stella demanded of Santiago books in Spanish and English. Her uncle acceded to her demands; perhaps thinking books a small price to pay for being rid of her. He was not about to permit Stella to live in Havana or travel to Baltimore to live with friends, though each letter she wrote him pleaded for that permission. Her consolation was what became the finest library in Viñales, which said little. It was then she began writing poetry, and Father Esteban read her verses and guided her. He became her best and only friend. Her poems drove her governess to distraction, since her English was insufficient in deciphering hidden meanings and references, and in that way Stella came to rule the woman, or so her girlish brain thought.

When she was thirteen, her uncle packed her off to a boarding school for girls in Troy, New York. Though Stella deeply regretted leaving Father Esteban, returning to America thrilled her. At Mrs. Willard's School, despite the strict and demanding regimen, she was a model student, always first in her class. Without caring or knowing, her uncle had provided her a fine education. Already fluent in Spanish, she became fluent also in French and Italian; she learned to read and write Latin. She translated portions of the *Aeneid* into English with such accomplishment that her teachers thought her translations suitable for publication. Stella became a devout classicist, and at fifteen, she fell in love. Ernest lived in Albany. He was two years older, dark hair, thin, bookish and somewhat sullen, but, in Stella's eyes, beautiful. He too loved the classics, and they spent long hours reading to each other, sitting on the lawn at Mrs. Willard's. Stella hated that she was so full-bodied, not overweight exactly, but too thick to appreciate her appearance and, because she was even larger than Ernest, she feared that he looked upon her as a friend only, not someone he might want to make love to. She was pretty enough—long, dark, excessively curly hair, full lips and breasts, and large eyes—she imagined them to be sensuous, lover's eyes. They were her best feature, and when she looked at Ernest, she concentrated on begging him with her eyes as if they alone could convey her desire. She ached for him to touch her. She had never been touched by a man and would have let Ernest do anything he wanted. She had no mother holding her back, lecturing her on the proper behavior of a young lady, only her teachers and the nuns at Our Lady of Grace where every day began with prayer, but by fifteen Stella had forsaken the Catholic Church for Sappho.

For several years now she suspected that her uncle was stealing the money and property she had inherited. Being in Cuba, he was beyond the reach of the laws governing her father's estate. Earlier, when she lived on the plantation in Viñales, he had added rooms onto his house in Old Havana on the pretense of providing for her, though he never permitted her to visit. Stella had been too young and naive then to grasp the implications; now she did. And now, two thousand miles away, she became incensed whenever she thought of having never once slept in those new rooms. She is certain that he helped himself to her inheritance with little or no regard for what was just. Therefore, anticipating graduation from Mrs. Willard's, Stella declared her independence from Santiago in a ponderously formal letter, punctuated with Latin phrases for purposes of ingraining the document with powers official. It was her *Magna Carta*.

Santiago responded in hastily written Spanish, brusquely refusing Stella's declaration on the basis that she was still underage. Defiant and willful, she explained her situation to Ernest who was understanding and sympathetic, but he withheld the hoped-for proposal that would have provided a solution. Stella would have married him, even knowing he might be marrying her for her money; she didn't require love. Need on his part, even greed, was acceptable. She had no one else.

After graduation, in the summer of 1841, she traveled to New York City to stay with a classmate for the summer and to decide about her future. She explained her predicament to her classmate's father, and he introduced her to an attorney friend. Sylvanus Lewis was more than twice Stella's age, and she thought him quite ugly. His face was clean-shaven, but a beard encircled his neck, beneath the line of his jaw, a style that Stella found pompous and unflattering. His eyes were his best feature, a deep penetrating blue; they were sincere and kindly. He listened, smiling sympathetically all the while as if he'd heard similar tales and knew the answers, but he remained silent, patiently letting Stella tell her story.

"My dear," he said when she finished, stroking the beard that concealed his Adam's apple, "you know enough of the law, I imagine. You seem a very bright young lady."

Stella looked down and away, frustrated and infuriated by the impotence his flattery implied. In fact she did not know enough of the law, but surely it was on her side.

"You have but one option," he said, and she turned back to him, hoping for some miracle. "Marry!"

She immediately thought of Ernest. If only. But she could not propose to him, nor could she entice him to propose to her beyond what she had done already.

"I take it," he added, rising from his chair, "that there are no acceptable suitors at this time?" He walked around his desk, took the chair next to Stella's, and breathed a deep sign of resignation. "I must say I'm surprised, seeing as I do such a beautiful young lady. Well then, here's the gist of it. You are the responsibility of your guardian until you reach the age of twenty-one or until such time as you marry and become the responsibility of your husband."

"Responsibility, Mr. Lewis?" she asked. "Or do you mean property?"

He laughed. "Property, Miss Robinson. Yes. It is the law of the land. Do you know the amounts? Have you asked for an accounting of the sources and uses of the funds? You have a right to that, and I could make inquiries, but bear in mind that your uncle will probably take offense. The situation could become confrontational, though I judge from what you say that it may already be. You shouldn't have written him yourself; it only served to put him on his guard. I'm sorry to say, the law is on his side. But, of course, if he has committed fraud, the court could dismiss him and appoint a new guardian. You would have recourse. It could become ugly, not to say costly. His being a resident and citizen of Cuba complicates the matter."

"I don't care," she said. Stella had introduced herself to Sylvanus Lewis as Estella Robinson, but now Sarah took charge. "I *do* wish you to make inquiries and without delay. I want to know."

He smiled, and she inferred from his smile that there was something she hadn't thought about. Yes, of course; his fee. Could she afford to pay him out of her allowance? No doubt Santiago would refuse to pay the expense. Nevertheless, Sylvanus Lewis agreed to represent her, ignoring, at least for the moment, the matter of his fee.

Stella met with him on several occasions thereafter. His inquiries yielded nothing; her uncle proved predictably intransigent and outraged. He refused even to supply a copy of her father's will, and Mr. Lewis was forced to obtain one by way of a colleague in Baltimore from the recorder of indentures. By the end of six weeks, she knew little more than she had to begin with; nevertheless, with each visit to Mr. Lewis's office at the corner of Broad and Exchange, he became friendlier and more gracious. His clerk greeted Stella as if she were a Broadway aristocrat, and she never had to wait to be ushered into his private office. And each time, his appearance became more dapper, his shirt and collar always starched, his waistcoat and suit coat buttoned, his boots shined, his beard evenly clipped, his fingernails cleaned and manicured. He would come around his desk, shake her hand warmly with both of his, and sit beside her while his clerk placed a service of tea and cakes on the little mahogany pedestal table that stood between their two chairs facing his desk which, unlike her first visit, was now neat and organized—twin polished brass oil lamps, their green lanterns wiped clean of soot, one or two legal portfolios beneath a bronze sundial paperweight, a silver inkstand, a neatly folded copy of the *American Whig Review*, and at one end, the knob atop his walking stick, leaning against the edge of his desk. Beyond his swivel brown leather desk chair, two opened windows looked out on the intersection, though from their second story vantage point, they could only see the windows of the building across the street and hear the sounds of traffic below.

There inevitably followed small talk—the weather, the latest fashions appearing on Broadway, the theater. Mr. Lewis loved the theater. He made a point of reminding Stella that he was a lifelong bachelor and seemed quite eager to know all about her. She confessed her passion for writing poetry, and he affected great interest, asking for samples of her work which she brought him. He was not a particularly literary man, but he made an effort for her sake. He seemed more interested in politics, but always apologized if the subject of their conversation turned in that direction. Such things were not suitable for a lady, he said, and they then got down to business, usually a litany of the same frustrations.

"Miss Robinson, I have a proposal," he said one sunny morning in mid-August. Stella took this to mean some clever legal stratagem he had devised, and she turned to him, eager to hear. He hesitated. The easy confidence that she had come to expect in him dissolved. Now he seemed quite nervous. He moved to the edge of his chair and with the palms of his hands, rubbed his knees as if he might spring forth from his chair and leap through the window. A shocking rush of realization gripped Stella, and she pictured Sylvanus Lewis jumping forth and whirling around, suspended in midair, his arms outstretched Jesus-fashion. Her savior? Her thoughts rushed to Ernest and the torture of loving him. She had clung to that hope and for the first time perceived it vanishing. She understood, in that instant, that youth ends badly, that happy-ever-afters are the fiction of dime novels. Bliss is airy and fleeting; torture is ponderous and plodding-slow like the excruciating pace of civil suits. Before he ever popped the question, she knew she must accept. She was nothing if not a plump young lamb on the market.

Recall that Stella was an orphan, that she had no one in the world except a thieving, profligate uncle who cared nothing for her. She had not heard from Ernest since before leaving school. The property her father left was all she had in the world, and she was seventeen, homeless, and frightened. She had heard that it was possible to *learn* to love someone, and, as Sylvanus laid out his plans, she gazed into his pleading blue eyes—that best feature of his—wondering if such were possible in his case. In the end there were more reasons to accept than decline. He seemed kind, knowledgeable, well educated, prominent, and she believed he wanted her. He promised her absolute control of her money. He gave her the names of attorneys and bankers, inviting her to choose for herself, and insisting that he, as her fiancée, would withdraw immediately to rise above a suspicion of conflict of interest.

"There are many women in this city," he said, "who have complete control of their wealth. It is not the least unusual. In fact, I've seen cases in which women manage their affairs far better than many men I know."

Short of breath, Stella begged time to consider. She hurried away, up Broadway, gripped by a fear that was palpable and wrenching. It blotted out all but the bleakest visions. For all she knew, in five years' time her uncle could bankrupt her. Which was worse—bankruptcy or lying beneath Sylvanus Lewis, his irksome beard suffocating her? She saw no choices but these. She abandoned hope and inside two months they were married.

As promised, her money was put in her name, but, because of her youth and lack of experience in money matters, it was immediately turned over to men of business acumen, men-friends of Sylvanus. And since lawyers and businessmen tend to be chummy and cozy, Stella *and* her money became, for all practical purposes, Sylvanus's property.

And like most girls her age, Stella was also inexperienced in matters of the flesh. Nothing, however, not even the bawdy novels that were hidden under mattresses, atop wardrobes, and covertly passed around Mrs. Willard's School prepared her for the demands Sylvanus made in their bedroom. He was patient at first with her refusals, but his patience wore thin. At the theater he pointed to the women in the upper balcony, the girls of the town. He did so for a reason. They were not merely soliciting, he confided. It was entirely possible that a certain act of oral gratification was taking place even during the performance. Stella could not imagine how it could be done without notice or without wrinkled and soiled skirts or without losing track of the plot. Such was her naiveté, but during the performance she reflected on it, becoming aroused by the idea of doing it to Ernest in the woods or in a particular grassy spot above the Hudson River near Mrs. Willard's where they had often been alone. She was not, however, about to do it to Sylvanus Lewis, though he suggested it again that night in the privacy of their bedroom. It was then she realized that poor Sylvanus had married Sarah; whereas, Estella remained fiercely loyal to Ernest. A marriage of convenience carries with it certain sacrifices that must be borne by both parties. Each has their cross to bear. In the case of Sylvanus Lewis, it was going without the pleasure of having his pizzle bussed, at least not by his wife.

Stella's Sarah quickly became a pragmatic, impatient, demanding, and plain-speaking woman. She has had a hard life. Throughout her sixteen years of marriage, she never ceased reminding Sylvanus of his promise that she would have complete control of her money, and by degrees she demanded that control and seized it. Stella's Estella, on the other hand, remained throughout, true to her mutable romanticism. In their entire lifetime, Sarah has attempted only one poem, and Estella had to finish it for her, as the italicized portion gives witness:

Man is the vainest creature Heaven has made,
Except the peacock, which unpicked would be
Of him a better definition, five to three,
Than Plato's on which classic stress is laid.
I hate his selfishness, effeminate weakness,
Because in him I look for something strong.
(Since strength's his boast), I hate the load of wrong
He legislates to make us tote in meekness,—

Yet, hath the God of Nature given to me
A soul so large, a heart so broadly fashioned
For all that's high, impetuous, and impassioned,
That I'm in love with half the swains I see.
Upbraid me not, cold hearts; mid toil and strife,
This love's the well-spring of my higher life in life.

No magazine would ever publish it. Estella never even bothered submitting it. It's only airing came in a collection of her poems in which her editor had no say, though he attempted to: "Do you think this is the sort of sentiment your readers expect of you? Why not reconsider."

Estella smiled, thinking she will not reconsider, that her editor doesn't know her readers half as well as she. They will applaud; they will laugh out loud; such are the secrets we share.

In moments of accord, Sylvanus, to his credit, tolerated Stella's mutability. He convinced her that, if she wanted to make a name for herself in the world of literature, she should stick with one name only. So she became for all time and for all the world, Estella Lewis, accepting "Stella," though she doesn't like nicknames, but what could she do? She introduced herself as Estella, and inevitably someone would ask, "May I call you Stella?" The confusion persisted in her first book. She is misnamed as the author, Estelle Lewis, but the engraving of her on the frontispiece is correctly captioned, Estella Lewis. At readings she was inevitably asked, "Which is it?"

Two years after their marriage Sylvanus was appointed Commissioner of Deeds for the city of Brooklyn. With Stella's money they purchased a large, three-story brownstone on Dean Street, hired servants, and, as they were some distance from the ferry landing, purchased a horse and cabriolet. Despite her youth, she (which is to say Sarah) discovered a facility for directing servants and managing a household, a skill perhaps resulting from her years in Cuba on an estate full of slaves. Estella was relegated to a small study on the third floor, being, as she was, a person so unlike Sarah as to have confused the servants. They would have taken every advantage of her; they would have laughed at her behind her back. So Stella hid Estella there in that study like a page in her copybook, a secret known only to her.

She emerged from that room only in her poetry, and, fortunately for her, most of the servants could not read and those who did, did not read poetry. From the vantage point of experience, it is a wonder to her that she has never been thought of by way of her poems, and long ago she decided that a poem is a frosted window—all is there revealed, though indistinct. People's actions reveal their outer selves, poetry, their inner. Consider the difference in perception as real versus romantic or day versus night or masculine versus feminine. For example, consider how differently Edgar Poe was perceived by men than by women. One would have thought him two different people not unlike Sarah and Estella, and that, depending solely on the gender of the speaker. But this is not precisely true either. Women can be manlike. Mrs. Clemm was exceedingly manlike. She judged people on the basis of actions and appearances alone with no regard for their more romantic side which is more feminine than manlike. Actions usually reveal our maleness; emotions, our feminine. It is a shame that there are not better words to describe this distinction, since most men refuse to admit that they have female qualities, but language fails us. Edgar Poe was an exception. Suffice it to say that Stella was often judged with *prejudice aforethought*. Having been the wife of an attorney for sixteen years, she is given to judicial phrases.

In 1844 Stella published her first book of poems, *Records of the Heart*. It was well received, and there followed invitations to literary soirees in New York. She was never comfortable at such gatherings, her insecurity stemming from uncertainty regarding which of her should attend, but she understood their importance in furthering her career and persuaded Sylvanus to take her. Crossing on the ferry made for a long evening, and since Sylvanus thought such affairs boring and a waste of time, they did not go often. One night in the late summer of 1845 at the home of Anne Lynch in Greenwich Village, she met Edgar Poe for the first time. At the end of the evening, he recited "The Raven," and she knew at once that she had met someone who could appreciate that part of her that she concealed from the world. She wrote to tell him, and he wrote back to say that he thought her poem, "The Forsaken," to be "inexpressibly beautiful."

It is impossible to describe the thrill she felt in knowing that Edgar knew of her work. In many ways the sentiment of "The Forsaken" mirrored that of "The Raven." She and Edgar continued to exchange letters, but as autumn came, her trips into the city for such evenings ceased. Then Edgar moved away, and she did not see him for nearly a year. One morning in October of 1846, Stella read N. P. Willis's column in the *Home Journal* which described Edgar's poverty and his wife's illness and asked for subscriptions for their aid. Stella resolved to do everything she could, and soon after she and Sylvanus made the journey to Fordham with gifts of food and one hundred dollars of her own money.

The November day was overcast and cold. Leaves had mostly fallen. The little cottage, a hermitage in the woods, was clean and cozy; a wood fire in the fireplace made it warm and cheery. Edgar did not recognize Stella at first, but once reminded, he seemed thrilled at their coming and beside himself with gratitude. His wife lay in a little bedroom off the parlor, and they visited with her for a few moments, but Mrs. Clemm warned them that she was having a bad day and should not be overtaxed. They spent the afternoon, therefore, in the parlor alone with Edgar, and it seemed to Stella that their presence took his mind off his wife's suffering. He became quite animated. He could not sit still. More than once he got up to stoke the fire or find a book.

"I have a new story in *Godey's,*" he said. "Shall I read it for you? Louis Godey believes it may be the best thing I've ever written."

In the corner of Stella's vision she could see Sylvanus reaching for his watch; it was getting late. "Yes, please, Edgar. We have time, don't we Sylvanus," she said as a way of instructing him to put away his watch.

Edgar fetched the magazine from among the periodicals on his writing table then resumed his chair. Thumbing the pages, he took a deep breath, glanced at the fire, then at Stella, and, after clearing his throat, he began. "*The thousand injuries of Fortunato I had borne as I best could; but when he ventured upon insult, I vowed revenge.*" And so he continued for twenty minutes, holding Stella spellbound to the final line, "*For half of a century no mortal has disturbed them. May he rest in peace!*"

Dropping the magazine to his lap, Edgar stared at it during a long silence, the only sounds, the crackling of the fire and the rattling of the casements.

"*In pace requiescat.*"

His words pierced the stillness. Aware that she was in the presence of greatness and in a moment of greatness performed, Stella watched, staring at Edgar, the magazine resting on his lap clutched by his thin genius fingers, the humble wooden chair that held him, the bookcase hanging on the wall behind him, and the silhouette portrait of a soldier hanging beside it. There are few still moments in a lifetime, and, though these particular few occurred nearly forty years ago, Stella can still evoke the emotion they contained.

From that day forward she and Edgar remained close friends. They had much in common in addition to being orphans. They had both attended boarding school at an early age; they had both spent youthful years in a foreign country; they both knew Baltimore. They had lived there at the same time, though under very different circumstances that may have precluded their knowing each other. He had been in his early twenties and lived with his aunt and cousin in a poorish neighborhood. Stella had been seven or eight at the time and lived on the bay in a more affluent suburb. She has often wondered if she might have passed him in the street or been in the same shop or eating house as he. Perhaps they even rode in the same horsecar. Baltimore was a large city but not so large that it would have been unlikely for them to cross paths. They reminisced often about the old city. "Do you remember my winning story in the *Saturday Visiter*, 'MS. Found in a Bottle'?" he once asked her. Stella told him she had, though she had not, and he smiled proudly, telling her about the competition that had won him fifty dollars. With part of that prize money he, his aunt, and cousin rode the B. & O. train to Ellicott's Mills, twenty-five miles out and back at the breathtaking speed of thirty miles per hour. His cousin— he called her Sissy—became his wife, of course. She was two years older than Stella, but they only met in the last stages of her illness.

After Sissy died Edgar became quite ill. He was unable to write, so there was no money coming in. Others helped, but Stella provided from her own funds and by the hospitality of her Brooklyn home, the primary source of sustenance and relief for Edgar and his mother-in-law. She went weekly to the cottage at Fordham with parcels containing the items on Mrs. Clemm's shopping list, and after visiting with her, she spent time with Edgar. Above all else, she and Edgar shared a love of literature. He was no classicist, but pride prevented his admitting this, and Stella found his knowledge of Shakespeare wanting. Nonetheless, his sensitivity on the subject of his literary limitations was too finely whetted for censure. Don't misunderstand. He was exceedingly well-read—far above other editors of the day—but his genius dwelt in his memory and power to retain. In this regard he had no peer. Others would point to his creativity and knowledge of his craft, and Stella doesn't disagree, but to converse with him was to be enthralled and astonished by his ability to recall and to quote flawlessly from almost any work or any poet one could name. This had accounted for his great popularity as a guest at the literary conversazione. On the subject of literature he was animated, entertaining, and loquacious, ready with a quote apt for the occasions, but never was he arrogant, never obtrusive. One cannot imagine how women adored him. A conversation with Edgar Poe was inevitably the highlight of an evening out.

After Sissy died, however, Edgar changed. Listless and depressed, he could hardly get out of bed, and he found conversation fatiguing and irksome. Stella went alone to Fordham one weekday in June of that year, 1847. It was not an easy matter, getting to Fordham. The only way there was to take the ferry into New York City, a brougham to the train station, the train—an hour and a half each way—then a twenty minute walk from the station at Fordham to the Poe cottage. And she did this always loaded with parcels. She was sweating like a car-horse by the time she arrived. Mrs. Clemm greeted her with the news that Edgar had a sore throat and that Loui Shew was expected. Stella had first met Loui at Virginia's funeral; she had come out with Mary Gove. Both women advertised themselves as doctors, and Stella was grateful to Loui for caring for Edgar and for her generosity. Apparently Loui did not return those feelings and told Mrs. Clemm that Stella's presence in the cottage vexed Edgar unnecessarily. It was a mean-spirited thing to say in light of Stella's assistance and so like Mrs. Clemm to report it, stirring up controversy. Her feelings hurt, Stella considered leaving and never coming back, but Mrs. Clemm insisted she stay.

She remained in the kitchen, also sensing from what Mrs. Clemm reported that Edgar was not up to a visit except by his doctor. Just at noon Loui arrived with Dr. Mulhenberg. After hellos were said, Loui and the minister went up, following Mrs. Clemm. Stella remained alone in the kitchen for about twenty minutes until Loui and Mrs. Clemm came back down. Loui seemed upset. "Edgar's not up for visitors," she told Mrs. Clemm at the door as she tied her bonnet strings, then she left, never even deigning to look Stella's way or say goodbye.

Mrs. Clemm busied herself in the kitchen, saying nothing. "Is he worse," Stella asked, genuinely alarmed, imaging last rites being administered.

"He'll be all right," Mrs. Clemm said. "He's had some bad news."

That is all she said, though Stella waited, hoping for some further explanation. Sensing that she was not wanted, she got up to go, placing an envelope containing ten dollars on the little green kitchen table. With this Mrs. Clemm became more attentive, falling all over herself with apologies and appreciation. She wants me to leave, Stella decided, but she also wants me to return. Despite hurt feelings, Stella knew she was needed, and not knowing what Edgar's bad news was, she endeavored to be sympathetic. She would have forgotten the incident altogether had it not been for the spiteful falsehoods that Loui later spread about her, injuries that she has borne to this day.

Perhaps Stella has lived too long alone. In the twenty years since her divorce from Mr. Lewis, Estella has given sway to Sarah. Were the rumors to blame?

Edgar claimed that Stella's translations of Petrarch were the best English-language translations yet of the great Renaissance poet. His favorite was "The Torture of Loving":

> If 'tis not love, what is it that I feel?
> But if 'tis love, whence these consuming pangs?
> If good, why goad me with these festering fangs?
> If ill, why with sweet torment do I reel?
> If bliss be mine, whence this eternal strife?

The sentiment belongs to Petrarch, but the poetry is hers. She and Edgar shared that also, the torture of loving. They had much in common. He claimed she was a fine poet. If words have been said to the contrary, consider the possibility of envy. Stella never asked him to praise her work, and he did not invariably do so. He was as critical of her as others, though, perhaps out of affection for her, he may have softened his criticism—blunted his tomahawk—but he did that with all the women poets, perhaps Fanny Osgood most of all.

It's true that Sylvanus Lewis assisted Wilmot Griswold, and for that service Stella was condemned by the women who so adored Edgar. What is not reported is that her husband acted on behalf of and at the behest of Mrs. Clemm. He was her advocate at Stella's insistence, for Edgar who had begged her to be a friend to his mother-in-law should some tragedy befall him. He had a premonition of such, and Stella had vowed to do all in her power. Sylvanus never asked for nor received a penny for all the work he did on behalf of Mrs. Clemm's interests, work that earned her a considerable sum which she, in turn, squandered. But is this taken into account by all the women who condemned Griswold? Of course, not. They only saw the Lewises as accessories to the crime. They were more than unkind; they were vicious in their attacks and thorough in their ostracism. For years Stella was isolated, an outcast of the very society to which she most longed to be included, and the grief she suffered for her victimization had no succor, not even from her husband. When her marriage failed, there was nothing left for her in New York. She could not wait to flee.

England proved unkind as well, but for different reasons at first. Stella wasn't prepared for the disdain with which Americans are held there, even more so for Americans with Caribbean roots. Her tawny complexion and full figure marked her as foreign, alien. Unwisely, she came to her own defense, citing Edgar's praise. He was popular there, and she couldn't resist trumpeting their long friendship. And when the English press accorded her praise for one of her poems, she could not resist a foolish bit of exaggerated braggadocio to an American friend, "the British press has placed me on a plane with Shakespeare—the highest position accorded to a woman since the Greeks seated Sappho by the side of Homer on the pinnacle of fame." It was pure Estella; Sarah would never have made such a boast, and perhaps that's why Sarah began to take over. Had Estella been joking or had it been a desperate plea for acceptance—somewhere, anywhere? When it miscarried, she withdrew as in her childhood, escaping into her own imagination, and practical considerations necessitated Sarah's emerging dominance.

Then Ingram came calling, and once again Estella found herself eager to speak. Why? For Edgar's sake? Perhaps. Perhaps she believes that his constant vision in her dreams portends their mutual redemptions, that their condemnations were also somehow joined together by the same act—a thirty-two-page memoir by a man who wished to cleanse his own soul and could only do so by condemning the man he loved—the man he loved unnaturally and, therefore, hated also. It must be remembered that Dr. Griswold was a man of the cloth, and to such a man, unnatural love was so despicable that it must be put at a distance, denounced, tormented, and sent to hell. So long as Edgar lived, such condemnation was impossible for Griswold, loving him as he did, but once Edgar died, it became easier. Still he grieved and hid his grief, but not well. Few knew of it. Griswold tried to hide it—tried and failed, for when he died and was found in bed, rigor mortis having set in, he was staring, not at Fanny's portrait as has been reported by some conspirators, but at the object of his affection, Edgar Poe. Of this Stella is certain, though still persistently reticent on the subject. Feeling herself to be a pariah in that society, she can only imagine that such a charge made public by her would only render her more of one.

(ITEM 53: *Sarah Anna Lewis*)
...

June 19, 1880
8 Bedford Place
Russell Square
London

Dear Lieut. Gayle,

Your letter finds me not only *extremely* ill of health but *exceedingly* out of sorts. I confess that Ingram's biography is the cause of the latter, a disappointment of tragic proportions. I hoped it would be fair in its treatment of Edgar, sympathetic even, but instead of being titled *The Life of Edgar Poe*, it might have been more appropriately titled *Song of Helen Whitman*. I expected her hand in it would be evident, but not in so self-serving a way and certainly not to my cost and the cost of others. How ungracious of her! I always thought of her as a friend. I wrote to her on numerous occasions, knowing she loved Edgar as I did. Since she lived in Providence, I didn't expect her opinions would carry the taint of the New York cabal so poisoned against me. I considered her above that, but I was much mistaken. She has proven true to their interests and the work she inspired—Ingram's biography—is as distorted as Griswold's, though at the opposite pole. Although this work, if it proves popular, may serve to redeem Edgar's character in the minds of a new generation of Poe admirers, it does little to promote the truth. It is for certain that the last word upon his life remains unwritten.

In a long letter to Mrs. Whitman that I have always presumed motivated her to have Ingram contact me, I told her details of Edgar's last night in New York in June of 1849 before he left on his ill-fated trip south. He and Mrs. Clemm came out from Fordham to my house in Brooklyn to spend the night. He was dejected, not only because he was worried about his mother-in-law, but I think also because he did not look forward to the purpose of his trip—to become engaged to Mrs. Shelton. The courtship had been prearranged, but Mrs. Clemm and I both knew that at the time Edgar was much taken with Annie Richmond [*sic*: Nancy Locke Heywood Richmond, 1820–1898]. I did not tell Mrs. Whitman this; in fact, Edgar did not even know that I knew of Mrs. Richmond's existence. Mrs. Clemm had confided in me that Edgar was in love with a married woman. She was distraught, certain of trouble, but Edgar would not cease his attentions. The night he arrived at my house, Mrs. Clemm told me that he had not wanted to leave Fordham, thinking he would have a letter from Annie that would preclude his trip south. I wondered if he had told Annie of his plans in hopes that she would write, begging him not to go, promising to leave her husband and marry him. This news would have broken Mrs. Whitman's heart. It was foolhardy of Edgar to think such a thing possible, so I spared Mrs. Whitman for her sake. I confess to wondering if "Annabel Lee" had been intended for Annie. I was not jealous of her. Truthfully, I thought Edgar more desperate than in love, desperate for an excuse not to marry the widow Shelton.

We did our best to cheer him up. I invited a young couple, new to our neighborhood, for dinner, having made sure in advance that they knew who Edgar was. They did and were keen to meet the author of "The Raven." Edgar loved being fawned over by new admirers, and I thought their presence would be a welcomed diversion. I was wrong. He remained sullen throughout the night, preoccupied by either Annie or his trip south. During dinner, he looked up at me as if there was no one else at the table. "You realize, Stella," he said, "that you will never see me again."

"Why would you say that?" I asked. "Do you want to hurt those who care for you?"

He laughed at this as if I had belittled his pessimism. Then he turned to the young wife of our new neighbor as if her presence at the table irked him, and I cursed myself for not having realized that his departure was much too personal to share with strangers. Sylvanus sat at the head of the table; I sat beside him, and Edgar sat at the other end. He turned back to me, clenched his teeth, and swallowed hard. "They'll kill me," he said and laughed sarcastically. "I have no prayer of surviving this. Don't you see? Are you all so blind?" He looked around the table at the baffled looks on the faces of our guests and Sylvanus. Only Mrs. Clemm did not return his gaze. She stared down at her soup, near tears, as if she accepted without question the prophecy. She always took his dramatic moods seriously. Not that I didn't, but it was Edgar's way to exaggerate things, and one had to talk him down gently.

On reflection, I don't think Mrs. Clemm suspected he would not survive. I think she knew only that Edgar was Edgar, as always given to dramatic pessimism, and she didn't want to betray that she urgently wanted the marriage; she *needed* the marriage. Mrs. Shelton was quite wealthy. I wanted to tell him not to go, but what was I to say? Don't marry if not for love? Sylvanus sat beside me. He smiled, shrugged off Edgar's questions, picked up his soupspoon, and returned to his slurping, guarding with his other hand his beard to keep it dry. I stared at Edgar, begging him with my eyes just as I had begged Ernest, wishing that I had the courage to say, "don't do what I did or it *will* kill you— your soul and your genius if not your person." And just like Ernest he could not read my thoughts or chose not to read them. Had I spoken those words instead of only thinking them, I might have saved his life.

It rained during the night, and at the ferry dock in the morning, fog was so thick on the river that it shrouded the metropolis beyond. We watched Edgar hand his trunk to the ferryman then climb aboard. Since the river was dead calm, he was able to stand in the boat even as they pushed off. He stared at us out of the mist of a gray morning— a man dressed in black, bareheaded, his hat in his hand, his posture stooped, his head tilted forlornly, his features downcast. When I recall that image, I think of him disappearing into the "misty-mid regions of Weir." Though I didn't then think of what he'd said the night before, the day was such that I could have easily believed I would never see him again. As the ferry reached the current, he sat down and waved but did not smile. Before five more pulls at the oars, he was lost in fog.

A week later I had a letter from him that included a note to Mrs. Clemm. In it he said that he had contracted cholera and suggested that we die together. I knew from both his bizarre proposition and unsteady handwriting that he was not ill, but in his cups. Thinking we'd have more sober news soon and since Mrs. Clemm was still staying with us, I dismissed it and hid the letter. When another did not come, I showed the letter to Mrs. Clemm who became furious with me, swearing she would have gone to Philadelphia immediately had she known. Fortunately we had another letter the following day to say that he had recovered and was on his way to Richmond. The strain caused Mrs. Clemm to leave us then, and I did not see her again until after Edgar died that October, four months later, when she came again to stay for some length of time to mourn the loss of her son. I cared for her, welcomed her always during the next several years until she began taking Sylvanus's side in the arguments that characterized our deteriorating marriage. She criticized me on niggling little matters to the point that I could abide her no longer. I made her a gift of money and attempted to part friends; she did not appear to return the sentiment, but she did write to me on occasion after that, as often as not, asking me to purchase some souvenir that had belonged to Edgar or Virginia.

If I am not mistaken, Lieutenant Gayle, I told you a few years ago that if you were persistent and if you proved yourself to be upright, then I would provide certain information of a sensitive nature. I have now gone far beyond my intention. I trust you realize this. You persist in your claim to be interested in Edgar Poe for curiosity's sake alone, and in the wake of our years of corresponding, I no longer doubt this. But I want you to understand, Lieutenant, that the true life of Edgar Allan Poe remains to be written. Ingram has failed. I believe I have revealed enough so that you cannot doubt me when I say this. He may not have written all he knows, but I assure you, you know more than he of matters that are of greater import. Who cares if so-and-so spent such-and-such a night at such-and-such a place? This is minutia. Do you understand what I mean? The larger picture remains obscure, and perhaps you are the very man to cast light upon it. If not now, then in time. Mrs. Whitman is dead as is Loui Shew, and I am not long for this world. I once told you that you were playing with fire. Well!—the fire is going out. A few more years and you won't risk burning your fingers.

Forgive the length of this letter, but, as it may well be my last, I wanted to end it having revealed all. If you have further questions, you'd best hurry!

Yours, fondly,
Estella

(ITEM 31: *Charlotte Ayers*)

...

June 29, 1878
12 Hope Street
Providence, Rhode Island

Dearest Eddy,

Mrs. Whitman died Tuesday, day before yesterday, early in the afternoon. I have been so busy in the last two days that only now, Thursday night, have I had a chance to write. As I stated in my last letter, I feared the end was near. She worked so hard this spring, preparing her last book of poetry; I think she felt she had to finish it before departing this world. She was a great, great lady, and I shall miss her. Our newspapers devoted their front pages to her, and I understand that all the great writers from Boston and New York will attend her funeral on Saturday. They will include the great Henry Wadsworth Longfellow. Imagine! He must be very old, but I'm told he is coming. I wish you could be here; I know you would like to be. She adored you, Eddy, and was so pleased that you and I are corresponding.

Her last two years were not happy. She has seemed depressed to me, and I must say that I date that depression to the night of your first visit. I have refrained from telling you my conclusions as to what transpired that night, and you have been kind enough not to ask, but I will tell you of one of those now. I believe she received a message that pertained to her relationship with Edgar Poe, something hurtful, perhaps even insulting. I have nothing to base it on; it's just an impression. It had something to do with Cato, and I believe this is why she could not abide Cato's presence after that. And she came to find her correspondence with Ingram intolerable. She would leave his letters unopened for days or weeks even, and her letters to him became brief and businesslike when she deigned to write to him at all. Perhaps this was a blessing in disguise, for she began spending more time composing new poems, and they are fine, though they lack the joy of her earlier work.

My sorrow is only tempered by knowing that I will see you in three short months. At times the wait seems interminable; at other times the days fly. You will stay three nights, won't you? Please! I can't imagine what it will be like to see you. When I read what you say about me, I begin to feel so insecure, feeling certain that I will disappoint you. Yes, of course, I remember having to fetch Cato out from under the couch. (I *did* close him up in the kitchen.) Doubtless it was Miss Power who let him out. She was always doing hurtful things to Mrs. Whitman; it was dreadful the way she treated her sometimes. She will be lost without Mrs. Whitman; I can't imagine what's to become of her. At any rate, I didn't have the presence of mind that first night to think that you might be looking while I was on my hands and knees. Shame on you, Eddy. Would it shock you to know that I am flattered? Does that scare you? Yes, you may kiss me if you still want to once you see me again, but I rather think it's that vision of petticoats that has turned your head. I hope I'm wrong.

I shouldn't be distracted by such thoughts in light of what's happened, but I can't help myself. I can't wait to see you. Would you believe that I dreamed about you last night? I dreamed that you were helping a child who needed your help and that you were wearing your blue military cap. I watched, loving that you were being so kind, but I wasn't in the least surprised. I know you are that way. Please wear that hat for me when we meet. I get teary thinking about it.

I will write again as soon as I can and often thereafter until September when I will be able to tell you in person all that is in my heart.

Yours,

Charlotte

August 4, 1878
12 Hope Street
Providence, Rhode Island

Dearest,

I received your wonderful birthday present—your carte de visite. What a glad surprise! I stare at it, thinking this is the man I long for more than any man alive. Handsome man! It is almost unfair of you. This is the happiest birthday of my life, because *you* are my birthday present and the *only* present I want. We will be together in 37 days. I try not to count, but I can't stop myself. Will you come by ferry or by train? You've said both. Cable me in advance so I can meet you. I couldn't bear for you to show up on my doorstep with me unprepared.

I must tell you that it has been hard, moving back home again. I had not realized how liberating it was for me to live with Mrs. Whitman until I had to move back. My mother and I do best at a considerable distance. I have hesitated to tell you certain things about me, but I feel I must before you arrive. I told you my father died when I was twelve. In truth he went missing, and when it became apparent he was not coming back, my mother, to preserve her dignity, professed that he had died at sea, but, Eddy, he is still alive—on rare occasions she receives money from him. As for me, I have neither heard from him nor seen him in eight years. In my heart I know that he abandoned us. My mother has never gotten over it, not because she missed him, but because of the "scandal" it nearly caused. I am certain she has told him not to return under any circumstances. I don't miss him. I tried to love him when I was a child, but he made that impossible. I have never told anyone this, and you must not let on that you know.

What is most important to my mother is to be accepted by the best people. It is all she cares about. I don't think my father could cope with this pressure. When we were growing up, she insisted that her children do nothing to embarrass her or jeopardize her sacred social position—more important to her than any of us. Whenever we failed her, she turned us over to our father and shut herself in her room. Perhaps my father found the task distasteful, but he obliged her to guard against her wrath falling on him. I won't tell you what he did. Suffice it to say that the vision of a razor strop frightens me to this day. Will you forgive me if I can't talk about that?

When I secured the position with Mrs. Whitman, Mother was thrilled. She viewed it as redemption. It is so bizarre; I wish I didn't have to tell you these things. It never occurred to Mother that I might have had something to do with obtaining the position. My high grades in school never mattered a whit to her; she paid no attention to my education. Mrs. Whitman was the most highly respected woman in Providence, so Mother was beside herself with glee. But thereafter, she was forever pestering me to tell her things about Mrs. Whitman that were truly none of her business, and I refused. She took that as disobedience, but what could I do? My father was long gone, and I was living in Mrs. Whitman's house. I avoided my mother, much preferring the Whitman house despite the unsettling presence of Miss Power. I know my mother had no compunction whatsoever about seeing to Cato's destruction. I wouldn't be surprised if she killed the cat herself, only there would have been no one to bury it. She would never dirty her hands with a task the likes of that.

Oh, Eddy, I hate this, but I have to tell you before you come. As you might expect, Mother is quite opinionated. I have answered her questions about you without volunteering anything. She is prejudiced against Southerners—not that she knows any. She is prejudiced against anyone who is not a white Anglo-American, does not own property—lots of property—and does not live in New England. She despises New Yorkers. If you and I could be together anywhere but my house I would, but she won't hear of it. It's not proper in her eyes. She won't let us out of her sight. I didn't respond when you wrote that you planned to have a kiss from me when you come. And it wasn't because—as you suspected—that I blushed at the notion. I would gladly give you all the kisses you want, but I don't know if it will be possible. I pray it will, but you must be prepared for what might happen.

My greatest fear is that learning this, you will change your mind about coming. I wouldn't blame you; I couldn't blame you. I would be heartbroken. Yes, I have told her that you are shorter than I. You know that doesn't matter to me, but I would be less than candid if I didn't tell you that I worry about her reaction to this also. If only Mrs. Whitman had lived a few more months. She was so fond of you. I miss her terribly. It makes me weep to think of that feeble, seventy-five-year-old woman going to brew coffee so you and I could be alone in the parlor. I know she planned the whole thing, even your coming. May God bless her for that act of kindness. Does it frighten you to know that with Mrs. Whitman gone, you are all I have left?

Since you asked I will tell you that Mrs. Whitman's papers are to go to Brown University, and they have taken over paying my stipend with a small increase for helping with the transfer and cataloguing. Since this has been my responsibility for two and a half years I am proud to say that her papers are in excellent order. And now that they will be available to the public, I feel at liberty to tell you anything you wish to know—and I know a lot, Eddy—and I promise to tell no one but you. Unfortunately the collection will not be open for viewing for many months; otherwise, I would have the excuse of taking you there to see the letters that you have a particular interest in—the Griswold letters. That would have been a perfect excuse to get away from Mother. As a consolation, before you come I will have them all copied out for you. I have never read them, but they are there, five of them—the last two postmarks are unopened; she never even read them. I suspect my hands will be shaking when I open them, but I can think of no reason why I shouldn't. In light of the séance we both experienced two years ago, I am as curious as you to know what they contain. Won't it be fun to discuss them? Perhaps we'll be able to decipher the dream I had that night. Gamblers betting with black coins—I will never forget that vision.

I have been approached by a woman who wishes to pay for my assisting her with a biography she wishes to write on Mrs. Whitman's life. I will, therefore, have employment when my engagement with Brown University ends this winter. Beyond that I don't know what I'll do. Teach perhaps. Teaching positions are difficult to come by in Providence, but I would prefer to go elsewhere anyway—as far from my mother as I can get. Are qualified teachers needed in the South or, better still, in Montana?

My dear Eddy, don't be discouraged by what I've told you. I am your best and truest friend, and I joy in my affection for you and in your affection for me.

With deepest devotion,
Charlotte

(ITEM 38: *Charlotte Ayers*)

...

August 22, 1878
12 Hope Street
Providence, Rhode Island

Dearest,

Your descriptions of Montana in summertime thrill me beyond expression. How I would love to see with my own eyes the grandeur you describe, but I know that also—though you are in a most beautiful part of the world—you are in a hostile place, and I worry for you so. I hurry to write, hoping this letter will reach you before you begin traveling here. I cannot believe that in a mere nineteen days I will see you. I am so nervous, darling, that I can't keep my hand from shaking as I hasten to write this.

First I must thank you for your kind understanding of the things I revealed in my last letter. Bless you for this. I hope you are correct— that you will "charm the shoelaces" off my mother. I wish I could believe that possible, but I wish it only for your sake. Don't be disappointed if it doesn't happen, dear. It won't matter to me one way or the other. I hope you understand this. I don't want you coming with that goal in mind. Please come with me in your thoughts and not with any determination to win over my mother. I turned eighteen earlier this month, Eddy. I am "of age" and fully intend to make my own decisions, regardless of my mother's strictures. Think ill of me if you must. I know you are from a strong and moral and close-knit family, but as for me, I will not spend my life trying to please my mother. I would die first. If this disappoints you, then the cost to me is dear, but it's a cost I have no choice but to pay, or I shall never be content. Believe me when I say I will not sacrifice my future—not even for you, my darling—though the depth of my grief for loss of you might far exceed any future gain in contentment; I cannot do it. Try to see this from my perspective.

You asked about my passions. I will tell you. I am passionate about truth and art and truth in art. Does this make any sense? First, truth. I believe we should be who we are and not some falseness viewed as acceptable to those whose attentions and favor we crave. Such craving is a sickness, debilitating and ultimately fatal to the soul. You, my dear, could not be more yourself, and that is a reason you bring me such joy. I know your heart; I read it in your letters when you describe the Indians and lament their horrible plight. I cried tears, Eddy, when you told me this spring of pleading with your captain to relinquish two worn-out and emaciated caisson mules in order to provide a bit of food for a starving tribe of Sioux whose young-men-hunters had all been victims of the previous summer's war. You carry your heart proudly before you unlike most men who view too great a show of heart as a sign of weakness and effeminacy. You are a man for your show of heart. True, I am young and not worldly wise, but my limited experience has taught me that in the eyes of most of my sex those other men I describe are less manly for repressing their feelings.

How fortunate I have been to have experienced the influence of Helen Whitman. I am certain that I saw her agonize over truth—it was that vital to her. In some ways it defeated her. In her last two years, I think she faced a truth that she had denied for many years, a truth that broke her heart and perhaps even took her life before her time. Oh, Eddy, she was so difficult and demanding in some ways, so inspiring in others. I will tell you more about this, as it relates to the particular matter of your interest. I know, for example, that she refrained from telling Ingram things, because she was torn between being fully truthful and being a *true* friend. What a terrible dilemma she faced in that regard. In the end, she came down on the side of true friendship, but the decision gave her no rest. I concluded from her distress that truth is a narrow and thorny path, but the only path that provides any glimmer of contentment.

Do I sound hoity-toity? I can imagine this letter giving you second thoughts about me. But do you understand now, darling, why I asked you not to tease me? There is something deceptive in teasing—albeit good-humored—it is deception just the same, and I am too gullible or naive or vulnerable to withstand it. Forgive me this. I wish I were more stout-hearted, but I had too much of deception growing up—a family aspiring to something we were not, some false ideal of my mother's ambition. Deception was what was expected of me, so now I have a particular contempt for it. Perhaps it's best you know these things about me before you come to avoid the risk of disappointment once you are here. Don't you think there might be benefit in the arena of passion in deeply truthful sharing? I believe you can depend on that, my dear, should passion inspire you.

As for art, I have told you of my passion for drawing. I have seen great works of art and understand at a profound level how uplifting true art can be. I am no artist, but I think I can recognize truth in art as well as deception in art. I cannot tell you how except with the most rudimentary of examples. Mrs. Whitman had her portrait painted by her friend and neighbor, Walter Brown. You remember Walter, of course, from the night of the séance. Perhaps you saw the portrait, though she removed it that night—purposefully, I am certain, for it was a lie, and I am just as certain that Mrs. Whitman loathed that painting. Were it not for her true affection for Walter, she would have burned it. Again, I present you with an example that begs the question: what is more important?—truth or true friendship? Much as I loved and respected Mrs. Whitman, I begin to come down on the former being the more important. She may have disagreed. I don't think the path is wider or less thorny either way.

For some reason, the giddiness I felt at the beginning of this letter—frothing as I was with the prospect of seeing you in 19 days—has evaporated. This doesn't mean I am less eager—on the contrary, I am *more* than eager to see you, darling. Perhaps I have told you so much that I fear you will have lost your own eager-edge to see me. Or perhaps—more likely, I think—I have convinced myself of my unfitness to be what I imagine you imagine—all soft petticoats and sweetness. I am not a girl, Eddy, nor am I a lady. I am a woman, and I pray you comprehend the difference and that such is what you want. If you don't, I pray that I can convince you. As I say this, I'm not even sure I know the difference myself. Perhaps I will lose my nerve and not post this letter. My emotions roil inside me. Do I even know what I'm saying?

In your first letter following your visit last March, you professed that you would overwhelm me with words, that you had time on your hands and loved letter writing. I fear I have bested you in the dubious art of overwhelming. I find that my capacity for it exceeds my expectations, but I too now have time on my hands, and I take no greater pleasure than in writing you. I have copied Griswold's letters for you and they are enclosed. I think you will be as disappointed as I am. I can understand why Mrs. Whitman did not bother to open the last two—they are more of the same—flattering and spurious attempts to regain her goodwill—a packet of deception. He obviously didn't know her well. I await your take on them. The only surprise was his remark about Longfellow. What do you make of that?

Travel safely, my dear. When you read this, you will be preparing to leave, and I will be preparing for your arrival. I almost can't believe that the time has finally arrived. In some ways it has seemed like forever getting here; in some ways not. In all ways, your coming is the long-sought landfall for someone who has spent a lifetime at sea. I will not know what to say or how to act. I can only hope that you value already what will appear at first a giddy, stupid, blubbering girl, for I'll be mesmerized by you—power-of-speech will have forsaken me. Be patient and understanding, and I promise to come to my senses and not disappoint you.

All my love is enclosed herewith,
Charlotte

5

MARY GOVE

::

(ITEM 13: *Mary Gove Nichols*)
...

January 30, 1877
Aldwyn Tower
Malvern, England

Dear Lieutenant Gayle,

From your letter I see that Mrs. W. continues to raise the hue and cry over Poe. I fear it has become her life's work, incredible considering his shabby treatment of her. It is remarkable, is it not, that a writer as gifted as Mrs. Whitman should spend her final efforts for such a cause? Perhaps—to her credit I confess—she possesses the wisdom to know that in the eyes of posterity, genius trumps character. Edgar was a friend and a gifted man, but no saint. Mrs. W.'s efforts to rectify Griswold will only lead to more distortion, for I am certain that, if in her power, she will stop at nothing short of having Poe bronzed and placed upon a pedestal in City Hall Park. One must be matter-of-fact, lieutenant, or else live in a dream world in which I fear Mrs. W. has lived since Edgar left her at the altar.

Yes, I read Griswold's memoir, though it was years ago. Perhaps there were inaccuracies, I can't say; neither can I say that it was unfair. Nevertheless, Griswold will have no rest so long as Mrs. W. lives. And poor Poe is trapped in the middle, so parsed and dissected that one wonders how there can be a morsel left for putting under the glass.

I am likewise familiar with Dr. Ingram and suspect he will do Mrs. W.'s bidding. He and I corresponded a year or so ago. I dictated several letters, providing answers to his questions, then quite suddenly he stopped writing. Later I had a nosy and conspiratorial letter from Stella Lewis—that detestable woman—to say that she too had been in correspondence with Ingram and that he had confided in her that I was "unreliable." With that I washed my hands of the entire affair.

Americans are naive, lieutenant. Being one myself, I can say that without compunction. Americans want their heroes pure. I will tell you the same thing I told Ingram—the answer to your question—Fanny Osgood. True, there were also debts and ill-will arising from unfavorable comments Poe made about Griswold's books and—I very strongly suspect—another matter that I am not so reckless as to mention, but the essence of Griswold's malice had to do with Fanny. Jealousy has caused worse things than vindictiveness. But Ingram will avoid the subject of Fanny Osgood. Mrs. W. will not be a party to dragging Fanny's name through the muck, much less Poe's. She is much too delicate for such a thing, and Ingram's silence on that matter is the price for her cooperation. So there you are. As for the other biography you mentioned, that by Gill, I know nothing of it.

Fanny Osgood was my delightful and incorrigible friend and I loved her like my own sister. It grieves me that you are not familiar with her work; she was a marvelous poet. Sadly, you are not alone. I will now reveal to you why she was so totally forgotten—Edgar Allan Poe. He was doubtless the love of her life, and she his. But they were both married, so there you have it. My instinct tells me that Fanny would want the truth known, but she was always careless when it came to matters of propriety, and she paid dearly for it. Honestly, lieutenant, I would not know the right thing to do were I attempting a biography of Poe or Fanny. I think the truth, but is that even possible now?

I hope I have answered your question, if not fully, at least sufficiently.

Yours,

Mary Nichols

:: THE HEART HEEDS NO COVENANT. Contrary as this notion may seem, I am certain of it. How dare the heart be so capricious? But there it is. For such rebellious ideas, I have been called every vile name—"shameless" being one of the milder ones. I have become inured to damnation. Like the leper in his den, such odious words as are hurled at me no longer belittle or pain.

The spirit of individual liberty is rarely nurtured in women, but it is, on occasion, thrust upon them by an unfortunate marriage, and so it was with me. In forsaking my husband, I incurred society's wrath and condemnation. My daughter and I were banished to poverty and exile, and I trained myself to suppress the clamor against me with strong faith in my own goodness.

My daughter, Elma, and I moved to New York City which, for all its liberality, could be in some respects as repressive as the Quaker New England village from which we fled. I say this, not because of any new misfortune that befell us in our new city, but because of the slanders that were soon after borne by one whom I came to know almost as soon as we arrived. I speak of Fanny. This dear friend came to me in hopes that the water-cure would alleviate the effects of a dangerous pregnancy, and almost at once we realized that we were soul mates in the truest sense of the word.

As I begin this tale, my first impulse is to call this friend by one of her many pen names and thereby conceal her identity. Kate Carol was one she used; Ida Grey, another. Before her death and ever since, writers have been careful of her reputation for reasons that will become apparent, but I fear that they may have done her a disservice. So much has been written about that brilliant society of literary folk in New York City in the years before the war. I think of that society as embodying an American Renaissance, and knowing Fanny as I did, I know that she would not want to be excluded. She was in many ways the heart and soul of that society. She could not bear missing a gathering of it, and she reveled in the literary repartee, wanting to be at the very center. Always radiant, smiling, laughing, she often provided the most colorful recitations. It would have been too cruel to leave her off the guest list; it would have broken her heart. I cannot do that. If I am to write about Poe, I must name Fanny Osgood by name, not by some *nom de plume*. She has been dead for many years and her three girls all died in childhood, so only her husband survives. Mr. Osgood will forgive me for saying that perhaps due to the demands of his profession—he was a portrait artist and a fine one—he became infected with wanderlust. He was away from home for most of the time that I knew Fanny, but he loved her deeply, and she loved him. Each had great respect for the artistic genius of the other, and I am certain that Mr. Osgood would prefer that his wife be remembered for her wonderful poems and stories even if the preservation of our memory of her be accompanied by revelation of her affair with Edgar Poe. I know firsthand that Mr. Osgood forgave that affair, and for that act of forgiveness and for the caring comfort he provided in her final illness, I cannot condemn him. Indeed, I came to have high regard for him. Though I have not seen him for many years, I feel certain that he would permit—nay, even encourage—a full recounting of those events. Furthermore, I believe that neither Fanny nor her husband would wish me to conceal her true identity in a recollection of the Edgar Allan Poe I knew.

I was thirty-five at that time—it was just after Christmas, 1846—and Fanny was thirty-four. She had two daughters, her oldest four years younger than my Elma. And like me, Fanny was a poet and writer of stories. As a writer, she far surpassed me; she was a highly regarded poet—among her sex, one of the most renowned in America. And like me also, she had endured unhappiness in her marriage, though at this particular time she and her husband had reconciled and were expecting a child. She confided in me, as I did in her, the disappointments of marriage, and it seemed that our experiences differed only in the nature of those disappointments. In her case, she had loved her husband, but his nomadic life kept them apart and subjected him to temptations he could not resist. My case was quite the opposite. I had never loved my husband—our marriage was more or less arranged in the Quaker tradition—and he had proved overbearing and demanding, and at the same time, indolent and incompetent. For our support, I became a teacher and later, a writer and lecturer, and, though my husband condemned me for writing novels and for the subjects about which I lectured, he demanded all my earnings which were his by law, and I never had a shilling for myself or my daughter for which I did not have to beg.

Fanny was a delight. Petite, precocious, and enthusiastic, she seemed overjoyed at my arrival in New York City. She made it her special project that I be introduced to every literary person. Almost before I was settled, I was receiving invitations to parties and literary soirées at which Fanny, leading me by the arm, introduced me to everyone, praising my work beyond its merits. She was quite beautiful. Her hair was a rich, chocolate brown; she had large gray eyes; and she was so coy as to seem almost childlike. Men and women alike adored her, and for her sake they were especially kind to me. I was, therefore, able to sell my stories, and it was only by the money I made by my pen that Elma and I could afford room and board. In short time I was able to make arrangements to resume teaching and lecturing.

Fanny and I were unlike in one important respect—dress. Fanny wore clothes and jewels that matched her beauty. I came from a Quaker background which meant simple clothing—drab earth tones—and no jewels, no lace, no ruffles, no ribbons. And, though I had been excommunicated by the Quakers, I found it difficult to modify habits and manners instilled in me for most of my life. Fanny would arrive at my house for her treatment in silk and satin, gloved and bonneted and tightly laced, though pregnant and despite my vociferous castigations against that dreadful practice. It was only by convincing her that she was choking her unborn child that I was able to make her give up her corset, but she was never happy about it.

Here I must explain how I came to be a physician, and I claim that title despite having had no formal medical training. Until recently such training was denied to women, and changes, though slow in coming, that allow women to attend medical school will be a boon to our sex. My older sister died when I was a girl of eleven. She died as a result of the vanity of tight lacing and the incompetence of a doctor whose remedy for every malady was the lancet and calomel. My sister made herself ill by crushing her ribs and lungs, then the doctor finished her off by bleeding her to death. I was saved from a similar fate by a more enlightened doctor who showed me drawings in his medical books of the effects of tight lacing, and his kind concern for me sparked my interest in anatomy. I ultimately borrowed every book in this gentleman's library, and my interest in a healthy lifestyle has never waned.

My sister had been a beauty. I was not. Squint eyes spoiled my looks, and, as an unpopular child, I found solace in reading books and reward in always being first in my class. Though I outgrew my crossed-eyes in adolescence, their effect on my temperament had been wrought. I found that I had a natural gift for teaching, and, as my pupils were all girls, I began teaching them about their bodies and the ill effects of tight lacing. The parents of my students were quick to criticize my lectures on anatomy which they considered improper, even indecent, but I perceived also that this subject fascinated my students even more than the standard curriculum of a Quaker school. I refused to stop, and I soon began lecturing to women also, and my lectures grew in popularity. I wrote articles that found a ready audience, and these articles were published in health and medical journals throughout New England. Though my motivations were born of suffering and loss, quite to my astonishment I found that I was doing what no woman had the knowledge and courage to do before me, but for which there was the sorest need—to instill in women dominion over their own bodies. By law a woman becomes the property of her husband when she marries, and thereafter her body must be always available to the satisfaction of his desires in whatever form that takes, but such a law is contrary to God's law and will never find acceptance in the hearts of women. I found rebellious spirits eager for information as if knowledge alone would set them free. So many women have come up to me after a lecture, expressing greater appreciation than I deserved, yet I could see, looking into those grateful eyes that their husbands would disapprove. Had my words only made their lives less happy or more miserable? Perhaps. But by such discord laws are changed, and that gave me heart and determination to persevere despite the fact that my husband, always insistent upon accompanying me to my lectures, was there to pocket the receipts.

My final break with him had its source in a monograph which I published in 1839 entitled, *The Solitary Vice*. Few had lectured or written on the subject of masturbation, and those few included no women. My position had become unique, and I found women desperate for someone in whom to confide their most intimate secrets. I listened and became alarmed by the prevalence of female masturbation; indeed I found it almost epidemic. Despite the delicate nature of the subject, I felt called upon to publically acknowledge that the practice was widespread and to urge women to exercise caution and restraint for fear of the possibility of unhealthy side effects. The Society of Friends was outraged, and I was excommunicated. My husband berated me for the effect my monograph had on him, and in a matter of months, I left him, and Elma and I returned to the home of my parents. I was ill—tuberculosis—and was convinced that my illness resulted from the anxiety and torment of my marriage, but leaving my husband brought neither recuperation nor comfort. A few months later he stole our child, and for three torturous months I did not know where she was or if she was even alive. With the help of right-thinking men, I stole her back and went into hiding, and for several years thereafter I spent the bulk of my modest earnings on lawyers and appeals. It was only when my husband decided to take a new wife that he agreed to a divorce, and my agony finally ended.

When I came to New York, I was still burdened with legal expenses, but I had become somewhat well-known as a result of my articles and lectures on anatomy and hygiene, so soon I had paying students and patients. Fanny was among them. By this time I had learned the techniques and miracle of the water-cure as the result of three months working at a water-cure sanatorium in Vermont. Fanny was less than three months pregnant when she first came for treatment in January of 1846. It had been our love of literature and writing that had sparked our friendship, and, when I learned of her condition and considering her age, I urged her to follow a hydropathic regimen for the sake of her health and to insure the birth of a robust baby. Fanny humored me. I think she had her doubts, but she came nonetheless to the Tenth Street house where I had established my practice thanks to the beneficence of a wealthy young man, Marx Lazarus, a medical student and devotee of philosopher Charles Fourier. Marx wished to establish a commune in the center of New York City where persons of like-mind could live and work together. A water-cure establishment seemed to him the perfect nucleus for the community he envisioned, and, with more haste and enthusiasm than prudence, he rented a house, hired a Irish serving girl, and installed Elma and I in rooms we could not have afforded otherwise. Until this time we had resided in a boarding house on Bond Street that also doubled as a water-cure establishment run by Joel and Louise Shew. While I adored Loui, as Louise was called, I could not abide her husband and was glad for the opportunity to leave his house despite the rather slapdash and impulsive preparations made by Marx Lazarus.

Fanny first came on a Tuesday in January. I remember it well, as she had promised to come the day before, and by her not coming, I had decided she had merely been polite the Saturday night before when we had been together at the home of Miss Anne Lynch for a party of literary types. It was in conversation at Miss Lynch's that Fanny whispered to me that she was with child. As she told me, I was horrified by the combination of this news and her tiny waist, knowing that she was too tightly laced for the health of her unborn child. I had asked if she understood the harmful effects of the corset she wore and urged her to consider hydrotherapy. She had smiled, and I wondered if she considered such treatment quackery, but she said she would come for a visit on Monday "to see what I was all about," and then she failed to appear.

As I descended the stairs upon her arrival on that Tuesday, Fanny was removing her bonnet. She wore an overcoat, and I suspected that underneath she was corseted. I decided she would prove recalcitrant, but in her case her vanity was almost charming. We went up to my room where we chatted for a while. Elma was in school; we were alone. Fanny seemed distracted and tired, and she apologized for not coming the day before when she had promised. She removed her overcoat, and indeed I perceived that she was corseted beneath her blue dress, a color I denied myself.

"Surely, Fanny," I began, "you know the harm you're doing to your child not to mention yourself."

"Don't preach to me, Mary," she said, shaking her head. "Not today. Please. Can't we talk about something else? I came for a visit and to see where you live. Can't you practice your medicine on me another time?"

"I don't practice medicine," I said smiling and thinking she was distracted by something—perhaps morning sickness had left her listless and depressed, but such was the confidence I had in relieving those symptoms that I took her by the hand. "Come," I said. "You can leave your coat and bonnet here. Come with me."

I led her to a room on the third floor, a room with fading blue wallpaper and no fireplace and a small window that faced the rear of the house. Against one wall was a narrow wooden cot with a pillow and blankets and against the opposite wall was a table and a ladder-back chair. In the middle of the room was a tin sitz bath and beside the bath were two pails of water. I opened the window, drew the curtains, lit the oil lamp, and turned to Fanny.

"Remove your clothes," I said, handing her a towel and smiling at the surprise on her face.

She obeyed, albeit reluctantly, as I poured a pail of water into the sitz tub. I took a linen sheet and plunged it into the other pail of water. When I turned back to Fanny, she was unlacing her corset. I helped her with the laces then lifted her chemise over her head and told her to remove her bloomers. Then I took the sheet from the pail and beckoned Fanny to me. She was shivering, her arms crossed over her chest for warmth. I wrapped the dripping sheet around her abdomen, tucked it in, and helped her to sit in the sitz tub. Goose bumps appeared on her arms and shoulders as she shivered in the cold water. I took a blanket from the bed and draped it over her knees and wrapped it under her feet, then with a wet washcloth I began scouring her shoulders, chest, and back. In so doing I felt her rib cage beneath the sheet in which she was wrapped for telltale signs of deformity, and indeed, her waist was tiny, her lower ribs pressed together constricting the lower portions of her lungs. I wondered if there was room for the child to develop, but in Fanny's case it was too late to do anything about it. I said nothing.

"Let's discuss your diet," I said instead. "During your pregnancy you are to eat no meat, no fowl—only course grain bread, fruits, and aspiring vegetables—those that grow above ground. Take no spirits or stimulants, no coffee or tea, and you are to drink lots of cold water—ten or more glasses a day." With this said, I stood, walked to the table, and took up Fanny's corset.

"What are you doing?" she asked.

"Soak for half an hour," I said, and I handed her a copy of the *Health Journal*, its pages turned to one of my articles on anatomy. "And read this."

"Where are you going?" she asked again.

"To burn your corset," I said.

"Mary!" she exclaimed. "I won't be able to button any of my dresses."

"Then buy new ones," I said and shut the door behind me.

When I returned, the magazine was lying on the floor, and Fanny was resting, her head against the back of the tub. There were tears in her eyes. I picked up the magazine, placed it on the table, and knelt beside her.

"What's the matter?" I asked.

She turned her head toward me and stared for a moment, her eyes searching mine.

"My child is not Sam's," she responded.

I must pause here to venture away from the path of my story in order to explain the intuition that develops in certain individuals who, by dint of their plainness or their deformity or their shyness, stand apart from the livelier crowd. Such was I, squint-eyed and sickly. Like a wallflower at a dance, such individuals choose not to gather amongst themselves; their nature is not gregarious. They prefer to stand alone and observe in the happy faces of others their own disappointment which is reflected there and which denies to such individuals the blissful naiveté of youth. They grow wise before their time. I recall lamenting why I was not pretty like my sister or why my hair was a mousey brown and not shiny, or why I could not have a pair of red shoes and a bonnet covered with silk violets. But I was not pretty, and my hair was dull and straight, and my father could not afford to buy me red shoes. And as these sad thoughts filled my mind, I studied those I envied, their eyes, their mouths, their gestures, and feelings of sorrow for myself gave way to a fascination with the drama before me. I would perceive that so-and-so did not love so-and-so, though he was her escort. I could see by his eyes as he danced with her that on every turn, he looked to find someone else, wondering who she was dancing with and would she look his way when the music ended. The wallflower became the seer. I became expert in nuance, in subtlety, and I learned by painful experience to keep such intelligence to myself. If the time ever comes when you must share a secret—when the burden of knowing something is too great to bear alone—but one single sharer only is desired—then share it with the plainest, most homely, most unfortunate, for there it will find a kindly sympathy, an understanding heart, and a resolute trust.

The instant I heard Fanny's confession, I knew who the father was. I need not ask, nor did I. Had she told me, her secret would have been as safe as had it been locked in a vault and dropped to the deepest pit of the ocean. I have kept that secret to this day, but as I have explained and shall further, I have become convinced that the keeping of that secret has denied Fanny her proper place in literary history, and I believe now that she would want it told.

I first met Edgar Poe at a New Year's Eve party at Caroline Kirkland's. As I thanked him for publishing one of my articles, I noticed that he kept looking beyond me, over my shoulder. I was used to this, and I paid it little mind. Men have been looking beyond me all my life. But when he turned away to speak with someone else, I glanced behind me in the direction his eyes had wandered, and there was Fanny.

I had not heard the rumors. Later I learned that Edgar and Fanny had been the subject of gossip, but on that night, one of my earliest in New York City, I knew nothing of such rumors.

Moments later Fanny found me, and I told her that I had just met the author of "The Raven," but that he had seemed preoccupied with her. She blushed with this news and looked away, but her lips gave me to know the pleasure she took in these tidings. I paid him some extravagant compliment just then, confident that in so doing, I would please Fanny, and I wanted to please her, for I would not have been invited but for her appeal to Mrs. Kirkland on my behalf.

"I must find him," she said, "to tell him what you said. It will thrill him, Mary. He says he doesn't like praise, but in that regard, he's like every other man in the world—he loves it!"

And with this, Fanny left me, the wallflower, and returned, as it were, to the mainstream current, leaving me to observe as I did as a girl those who, as a girl, I had envied. I watched her take his elbow and draw him away from his conversation with others. I saw their eyes meet, the glad surprise, the unheard words, the smiles, and I knew from years of lonely observation that they were in love.

I was thrilled for them—not shocked, not outraged—I was even envious, though I knew they were both married. I was still married also. But I would have sacrificed my soul to know the love I saw when their eyes met. Can Heaven offer greater joy than such love on earth? I think not.

Now, as I helped Fanny from the bath, removed the wet sheet with which I had bound her abdomen, and covered her in blankets to restore warmth, I sensed ambivalence in her thoughts. I led her to the bed and rubbed her dry with the blankets. Had she wanted to lose the child, she would not have come at all, yet she arrived laced so tightly that she knew the child must suffer. I could sympathize, I knew the heartbreak of losing a child. I had lost three before their time—cold, wet, limp. Those memories are awful.

"You must resolve to have this child," I whispered covering her on the bed with blankets. "Painful as it may be, the pain of losing it by carelessness or fear of what others might say would be worse. Give this child everything you can and love it for its innocence. It is no longer its father's child, it is yours. A child is an innocent thing no matter the father."

"Or the mother?" Fanny asked, her teary gaze fixed on the ceiling.

"Or the mother," I said, "but what child would not be overjoyed with you as a mother?" Fanny closed her eyes. Her pouting mouth told me tears would pour were I to say more. "Sleep," I said, and I doused the oil lamp and left her alone.

When I returned in half an hour, the curtains were opened, and Fanny was dressed and staring out the window. "Help me button my dress, Mary," she said. "I must get back."

We did the best we could, and I led her to my room for her coat and bonnet.

"Mary," she said as she tied her bonnet strings, "you must forget what I told you."

"It is forgotten," I said, "but will you heed my advice and come again?"

"Yes. I suppose," she said, and she closed her eyes and shook her head as if trying to erase everything from her mind. "If only I could leave New York, but I can't. And I can't be seen, so I suppose it doesn't matter that I can't button my dresses."

I asked her why she couldn't be seen, and she explained. On Monday a certain lady of Fanny's acquaintance had paid a call to advise Fanny that she had been indiscreet in a letter which she had sent to Edgar Poe and cautioned her to ask for its return. Though Fanny had not yet publically announced her pregnancy, it seemed that this lady knew the contents of the letter and implied that gossips would suspect Poe to be the father of her child. It seemed Fanny was powerless to stanch the rumors, and she had spent the day before agonizing over what to do, thus explaining her failure to appear at my house. She related all this and then praised her husband for his understanding. He had agreed to take her back and be the child's father in the eyes of the world. He was, however, so she explained, not a man to bear lightly the insulting presumption of that certain lady. Fanny had not yet told her husband of the visit, and she dreaded the task. I wondered further if her husband knew the identity of the child's father, but she said nothing regarding this. I could imagine the agony of her situation and the horror of the possible outcome.

Just at that time, shortly after I had moved into this house leased by Marx Lazarus, my husband, getting wind of it, had bruited it about that I had opened a brothel. He had sued one of the men who had helped me rescue Elma, and he was out to blacken my name in advance of his suit coming to trial. I could, therefore, sympathize with Fanny's plight, and I grieved for her. I begged her to move into my house until arrangements were made with her husband for a suitable place for her family to live. She listened and promised to consider the idea.

She did not move in with me, however, and I was not surprised by this. A commune was not to Fanny's taste; she was rather too worldly I think, but I loved her no less for this. She did come for treatment, though I think she came more for my company than for her health. She considered me safe. During that winter and spring she shunned society, and I think she was lonely. Without her sponsorship, I ceased to receive invitations to the literary soirées; therefore, I was in no position to hear the rumors about her, but inevitably she got wind of them and would recount them to me as I washed her and instructed her on the benefits and procedures of cold water ablution. She blushed red as a radish when I introduced the douche. She would cover her eyes, peeking between her fingers, as I inserted the syringe, and the jet of cold water took her breath away, and, though she feigned being horrified by the procedure, I think she found reassurance in both my treatment and my company.

Edgar Poe left New York City in the early spring of that year, and with his departure, the rumors subsided. Though Fanny's husband played his part until the birth of her daughter in late June, he ultimately found excuses to travel again. In the course of those six months, Fanny and I became best friends. It was our habit to unburden ourselves of painful thoughts. I told her of an incident that had occurred nearly two years before when, answering a question after one of my lectures, I made the statement with which I began this story—that the heart heeds no covenant. I had gone on to explain my belief that love flows freely, ungoverned by reason or by law. My husband, attending as he always did in order to collect the lecture receipts, overheard my words, and now for purposes of blackening my name, professed that I was an advocate for free love.

The effects of such an accusation coupled with my moving to New York go without saying. These things, on top of my leaving him and, by trickery, winning back my daughter, made me a pariah in the eyes of New England Quakers. Nothing I could say or do could redeem their opinion of me. Perhaps, therefore, they could imagine that I would become the madam of a brothel. The people of small New England towns believed that New York City was a hotbed of such establishments, and perhaps it was. I wouldn't know.

For this reason Fanny and I had much in common, for she was, so she explained, being spoken of in New York society as Edgar Poe's whore. I doubted that, thinking Fanny was exaggerating, knowing she was truly loved by many. But when her husband left her again after the birth of her daughter, his departure served to confirm those vicious slanders in some circles.

Having been a wallflower all my life, I was better prepared for ostracism than was Fanny. She was devastated by it, and I think she lost the will to survive. Though I cajoled and nagged and argued, no amount of wet-sheet packs, plunges, sponges, enemas, douches, or baths could overcome a loss of hope. She suffered my ministrations with no more energy than a penny candle.

One day not long after Fanny's daughter's birth, as she lay on her stomach while I massaged her back, she turned her head to me. "Mary," she said, "I want you to visit the Poes."

"The Edgar Poes?" I asked.

"Yes," she said. "Did you ever meet Virginia? His wife?"

I shook my head.

"She has the consumption. I've just had a letter from him, saying that her suffering is awful. No doubt she's incurable, but you could, at least, ease her pain. He would be grateful as would I."

This was in August, and Edgar Poe was back in the news. He had published a series of articles in *Godey's Ladies Book* that had incurred the wrath of a particular New York editor whose response to Poe's article about him was vicious in its condemnation.

"I can't go, Mary," she said, "for obvious reasons. Anyway, there is little I could do, but you could do a great deal. I think Edgar may be ill also. Please."

I agreed, but I could not go alone, and I had patients and obligations. Within a few weeks, however, with Fanny's help, George Colton agreed to escort me with a young friend of his—his "greenhorn protégé" so he called him. Colton was an entertaining and amiable man of about my age, the editor of a magazine. He was short, roly-poly, and had a waxed and twirled mustache that gave his round face the aspect of innate good humor. A confirmed bachelor, Colton arrived at the station with a picnic basket filled with sandwiches and cakes, a varnished walking stick and umbrella, and a carpet bag containing bottles of water and red wine, lemons, and packages of coffee, tea, and sugar, all gifts for the Poes.

Colton's young friend had recently arrived in New York from his birthplace in New Hampshire.

"I saved him from all manner of evils," Colton explained, catching his breath and moping his brow with his handkerchief as he introduced his friend, a Mr. Freemon. "Without my help, the poor boy would have been swindled and robbed by the droppers, sharpers, and blacklegs of our fair city. I found him wandering Washington Parade Ground like a wet puppy, down to his last sawbuck, with a portfolio of stories he brought to New York to sell. I'm turning him into a printer's devil at ten dollars a week. You see, Mary, I'm a soft touch."

Freemon was in his early twenties—blond, tall, shy, and quite handsome. His suit was homespun and too tight for his build, and his collar kept coming unstayed. He wore neither mustache nor hat, and he carried Colton's picnic basket and carpet bag, one in each hand. He was forever setting down his parcels, fixing his collar stay, and retying his tie. The two were an odd but willing pair, and I was grateful for their company.

It was a hot, humid, and cloudless morning in late August. We took the Harlem train out to Fordham, and, with directions from the stationmaster, made our way to the Poe cottage on a path through woods smelling of woodbine and skunk and wet from thundershowers the previous evening. After hiking uphill for perhaps twenty minutes, we emerged into a pasture from which we espied the cottage sitting at the top, surrounded by a pleasant acre of greensward. From appearances the cottage, overgrown with grape ivy, was dilapidated and abandoned except for a trickle of white smoke rising from the chimney. The gray clapboards were warped, and the roof shingles covered with lichen. It was as if we had stumbled upon the hermitage of these woods.

The three of us stared for a moment, standing at the edge of the woods and wondering if we had taken the wrong path. I turned and smiled at Colton who was breathless from our climb, his suit coat thrown over his shoulder, and his shirt wet with perspiration. There were questions in his eyes as he mopped his face with his handkerchief. Could it be that here, as it were on the edge of the frontier, lived the author of "The Raven"?

"Hello!" Colton shouted across the clearing toward the cottage. "Is anyone home?"

A lone figure appeared on the piazza in shirt sleeves and suspenders, bareheaded and mustachioed. He took hold of one of the posts supporting the porch and peered down at us. "Who's there?" he shouted.

"Poe? Is that you?" Colton yelled, and by his squinting I realized that my companion was quite nearsighted. "It's George Colton and Mrs. Gove. We've come out to see you."

Poe jumped off the porch and came running down to meet us. He leaped the split rail fence that enclosed the pasture, and we met him part way up. He was overjoyed to see us.

"By Jove, Mary!" he said, clasping my hand in both of his. "How are you? And George, old boy. What a wonderful surprise. Come up to the house and see Sissy and Muddy. They'll be delighted."

Colton introduced Freemon, and Poe pumped his hand, insisting on helping with the parcels. We crossed the tall wet grass of the pasture, then Poe helped me across the fence. As the others climbed over, I noticed hanging nearby from the limb of a cherry tree, a crudely made bird cage with a restless bobolink inside.

"You must tell me all the news," Poe said as we approached the piazza. "I haven't seen a newspaper in a week. Muddy! We have visitors."

A smiling Mrs. Clemm appeared in the doorway, wiping her hands on her apron. She wore a black dress and widow's cap, and she curtsied as we stepped up onto the porch. She was a sturdy woman with thick features and snow white hair. Poe introduced us all around.

We entered the house and met Poe's wife, Virginia, in the parlor. She stood, spilling a black and orange tabby that must have been curled in her lap, and she too curtsied as Poe made introductions. Her appearance startled me. At once I saw that Fanny was correct in speaking of her illness as incurable, but she had a lovely face despite the unearthly pallor of her complexion. So unlike her mother, Virginia was frail and shy. Her hair was black as a crow's wing, and the impression of this thick, jetty blackness with her ashen face was ghostly. I approached her at once, embraced her, and we sat down beside each other. As Poe conversed with Colton and young Freemon, Virginia and I exchanged pleasantries. I did not reveal to her that I was a physician, thinking the opportunity might arise for discussing health issues with Poe or Mrs. Clemm instead, but all the while, as we spoke, I was conscious of her condition and considered ways to alleviate her suffering. She was charming and articulate, and she asked about Fanny and her new baby, speaking of Fanny in fond terms. One would have thought them great friends.

The parlor was spare. There were four chairs, two small side tables, a writing table, and a hanging bookshelf that contained Poe's collection of books. The floor was covered with a checked matting, and the room's fresh neatness told of their poor but proud circumstances. Colton brought out his presents to Poe's delight.

"Look, Muddy," he exclaimed with each item, handing them in turn to his mother-in-law. "Let's have some lemonade," he said when Colton produced three lemons from his bag. With this, Mrs. Clemm repaired to the kitchen, and I followed to help.

There were just three rooms on the first floor, and a narrow staircase indicated a loft above.

Mrs. Clemm and I returned to the parlor with a pitcher of lemonade and found Poe showing Colton a leather bound copy of Elizabeth Barrett Browning's poems received from her along with a letter in which she extolled his "Raven," marveling at the sensation it had caused in England, lines that Poe read aloud with great pride. Fanny had been right. He was always thrilled with praise, but there was nothing boastful in his manner. On the contrary he was a perfect gentleman, eager to talk, modest to the point of shyness, generous in his praise of others. His conversation was always interesting; he spoke in a soft tone so respectful that it was difficult to conceive how he could be so maligned.

His demeanor belied his tomahawking reputation as a critic. I was quite taken with him.

When refreshments were over, Poe suggested a walk through the woods to the Bronx River, and the four of us—Poe, Colton, and I, with Freemon carrying the picnic basket—left Mrs. Clemm and Virginia in the cottage. Once outside I admired the pastoral view from the piazza. The cottage was surrounded by an acre or more of grass and clover shaded by two gnarled cherry trees. The lawn, a perfect green, was bordered all around by fenced-in pasture where sheep and Poe's landlord's two cows grazed. My attention was again drawn to the bobolink whose cage, hanging from one of the cherries, rustled and swung with the attempts of the bird to free itself. I suggested to Poe that he should release the poor creature, a thing not meant to be caged.

"I have named him, Robert of Lincoln Green," Poe said, ignoring my request, "and you are wrong, Mary. He is well fed and a splendid songster. He will grow accustomed to his little home, and in the fall I'll take him inside where we will enjoy his melodies all winter long."

I said no more, but I thought it cruel of Poe to imprison a thing meant for the wild.

We strolled through the woods as if on holiday. At my urging Freemon undid his tie and let his collar fly, putting him more at ease. Poe extolled the benefits of country living and a walk in the woods. He was writing again, he said; he had a story coming in *Godey's* that he claimed was his best ever. Questions to Colton about friends in New York City led Colton to mention Poe's recent lawsuit against the New York editor referred to earlier. Poe didn't care to talk about that, nor did he care to talk about the series of articles that had given rise to the controversy. He had spoken well of me in that series, though less well of Colton which I had thought unfair, since Colton had been first to publish "The Raven." I thought it ill-advised to do what Poe had done, but I held my tongue.

At the river, after taking in the scene—on the far side the woods of upper Manhattan, lush beneath the midday sun—to Colton's amazement, Poe suggested a swim.

"Come, George," Poe urged. "It will refresh you, will it not, Mary?" he said, smiling at me, acknowledging my appreciation for a cold water bath.

Poe slipped out of his suspenders and unbuttoned his shirt. I turned my head, pretending not to watch, but so amused by the prospect that I could not resist peeking. Soon Poe and Freemon were barefoot and shirtless, and, in nothing but their drawers, they waded out into the current. Colton hung back, reluctant at first, then he followed their lead, undressed and tiptoed to the water's edge. After testing the temperature of the water, he waded out, complaining about every hazard imaginable. Soon the three men were waist-deep, laughing and splashing one another.

"Mary, won't you come in," Poe urged, looking up at me on my rocky perch. "We'll hide our eyes, won't we George. The water's fine, and you'll be saved the chore of a bath tonight. And George will swear to report nothing of this in the *American Review*, won't you old boy?"

I laughed, shaking my head to decline his offer, and for a half-hour I enjoyed their high-spirited horseplay. Poe swam out into the current, showing off his skill as a swimmer. Colton demanded that he return, fretful and anxious. Freemon also remained close to shore, admitting he could not swim, but he did dare to put his head under water, then paraded like a peacock in front of Colton who eyed him with obvious admiration.

The three finally emerged, dripping wet and no longer mindful of their state of undress. Poe then suggested a game of leapfrog, and again Colton was shocked.

"It'll be just the thing to dry us off," Poe said, "and Freemon here must be a great leaper. Mary will judge the winner. Come."

Whether it was Poe's challenge or the notion of touching the naked back of his young friend, Colton agreed. The three put on their shoes and stockings so as not to hurt their feet on the gravelly beach, then Poe drew a line with a stick, bent over with his toes touching the line and braced himself, his hands on his knees. Then he invited Freemon to go first. With a running start, Freemon leaped Poe, his superior weight nearly pushing the skinny poet to the ground. Carefully Poe measured the length of Freemon's leap and reported his findings to me, then he invited Colton to go next, squatting again in frog position. Colton did the best he could, and I imagined his disappointment that he must leap over Poe and not Freemon. Again Poe measured and reported a leap far short of Colton's more agile friend.

"Now it's my turn," Poe insisted, motioning to Freemon to take his place at the line. Poe's determination was enlightening. It was then I realized that he was much too competitive to be a fair and impartial critic. For one so intent on winning, it was no wonder others claimed he wrote his reviews with a tomahawk.

With a long running start he leaped over Freemon, extended his legs to broaden his jump, and beat the others by good measure. The skill of his form, however, was not matched by the fortitude of his gaiters, and both of them snapped when his feet hit the ground. Open-mouthed, Poe looked first at his winning margin evident in the gravel, and then at his broken gaiters. His victory was undone by the ruining of his shoes, and by the look on his face, I knew they must be his only pair.

The contest over, the three men dressed. Poe made light of the mishap, and Colton covered over Poe's embarrassment by suggesting that we eat our picnic, and we sat down on the bank and ate our lunch. With this Colton uncorked a bottle of wine which only Poe refused, and there followed a pleasant hour that I shall never forget. In the course of our conversation, Poe professed to us that fame meant nothing to him. As if to spurn notoriety and explain his hermit life, he spoke of fame with such disdain that I decided his comments were an affectation. I didn't believe him, but I said nothing. Then, as if to change the subject, he began reciting poetry, one poem after another, an amazing repertoire of poems appropriate for a sunny summer's day. He had a soft voice, and when he recited, he lifted his eyes to the sky, and the three of us watched and listened in awe. I think we sensed that we were the recipients of an unexpected and special gift. The last poem, the only one I recall, contained a verse that I thought more beautiful than all the others.

> I will not waste these summer hours,
> The gift that He has given;
> I'll find philosophy in flowers,
> Astronomy in heaven!

"That's lovely," I said when he had finished his recitation. "Edgar, that is really beautiful! Who wrote it?"

From between his feet he selected a small stone and threw it so that it skipped over the surface of the water. It was almost as if he could not say. "Fanny wrote it," he said at last, reaching for another stone.

No one moved or said a word. Freemon turned to Colton as if to ask, "Who is Fanny?" but Colton slowly shook his head at the boy as if to warn him not to. Then he and I eyed each other.

Thoughts of Fanny seemed to occupy Poe's mind for a moment, and the recitations ended. He had lost his enthusiasm, and soon he was again lamenting the sad state of his shoes. He reminded me of the little boy who tears a hole in his best britches and dreads telling his mother.

Indeed, when we returned to the cottage, Mrs. Clemm was distraught.

"Oh, Eddy, how did you break your gaiters?" she asked.

His head hung in shame, Poe refused to admit that the game of leap-frog was his idea. Mrs. Clemm seemed to suspect as much, but pride prevented further questions and chiding. I felt more sorrow for him now than the poor caged bobolink. Drawing me aside, Mrs. Clemm pleaded for my help in persuading Colton to purchase Poe's new poem that she had delivered to Colton two weeks earlier. I knew the one. Colton carried it in his coat pocket; we had read it together on the train out to Harlem. It could have been Sanskrit for all we could make of it.

"If he would buy the poem," Mrs. Clemm pleaded, "Eddy could have a new pair of shoes."

I promised to do what I could, and later Colton did buy the poem, and Poe got new shoes and five dollars over.

We moved the parlor chairs to the porch and had a pleasant afternoon, leaving in time to catch the four o'clock train. In those few hours Poe had seemed content despite his broken gaiters, his poverty, and even despite Virginia's illness. She was napping and, therefore, not foremost in his thoughts just then. I envied him the bucolic setting—the lawn and pasture sloping away to woods, the smell of pine straw and wood smoke, and the silence except for the birds—Poe's imprisoned bobolink in particular. Poor proud Poe, cared for by a wife and mother who doted on him. He wasn't unhappy, and I thought how the mind can be a happy refuge for the poor as well as the wallflower. Were I rich, I would have bought him new shoes and what comforts were necessary to ease Virginia's suffering, but the cost of my trip to Fordham entailed, at least for a time, going without a clean dress and fewer oysters in my stew.

Colton's presence and my meager resources prevented me from prescribing a regimen for Virginia that day. As we said goodbye on the path at the edge of the woods, I suggested to Poe that Mrs. Clemm should bathe Virginia daily in cold water. I stopped at that, but I had concocted a strategy in my mind which I planned to put into action as soon as I returned to the city. There was someone with more resources than I, whose care would be equally efficacious, but I withheld mention of this. I had in mind Loui Shew, and I was certain she would prove a godsend for the Poes.

I returned to Fordham three times that fall and winter—the next time with Loui and the last time for Virginia's funeral. Loui and I found Virginia's condition had deteriorated to the point that she could not climb or descend the narrow stairs without assistance. There was no tub in which to bathe her, only a pail for water, but we managed. To Mrs. Clemm's credit, she had given Virginia a daily sponge bath, but this merely kept the patient clean. It did little to alleviate her pain. Loui took over and necessity forced me to let her. She raised a subscription of sixty dollars and donated many of her own possessions—a mattress and comforter and, at the end, a linen dress in which to bury Virginia. Poe was quite taken with Loui.

On my last trip out before Virginia died, Poe and I walked alone through woods painted in late autumn colors. Now on a perfect Indian summer day he confessed that he had deceived Colton and me on our visit to Fordham in August.

"In truth I cherish fame," he said. "I idolize it."

I think he felt the need just then to bare his soul, for he was pensive and frightened. It was as if he were confessing a sin. He was tired, his eyes, ringed with dark, bloated circles. His decline was shocking. No more the eager host with energy for a swim and a game of leapfrog. He had aged years in those two months, and there was nothing to be done that wasn't already being done. I urged him to write, but he was adamant in dismissing the idea.

"I cannot write," he said, shaking his head as if the idea was ludicrous. "I will never write again. To write one must have hope, and hope is dead."

I left his words as they fell. We walked on through the woods into the tiny village of Fordham. Poe wanted to show me Virginia's final resting place, for arrangements had been made. The Valentine family who owned the cottage rented by the Poes had offered a place in their vault in the cemetery of the Dutch Reformed Church. There were tears in his eyes when he showed me the spot.

These events occurred thirty-five years ago in the autumn before Virginia died in January 1847. Poe outlived her less than three years. Mrs. Clemm outlived them both, surviving many years in rather dreadful circumstances so I have been told. But these are not the stories I have to tell. No, the end of my story relates not to Poe but to Fanny whose memory is in total eclipse.

Whenever I returned to New York from Fordham, she insisted on knowing every detail, every word spoken. Did he ask about her? No, he hadn't. I did not lie to her. Hurt by this news, she tried to hide it. She tossed her head as if to say it didn't matter, but it did. The wallflower sees, and, sensing this, Fanny waved me off, insisting that his interest in her had no significance. It was her admiration, so she said—for his genius—that mattered. And I professed understanding and sympathy.

With requisite dispassion I laid out my plan regarding Loui Shew. Fanny listened. My words were clinical, precise—this should be done—that should be done. She nodded agreement, but, though she did care about Virginia, she loved Poe, and nothing I could say would feed those feelings. Those feelings must be starved, I decided, for her own good.

Who am I? An advocate of free love to hear my husband tell it. Yet in this instance, to one I considered my best friend in the world, I was manipulative and deceitful. No, he hadn't asked about her, and it was for that reason and other reasons that I endeavored to dissuade Fanny's affections away from the man I knew she loved above all others. This has preyed on my mind. Had I given her some hope, things might have turned out differently. I am no advocate of free love; in so many ways I am as conventional as those narrow-minded Quakers who shunned and condemned me.

Fanny's baby—a daughter—her namesake—would not live long.

Even in June of 1847 when we celebrated Fanny Fay's first birthday, we knew. In the presence of her other daughters, Fanny denied the possibility, putting on her most cheerful face. Her husband stayed away; I was more of a father than he. The night the child died, in late October, Fanny's oldest daughter, Ellen, was downstairs playing the piano while upstairs Fanny sang, rocking her daughter in her arms, a lullaby to spirit her into heaven. I sat on the stairs with May, the middle daughter, wiping both our tears, praising the joys of heaven, and silently cursing my own feeble incompetence.

To make matters worse, Fanny was dying too. I knew it even then. She was coughing up blood, and her constricted lungs had no room to expand and compensate. There was nothing I could do for Fanny or her daughter.

But Fanny had pluck. Devastated as she was by the death of her daughter and by her own illness, she refused to be downcast. In early December, still dressed in mourning, she came to see me to inform me that she was planning an elaborate Christmas party, and, as her apartment was too small for the crowd she envisioned, she had decided on my house, or should I say Marx Lazarus's house. She had a hundred ideas—there would be charades, guessing games, and theatricals, and everyone would be required to compose something farcical or some riddle or conundrum to be solved. The guest list already surpassed fifty, and she had only just begun, and the list would include a certain gentleman that she had especially in mind for me to meet. Fanny was playing matchmaker. No, she said, I did not know him, but he was intelligent and handsome and eager to meet me. She would not reveal his name, as there was the possibility that I might have heard of him before, and she didn't want to spoil the surprise.

"And—Oh, yes!" she added, "—I've invited Edgar. And I've asked him to recite 'The Raven.'"

I wondered about her motive. Fanny had not seen Edgar Poe since his self-imposed exile to Fordham two years earlier. I sensed that so long as her daughter lived, she avoided him on purpose. Perhaps she thought it would have been too awkward for her, or, I wondered, perhaps he knew the child was his in which case it would be too awkward for them both. More likely, in that year and four months that her daughter lived, Fanny was at first content to nurse her child and later, when it became apparent that the child was too delicate to survive, she had no other thought but to comfort her. And now both her daughter and Poe's wife were in the ground, and I think Fanny had become curious. How did he look? Would those feelings that were so evident the night I first saw them together at Caroline Kirkland's—could they be rekindled. I did not know, but Fanny seemed eager to see him, and I was not about to dash her enthusiasm.

Marx Lazarus was shocked. He could not believe that I was planning a gala ball to be given in a commune and water-cure establishment. I reminded him that Fourier encouraged such celebrations and that everyone who lived with us would be invited too. I gave him no opportunity to object or decline.

Seventy guests appeared. The women brought wine, jelly, comfits, cakes, nuts, raisins, and apples, and Fanny, dressed in a satin dress with long sleeves and lace to her fingertips, played the piano while the men sang and couples danced.

It was during the dances that Fanny introduced me to the man she had singled out for me. The experience was disconcerting, and I wondered how Fanny could have imagined that I would be interested in such a man. He was dressed in the latest fashion, wore military whiskers, and he was much too precise and gallant for my taste. What could Fanny have possibly been thinking? But this man, Mr. Nichols, would not leave me alone. It seemed that Fanny had primed him too, and he was out to please her by showering me with attention.

"He is nothing more than a dandy," I said to her when I was able to break free of him.

"He is a gentleman," she said, "as are all the men here. Don't condemn him for that. Scratch the surface, and I think you'll find a depth to match your own. But in any event, please yourself."

Just as the recitations were to begin, Fanny decided the lamps were insufficient, so she disappeared into the kitchen and returned with a dozen raw potatoes, a tray of penny candles, and a paring knife. When she finished, the lighting was augmented by her novel candlesticks. These preparations done, she began the readings with a letter from President Polk, regretting that he could not attend due to pressing matters of state, but expressing great admiration for her poetry. The make-believe was so convincing that some could not decide if it was real or her own concoction. Others read notices equally comic, or they sang to the accompaniment of the piano, or they recited poetry. Then, as midnight approached, Fanny demanded that the lamps be doused so that only candlelight lit the room.

With no introduction Edgar stepped forward, and with no copy for reference, he began "The Raven." I had never heard him recite it, and the effect was astonishing. So singular was the performance that, as I listened, I decided that the world must be divided into two parts—those who had heard Edgar Poe recite his most famous poem and those who had not. He stood erect beside the piano, unmoving throughout the recital except for the occasional tilt of his head up or down. The light of the candles and the coals seemed to play on his broad forehead, and there was not a sound in the room—no cough, no sniffle. His soft voice modulated with the emotion of his words; there were tears in his eyes; and everyone present seemed acutely aware of the pain he must have felt for the loss of his young wife.

There was a long silence when he finished, and this was followed by an eruption of applause. Thereafter, the mood was more subdued and guests began to leave.

In the course of that entire evening I do not recall seeing Edgar and Fanny together. I admit that I was curious; I wanted to watch like the wallflower of old, but Mr. Nichols's attention left me little opportunity. Fanny was right about him, of course, as time has proven, and our names became inextricably linked as they are to this day. At that time I was still a married woman, but in time, as I have said, my husband agreed to a divorce, and I married Thomas Nichols, reserving as I did the right to my name and to be a human being distinct from him, entering no compact to be faithful but promising to be faithful to the deepest love of my heart, and demanding a room of my own. He agreed to all these conditions and has been faithful to them as I have been to him, the deepest love of my heart.

Thomas and I had much in common. He was a writer also—he had published novels with which I was familiar, and after our marriage he studied to become a doctor. We planned and worked together to establish our own water-cure journal and sanatorium, and we have been equally dedicated to that work.

At the time of our marriage, in the summer of 1848, Fanny was away from the city. She went alternately to Albany and Saratoga, escaping the heat of the city and seeking the healthful effects of fresh air and the waters. Her husband was only occasionally on the scene—his portrait painting kept him on the go—and I seldom heard her speak of him in her letters. She did, however, write to me once about Edgar. It seems she and her daughters were staying with her sister's family, the Harringtons, in Albany when Edgar appeared unexpectedly and asked to speak to her privately.

"Mary, you cannot guess what happened," she wrote. "As soon as my sister and brother-in-law left us alone in the parlor, Edgar dropped to one knee and, in his formal manner, began what I knew to be the preface of a proposal of marriage. I was aghast and begged him to rise and stop at once. I even wondered if he'd been drinking. He stood, hung his head, refusing to look at me, and I felt sorry for having disappointed him. He was nothing if not lost and desperate, and my refusal appeared to humiliate him. He made hasty excuses to leave the house, and I haven't seen him since. You can imagine how I stammered and stuttered as I tried to explain all this to my sister and brother-in-law. Mr. Harrington, who disapproves of Edgar, was most upset and would have gone after him had I not stopped him."

I wonder if Fanny ever saw him again after that. She could not resist praising him when, by saying nothing, she might have stanched the old rumors that still persisted, rumors that shadowed her to the end of her life. But she was also unwell. She never had the patience for careful attention to her diet or long sessions in the sitz tub or wrapped in a wet sheet pack. I saw less of her after my marriage. In February of the following year her husband left her again, this time for California to search for gold. Fanny and her daughters had an apartment in Brooklyn, and she became the particular favorite of Wilmot Griswold. Griswold was divorced and in his anthology devoted to the female poets, he praised her above all other women poets in America. On the occasions that I did visit her, Gris, as Fanny called him, was there also. He doted on her. I liked him; he was handsome, tall, thin, intelligent looking. He had a contagious laugh, but he would quickly become serious and sincere, lowering his head and peering earnestly at Fanny as if he would have done anything she asked.

By a very odd circumstance, Gris had been named Edgar's literary executor after his death in October of that year. I say strange, because his obituary of Poe in Horace Greeley's *Tribune*—and afterward reprinted in many newspapers and magazines—was bitter and unkind, much more so, I think, than the memoir he later published. I cannot say what Fanny thought of this, for by this time she was confined to her rooms, so ill that I dared not raise the subject. For the life of me I could not understand why Griswold would have been so cruel, and I wondered if it could have been jealousy of Fanny's regard for Edgar.

Griswold arranged for publication of a large volume of Fanny's poetry late that same year, but Fanny was so weak that she did not even bother to review the list of poems selected. When she finally saw the galleys, she was so disappointed that she wrote a note to preface the edition, a note of apology. The book would be her last.

By the end of the year, her husband had returned, and he moved his family back into Manhattan. Fanny took on the responsibility for choosing paint color and fabrics for decorating her new apartment with all the joy and enthusiasm of one who had years to live, but she was failing fast. Griswold continued to be a frequent visitor, and in the end, Sam Osgood, being unable to bring himself to inform her of her hopeless condition, asked Griswold to do so. He wrote her a brief note to tell her that her end was near and handed it to her as she lay in her bed. After reading it, she turned her face to her pillow and cried. She died on the 12th of May, a month shy of her fortieth birthday. In little more than a year, both her surviving daughters died also, Ellen, fifteen, and May, eleven.

It is a tragedy, I think, that in the thirty years since her death Fanny is so forgotten. At least two men—Edgar and Griswold—had called her the best American poetess of her time. Another writer, Mary Hewitt, who knew and loved Fanny and esteemed her work as so many of us did, conceived of a memorial—a gift book which would contain memorial sketches and poems and original work contributed by the most important writers of the day. The proceeds of this publication were to go to a fitting monument to be erected on Fanny's grave in Mt. Auburn Cemetery in Cambridge. Before his own death, Griswold wrote the opening sketch which, to this day, is the only record of Fanny's life. Unfortunately, Mrs. Hewitt's efforts were for naught, a publisher could not be found, and the effort failed.

What things conspired against Fanny? There are reasons why the work of one writer survives and that of another, disappears—reasons that do not always pertain to the merit of their work. In Fanny's case, too many people in her circle of literary friends knew too much. Whether out of love for her or decency or propriety, they said and wrote nothing. Perhaps they thought it best to let her memory fade than to have it linked with Edgar Poe, since Griswold had so blackened Edgar's memory. In his case, however, respect for his work, albeit in some quarters, grudging respect, kept his name alive. In other words, if Edgar's genius required that his life be the subject of study and understanding, then it became all the more necessary to suppress any mention of Fanny and the child. And how could the memory of Fanny die if her poetry did not die also?

It is painful for me to think that I might have been a conspirator with those others who would have her disappear. I can no longer do that. I am aware of the fact that the distance may make it easier for me to break a silence. I have lived in England for over twenty years now, never once returning. My husband and I chose not to take sides in what is referred to here as the American Civil War; we decided to leave instead. I do not regret that decision, but that's another story. You asked about Edgar and Fanny, and I have told you what I know. He is today as popular here as in America, and that is a testament to his genius. But in America women writers are not as highly regarded as they are here in England, and I consider that a grave disservice to my sex. Perhaps this is the truer reason that I have told you what I have about Fanny, for I believe most deeply that her work, like Poe's, deserves a place among the first rank of American writers. But most of all, I remember Edgar and Fanny that first time I saw them together—from my watchful, wallflower perch. They were lovers whose free hearts found treasure in one another.

September 30, 1883
Aldwyn Tower
Malvern, England

Dear Eddy,

Mrs. Lewis has been dead for almost three years now, so I can't help but wonder how long ago she told you this. Have you posed this question to anyone else? I pray you haven't. Just as I believe we cannot dictate the object of our affection, I have come to the conclusion that we cannot dictate certain sexual choices. In counseling women over many years, I have come to know that many—unmarried or saddled with unhappy marriages—would have been happier married to members of their own sex. I am certain the same holds true for men. It is not a sin, though society and particularly the church dictate that it is. I can't help but wonder about your take on this issue. Probably, I shock you. It is a fact, Eddy, undeniable. It is the way God made them. So if anyone is at fault, it is He. Do I blaspheme? I think not, but by all means, you are free to think what you like.

I sincerely doubt that Mrs. Lewis revealed to you her own sexual proclivities, but I must tell you there were rumors regarding her here in England. Perhaps the rumors arose from the fact that she never tired of reciting her "The Last Hour of Sappho." Lie down with dogs, &c. I don't mean this in a hateful way. I never paid any attention to the rumors about her; it didn't matter to me which side of the bed she preferred. That was her business.

Eddy! Eddy! Eddy! Dear boy, what would you have me do? Corroborate Mrs. Lewis's contention regarding Griswold? Surely you know me well enough to know that I would never do such a thing even if I knew, and I do not. The story of the portraits is well-known, but it's not so bizarre as you think. The portrait of Edgar was painted by Sam Osgood, and it remained in Fanny's possession until she died. Griswold greatly admired one of several portraits that Sam had painted of her—the one painted when she was twenty-three before she married Sam. Griswold asked Fanny if she would leave it to him, saying he could not bear to live without a likeness of her. So she left a letter, bequeathing it to him along with the portrait of Edgar on the condition that the two must always hang side-by-side. They were both oval and of exactly the same size; they made a handsome pair. I know this, because she told me shortly before she died. She seemed to take comfort and pleasure in the arrangement, and she was either mindless or dismissive of Griswold's animosity toward Edgar. It was as if she wanted the world to see her and Edgar together once she was gone. It was daring of her, but that was so Fanny. It is for this reason, among others, that I told you in one of my earliest letters that I believe Fanny wanted the world to know the truth, not only about her and Edgar, but also about their love child, Fanny Fay. In this way she would bequeath a degree of immortality upon her dead child.

So, you see, it wasn't Edgar's portrait that Griswold wanted. It was Fanny's. That he obeyed her wishes to hang them side-by-side speaks well for him. As for Mrs. Lewis's contention that in death Griswold was found staring at Edgar and not Fanny, it is pure balderdash. And as for Griswold being in love with Edgar, PLEASE! Pure and unadulterated rubbish, I assure you. He may have had a preference for the intimacy of men over women—as I said I don't know—but if he did, Edgar Poe, above all men, would *not* have been the object of Griswold's affection.

There is something in this that disturbs me greatly, and it is that such a charge leveled against Griswold would quite naturally call into question Edgar's own sexuality. Much has already been made of the fact that he married Virginia when she was a mere slip of a girl—thirteen years old. And much has been made of the fact that his poetry and stories so often describe beautiful, young, dead women. I overheard two men comparing these things once; one of them said: "He must have been something of an odd fish." I was infuriated, stepped between them, and gave them what for. Edgar, for all his passion, was one of the manliest men I ever knew. Believe me, from a woman's perspective, the test of manliness is quite a different thing than a man would guess. Men don't know women one-tenth as well as they think they do.

My point is this, Eddy, were you to write about this or to reveal it to someone else who might write about it, you might well be doing Edgar a grave disservice. Think about it, and I feel certain you will agree. Furthermore, you have nothing more substantial than the word of a woman of dubious reliability and reputation and who was thought to be quite daft.

You seem reluctant to accept the answer I gave you at the very beginning of our correspondence—Fanny Osgood. Did I not say that in my very first letter? Don't you see that by imposing upon Griswold the condition that her portrait—the one he begged of her—must hang forever beside the portrait of Edgar, Fanny was in effect saying that she could never love Griswold as well as she loved Edgar, dead or alive. That must have been a bitter pill for Griswold to swallow, for, regardless of his sexual preference, he loved Fanny and desired to be foremost in her estimation.

I believe the greater story is Fanny's. I have told you things about her that I have never told anyone with the exception of my husband and daughter. I might have told John Ingram had he asked, but I am certain Mrs. Whitman had already forbidden the subject. I have long thought you planned to write a book, and I have cooperated with you for one reason and one reason only—to see justice done to Fanny. The time has come for the world to remember her, and if that means telling the story of Edgar and Fanny, so be it.

Yours,
Mary

6

JANE LOCKE

::

(ITEM 29: *Jane Ermina Starkweather Locke*)
...

June 8th (1878)
Boston

Dear Mr. Gayle,

"Imbroglio!" Is that truly how others perceive my relationship with Edgar Poe? I confess I am dismayed, perhaps a little disheartened, though I cannot say I am surprised. In all probability your information regarding me comes from my husband's cousin, Nancy Richmond. I am aware that she now goes by the name, "Annie." Though we are related by marriage and were neighbors prior to my removal to Boston in 1850, we have not exchanged a dozen words since a certain night thirty years ago this coming October. Such is her bitterness toward me, but be that as it may, I cannot help but feel sorry for her.

For years my motives regarding Edgar have been twisted to the point that the truth has been lost in a sea of distortions and half-truths while the perpetrators of this calumny have been lionized as noble defenders of the much-maligned Mr. Poe. They would have you believe that Griswold's memoir must be thoroughly dismissed as a flagrant prevarication, but I hope you understand that the truth of all matters most often dwells at some mid-point between pros and cons.

Are you aware of the dire need in which Edgar Poe found himself following the death of his wife? He had no money, he was ill, and he had alienated every editor from Philadelphia to Boston. The series of articles he published in *Godey's* in the summer and fall before his wife died was the equivalent of literary suicide—an exposé of New York's most respected writers, so it was labeled by the Boston press. To say the least, it was ill-conceived and poisonous to his future prospects.

He became an outcast, untouchable. I believe, however, that his motive was desperation. He mortgaged his future for the sake of a dying wife.

In the wake of this, few came to his aid. One was N. P. Willis whose column in the *Home Journal* appealed for tributes to the Poes' relief. When I read that, I was so moved by his plight that, without hesitation, I sent money and moral support in the form of a poem that his circumstances inspired. My poem touched his heart, and a warm friendship developed between us. That friendship ended due to circumstances beyond my control and by Edgar's own perverse nature, a trait he possessed that no serious biographer could ignore. Even Edgar, himself, admitted it—read his "Imp of the Perverse" if you have not. All writers write from their own life experiences; I think not doing so must be impossible. "Imp" was a made-up tale, but its source was factual.

I understand that William Gill has a biography of Edgar coming this fall. I know Mr. Gill, and he knows me, but he has not contacted me regarding Edgar. Furthermore I understand that a man in England and one in Baltimore are preparing others. Surely an important inspiration and source of this renewed interest in Edgar's life has been Helen Whitman who has labored for years on Edgar's behalf. I understand that Mrs. Whitman is very near death in Providence, and I am grieved to hear it. She was a guest in my house in Lowell the year Edgar died. As Helen knows of my relationship with Edgar, it grieves me that she has not pointed these biographers in my direction. It is, I feel, impossible to tell the story of the man without consulting all who knew him, friends, enemies, and those who fall in neither camp. I assure you I was a friend, though it seems others disagree.

I would be happy to answer your questions; therefore, as I understand from your letter that you are an officer in the artillery, fire at will!

Yrs truly,

Jane Locke

August (1878)
Boston

Dear Lt. Gayle,

Yes, I knew Griswold. I met him on a couple of occasions, and, need-less to say, every poet in America knew of him at the very least. By reason of his anthologies, he became a very powerful man, and, unlike other anthologists of the day—Caroline May for instance—Griswold's works had the blessings of the Boston clique—the "Frogpondians" as Edgar foolishly called them. If I am not mistaken, Griswold was born in Vermont and lived most of his life in Philadelphia and New York, but he knew Boston well and was tight with James Russell Lowell. Consider the implications of this friendship by understanding that in Boston it is said, "Lowell speaks only to Longfellow, and Longfellow speaks only to God."

Griswold was a secretive man and generally considered by women writers to be a misogynist. This may sound cruel, but such it was. He was polite and gracious enough when it came to the "weaker vessel," but, though he praised our poetry on occasion, he did so disingenu-ously. He spurned our opinions and relegated our work to a decidedly second rank. He was, of course, not the only man to do so, but that does nothing to redeem him in my mind. There were always rumors concerning "Gris" as he was called, having to do with his strange sec-ond marriage and a certain unnatural proclivity regarding his romantic interests. I do not know if there is any truth to this.

I know little more than hearsay about the ill-will that existed be-tween Griswold and Edgar, but it was deep-seated and rooted as far back as their time together in Philadelphia before either moved to New York City. I became curious as a result of your letter, so I decided to reread Griswold's memoir, a thing I have refused to do since its ini-tial publication for a reason which I shall explain later. On reading it again I find that my original opinion has not changed. It is unkind to the point of scandalmongering. Perhaps there are inaccuracies. I can't speak to details, but the general slant is mean-spirited. One sentence alone proves this point: "Poe exhibits scarcely any virtue in either his life or his writings." How could anyone have written such a falsehood?

My cousin by marriage, Frances Locke Osgood, had great influence with Griswold, and knowing the tone he intended to take with Edgar, I think Fanny must have demanded his permission to add her own comments at the end of his memoir. Were it not for her sentiments, the piece would have nothing whatsoever to commend it.

My reason referred to above for refusing to read the memoir again during all these years had to do with the letter Griswold reprinted that I had received from Edgar. Perhaps you noticed it. I am identified only as Mrs. L——of Massachusetts. At the time I thought it odd indeed that Griswold would solicit *me* for material. So many others would have been above me on a list of contributors, but at the time I was flattered and did not know, of course, what his intentions were. Once I read it, of course, I knew precisely. You must realize that it was commonly believed that I hated Edgar for what had transpired between us, and I believe Griswold sought out only those he believed would share his enmity. I am proud to say that my contribution did not play into his hands. The letter reprinted is both kind and thoughtful, and its tone contradicts Griswold's general condemnation, though I imagine this subtlety went unnoticed by the majority of readers.

I did not, in fact, hate Edgar for what transpired between us. I have never hated him. I don't know what you know about us. You may know nothing, so I will spare you an explanation. It is enough to say he hurt me deeply, but in affairs of the heart, such things are a common occurrence. In time I forgave him. Had his life not been cut short, I believe we would have become friends again.

I hope this information helps in your efforts, and, if I may be so bold as to ask, what are those efforts?

Yrs ever, Jane Locke

September 12th (1878)
Boston

Dear Lt. Gayle,

Herewith as per your request is a copy of the collection of my poems, *The Recalled*, published in 1854 in Boston. You asked to see poems I wrote related to Edgar. I would point you to four. Read first "An Invocation for Suffering Genius," the poem I referred to in my first letter, written when I learned from Willis's column in the *Home Journal* of Edgar's distress during the time just prior to the death of his wife. Next read "The True Poet" written in June of 1848 after the exchange of numerous letters through which our friendship had grown considerably closer as you will conclude. Both of these poems were written prior to our first meeting that July.

The other two, "Requiem for Edgar A. Poe" and "Lady and Poet" were both written after Edgar died. Read them and you will see proof-beyond-doubt of my affection for Edgar even after our brief affair. I wrote other poems to him not included in this collection, but these should avail.

Yrs,
Jane Locke

:: IT HAS NOT BEEN EASY BEING JANE LOCKE, and no one knew that better than her late husband, John. Her greatest fear and, consequently, the catalyst for her life's work, has been that she would accomplish nothing of note. Perhaps this fear grew out of a feeling as a child that she had been cut off from her parents, abandoned as it were, and in her hopeless despair, she fantasized herself a great lady, admired and loved for some great accomplishment, she knew not what. She often played at being a dying princess, adored by tearful subjects whose lives would turn to such misery once she was gone that they erected a statue of her, unveiled just before she died so that she could see for herself the depth of their love for her. She even posed as the statue, assuming numerous positions, usually with her left hand propped against the bedpost that served as a fluted stone pillar to give her weakened body support and with the back of her right hand pressed against her forehead, her fingers weak and limp. She posed naked, of course, and imagined small breasts as befit a dying young princess. She suffered exquisitely. After blowing out her candle she rocked back and forth on her bed, not wanting to sleep, but to re-create in her mind the amazing story of her life cut short in the beauty of her youth.

No one understood the degree to which Jane suffered—not her parents, not her sisters and brothers, not her classmates and teachers; indeed, no one in all of Worthington, Massachusetts, where she grew up. They knew only that Jane had special needs—time to herself being first among them. By virtue or by dint of her singularity, Jane learned that she could wield a certain power—her princess-power. She learned that she could have her way, that others would step aside for her, and so she made demands, rebelled as it were. She demanded to go to school even beyond the age when most girls left to marry and start families. She easily bested her classmates. Her teachers called her precocious, which she took to mean precious. It made her feel significant, and her fears were thus alleviated.

Jane was courted by many men, young and not-so-young, all of whom told her she was beautiful, which she was, and at twenty-one she married John Locke because he was handsome and from a prominent family in Lowell and because he thought her unreasonably beautiful and because he had a magnificent name. She hated her own name, Ermina Starkweather. She settled on "Jane," added it on the eve of her wedding day, and insisted that the minister ask, "Do you, Jane..." She had her way and thus became Jane Locke.

Marriage proved heartbreaking at first. Notions of a princess-life evaporated overnight in a grim reality of chores and pregnancy. After four children her body turned to mush, ruining her beauty, so she thought, and her weeks were filled with the mundane exigencies of household life. One late autumn afternoon Jane looked out through the kitchen window at the yellow-brown leaves and prickly balls of the sweet gum in the yard and realized that she was commonplace after all. She cried for days. Her greatest fear had been realized.

Without a thought that she was doing anything to remedy her crushing ordinariness, she poured out her grief onto the blank pages of her commonplace book, and without a thought that such a transfiguration could occur, she found that her grief became poetry. The instant of consciousness that this metamorphosis had occurred was nothing short of a miracle. The same words that had before been so fearful, so fraught with anxiety, so ominous and foreboding, so demeaning and awful were suddenly invigorating and uplifting—the very, *very* same words. With *work* that seemed much too easy and pleasurable to be called by such a name, Jane found that she could transform drudgery to joy, that she could express her inmost self—her greatest fears and desires—creatively. Her princess, precious self thus reborn, she began writing, devoting hours every day to the task, certain that she had found the thing that would give her life significance. It became her passion, and by far the most important thing in her life.

Blessed with a good education, insofar as a girl's education went in those days, and with having excelled in the classroom and with the impetus of an early childhood in which she had striven with all her might to be noticed, Jane found a facility for composition. But also, by virtue of life experience, she respected the magnitude of the challenge and the limitations imposed by her shortcomings. With a voracious appetite she read the great poets, both of her time and of time immemorial. To the exclusion of all else, she read, studied, and wrote, imitating the masters in her own words. Thus inspired she also transformed her world, intent on surrounding herself with beauty to match the beauty flowing through her pen. The Locke's rustic log home on the north bank of the Concord River just north of Lowell was transformed into Wamesit Cottage—a name she liked, inherited from some previous owner—with a rock garden of ferns and peonies and flowering vines climbing at every corner of the house, greensward sloping down to the river kept shorn by a small herd of coddled and groomed black-faced sheep. Jane spared none of John's expense, including a small addition to the house, added beyond the kitchen with a view from one window of the rock garden and from the other, the river—Jane's writing room, a room of her own, entry forbidden to all but her. John went along for the sake of harmony, and here she wrote her letters, kept her journal, composed her poems, and dreamed of her name in *Godey's Ladies Book*, *Graham's Ladies & Gentleman's Magazine*, and *The Home Journal*. To everyone's surprise and amazement, it did not take her long.

Something instinctual told Jane that poems are like capillaries that flood and ebb with emotions borne from the heart. She looked there for inspiration and wrote what she found. Early attempts were awkward and banal and met with rejection. When, at last, one of her poems was accepted and published in the *Lowell Journal & Courier*, John was so undone by its sentiment that he stormed out of his office, mid-morning, and came home to confront his wife, even violating the sanctity of her writing room.

"What is the meaning of this?" or some such was the demand with which he greeted her.

There followed a heated discussion that only ended when the children clamored for their lunch. The debate defined the rest of their lives together. Though Jane doesn't characterize it at all in this way—she won. It turned out to be a repeat of her youthful struggles with siblings and parents, which is not to say that she gained an upper hand. What she gained was a right, and likely it was to John's credit that he granted it, though it is equally likely that, at the time at least, he had no idea just how far that right would be extended. The crux of it was that Jane could be her own person, free to do as she chose (roughly within socially acceptable limits), and free to express herself (in print if she wished) in return for breakfast, lunch, and supper being served at the appropriate hour, the children cared for in the appropriate manner, and John's bedroom needs satisfied with alacrity and without resort to headache. The bargain was struck.

In time Jane achieved a modicum of success. She became a more-or-less regular contributor to several local newspapers in the region, and her poems were often accepted for publication in a half dozen of the lesser New England magazines and literary journals, though there was no pay involved. Remuneration came in the form of having one's name in print, but money is not, nor has it ever been, the object of Jane's pursuit. Nor is fame her objective, or so she reasons. It is, rather, doing something of note, something conspicuous and extraordinary, something that justifies a life. Though often in her mind this distinction is confusedly muddled, outwardly she professes that it is not, and nothing could be truer. What Jane loves—loves above all else, is the act of creation. She doesn't necessarily mean by this, the taking of God-given talents for use in the creation of something to impact in a positive way

the lives of others, though there is doubtless a certain nobility in so doing. What she means precisely—if such can be described *precisely*—is
the process of employing mind, body, soul, and spirit in the creation
of a work of art. This is Creativity with a capital "C." And Jane has
devoted her adult life to it. Furthermore, Jane feels that she can read a
work of literature and determine if the writer is merely a writer or an
artist, the latter being, more precisely, a Creator. It is there, somewhere
in the work, gleaned by intuition and difficult, if not impossible, to
pinpoint, but *it is there*. How she learned to perceive it, she has not
the foggiest idea, but she will invite you to show her a poem, and she
can tell you with certainty whether the author is a writer or a Creator.

The first poem she ever read by Edgar Poe was "The Raven." She
knew of him. Jane had been a longtime subscriber to *Graham's* when
he was editor of that magazine. She had read many of his tales which
were often published while he was employed there before he left and
Griswold took his place. She had never submitted a poem to *Graham's*
when Edgar had the chair, though she did later with occasional success. Griswold had admired her work, or so he said, and he had been
kind enough to include her in his anthology of female poets, though
so many were included—more than one hundred—more names that
were unfamiliar than familiar to Jane—that her inclusion had seemed
nothing of particular note. On the contrary, had she been left out, she
would have been mortified. But, regarding Edgar Poe, what little she
knew led her to believe that he was a writer of tales, not a poet.

"The Raven" was so incredible as to seem seminal to Jane's thinking. Here, without doubt, was a Creator. Poetry had a new standard.
Wanting more, she took a subscription to the *New York Mirror*, and
followed his long series of reviews of Longfellow's poetry with fascination. How could anyone so thoroughly dismiss Longfellow? It seemed
sacrilege. But "The Raven" gave Edgar authority, and Jane hung on
every word he wrote. His mastery of the art of poetry was astonishing;
his knowledge of the complexities and intricacies of construction, un-
paralleled. His amazing recall not only exposed plagiarists, it reduced
them to the level of common criminals; it gave irrefutable evidence of
his superior education and vast knowledge. His uncanny ability to discern infinitesimal flaws was remarkable. Jane decided that Edgar Poe
was unquestionably the English language authority on versification.

How she missed finding out that Poe left the *Mirror* to start the *Broadway Journal*, she attributes to the fact that at the time she was not attuned to happenings in New York City. The focus of her attention in matters literary had always been Boston; she thought of herself as a New England poet and of Boston as the epicenter of what mattered in America in the arena of things poetic. Had she known, needless to say, she would have taken a subscription at once, but she did not know until after the *Broadway Journal* had become defunct. Therefore she missed the exchange of poems between Edgar and her cousin by marriage, Fanny Osgood. Jane was beyond earshot of the rumors that arose regarding their "affair of the plume." Despite the familial connection, she hardly knew Fanny. What she ultimately learned, she learned from Helen Whitman and never suspected for a minute that what Helen told her had been sanitized. It made no matter. On the contrary, it made matters somewhat more bearable later on, if that can be believed.

It was in December of 1846 when she read N. P. Willis's card in the *Home Journal* relating the Poes' desperate situation and calling for tributes for their relief. Shocked and distraught by the news, Jane latched the door to her writing room and immediately began composing a poem. From a short sketch of Edgar's life that included a likeness of him published in *Graham's* two years earlier, just after "The Raven" appeared, Jane had some knowledge of his background and physical appearance. She thought him handsome and knew his approximate age—a few years younger than was she. All of this had served to enhance her admiration, but learning now of his poverty and the deathly illness of his wife, admiration turned to empathy and empathy to profound affection. It seemed to her that they shared something kindred, something just beyond Jane's grasp but that related to her own deeply rooted fear of losing the ability to achieve self-justification. In fact his past successes and present poverty served to enliven her fears. She could feel the fingers of fear wrap themselves around her esophagus such that she could not breathe. She loosened their grip the only way she knew how and did not stop writing until sunup when she decided her poem was finished and as polished as her abilities allowed. Even so, her insecurities rose up out of knowing her lines would be read by *him*—the world's most exacting critic whose "tomahawking" reviews had become legendary. "An Invocation for Suffering Genius," as she titled her poem, was long—ten, rhyming four-line stanzas. It was a plea to "Charity." It placed Edgar next to "Royalty." The following morning she posted it to him in care of Willis at the *Home Journal*, enclosing a twenty-dollar bill and a brief covering note that included her name and address.

Though there was no immediate response, Willis published a letter he received from Edgar in the *Home Journal* in mid-January in which he thanked Willis for forwarding "the beautiful lines by Mrs.——and those by Mrs.——, &c." Jane presumed that she was one of the Mrs. Still, she would have liked a personal letter, but none came. Then in early February she read of Virginia Poe's death in the same magazine, and, though she was moved to write again, she hesitated.

Another month passed.

When a letter finally came, it was apologetic and disappointing at first, but in the penultimate paragraph, to her delight, came evidence of Edgar's familiarity and appreciation for her work—not just for the poem she had sent in care of Willis, but for her work in general. She hadn't supposed that Edgar would have been familiar with her work, but now that she considered it, knowing how well-read the man was, why should she be surprised. He said of her poems that they "evinced a fervid and generous spirit." While this could not be construed as high praise for command of craft, it at least demonstrated an appreciation and familiarity, and, after all, Edgar was not likely to include a review in a letter of thanks. He said, further, that his delay in responding was due to utter incapacity in the aftermath of his recent "sorrow"— without naming his wife's death—and ended by calling her "dear Mrs. Locke" and saying that he was "already ceasing to regard those difficulties as misfortune" by virtue of this correspondence. Jane could not be certain precisely what difficulties he referred to; the reference was vague—surely not his wife's recent death—more likely he was referring to his own utter incapacity in the wake of his wife's death.

Jane wrote back immediately, detailing every emotion she had felt for all his suffering, confessing her great admiration for his work as a poet, storyteller, and critic, and digressing into the area of her own private philosophy regarding artistic creation. She even quoted one of his reviews, agreeing totally with the quote selected, the gist of which was that the sole duty of a poem was to express beauty. Moreover, she also boldly confessed that, on occasion, she was so overcome by beauty that she suffered brief periods of fatigue and emotional paralysis resulting from having indulged erotic daydreams of an imaginative lover as appreciative as she of beauty and the beauty of creation. Her letter ran to six pages, and she purposefully omitted any details about herself other than what is here described.

Again she waited for a response for what seemed like forever. Arriving mid-summer, it was brief and apologetic, citing the press of illness and "niggling, trivial concerns" which Jane took to mean money. He did not reference the bold confession of her letter of mid-March—perhaps he had misplaced it. Nevertheless, near the end, he begged her to write again soon, a clear indication of interest and assured her that the content of her letter had not been forgotten. Furthermore, he closed "With deepest devotion & affection, *Edgar*"—not "E. A. Poe" as he had signed his earlier letter to her or "Edgar A. Poe" as he had signed the letter Willis reprinted in the *Home Journal*—the only two of Edgar's letters Jane had ever seen.

Sitting at her writing table in her writing room, Jane raised her eyes to the northern window, searching for the breeze that she could see blowing the ferns in the rock garden. She was perspiring and wondered if it was the heat or the swelling in her chest that inevitably came when she thought of her ideal lover—*that man*—for years amorphous in her imagination—now aggregated into the face, form, and mind of Edgar Poe. She was certain she loved him.

She wrote again, sending more money and promising undying affection and a gift of creation in the very near future, and with this posted, she went to work on another poem, a poem that would reveal everything. It would be, she resolved, her greatest poem ever.

Jane worked on it night and day for a month. When finished it stretched to thirty-one four-line stanzas—her longest ever—and it laid bare the emotions that had before been veiled.

> Then *deep, deep* down within my *wondering* heart,
> There woke a *thought*—a *dream*—a picture e'en,—
> *Like to that figure*, drawn in *youth*, apart,
> *My soul's ideal had my clear eye seen!*

I felt his clasp, as lip to lip he pressed,
Listened, beguiled as to an angel's tone,
To his impassioned words;—then sank to rest
In trance divine my heart upon his own!

Jane entitled her poem, "Ermina's Tale." With respect to Edgar, she
was not Jane Locke. She posted it in late August, accompanied only
with a brief note, emphasizing that the sentiments of the poem were
hers and unmistakable, promising that anything he said in response
was theirs for safekeeping, and asking that he acknowledge receipt *immediately*. Since Edgar's previous responses had been slow in coming,
Jane knew she would not be able to wait a month or longer for a reply.
She would go mad if she had to wait so long. Her fingers trembled as
she posted it; she would be on tenterhooks until his reply came.

Still she waited. When a letter finally came in mid-October, its
greeting plunged her to deepest depths—"My dear lady," it began. But
its tone was appreciative and congratulatory, and Jane decided that
the greeting indicated he had become uncertain as to how to address
her—"Jane" or "Ermina." He praised her poem, urged her to seek publication of it "in one of the better magazines," but there was something
lacking in his response that portended uncertainty and caution on his
part. Or was there someone else in his life? Had he already found a
new love? Jane still knew nothing of the rumors that had circulated
in New York City two years earlier regarding Edgar and Fanny; otherwise, she might have suspected her own relative of winning his heart,
thus preempting her. As it was, she could not guess why he had failed
to respond in a more definite manner, moving toward her if interested
or away if not. What must she do to elicit a declaration?

During the ensuing winter and spring letters were exchanged. A
few. Far too few to Jane's way of thinking, but he refused to hurry his
responses, making it awkward for her to do so. Not only this, the relationship took a giant step backward. In December he wrote of budding
friendship, and, horrified suddenly, Jane realized that she had moved
too quickly to profess her heart-felt feelings. Perhaps, she reasoned
now, "Ermina's Tale" arrived while he was still grieving for his wife.
After all, she had only been dead six months.

Though discouraged, she could not give up. With measured discretion, she encouraged him as if they were beginning again, feeling now that she had thrown herself shamelessly at him with "Ermina's Tale." What must he have thought? His responses grew ever more interested but also curious. In May he wrote a long letter addressed to "My Dear Friend," apparently still uncertain as to her given name, presumably because she had been reluctant to commit herself to one. The letter was long due mainly to Edgar's tiptoeing around his questions pertaining to his "sweet, dear friend," as he called her. "Tell me only of the ties," he asked, "—if any exist—that bind you to the world:—and yet I perceive that I may have done very wrong in asking you this:—now that I have asked it, it seems to me the maddest of questions, involving, possibly, the most visionary of hopes?"

How Jane's spirits soared reading these last words—"*the most visionary of hopes.*" The two of them were so alike. She was certain of this. The similarities of their temperaments seemed everywhere evident, most notably in his poems—the search for an ideal love. She had purposefully deflected his questions about her "ties," reasoning that they would discourage him prematurely, and she was certain that a meeting between the two of them would render all ties immaterial anyway. As Jane saw it, their similarities of disposition, their love of poetry and concomitant appreciation of beauty, and their shared passion for creating art through inner experience would render all other ties to the world of little consequence. She had no plan as to where it would go from there, such matters as that could not have been less important to her. She had found her ideal love and the devil with the consequences.

The time had come to meet, and for that, Jane had a plan, one she had mulled and shaped for months. She would arrange for Edgar to deliver a lecture in Lowell, using her influence to gain sponsorship by the *Journal & Courier*. Lowell had an appropriate lecture hall, Wentworth's Hall, that would easily accommodate two hundred at a ticket price of fifty cents a head. She reasoned that Edgar would certainly come if guaranteed a fee of fifty dollars, and she reasoned that by her efforts alone she could fill one hundred seats. She had even made a list of those she would approach. Putting her plan into action, she had little difficulty making the arrangements, and before the end of May, she wrote to ask if she might pay a call on Edgar at Fordham for the purpose of introductions and to make a proposal that she felt certain would be of interest. She named the date, and, not waiting for a response, took the train into New York, spent the night at the Astor House, and the following morning took the train out to Fordham.

Jane was not accustomed to traveling by herself, but her plan precluded John traveling with her. He had questioned her need for traveling without escort, but Jane was insistent. She could not take John along. There were too many things about her "ties to the world" that she feared Edgar would find off-putting. She could not spring them on him all at once. She had good reason to go—to arrange for his lecture—and if they found each other agreeable both in terms of the proposed engagement and to each other personally, then other "ties" would later prove less of an impediment to the relationship Jane envisioned. Just what that relationship might be remained vague in her mind. Though, if she must, she would agree to something in a platonic vein, Jane longed for passion.

At Fordham the station manager found a boy who, for a nickel, led Jane to the Poe cottage. The day was ideal for a walk through the woods, following behind the boy who seemed eager for her to hurry so he could go spend his nickel on licorice or candy, she supposed. She refused to hurry, wanting to savor the experience, knowing she would remember it all her life, the anticipation building with every step. When they emerged from the woods into pasture, the Poe cottage was seen up ahead, humble but quaint. A heavyset woman stood on the porch, beating with a broom a throw rug draped over the porch rail. She saw the visitors approaching and called to someone inside, and with this the boy turned, pointed, and was gone. Jane approached, bidding Mrs. Clemm a good morning.

Edgar appeared just as Jane reached the steps. "Mrs. Locke, I presume. Won't you come in?"

"Mr. Poe. At long, long last!" She smiled up at him, thrilled by his calling her name. "So *this* is the *raven's lair*," she said—words she had carefully planned and rehearsed.

He ushered her into the house, introduced her to his mother-in-law, and led her to a chair in the parlor. Just as Mrs. Clemm was about to excuse herself to brew tea, Jane presented her with a small basket she had brought containing wrapped packages of cold beef, cheese, and bread, enough for their lunch with ample left over for the Poes' supper.

The two of them sat and smiled at each other for an instant. "I have looked forward to this day," she said, feeling confident, feeling beautiful.

"As have I," he said, seeming pleased with her appearance, or so Jane thought. She was pleased with his. He was in shirt sleeves, no vest. He explained that he'd been working, proofreading an original work of scientific detail that necessitated absolute perfection lest it should prove an embarrassment to him. He was self-conscious, timid, quite thin but otherwise hale and cheerful. He was even handsomer than she had imagined and more personable and approachable in a way that almost surprised her. It was going well.

She laid out her plan for the lecture. The date set was July 10, and she handed Edgar a letter from the editor of the *Lowell Journal & Courier* that outlined their proposal and the terms. Depending on the number of seats sold, he could make as much as fifty dollars, but in no case less than thirty. He studied it, seeming to be less enthusiastic than Jane had hoped. For a brief instant she worried that he might refuse or, at the least, make a counteroffer, something she hadn't counted on, but he carefully folded the letter and returned it to the envelope and nodded his head, indicating his agreement.

Jane's smile revealed her relief and thrill. She asked what he proposed as the subject of the lecture and pleaded with him to recite "The Raven" whatever the subject. At any rate, she explained, she must return to Lowell knowing the title in order for the newspaper to prepare appropriate copy for their advertisements. Edgar named it: "The Poets and Poetry of America." And he agreed to her request regarding "The Raven." Their business concluded, Jane started in on her questions, having saved them up for more than year, just for this occasion. Her questions were exclusively of a literary nature, and they spent the afternoon discussing many works and poets. He surprised her, both by those of whom he spoke well and those he censured. He spoke well of Longfellow's "Evangeline"; he criticized Lowell and Elizabeth Barrett Browning, and he confessed to Jane that reviews of the poetry of women were not worth the effort of reading—that no critic, man or woman, had the nerve to treat honestly the fairer sex. Jane shrank from asking him about her own poetry, and he refrained from volunteering.

At two Mrs. Clemm served lunch and immediately thereafter, Edgar escorted Jane back to the train station. Before leaving the Poe cottage, however, she slipped unnoticed an envelope beneath papers on Edgar's desk. Inside were a twenty dollar gold piece and a poem she had finished and written out in her hotel just the night before. Entitled "The True Poet," it was both encouraging and reverential: "And when thou thy work hast done / Earth shall feel thy presence gone."

At the station, as Jane stepped up into the car and turned to wave goodbye, she felt—by the urgent look in his eyes—that he was much taken with her. Their first meeting might even have surpassed her hopes. But on the trip back into the city, she reminded herself that he was still uncertain of her age, that he still did not know there was a Mr. Locke and assorted Locke children. One hurdle at a time, she reminded herself. One hurdle at a time.

Has it been said that at this time Jane was forty-two? She had given birth to five children, all living, who now ranged in age from eleven to eighteen—three girls and two boys about whom little has been said. Jane adored her children and considered herself a good mother. They were healthy, well-adjusted, and receiving good educations. As they were growing up, she put her highest priority on reading to them or seeing to it that they read themselves once they outgrew her lap. She encouraged their imaginations and fantasies, playfully enjoying her own role in them when invited in. As a result her children excelled; they were bright, confident, and precocious just as Jane had been. And like Jane also, they were exceedingly tolerant—shall she say, liberal, in their thinking. This tendency ran somewhat counter to John's strict New England conservatism, but as in most middle-class New England households, care of the children was the responsibility of the mother. In the Locke's case, the difference was that few New England mothers possessed Jane's independent spirit, or, at least, few prevailed to the degree that she did.

Considering these things plus Jane's modest success as a poet, it is not surprising that outwardly, she appeared to possess a full quotient of confidence. She could hold her own in conversation with any man, and she was still a handsome woman despite her forty-two years. Though she had given birth to five children and witnessed for herself the effects of childbirth on her body over time, she had kept thin and when tightly trussed, her youthful figure was restored. But Jane's inmost self struggled with insecurity and cried out for rescue before it was too late, before others realized that she was not really a princess, that she was merely a poser. They would abandon her then, robbing her of the justification she had worked so hard to achieve.

It was for this reason, therefore, that she both eagerly and nervously anticipated Edgar's visit to Lowell. She had no illusions that he would be a rescuer in the sense of saving her from a dire situation. It was *his* situation that was dire, not hers, and in this respect, she thought he might even view *her* as a rescuer. What she hoped for was not a rescuer in the traditional sense, but a rescuer in the Romantic sense—a soul mate. That is all Jane wanted. It was something she had never had. It was her soul's ideal.

She anticipated his dismay, and it was there, in his eyes, when he stepped down from the train car. After greeting him, she turned to the man standing beside her and introduced John Locke. They shook hands, and John insisted on carrying Edgar's valise. His dismay became even more apparent when the carriage wheeled up to Wamesit cottage, and her sons and daughters emerged onto the porch.

Needless to say, John Locke knew nothing of the content of Jane and Edgar's correspondence, nor was he aware of even the existence of "Ermina's Tale," but, of course, Edgar did not know this, and his discomfort was apparent. Jane had planned everything down to the minute and had given strict instructions. John was to take Edgar's valise up to the guest room and supervise the children while Jane walked Edgar down to the river, ostensibly for a tour of the Wamesit cottage grounds and a view of the river. This began without a hitch. At the river, Jane and Edgar turned to look back toward the cottage, and, assured that no one had followed, Jane delivered a little speech she had rehearsed for months.

"You are surprised, Edgar," she began. "I can see it in your eyes. And, of course, I expected it. You mustn't be unsettled by what you have found here. As I told you in one of my letters, our correspondence is kept safe." There Jane paused and turned back toward the river just as she had planned. Emotions rose inside her as she knew they would. She took a deep breath. "I am a poet, Edgar. Poetry is my life's work and my life." There she turned back to him, rubbing her hands together to allay the tension she felt, and looked him squarely in the eyes. "You can't imagine what it's like to be a poet in a place like Lowell. I'm not being critical. It is a fine town; I have a fine life as you can see. I have a fine family. But, as I think you understand, a true poet dwells apart—at the margin, so to speak—looking in. Not by choice, but by *no* choice. Despite all you see, understand that for all intents and purposes, I exist alone."

Jane had practiced her speech out loud, even coming to this point of greensward, the point farthest from the house where the river made a slight turn in its course from south to east. She had imagined what would come next, even thinking of words he might say in response, always words of understanding, but she had not rehearsed further, thinking it best to let things take their course. But Edgar's discomfort remained. He seemed not to know what to say, and Jane felt compelled to beat a retreat. She suggested that perhaps they go in and dress for the lecture and that they could talk more about these things later. He agreed; Jane feared he agreed too readily, but as they walked back to the house, she comforted herself with the knowledge that the lecture was sold out and that Edgar would be pleased. Perhaps his discomfort was nothing more than nervousness, and she chided herself for not having anticipated this. She should have saved her speech for later, after the lecture, beneath a starlit sky. That would have been much the better.

The lecture went well. Wentworth's Hall was filled to capacity with at least thirty persons occupying standing-room at the back. But twenty minutes into the lecture, Jane's attention wandered. Worrying for him, she became attuned to telltale noises in the crowd, but thankfully just then he began reciting, and the murmurs died. When he began "The Raven," Jane could not contain a smile. Its magnificence shushed the crowd. She knew the event was a ten-strike before he ever got to the second verse.

The eruption of applause served to reinvigorate her confidence. As she herself applauded, watching Edgar's polite and nonplused acknowledgment to the crowd, she hoped he remembered what she had said beside the river but feared he had not heard a word. But how could he in his nervous state? How stupid of her not to realize that he would be otherwise preoccupied. At the prospect of such an event, she would, herself, have been distracted beyond reason, and was he not like her in that regard? She smiled up at him, wishing he would catch her eye and return the favor. After all, this was her doing.

Instinct told Jane to hang back. Let others rush forward with their congratulations. Let Edgar bask in the spotlight for a time. Her compensation would come. His appreciation would be fullest after being satiated by well-wishing. That she did, enjoying the scene until she noticed relatives she had intended to introduce rushing forward. Among them was her cousin, Nancy Richmond, whose youth and beauty unnerved Jane suddenly. On impulse she rushed to intervene, hastily making introductions, conscious that by so doing she might have seemed, in a way, condescending. It was a momentary loss of control, and she cursed herself even as she introduced Nancy. It was somehow graceless on her part, and she sensed the impropriety was not lost on Edgar. Jane turned to look at him just then, and his expression was pained. He explained that Nancy's brother had invited him to their home for a late supper and that he had gladly accepted the invitation in light of the Richmonds being Jane's cousins.

"But of course," Jane said. "How kind of them to invite you." Here she paused, swelling to her full height. "Then we shall see you 'on the morrow' as they say? Enjoy."

And with this Jane turned away. What else could she do? She looked for John in the crowd. He was loitering near the exit. And her children, all five of whom she had pressed into service for this occasion and for what reason, she wondered now? Where were they? She would corral them, rush them home and to bed. Jane craved darkness just then. She would not sleep, of course, but darkness would bathe her.

Morning came. Edgar did not come down from his room until nearly noon. Jane had planned a repeat of their conversation of the previous afternoon, but he declined her invitation to walk. Instead, he declared the need to go into Lowell to seek out potential prospects for serving as a local agent in lining up subscribers for a literary journal he hoped to found later in the fall, by year-end at the latest, he explained. Jane was hurt that he did not consider her for the position, but he apparently did not, and he stayed gone all afternoon. The next morning he was up and gone early, again on an errand of business, and did not return until time to catch his train back to New York. Both evenings since the night of his lecture had been spent in the company of Jane's relatives, the Richmonds, and Edgar left Lowell having spoken not a word to Jane in confidence.

For days after his visit Jane sat at her desk in her writing room, staring out the window. What had gone wrong? Was it Edgar's realization that she was four years older than he, that she had a husband and five children. Yes, she supposed, that must be it, but in alternate moods she was equally convinced that it had been something else, something to do with Nancy Richmond. Lowell was too small a town and Nancy's brother too boastful a talker for word not to have spread of Edgar's several visits to the Richmond house on Ames Street. Nancy was still young and beautiful, and Jane now felt intense jealousy for her husband's cousin. But despite her beauty, how could Nancy Richmond hold any sustainable attraction for a mind like Edgar's? Was she even literate? Jane dismissed the possibility and wrote Edgar a long letter in which she repeated the anguished confession she'd made on the bank of the Concord River that first afternoon—"Not by choice, but by *no* choice, I exist *alone.*"

August and September came and went with no response. One late September night Jane stood by herself on her porch, one arm wrapped around the post supporting the porch roof and staring into puddling plashes of steady rain. She felt abject hopelessness; life seemed over. For years she had dreamed of an ideal love, certain that he would come and equally certain now that Edgar was that love. And were they not ideally matched?

In the days that followed panic set in, brought on by Jane's rising anger for having wasted years in what now appeared to be a futile search. She felt she had to take some action— any action—or she would surely go mad. She determined to arrange another lecture, suspecting that only the promise of money could bring Edgar back to Lowell and certain that given time, he would come to understand. She was ready to leave John. As her children were nearly grown, she was even ready to leave them too in order to move to Fordham. She didn't know how they'd live except for a sense, or perhaps merely a hope, that John would not be ungenerous. She and Edgar would manage somehow, but so idyllic did a life with him seem, she couldn't imagine they would need much. She would care for him, cure his intemperance, and provide him with the freedom and peace of mind to write. That alone could sustain them, since Jane could take care of all the bothersome details that took him away from Creation. Yes, it would work.

He arrived on the 20th of October for a lecture to be delivered that night entitled "The Poetic Principal," and once again "The Raven" was promised. Edgar's sold-out and standing-room-only performance the previous July made it easy for Jane to arrange for a repeat on very similar terms. Again he settled in at Wamesit cottage, welcomed by the Locke family. He seemed quite cheerful and happy to be back, and Jane's hopes rose. She kept herself calm, reserved even. There was no need to press her feelings; they had been made clear. Jane could only trust in matters to advance along the lines of her fantasy. Oddly, she found herself prepared for any outcome.

Immediately upon arriving at Wentworth's Hall, Jane realized that the house would be disappointing. As they entered the hall, the editor of the *Journal & Courier* who had again underwritten the lecture whispered to Jane something about a rally being held that same night by the supporters of Zachary Taylor's run for the presidency. It had been hastily scheduled; he had not known. The seats were far less than half-filled. Edgar's delivery was pained; he seemed embarrassed by the paucity of attendees. He concluded rather abruptly, and his recitation of "The Raven"—the only poem he recited—was hurried and without the anticipated effect.

Jane rushed to him as soon as it ended, thinking to congratulate him and to explain and apologize for the small crowd. He was not to be mollified, and his anger was obviously aimed at her, but all he said to her was that he planned to spend the evening at the Richmond's. Shocked, Jane could not resist turning to see Nancy Richmond as if expecting to discover from the look on her face something prearranged. It was there, in her eyes, that and a look of alarm. Jane's resentment toward Nancy had caused her to avoid the Richmonds since Edgar's visit in July, and now she gathered that there must have been some intervening correspondence between the two of them. Was it Nancy or her brother who had corresponded? And did that explain Edgar's cheerfulness earlier? It must have been Nancy, and Jane could not resist lashing out. Turning back to Edgar, she said, "The Richmonds are not like us, Edgar." She meant by this that they were not of a literary bent, but the words came out wrong. He stiffened perceptibly; his eyes flashed, and he asked what she meant by that, then gave her no time to speak.

"I will accept that from no one, least of all—*You*! You deceived me. I don't believe a word you say, and I'll not spend another night beneath your roof."

Though he waited for a response from her, Jane could not speak. It occurred to her that he had not listened to a word she had said. In all her letters and poems in which she had poured out her heart, he had not heard a single word. She turned and left the hall. She found herself out on the road, prepared to walk home if necessary. She had to get away. Her children caught up with her before she had gone far. John had gone to get the carriage and soon arrived. Not one of them asked what had happened. They sensed something dreadful and knew better.

When they arrived back at Wamesit cottage, Jane sent her oldest child, her son John, up to pack Edgar's trunk for him with further instructions that he should bring it down and set it on the porch, and with this said, Jane locked herself into her writing room and remained there, sitting in the dark for what must have been hours. She lost track of time. In those hours she tried to beat down the envy and resentment that overwhelmed her. Her sense of rejection was crushing but not so crushing as a feeling that rose from deep inside, a feeling of total and utter obscurity.

On her way up to bed just at daybreak, she looked out the front window onto the porch to see that Edgar's trunk was gone.

For a time Jane abandoned poetry. The whole idea of writing made her nauseous. Her family sensed something dreadful had happened, and they tiptoed around her all through the Christmas holidays. John seemed to realize in his wife's despair that there was more to it than merely a matter literary, but he said nothing, evinced sympathetic understanding, and in her domestic efforts during the holidays, he seemed happy to have his wife back. His cheeriness gave her some comfort even.

In January Jane learned that Edgar was engaged to Helen Whitman and that he had been courting her for some months. Jane did not know Helen, but she knew of her. She not only wondered why he had said nothing about it, she decided it was deceptive on his part—certainly more deceptive than anything for which she could be accused—and she felt bitterness toward him. Then she heard rumors that he had returned to Lowell in December to visit the Richmonds and that his marriage to Helen had been called off. There was gossip having to do with his intemperance again and that such had been the cause of the breakup with Helen. This gave rise to perceiving Edgar in a somewhat different light. Had she judged him fairly or had she elevated him unreasonably? Questions persisted, and as the winter and spring passed, Jane realized that she still had not let go, that she could not let go. She replayed over and over in her mind her afternoon spent with him at Fordham and the fantasies she had entertained about a life with him there. Perhaps, she thought, his commitment to Mrs. Whitman had precluded his entertaining thoughts of loving her. Could it be simply that her timing had been bad?

She could not lure him with another lecture, of course. Another idea had come as a result of writing again. Not poetry; she was in no way inspired to write poems. But during March and early April she returned to her journal, seeking to find there relief from her grief by recording events. She found in her responses to those events, as she had in earlier years, relief from the cares of early married life. Jane decided to write a novel, a romance, based on her affair with Edgar. She had never written prose and was suddenly reinvigorated by the notion.

Conscious that the project could be perceived as assuaging her sense of hurt and ill-treatment, she resolved that it would not be a yellow novel. Such a thing was beneath her. This brought to mind Edgar's series of articles in *Graham's* two years earlier when the featured New York writers were so undone and offended. Now, thinking about that series, she took a certain license from it, but such feelings smacked too much of revenge, so she conceived of something more noble, a true romantic novel. She would have to change their names and certain other details and, of course, adopt a pen name, and she gave considerable thought to what this should be, trying on many different names to see what fit.

She wrote. The words flowed fast and with facility. Jane decided she had a knack for the genre and imagined a major turning point in her writing career. It seemed to her that by virtue of long years of poetic discipline, she had a greater appreciation for words than the popular novelists of the day—most of who were hacks anyway—the genre having been of rather ill-repute. But Dickens and Hawthorn had brought it respectability, and Jane felt confident that she could excel. Then it occurred to her that Edgar might even collaborate. Somehow it didn't seem too farfetched a notion, so she wrote to him, laying out her plan and suggesting that she would gladly come to Fordham to discuss the project with him. Her reservations, however, motivated her to add at the end of her letter that if she didn't hear from him, she would proceed with publication on her own. She had not heard from him by the end of April when the project died for want of resolution.

In early May, Jane heard gossip that Edgar was coming to Lowell to visit the Richmonds again. It seemed to her now that he had adopted the Richmonds as a sort of second family. The news came through Nancy Richmond's brother, Bardwell Heywood, who had secured a position in Lowell and recently moved there. Bardwell was quite proud of his celebrity friend and enjoyed bruiting it about town as if to elevate his own importance. The intelligence served to renew Jane's deep sense of hurt of the previous October, and on impulse she wrote to Helen Whitman, inviting her to spend a week at Wamesit cottage, promising to tell things that could not be revealed in a letter. At first Mrs. Whitman politely refused, but when pressed and informed of the possibility that Edgar might also be in Lowell at the same time, she changed her mind and came, arriving near the end of the month. Edgar had not appeared, but was expected.

Jane and Helen Whitman were almost exactly the same age. There were similarities in their growing up years—Jane had felt alienated by her parents and Helen's family had been abandoned by her father—and they were both poets of some note; although, Helen Whitman was much more widely known and respected. They got on well at first, Jane being careful in the first few days of Helen's visit to avoid the subject of Edgar altogether, but inevitably it came up and with it the atmosphere became exceedingly tense. It quickly became apparent that both women held closely guarded secrets and mutual suspicions. Jane sensed Helen still held deep feelings of affection for Edgar, and, since she did also, she realized they were rivals, equally anticipating his arrival. The tension became untenable, and one morning Helen declared that she *had* to return to Providence, but for reasons Jane can hardly explain, she begged Helen to stay. She wonders now if she sought to foil what she perceived as a budding romance between Edgar and Nancy Richmond whom she learned that Edgar had come to address by a pet name, "Annie." Or did she think that the presence of a triangle of lovers would so embarrass Edgar as to put him in his place, repay him for his shabby treatment of both her *and* Helen Whitman. She can't say. When, two days later, Edgar had still not arrived, Helen left on the train, and just as her train left the station, Edgar's arrived. Jane learned this by the arrival at the train station of Bardwell Heywood, so she hurried away, her heart pounding as if it would burst through her rib cage.

In this way Jane missed Edgar by a matter of minutes. Had she seen him, it would have been the last time, and she almost regrets now that she did not. As it was, her last vision of Edgar Poe was the anger with which he shunned her after his lecture the previous October.

As she looks back, the idea of a romantic novel and her invitation to Helen Whitman to visit Lowell were foolish and desperate attempts on her part to salvage some degree of dignity and grace in her relationship with Edgar. But the vantage of thirty years has made her see how ill-conceived these things were. She admits that at the time she felt as if she was fighting for her very existence.

Jane learned of Edgar's death by a brief note from Nancy Richmond, written and hand-delivered the same morning—the 8th of October, almost one year to the day after Jane last saw him. The note said only that Nancy had learned just that morning that Edgar had died the day before in Baltimore following a brief illness and that she knew Jane would want to know. The note was a kindness that Jane never forgot, though she and Nancy have seen almost nothing of each other since—an occasional funeral or wedding, and then only to nod polite recognition or greet each other with as few words as possible. Jane doesn't want to know more.

Isn't it all so odd?

Jane Locke has not written a poem in over thirty years. She wrote her last one in 1857. When asked why, she says with disarming honesty, that she got them all out, that there were none left to write. What's more she gave up writing altogether. But not creativity. For the last thirty years, she has painted clouds. She laughs telling how this came about as if a pursuit of thirty years is nothing about which to brag. She is modest regarding her skill as an artist, but her canvasses are quite good. It seems that when her family moved from Lowell to Boston in 1850, Jane so missed country life that on walks in the city she inevitably found herself looking up at the sky, and she became fascinated by the ever-changing nature of clouds. At first she wrote about them then realized that she could not capture them with words. She had never painted in her life, and her early efforts were as crude and childlike as her early poems. But in time and with lessons she acquired some skill, though it was not in perfecting the craft that she found pleasure so much as it was the process of creating. Now, in her late seventies, living comfortably with her grandson and his family, free of chores except for reading to her great-grandchildren, which is no chore at all, she still paints almost every day.

She will add that—also in time—she entirely forgave Edgar, having come to a greater understanding about the character of the man. This is in no way saying that Jane agreed with Wilmot Griswold's characterization. She does not at all. How can she say what she means? Edgar had special needs, but such in no way can be subtracted from his genius.

She is well aware of efforts made by others who knew Edgar to correct the twisted imprint Griswold was apparently so determined to make. For what reason was Griswold so possessed with vitriol, she cannot imagine. She admits to hurt feelings that she, too, was not enlisted into the mainstream of this effort to redeem Edgar's character. She would have been eager and willing to do so. She would have thought that two of the poems she wrote and that were included in her book, *The Recalled*, would have qualified her for inclusion, but she suspects that her last one might have seemed self-serving to his other friends. She didn't mean it that way at all, she explains, as she puts on her glasses to read. Yes, she *did* put the word "forgive" in Edgar's mouth, but she also believes that the poem expresses her own forgiveness as well.

> A poet in dread
> Pressed his dying bed—
> Afar 'neath a southern sun,—
> Yet a missive he sent,
> Ere his life's day was spent,

To an early worshiped one.
'It haunteth me e'er,
O, Lady fair'—
('Twas thus that the missive ran,)
'That a wrong I spoke, a vow I broke,
Mournful the past I scan.
'My words pure were they,
And my heart true as day,—
('Twas thus that the missive ran,)
'But a demon awoke,
And a wrong I spoke,
Thus pining my life fills its span.
'They fall as 'tis meet,
Tears—tears on the sheet—
(So the words of the missive ran,)
'That with beckoning hand
Now to thee I send—
Forgive, gentle one, if you can.'

Boston Evening Transcript

Friday, May 14, 1879

~ OBITUARY ~ Jane Ermina Starkweather, noted poet and wife of the late John Goodwin Locke of Lowell, Mass. and this city, yesterday, late PM. A native of Worthington, Mass., Mrs. Locke was widely published in the literary journals and newspapers of this region. She authored *The Recalled*, a collection of poems published by James Munroe & Company in 1854. Mrs. Locke is survived by a daughter, Grace Le Baron Upham of this city, fourteen grandchildren, and eleven great grandchildren.

7

ANNIE RICHMOND

::

(ITEM 39: *Nancy Locke Heywood Richmond*)
...

P. Office Box № 84
Lowell, Mass.
Aug. 22 / '78

Dear Sir,

Please believe me when I say that I cannot help you. I was not one of Mr. Poe's literary friends & never personally knew any of them excepting Mrs. Locke & Mrs. Osgood who were cousins by marriage and Mrs. Sylvanus Lewis who visited me briefly at the request of Mr. Poe. The late Mrs. Whitman came to Lowell to lecture in 1849, but I was unable to attend and never met her. Nor was I acquainted with Mr. Griswold, though I am familiar with his unfortunate memoir of Mr. Poe. As one of many who knew Mr. Poe &, as did they, wished to correct erroneous impressions regarding his character, I have in the past provided information. My willingness to do so returned to haunt me. I no longer speak nor do I wish to be consulted on the matter. Please understand that by this I mean no disrespect.
   Yours very truly,
   A. L. Richmond

P. Office Box № 84
Lowell, Mass.
Sept. 30 / '78
Lieutenant Edward E. Gayle

Dear Sir,

Please accept my apology for asking that you not write to me again. I do not wish to be rude, &, owing to the sincerity & engaging tone of your recent letter, I find it impossible to refrain from responding. Allow me to explain why I make this request, & please understand that I do so *only* for the sake of politeness.

Years ago my sister wrote certain recollections of Mr. Poe based on things he told her. It was *not* something written for publication. Shortly after his death—out of affection for him & wishing not to forget the things he told her—she decided to write down what she could remember of their many conversations. She was still in her teens at the time. It was meant as a keepsake, nothing more. Please understand that Mr. Poe was a dear friend of my family. He found comfort in our home in Lowell & also in my parents' home in Westford. He was a not infrequent visitor in the year following his dear wife's death & a man highly esteemed in our community where he lectured on three occasions. Some eight years ago, I had inquiries from a gentleman who wished to write a memoir of Mr. Poe, his purpose being to right the wrongful imputations of Mr. Griswold's cruel and unjust memoir with which you are apparently familiar. As I felt duty bound to assist any effort associated with putting to rest those atrocious falsehoods, I prevailed upon my sister to allow me to send the gentleman her "Recollections," & she reluctantly agreed on the two conditions that she not be quoted or named & that the manuscript be returned promptly without markings or defacements. As these conditions were acceptable to the gentleman, the pages were sent. It pains me to report that both conditions were violated.

Then again, more than two years ago, I received yet another inquiry from a gentleman bent on the same purpose—to right the wrongs of Mr. Griswold's memoir. This time, however, the writer carried the weight of a personal endorsement from Mrs. W——, a woman of un-impeachable character, & by this I was persuaded that the gentleman was a man of honor & integrity. To this gentleman I entrusted precious mementos & copies of private letters received by me from Mr. Poe on the condition that the letters not be quoted or reprinted, that they were offered solely for the gentleman to judge by their content the purity and high-mindedness of Mr. Poe's character which was so at odds with the infamous portrait by Griswold. You can imagine my consternation, disillusionment, & heartrending disappointment when I found shortly thereafter—& with no forewarning whatsoever—my letters published word-for-word in a popular magazine. As a result, I ceased all correspondence with the gentleman, if such he may be called, & I burned all letters written to me by Mr. Poe to prevent such a thing from ever recurring. I will tell you that those flames consumed my most precious possessions.

It grieves me to be distrustful, Lieutenant. Such is not my usual nature. But I have learned by painful experience the correctness of something Mr. Poe once told me regarding the publishing profession—that "trust is betrayed routinely & unconscionably." I will not name names, for such lowers me to the level of those who have betrayed my trust. I was naive in not taking Mr. Poe's words to heart for surely he knew. I will not make that mistake again; I have neither the constitution nor the authority to subject to public view matters of the heart of those, both living and dead, for whom I care deeply. I hope you can find it in *your* heart to understand.

Yours truly,

A. L. Richmond

P. Office Box № 84
Lowell, Mass.
Oct. 11 / '80
Lieutenant E. E. Gayle

Dear Sir,

I have your kind favor of the 31st ultimo. It is considerate of you to inquire as to my health. I am well, thank you, but I glean from your letter that your true reason for writing is to inquire as to my opinion of Mr. Ingram's recently published biography of Mr. Poe. I hesitate to do so. How can I without seeming to violate my resolve not to speak on this subject? I will go at it in this way: Love is a highly complex emotion. It seems to me that there are many kinds of love. I am told that the English language contains more than double the number of words as French or Spanish, but I think when it comes to the word, "love," our language is inadequate. One single word to express something so complex leaves open a multitude of interpretations, &, therefore, misunderstandings abound. Mr. Poe possessed an immense capacity for love—larger by far than any man I have ever known. By virtue of this, he was more at ease in the presence of women than men. No doubt you are familiar with the science of Phrenology which has proven that women possess larger organs of amativeness than men. My observations tell me this is true. Mr. Poe possessed a far larger organ of amativeness than most men, & I believe this may explain, among other things, his genius in the Art of Poetry. I am neither a scientist nor a scholar, but my faith in this conclusion is unshakable. I might add that we must learn wisdom through bitter experience; therefore, I ought to be wiser than Solomon!

Furthermore, Lieutenant, I believe that, because of Mr. Poe's unique propensity in the above regard, his true character is difficult—if not impossible—for most men to comprehend, much less find sympathy with. Men tend to view things as black or white; whereas, women are more apt to view shades of gray. I am aware that numerous women acquainted with Mr. Poe eagerly assisted Mr. Ingram in his biography out of a feeling that Griswold had done a grievous injustice to Mr. Poe's character. I was of like mind and felt compelled to assist also.

My first impulse upon reading Mr. Ingram's biography was one of having been entrapped, but on reflection & in a more generous frame of mind, I decided that the man had been motivated by a genuine desire to right the said grievous wrong, that his sympathies were with Mr. Poe. This notwithstanding, the most noble & lofty intentions are easily undermined by a failure to comprehend—in this case—in my humble opinion—for reasons stated above.

I hope this answers your question. I will offer one final opinion that may seem at odds with the general view: it is quite possible that only a *woman* who knew him personally could do true justice to the character of Edgar Allan Poe, but sadly that time has passed. With this I will wish you well in your endeavors, & I remain,

Very truly yours—
Annie Richmond

(ITEM 58: *Annie Richmond*)
...

P. Office Box № 8
4 Lowell, Mass.
Nov. 18 / '80
Lieutenant E. E. Gayle

Sir,

Your favor of the 13th ult. just arrived. Did I, indeed, leave you perplexed? What did I say? I hardly remember. I warrant you are a flatterer, Lieutenant Gayle, judging from your carefully worded roundabout way of telling me that I posed more questions than I answered. As I think about it, I do recall saying something about "shades of gray." Did that not suffice? I won't spell it out for you; I have told you that I will not speak on this subject again. Do you not recall that I have cause for caution?

I confess that I am intrigued by what you say about having some insight into why Mr. Griswold did what he did, though I may know the answer to that already. That you appear willing to share your news, as you call it, is most kind of you, but it seems your "sharing" comes at the cost of information I possess. In short, you are proposing a trade. I find that highly suspicious. You tell me that you once considered writing a book but that you've abandoned that idea, that your interest is mere curiosity, but I find that difficult to believe. Forgive me. You seem sincere, & I would very much like to think of you as an honest, sincere person, but I have experienced too much of false sincerity by men interested in Edgar Allan Poe.

If you wish to persist, then you may come to Lowell as you propose. If you do so, be on your guard, for I will put your sincerity to the test. A "picture," as is said, "is worth a thousand words"—which is to say that all the letters in the world will not persuade me that you are different from others—namely Messrs. Gill & Ingram. Why Edgar's peers never came to his defense in the wake of Griswold's wicked biography has & will always remain to me a profound & unfathomable mystery. It is for this reason, and this reason only, that I might have some interest in your "news."

I do not wish, by my suspicions, to insult you, Lieutenant Gayle. On the contrary, I have come to enjoy your letters & the things you say about yourself of a personal nature. I would like nothing more than to trust you, but please understand that on two occasions my trust in this matter has been betrayed, & I will not again be subjected to such deception.

If you are sincere, you may come. If you are not, save your fare.—closed in haste for today's mail, I am,

Yours truly,

Annie Richmond

:: "ANNABEL LEE" WAS NOT WRITTEN FOR ME. It was, rather, the other way round as you shall see. My cousin, Jane Locke, invited Edgar Allan Poe to come to Lowell one summer in the late 1840s for the purpose of delivering a lecture on the subject of American poetry. Jane was a poet herself, but no one had any idea that she had the influence and prestige to attract someone of Mr. Poe's stature. Suddenly we were all quite in awe of her, the entire town abuzz with excitement. "Will he recite 'The Raven'?" we all asked, hoping against hope that he would, for everyone knew by then that his recitations of the poem were legendary. Then the *Journal & Courier* announced that he would recite a selection of poems by American poets, including his own "beautiful and popular poem, 'The Raven.'" In short time all available seats were sold, and Wentworth's Hall announced standing room only. Jane had kindly seen to it that Charles and I had front row seats, and I cannot describe my excitement. I had never met a celebrity the likes of the great Edgar Allan Poe, and I felt certain that Jane would introduce us. As she was fifteen years my senior and of a literary compulsion, she had always been somewhat aloof, but we got on well enough.

I dressed in my very best, and I remember the difficulty with which I explained to our three-year-old, Caddy, why she could not go with us. I imagined nightmares were she to hear "The Raven" just as I imagined Mr. Poe's recitation would be ruined by an outburst of juvenile sobs.

When Jane saw me at the hall, our eyes met briefly, then she turned away, concern clouding her expression. I glanced down at my dress, wondering if I'd missed a pin or button, then it occurred to me that Jane was jealous. I could not explain it any other way. On the surface she had no need to be jealous; she was quite a handsome woman, but at twenty-eight I suppose I had the advantage of youth. Before that instant, however, it had not dawned on me that Jane felt such affection for Mr. Poe that another woman might be viewed as a rival. I had often been told that I was beautiful; my husband, Charles, often said it, though I rather think this had become something of a habit. I am above the average height for a woman, light-brown hair (or so it was at the time), and I suppose my eyes are my best feature, gray but with hues of other colors and so light in tone that they are considered unusual. People often stare to the point that I become self-conscious until I realize that they are merely curious as to the color of my eyes, a shade perhaps they have never seen before. I was even told by an old suitor that my eyes were so clear he could peer into the deepest recesses of my heart, though I think he was merely trying to see how far the familiarity would take him.

Of course I could not be certain I had correctly read Jane's thoughts, but out of caution, I resolved to sit some distance away and prevailed upon Charles to exchange seats with another couple, friends of ours, who were more than happy to do so in view of ours being preferable.

We sat on the third row at the very end, a discreet distance from Jane, and when Charles asked why, I explained that I did not wish to spoil the evening for Jane, though this didn't seem to satisfy his curiosity. He was not overly fond of Jane, but happily the program began, sparing me further explanation. Having been introduced, Mr. Poe began his remarks, seeming at first to be exceedingly ill at ease. He stood, stiffly formal, and warily eyed the audience as if carefully measuring our response. Not once did I see him refer to notes, and I judged his mastery of the subject such that written notes were unnecessary. For the first twenty minutes or so, I was more taken by his manner and delivery than by the content. What at first seemed to me to be an unfriendliness or detached reserve, came to seem an engaging timidity. It occurred to me that Mr. Poe was shy. I found this remarkable, and the more I watched, the more certain I became that underpinning the mastery of his subject was intense insecurity. I began feeling sorry for him. I was aware that he had lost his wife the previous year, and putting this together with my other impressions, I decided that perhaps Mr. Poe was lonely. So intense was my apprehension at one point that I began to worry if the man would be able to go on. This alarming concern came just as he turned his comments to the poet, Longfellow, and a certain obese gentleman sitting immediately behind Charles was taken with an unpleasant choking-cough that seemed to persist unnaturally. Mr. Poe turned his gaze to the gentleman as if he thought the cough was censure on behalf of Longfellow. I then recalled Mr. Poe's disdain for the New England poets and the Boston press who had derided his work and viciously attacked him several years earlier. Then the whole thing came clear to me: insofar as Mr. Poe was concerned, Massachusetts was hostile terrain. He continued, however, with what appeared the utmost effort on his part, and, as he did, his eyes traversed the aisle from the coughing gentleman to me. He then stared at me for a time longer than would have been natural, and I returned his gaze with an expression that must have conveyed my anxiety, for when at last he looked away, a trace of a smile was visible on his lips. Thereafter his confidence revived. I concluded that he had not been as apprehensive as I feared. Just then, as if on impulse, he cut short his lecture, began his recitals, and from that point and for the remainder of the evening, he kept his audience enthralled. I cannot recall the poems he recited—one by Longfellow, one by Frances Osgood, the others I don't remember—but with each one he became more animated, more confident, more captivating until, at last, he paused, clasped his hands behind his back, bowed his head, and took several very deep breaths, his lips pursed tightly together. Then, looking up at the highest point in the hall, he began,

> Once upon a midnight dreary,
> While I pondered, weak and weary,
> Over many a quaint and curious
> Volume of forgotten lore—

It was so totally unexpected that it took my breath away. Yes, I knew he was going to recite "The Raven," but I had expected at least a few words of introduction, perhaps an explanation of his inspiration or the difficulty of its composition, but there was nothing of the sort. He began in a voice so soft that had I been unfamiliar with the poem, I would have thought he spoke of something of little consequence, but by its familiarity the effect was thrilling. It was as if I heard for the first time my favorite Mozart melody played by Mozart himself. I was with him all the way. He plunged me into every emotional trough even as I soared with wondrous elation at words assembled and ordered with such genius—words I knew, words that had never stopped my breath before, but now, by their captivating arrangement, they arrested me. I cannot adequately describe the effect, not just on me, but on the entire audience. We were spellbound, caught up in an intricate web of words, the meaningful effects of which bore hopeless despair. Never before had I seen its like and never have I since.

When he ended he bowed his head, seemingly spent and grief stricken, and truly I believe he was. No one in the audience could possibly doubt that the man had revealed his inmost self, and by his so doing it seemed cruel that anyone would not feel utter compassion for the man whatever their prejudices might have been before. Proof of this, without doubt, was the uproarious applause and shouts of "Bravo!" which erupted from the audience. The reception thrilled me beyond measure; I could not resist laughing out loud at the thrill I felt for him. I was his from that instant, though I never hoped to be but one of a throng of well-wishers. As the applause died finally, I searched for Jane, and, though I could only see her from aside and a little behind, the admiration I perceived in her face—no, it was not admiration alone; it was also *adoration*—told me that my earlier impression had been correct. She loved Edgar Poe.

He was immediately surrounded by a crowd, wishing to congratulate him. I watched as he accepted the accolades with modesty bordering on embarrassment, continually nodding his head, smiling now with consummate generosity, though his cautious reserve remained. I found this even more fascinating than what had come before. There was nothing in the least expansive or arrogant in his manner that one might naturally expect from a performance received with such acclaim. He was modest and humble in his acceptance, never more polite than with a gushing, rather officious matron who wished to appropriate him entirely with tales of her youth in Portland where she claimed to have been a childhood playmate of Mr. Poe's friend and former associate, N. P. Willis. Charles and I lingered. I held him back by his elbow, still sensitive to the emotions I sensed in Jane. He kept turning to me for some explanation as to my reticence, but I avoided his eyes, thinking I would reveal all later, after prayers and lights out. I then felt someone take my other arm and turned to see my brother, Bardwell. "We should have him over, Nan," he said, "to your house for tea tomorrow. He's here for several days, I'm told. Surely he'll come. May I invite him, Charles?" he asked, turning to my husband.

"By all means," Mr. Richmond said enthusiastically.

And with that Bardwell advanced to the crowd surrounding Mr. Poe.

"That may not be such a good idea," I said to Charles.

"Why?" he asked.

I didn't want to say why; I worried that Jane might object, but the matter was now out of my hands. A moment later Bardwell was motioning us over, his hand on Mr. Poe's shoulder. We approached as bid, and Mr. Poe turned to us and smiled more broadly this time, but just then Jane appeared, inserting herself, determinedly eager to usurp Bardwell's introduction. She spoke hastily.

"Mr. Poe," she said, "may I present my cousin, Nancy Richmond, and her husband, Charles, her brother, Bardwell, and here comes Sarah, Nancy's and Bardwell's younger sister, and I'm afraid you must all excuse us, as the reporter from the *Journal & Courier* wishes to interview Mr. Poe. This way. Please, Edgar."

Before leaving, Mr. Poe turned to Bardwell, nodded and said, "It would be my pleasure, Mr. Heywood, as soon as I have concluded my interview with the newspaper."

Jane shot Bardwell a spiteful glance, then led Edgar away, questioning him as they went, doubtless concerning whatever invitation Bardwell had proffered. I was quite certain Bardwell had created a muddle, but it was too late now.

"He's coming tonight," Bardwell announced as soon as Jane and Edgar were out of earshot. "He may leave tomorrow, so he's coming tonight. Will that be convenient?"

Bardwell addressed his question to me, but I immediately turned to Charles. Did he understand? I could see he did not. Charles was not an overly sensitive man, and even if he had perceived Jane's desire to appropriate Edgar, he would have thought such a thing frivolous and selfish of her.

Jane could hardly object, but before leaving the hall that night, she made it abundantly clear that she was miffed by the arrangement, and the focus of her ire seemed bent on me. To this point I had said not one word to Edgar, but he had looked my way during the introductions, and Jane had taken notice. I had been caught up in the middle despite the considerate diplomacy that had governed my actions, and, at that point, I would have gladly forgone meeting Edgar altogether for the sake of family harmony, but events had overshot my control. Bardwell was beside himself; Charles was agreeable, even enthusiastic; and Sarah, my teenage sister, was agape—positively starstruck. At that point, I was a pawn and never a more reluctant one.

I haven't described Edgar's physical appearance. (By his invitation that night I came to call him Edgar, though later he insisted I address him as "Eddy.") He wore a black suit, vest, and tie, a white shirt. His face was careworn—that's the best word to describe it—and thin. His photographs do not do him justice; they make his face appear broad which it was not at all. He was rather more regal than handsome, I thought. He bore himself rigidly at first as if on his guard and with pride but not false pride. Always a bit ill at ease, he seemed to go out of his way to be polite, but he gave easy answers to questions, quite comfortable with conversation of a general nature. Never did he initiate conversation, and, at first, when the subject of such centered on him, he deftly deflected it away, inquiring about others' interests or the town or some topic current in the news. In this way, he put us at our ease in the kindest way. Once in our home, a snack having been offered and declined, he seemed to relax a bit, though he kept his coat and vest buttoned, his tie tied, even as Bardwell and Charles stripped to shirtsleeves.

It was near ten o'clock when we settled into the parlor with coffee cups or bowls of ice cream in our laps, a silver tray of cookies on a linen doily on the tea table. As the evening temperature was pleasant, the windows were opened and crickets chirped outside. While Sarah played a waltz on the piano, I went upstairs to check on Caddy, and when I came down Edgar was saying that his recently published poem, "Eureka," was the most important work of his lifetime, that it would far outlive anything else he'd ever written.

When Bardwell asked why he had not recited it that very evening, Edgar explained that it was too long and that the subject too complex for a general audience. "Still, you should do it," Bardwell insisted. "Come to Cambridge; I'll persuade my professors to arrange for a lecture on 'Eureka.'"

Edgar became somber suddenly, and I regretted that Bradwell was too young and impulsive to be sensitive to the fact that to Edgar, Harvard meant Longfellow. He would not be welcomed there. As it turned out, this was not what had changed Edgar's mood.

"I was born in Boston," he said. "Not many people know what special affection I have for the place. My mother claimed her best audience was in Boston and that I should always appreciate the city in which she had her most enthusiastic reception."

This remark was followed by silence. Was his mother a singer or actress, I wondered? When Bardwell posed another question; I don't remember precisely what, one of those broad questions that require an answer encompassing the whole of life's experience. Were I to ask, for example, *who are you*? Would you respond in a flippant manner?—summing up with some witty retort all that you wish others to know?—some remark that deflects rather than informs? There was never anything flippant in Edgar's answers. He felt called upon to tell his story whether out of a sense of obligation to his host or out of some pent-up need to lighten his burden. Perhaps at that precise moment in time Edgar needed to tell what he told. I think such things happen. Emotions well up to such a degree that the most important—perhaps the sole—listeners are those nearest at hand, be they lifelong friends or total strangers.

It was thus he began his story, and for an hour or more he talked nonstop, telling us about his parents' early death, his adoption, schooling in England, disinheritance, the intimacy that developed with his young cousin, Virginia, when he moved in with his aunt in Baltimore in his early twenties. As he spoke of Virginia, tears welled in his eyes and began running down his cheeks. It had been the affection of brother and sister, he explained with emphasis—nothing more or less—but others had put pressure on him to marry her, and he finally yielded to those importunities. How could he not, he asked rhetorically, and I wondered how he *could*, for I imagined many reasons, not the least of which was Virginia's tender age. We, his small audience, remained as enthralled as we had been listening to "The Raven." No one interrupted, and on numerous occasions his gaze moved to me, staring at me with a kind expression as if he perceived in my eyes a willing listener and sympathetic heart. His story was incomparable yet sad beyond belief. The events of his life had an aspect of unreality or other worldliness so like his tales. When at last he stopped—the same despair in his expression with which he had ended "The Raven"—I felt as if I'd finished a long and beautiful novel, and, unwilling to put it down, I wanted to start at the beginning again. He then looked at me again, and I felt his gaze penetrate me, still we had not directly exchanged a word.

Toward midnight Bardwell walked Edgar the mile back to Wamesit cottage, the home of the Lockes. I did not expect that we would see him again, and as we prepared for bed, I explained to Charles my certainty that we had hurt Jane's feelings by spiriting away her honored guest. That we had done so troubled me, and I resolved to write a note of apology first thing in the morning despite Charles's expressed opinion that I was blowing the whole thing out of proportion. I did write to Jane, but before even posting my note, Edgar appeared at our front door. He was alone.

It was just after noon on a Tuesday, and I was alone in the house save for Caddy who was napping and the servants. Charles was at his office, Bardwell had returned to Cambridge, and Sarah to Westford. They had only come down for the night of the lecture. I greeted him politely and invited him into the parlor where we sat in silence for an awkward moment.

"Mrs. Richmond," he said, "forgive me if I seemed to stare at you last night. It was rude of me, and I came to apologize. You see, I felt a certain connection that I can't explain. It was, at first, borne of a feeling that we had met previously, and I studied you, trying to recall the time or place. I realize, of course, that such could not be the case, yet the sensation is too vivid to be ignored. I presume you never lived in New York or Philadelphia?"

I explained that I had not, that I had spent my entire life in Westford and Lowell and that I seldom ventured farther than Rye Beach for a holiday. This made him laugh, and easy conversation ensued. We talked of many things. He inquired as to my appreciation for literature, my hopes and aspirations. I explained that I was involved in several charities, my pet one being the Lowell orphanage, "The Home," as we called it. All the while I was conscious of our fine house which must have made our situation seem very prosperous to Edgar, and, indeed, Charles's business success had provided many advantages. I was relatively certain that Edgar was poor. One could tell by numerous little details that arose in conversation or even by the clothes he wore, which is not to say that his attire was not neat and clean. It was. But it also told of frugality and economy. I felt so sorry for him that I wanted to compensate in some way, but I knew not how. Just then a ready and sympathetic ear seemed to be of greatest importance to him, and intuition told me that he had come in hopes of finding just that, but perhaps also something more—an attractive, younger woman. I do not impute by this anything of an offensive nature, though for a brief instant I did wonder if he'd made some comparison between Jane Locke and me and chosen me for the same reason that most widowed males prefer to court a younger face and figure. It was a silly response on my part; Jane and I were both married, so what would Edgar hope to gain by choosing either of us.

At two o'clock Charles arrived for lunch and was quite surprised to find Edgar and I conversing. I invited Edgar to lunch with us, but he refused, saying he had business to attend to, that he had already overstayed his welcome.

As Charles and I lunched, he inquired as to an explanation of Edgar's visit, and I answered with what I truly believed—that he merely wanted congenial company.

Edgar returned the next day for the purpose of bidding me goodbye, but he stayed for two hours during which time he imparted many things of an intimate nature. He wished to marry again, he said, and he mentioned Helen Whitman as a possible object in that regard, but by things he said, I inferred reluctance on his part, not merely insofar as Mrs. Whitman was concerned, but a reluctance of a more general nature, the essence of which I was at a loss to fathom. When he left for the last time, he expressed the hope that we would meet again, and he asked if I would agree to his calling me by the name, Annie. I smiled at this request, almost laughing out loud to be truthful, for I couldn't imagine why he would want to do such a thing.

"Annie is a name that is dear to me," he said, "as you shall learn soon enough."

I consented, feeling flattered I should add, for it seemed a particularly affectionate gesture on his part to wish to call me by a pet name. There was a certain intimacy attached to the request that endeared him to me, but, though he left me with "Goodbye, Annie," I didn't suppose I would see him again or ever again hear myself referred to by that name.

Edgar returned in October. Jane Locke arranged yet another lecture, and he consented to come, but immediately upon seeing him I knew he had come for the sole purpose of seeing me. By her reaction to the events in July, I had become certain that Jane was in love with Edgar Poe. Relations between our families had been strained as a result of Edgar's several visits to our house, but Jane's own marital situation was strained as well, adding to the discomfort. I considered it careless beyond prudence of her to invite him again, to insist that he stay under her roof when it was so apparent that she was in love with him. I was not the only one who suspected. It seemed to many of her friends and relatives that Jane had lost touch with reality. She now lived in a dream world, disregarding the needs of her husband and children, turning Wamesit cottage into a fairy tale. She was demanding and extravagant and would not be denied. I avoided her, and when I heard that Edgar had been invited for a return engagement, I resolved not to go. It proved impossible. Jane wanted me to come, demanded that we come, again as her guests, and I suspected she had a plan to draw attention to herself and away from me as if to prove to Edgar, in some perverse way, that she was the more worthy. It was a bizarre arrangement, but Charles proved intractable. He could not credit her strange behavior as having anything to do with me, but merely the product of a too literary and fanciful frame of mind. Also, Charles was mindful of appearances. Lowell's best and wealthiest citizens would be in attendance; therefore, we must be in attendance also. My warnings fell on deaf ears.

As it turned out, Charles was wrong. Wentworth's Hall was far from filled. Ticket sales must have been disheartening to Edgar. The title of his lecture was "The Poetic Principal," and, though it might have been brilliant and the source of fascination to scholars, it left the more industrious citizens of Lowell scratching their heads. At the end there was no eruption of applause, not the first shout of "Bravo!" The tentative and polite clapping made me grieve for him. Jane was the first to greet him at the podium when it was over, and I watched an exchange between the two of them that was obviously strained and soon became heated. Jane thrust her chin into the air, turned, and left the hall, not bothering to wait for her husband who soon followed in a fit of pique.

Edgar then walked over to where Charles and I stood and reported that Jane had insulted us, and, refusing to be a party to such indignity, he had declined the Locke's invitation to board at Wamesit cottage. Would we put him up, he asked? Hearing this, Charles's eyes flashed, and he agreed immediately, turning to me as if to ask what in the world had gotten into my cousin. On our way home, he asked Edgar to reveal the nature of the insult. Hesitant at first, he refused to repeat word-for-word what Jane had said, but he revealed that the gist of it had to do with Charles and I being admitted to society only though the patronage of the Lockes. I learned later that Jane had called Charles "despicable." It was not unlike Jane to be petty in this way; she considered herself quite the bluestocking. But at the time I considered the possibility that Edgar's disappointment in the attendance at his lecture played some role in the quarrel.

When we arrived home, Charles sent a servant to fetch Edgar's trunk from Wamesit cottage, and as soon as it arrived, we went up to our rooms. As we prepared for bed, Charles and I exchanged not a word, for I was furious with the outcome and not in the mood to discuss it. The whole evening was a disaster in my opinion.

The next morning Charles went off to work, leaving me to attend to Edgar and the household. I put Caddy in the care of a serving girl with intentions of speaking to Edgar privately about the difficulties his visit had caused, though I considered his actions inadvertent and by no means his fault and fully intended telling him this, but the opportunity never arose. Instead I listened to a stream of confessions and pleas for understanding. I had not heard from Edgar since July; therefore, I assumed that he had given me little thought, but I now realized how wrong I was. We sat in two chairs, beside each other, in front of a wood fire. He spoke, haltingly, perhaps uncertain as to how his words would be received. I listened to him confess that for months he had thought of me constantly, that our conversations the previous summer had convinced him that I alone understood him.

"You understand me better than anyone alive," he said, "with the possible exception of Fanny." I knew he was speaking of Frances Osgood. "Fanny understands me," he continued, "but we cannot speak or write for reasons that I cannot say. Please understand, my dear Annie. I would tell you if I could, but I promised her—I swore to her—and I will not break my pledge to Fanny. She is as dear to me as you. In all the world, I have but you and Fanny, and I am forbidden even to see her, so I beg you, Annie, dear, *dear* Annie, be my friend. I have *only* you."

I did not know how in the world to respond to this; I was uncertain about what he meant by "friend." His need seemed great, however, and I didn't want to hurt him. I promised, not knowing precisely what I was promising. And with my promise, he reached out and took my hand, and for a long while we sat before the fire, my hand in his, not a word being said. He stared at our joined hands, caressing mine and seeming to take much comfort in the sensation. Though I was uncomfortable with this familiarity—thinking one of the servants might appear or even Charles—I dared not pull away.

"Let me tell you something about love, Annie," Edgar said, turning to me finally and peering into my eyes—"something I have learned in my nearly forty years." His gaze frightened me. His eyes had a burning intensity, unsettling to say the least. The same confidence returned that had appeared suddenly at that point in his first lecture when he had begun reciting, but there was also something else, something abject and hopeless. Just then he was no longer the needy, insecure person of the moment before; he was now the other-worldly person of his poems and tales. How else can I say it?—There was in his eyes some awful truth.

Here, I dreaded to think as I returned his gaze, was someone who knew death too well. What followed was a torrent of words, which, had they been an essay, far, *far* exceeded my capacity to comprehend. I felt my hand in his; I watched him, fascinated, but the only words that registered in my small brain were "purity, beauty, love, death." "Purity, Beauty, Love, Death." Repeated continually, they clanged like cymbals, almost deafening, uplifting yet tragic. I strained to follow his meaning; I wanted desperately to understand, but I couldn't, and the anxiety brought tears to my eyes—a cry for help. Edgar seemed to understand or, at least, sympathize. He ceased his harangue, turned to the fire, and squeezed my hand so tightly that it hurt. I winced perceptibly. With this, apologies followed in the softest words, "Oh! Annie, I'm sorry. I have frightened you. Please—please forgive me. I would not hurt you for the world. I care for you more than anyone alive. Do you not know how dear you are to me, how much I love you?"

I freed my hand, rubbed my tears away, and tried to compose myself, still fretting over the possibility of someone discovering us. I sensed, nevertheless, that the love of which he spoke was of a different kind— "purity, beauty"—that was the description that came to mind, and I reasoned that Edgar was not making love to me. Such was neither his desire nor his intent.

For hours after, he told me things about his life. Choosing his words with exceeding care, he described in vivid detail the loves of his life as a way of explaining his love for me. He described in intimate details his love for Virginia, Fanny Osgood, the mother of a boyhood friend, his experiences with prostitutes in Richmond, Baltimore, Charleston, and West Point, with someone named Eliza, someone named Mary, someone named Catherine, someone he referred to as "Holy Eyes." I was both appalled and titillated by so many loves until I realized that few of them had been physically consummated. I came to understand that Edgar was not experienced in that way, nor did he profess to be. It did not seem a thing important to him. On the contrary, it seemed a thing even a little distasteful. I followed his tales of love with increasing interest and realization that his definition of "love" was something more rarefied.

Abruptly he changed the subject as if worried that it had been talk of love that distressed me. Now he talked of family, retelling things he had talked about in July, his mother's death, his being taken in by the Allans—"like a pet dog," he described it with venom in his voice—though later he talked of his foster mother with such affection that I inferred his bitter feelings had been associated solely with his foster father. He spoke of his attachment to the mother of a boyhood friend, her death when he was sixteen, and the many nights he had spent beside her grave in Richmond.

"I have never had a family in the truest sense of the word," he said. "You cannot know, Annie, how a child denied a true family longs for one."

I reminded him of my charitable work at the Lowell orphanage and how that had taught me something of the sense of incompleteness about which he spoke. He was exceedingly pleased with this reminder.

"Then you *do* know," he said happily. "Something told me you did. Something I perceived in your expression the very first time I saw you. Perhaps this explains the sense of connection that seemed present even when we first met. Do you agree, Annie?"

I was still unsure as to how all he had said was connected, but I did agree, and I found suddenly a new perspective on both my own upbringing and my interest in the orphanage. Perhaps my sensitive nature rendered me susceptible to the particular needs of young girls and boys who have no family. I had never considered these things quite in this way, and I wondered if it could be that my intuition had somehow told me that Edgar, too, was an orphan. Then it dawned on me that Edgar was just a child with no family. He had adopted his mother-in-law as a mother. He had married his cousin in order to provide a sister. These actions provided him a family to replace all the families he'd lost. And by those losses so early in his life, he had been arrested in a childlike state. It dawned on me suddenly that Edgar, poor man, having been denied a family, had never grown up.

This seemed a great revelation. It explained all his talk of loving the women he had mentioned. Edgar did not want a lover; he wanted a sister, someone to take Virginia's place. It was a role I could take on; indeed, it was a role I would cherish. But how to explain it to others? Could they possibly understand? I was quite certain that holding hands was as far as it would ever go.

That night, after Caddy had been put to bed and Edgar had retired, I told Charles all that had occurred, including the hand-holding and my impressions as to Edgar's interest in me. My attempt at an explanation sounded farfetched, even to me. Quite naturally Charles was skeptical and leery of Edgar's intentions, and he cautioned me not to be naive and to consider appearances, but beyond that, he voiced no objections, though I had thought it quite possible he would ask Edgar to leave the house. He was, rather, more concerned with having it out with John Locke for his wife's tongue. Determined to repay Jane's insult, he insisted that Edgar could stay and hold my hand for as long as he liked. For another thing, I think Charles was pleased to have a celebrity under his roof, as the situation was serving to call attention to him in the community, a thing he valued highly.

During the days that followed, Edgar and I sat for long hours together, he always insisting that we hold hands. We talked, or rather he talked. I marveled at the ease with which he revealed the most intimate things about himself, even including conjugal relations with his wife which I shall not repeat, as they were said to me in private. It was apparent, however, that his overriding perception of her was as a sister, though the relationship was such that the distinction between sister and wife became blurred. Suffice it to say, Sissy—as he called Virginia—never became pregnant, and that not solely for reasons of her young age or ill-health. We sat, holding hands even in the presence of Caddy and Charles, though whenever someone else entered the room, all talk ceased, and we would sit in silence, watching the fire. One evening, in fact, this scene was repeated even as Charles sat across from us reading his newspaper.

At this time, my brother Bardwell had finish his schooling and returned to my parents' home in Westford, and by his urging Edgar, Caddy, and I went there to spend three days. Each evening Bardwell hosted a "reading circle," having invited friends including Mr. Williard, the Unitarian minister, and others, all of whom were impressed by the depth of Edgar's knowledge and intellect. On demand he recited poems, including again, "The Raven." Bardwell even prevailed upon him to read "Eureka." Our days were mostly spent walking, climbing, and horseback riding; Edgar even walked my sister, Sarah, to school one day, but not a morning went by that he and I didn't sit before the wood fire, holding hands. I later concluded by his story, "Landor's Cottage" and by his desire expressed in letters to me to move with his mother-in-law into a cottage near Lowell that those three days in Westford yielded great contentment for him.

Before leaving to return to New York as the end of October approached, Edger confessed to me that he had made a proposal of marriage to Helen Whitman. Knowing her reply would await him by letter on his arrival back at Fordham, he lamented the necessity to return home. Our days together had been so idyllic, for both of us, but now the realities and fever of existence were about to descend again.

He was back in Lowell two weeks later in an agitated state of mind. He came, so he said, to beg my advice regarding his intended marriage to Helen Whitman. I had by now gained considerable insight into why, on the one hand, he would profess love and desire to marry and, on the other hand, shrink from it. In twenty-four hours he was due in Providence to seal the engagement, but a foreboding of doom had brought him first to me. Before speaking of the impending event, I soothed him with tea and a long talk before the fire, holding hands as always, and reminiscing about his recent trip here and the enjoyments we had shared. I avoided the subject of Jane Locke, and, for a time at least, the subject of Helen Whitman. Once he was calm and more himself, I asked him if he loved Helen. He demurred. Instead, he talked about her finer qualities and her situation which would afford him relief from the pecuniary difficulties that had beset him since before Virginia's death. By this I understood more clearly the nature of the match, and, though I presumed that he did not love her, I decided that her guiding influence and comfortable income would be in his best interests. I urged him to marry her. I even went so far as to suggest things he might say to her.

A look of dejected resignation came over him. "Would that she were nearer you, Annie," he said. "I could endure anything if only I could see you occasionally."

I could not wish for such a thing. People would not understand. But I did not say this. Instead, I allowed that he could write to me and I even promised to write to him on occasion. As he prepared to bid farewell, he extracted another promise—that I would come to him on his deathbed, wherever that might be. I vowed that I would.

Two weeks later I had a long, frantic, disjointed letter written on the 16th of November from Fordham retelling a night of horror and all that followed. He told me that when he arrived in Providence, his resolve abandoned him, and he immediately left and returned by train to Boston where he purchased two ounces of laudanum with the intention of killing himself. Renting a hotel room for the purpose, he wrote me a letter to say that he was dying, reminding me of my promise to come to him, and giving me the address. After writing the letter, he swallowed an ounce of the laudanum, but its effect was immediate and such that he could not even make his way to the post office. At some point in the odyssey from his hotel to the post office, he lost the letter, and immediately upon returning to his hotel his stomach rejected the potion, though he remained out of his mind for two days. On the 7th, having somewhat recovered the ordeal, he returned to Providence where he stayed until the 13th, then engaged to be married.

Still there persisted serious misgivings. Visions of a cottage in Westford had arisen again—"oh *so* small—so *very* humble," he wrote. As if this was all that was necessary for sober and contented life, he vowed to labor night and day so long as he could be nearby and on occasions be with "my *pure, virtuous, generous, beautiful, sister* Annie!" His pleas were pitiful, yet they tore at my heart, and I began to have misgivings. Though for reasons stated, the match with Mrs. Whitman had advantages, no advantage in the world was worth the gloom and misery he foresaw. What had compelled him to seek the match, I wondered? But for dire pecuniary straits, I could not imagine a reason unless he feared a loss of control in the absence of a strong will to keep him in check. He ended his letter by begging me to come to Fordham for a week, saying he was ill and feared impending death or madness. Not knowing how to respond, I did not. What could I say beyond what I had already said? A consequence of advising him to call off the engagement might be his arrival on our doorstep with intentions of living close to us, and I could not accept that.

Little more than a week later, my sister had a begging letter from him, wanting to know why I hadn't written. Sarah was so distressed by the tone of the letter that she made my father bring her to Lowell to beg me to respond. I did so, professing my love and support and chiding him for failing to take better care of himself. This last remark was calculated to bring him to his senses, and I suppose it had some effect, for when he wrote next he indicated all was well, that a lecture in Providence had gone very well, and he wished us all a merry Christmas, this despite the fact of that day being his wedding day.

I had a letter from Mrs. Clemm shortly after Christmas to say that the wedding had been called off, but I did not hear from Edgar until mid-January when he merely said, referring to the broken engagement, that a burden had been lifted from his heart. He renewed his pledges of love for his "own dear sister Annie!" It was only when Charles heard from members of his family who live in Providence that details were forthcoming, and those details caused me more unhappiness than anything I had ever experienced. The gossip had it that Edgar had behaved shamefully, drunkenness plus rude and disorderly behavior bordering on sheer madness. It was reported that, at one point, the police had to be called to the Whitman house to subdue him, and that Mrs. Whitman had called off the marriage the day before it was to take place, because Edgar had broken his pledge to her not to drink wine. I could not believe these to be the actions of someone who professed to call me sister, and I wrote to him immediately to ask for an explanation. I should add that Charles was so undone by the reports that he apologized to the Lockes for the unpleasantness of the previous autumn. As for me, I was prepared to end all correspondence with Edgar and told him so.

Edgar's response was wounded, indignant, but without apology. He refuted all that we had heard except for some difficulty that had arisen as a result of Helen's mother, Mrs. Power, who had insisted that he sign papers renouncing all claim to any properties belonging to Helen or any member of her family. He bemoaned the humiliation of the ordeal and insisted that from beginning to end Mrs. Power had been hostile to him and to the match. He professed to be very busy and energetic, saying that he was daily receiving requests for original work "from every magazine in the country save *Peterson's National*." I couldn't imagine that this could be true. He ended by saying that he had foresworn forever the "pestilential society of literary women" with the single exception of Fanny Osgood, and to that he added kisses, a hundred for me and fifty for Sarah.

In time, largely by his efforts, we learned that much of what we'd heard from Providence had been distortions and exaggerations, and soon our correspondence returned to a more or less regular basis, his letters always full of love and adoration for his "lovely" and "unworld-ly" Annie. He planned a trip to Lowell in the spring, but had to cancel. I do not know why, but I suspect it had to do with a lack of the necessary funds for travel. In March he sent a letter that he had recently received from Jane Locke in which she alluded to having cautioned Edgar against Charles and I, and with this proof in hand, as I feared it would, the feud between the Lockes and the Richmonds resumed. In the same letter he sent a manuscript of a poem entitled "For Annie," a poem that envisions the scene evoked by his departing wish that I come to him on his deathbed. I will not comment on it except to say that I could not, in the end, when he lay dying in a Baltimore hospital—for the reason that I did not know—fulfill my pledge. But had I known, I would have moved heaven and earth to be with him.

In April he wrote of a secret terror that plagued him, borne of the notion that he would never see me again. He also professed a "dark foreboding." He had heard again from Jane Locke who was threatening to publish a romantic novel based on their affair and was also threatening to show up at Fordham. I had avoided Jane for some time, and I decided she must have fallen over the edge. I would not have been surprised by news that she had been committed to a madhouse.

Edgar came again in late May to stay for a week. Sarah was now living with me and Bardwell had just been elected principal of Franklin Grammar School, so all of us were in Lowell for his visit. At this time he had renewed his efforts to form a literary journal which he intended to call *The Stylus*. He had suffered numerous publishing disappointments during the spring—one or two magazines had failed; two others were in such straits that they could not pay for work already published; etc. Edgar claimed to have monies due from a half dozen such rags. Perhaps his resolve to start his own journal was an attempt to remedy the situation. At any rate, he made the rounds in Lowell, both for underwriters and subscribers. On two occasions he visited Franklin Grammar School, the first time to be introduced by Bardwell to a young teacher, Eliza Butterfield, who was much taken with Edgar. Deciding to play the matchmaker, Bardwell invited Edgar back and saw to it that the couple had some time alone together. That Bardwell did this, of course, indicates that he knew full well the true nature of my relationship with Edgar, and, though I said nothing, I confess that I did feel a pang of jealousy. I have described how the line between sister and wife became blurred in the case of Virginia and Edgar. I had taken Virginia's place in his affections; I was the new Sissy, though such an utterance would never have crossed our lips. We both knew it. Therefore, it was difficult for me not to have certain wifely feelings toward him. I don't refer to anything of a carnal nature, but I had come to know the joy in being foremost in his affections, and I relished my role. Edgar perceived my disquiet when Bardwell, during supper, made light of the mating game he had orchestrated, describing the blush on Miss Butterfield's face when she exited the classroom where the two had been conversing. Edgar looked every bit the guilty lover, and I hated myself for feeling so bothered by it, continually reminding myself that we were like brother and sister, nothing more or less. It was the only time in our entire relationship that I wished we were, indeed, married.

While he was with us, I insisted on his sitting for a daguerreotype at Mr. Gilchrest's on Merrimack Street. I wanted a keepsake of my own, as did Sarah, so Mr. Gilchrest made two plates, but as I've said, his photographs do not do him justice, and I have never been particularly partial to it.

My last letter from him was written in June from Fordham, shortly before he left for Richmond. I have considered that the reason for not hearing from him again was his courtship of Mrs. Shelton, but I was in no way jealous of her. On the contrary I would very much like to meet her and Mrs. Houghton also of whom Edgar spoke with such affection. I never wanted to meet Mrs. Whitman after the debacle in Providence, nor did I care for Mrs. Lewis. I am the possessor of a soft heart, and I suppose I am more comfortable with those who are as sensitive as I. Those of keen sensitivity are attracted or repelled intuitively, without having any reason for our likes or dislikes of people.

I heard from Mrs. Clemm on occasion during that summer, 1849, always up or down in spirits, all depending on how her precious Eddy was doing. It's curious that, though we'd never met, she called me "daughter" and showered me with motherly affection in her all her letters. I was busy throughout that time with my charitable pursuits and my larger household, now that Sarah had moved in with us. With no letters or visits, my thoughts turned to Eddy less and less. It was hard to believe that I had only known him one year. Then in early October that letter came from Mrs. Clemm—"*Annie my Eddy is dead; he died in Baltimore yesterday.*"

During one of our hand-holding talks, Edgar told me this story: that as a little boy he was in the habit of playing in the nursery of the home of his foster mother's goddaughter, Catherine Poitiaux, with Catherine and her older sister, Mary Jane. He pronounced their name, "Poycha." This was before he left for England with his foster parents, so in age he was not more than five or six. Their usual game was marrying Edgar to his little godsister, and he would call her his "sweetheart."

He told me so much about so much of his life, but, despite our many, many private conversations, he could not tell me everything. I decided that those things he selected to tell me had some bearing on his affection for me or they were intended to elicit my affection for him. I find now that certain of the things he told me have stayed in my mind for these thirty years and for a reason. They are important in defining my relationship with him, and I, therefore, pay attention to them. This story of Catherine Poitiaux tells me so much now. Sisters and sweethearts. The scene in the nursery he described is filled with purity, beauty, and love. These things were so important to him that I believe he spent the rest of his life trying to recapture them. If ever he did, it was his brief time with Virginia, though I suspect that in some respects having re-created it with her, he was left unsatisfied. Or perhaps I'm wrong. His desire for a humble cottage makes me think sometimes that his final year with Virginia—there in the humble little cottage in Fordham, despite abject poverty and her illness—was the happiest year of his life. One need only read "Landor's Cottage" to understand that he wished to re-create it.

When I first saw the poem "Annabel Lee" published shortly after his death, I suspected I might have been the inspiration. I had a vague knowledge of the poem's existence. Perhaps he had told me about it before, and I had remembered that he'd said when we met that the name "Annie" was very dear to him. He had never explained, and now I suspected that his naming me "Annie" had been inspired by a poem that he was perhaps working on at the very time we met. I don't know this for sure, but when I read the line, "I was a child and she was a child," I knew, at least, that something else I'd suspected was true, for here he was, back in the nursery, marrying his little godsister, Catherine Poitiaux. Of course, Annabel Lee dies and in "For Annie" Edgar dies, so there is the very word that completes the string of words that had so struck me in our very first conversation—Purity, Beauty, Love, Death.

I don't pretend to understand all these things, only that they were somehow connected in that brilliant, complicated, and deeply troubled mind. Of this I am certain, however, there was nothing mean or malicious about him, nothing wicked or evil, nor was he capable of acting dishonorably toward any human being. So why did Griswold portray him in this way and why did his peers, knowing his better nature, not come to his defense?

I suppose John Henry Ingram got his facts right, but so much of what is presented as fact in his biography is nothing more than opinion and should be read with skepticism. Ingram did not know Edgar; therefore, his opinions are based on hearsay, but I venture to say that they will be read as truth. That his characterization was truer than Griswold's is a welcomed thing for those of us who knew Edgar and have for years desired a more truthful telling, but that doesn't make it all true. That he reprinted against my will so many of Edgar's letters to me, leaving the reader to draw conclusions without presenting the whole story, was not only a betrayal of my trust, it was a disservice to the man he hoped to champion. In light of this I have no choice but to consider his work a failure, for I must expect that he took similar liberties with others of his correspondents, including Helen Whitman who I understand became equally distrustful of the man when all was said and done.

I have agreed to reveal these things, breaking my silence on the subject, for a very different reason than that which motivated me to assist Gill and Ingram. Then I hoped to redeem the good character of Edgar Poe. Now, sadly, I have my own character to defend, that thanks to my naive generosity. Mr. Ingram begged of me everything I had related to Edgar, but there were things too precious for me to part with or risk sending to England on loan. Two of these things were original manuscripts of Edgar's "The Bells" and "A Dream Within a Dream." Acceding to Mr. Ingram's wishes, in January of 1878 I took both manuscripts to Mr. Sanborn to have photographic copies made for him, but before the work was done, Mr. Sanborn lost them. I was frantic and devastated, and he even more than I. He offered a generous reward for their return, printing an ad in the Lowell *Courier* without naming my name or any details about the lost manuscripts. Happily they were found in the dead letter file at the post office, posted inadvertently by Mr. Sandborn himself. Later the *Courier* reported a follow-up story stating that the lost manuscript had been the original of Poe's "The Bells," and this was the cause of considerable interest throughout the region. Then the Boston Sunday papers reported that the manuscript belonged to me, naming me by name. Although I cannot prove it, I feel certain that the source who divulged my name was William Gill, done out of jealousy for my cooperation with his rival biographer, John Ingram. As if this wasn't enough, in May of the same year, John Ingram published Edgar's letters to me in *Appleton's Magazine*. Though he referred to me only as "Annie," he provided enough additional details to enable the local papers, including those in Boston, to make the connection with me. Edgar's numerous professions of love for me in those letters would have been more than enough to embarrass me and my family, but in one of his letters he says, "Oh, Annie, in spite of so many worldly sorrows—in spite of all the trouble and *misrepresentation* (so hard to bear) that Poverty has entailed on me for so long a time—in spite of *all* this I am *so*—*so* happy to think that you *really* love me." The effect was devastating. The world, of course, could not, would not understand the nature of our relationship. They could draw but one conclusion based upon those letters, and I need not say what that conclusion was and is even to this day. I was left in a position of defending my honor and that of a deceased husband. I chose to say nothing at first, feeling certain that my protestations would only make matters worse, but knowing at the same time that I was being perceived as an unfaithful wife or worse, a harlot, and all because I was so innocent and naive as to think that I was rendering Edgar a service by my cooperation with Gill and Ingram. Can you now understand my sense of utter betrayal? I was bitter. How could I think those two or anyone seeking to achieve money and fame from a biography were anything but extortionists and mountebanks. I felt that they had taken advantage of my sensitive and generous nature and stripped me naked. I decided they were no better than Griswold, and I turned away from the matter, hoping it would go away, wishing I had never heard of Edgar Poe, and wishing also to spend my remaining few years in relative peace.

There are hearts that never give up, and I suppose I possess one. In addition, I must tell you that I am the sort of person who keeps a neat and clean house. I much prefer that matters be resolved, loose ends tied neatly. I don't want to let go this life, leaving the most important part of it at sixes and sevens. I would feel a failure. Yes, it *was* the most important part of my life—that one year of romance with Edgar Poe, and romance it was. Not romance in the common sense, but *Romance* in a much more lofty sense. I was so careful during the time I knew him. I didn't refer to him as a friend, but as an acquaintance. The distinction seemed to me to put an appropriate distance between us which in my mind distinguished the love we felt for each other from the more common love of lovers. I want this distinction known, but is such a thing even possible?

I have said that Edgar told me many intimate things regarding his relationships with other women. In an effort to try to explain what I mean, I will say what he told me regarding Fanny Osgood. He loved her very much. She possessed many of the traits of his *ideal love*. She had a youthful innocence about her that had initially provided the attraction. And her brilliance and witty mind provided added attractions. That she was a fine poet, of course, meant that they shared much in common. But in the end, Fanny was too much of a woman for Edgar. She was sensitive to his own keen sensitivity, but she was also sensuous and sophisticated, and I believe these additional traits intimidated Edgar, though they also appealed to his baser instincts. I have said that he was, in so many ways, still an innocent boy, but he was a boy in a man's body, and the man in him was seduced by her. It might have ended tragically—perhaps it did—but I believe that Fanny's sensitivity prevented a break in their relationship. Once she realized his special needs, she withdrew her own, and thereafter, for the rest of their lives, they remained dear, understanding friends, though for reasons of the interference of others, they could not remain close friends. I know he missed her; he as much as said so, but they would not have been well-matched. Edgar wanted a sister, not a lover, and Fanny was very much a lover.

These distinctions I draw may seem too precious to some. For someone with keen sensitivity the difference between aqua and aquamarine is night and day; to others, they are merely shades of blue.

(ITEM 98: *Annie Richmond*)

...

14 Ames Street
Lowell, Mass.
May 16 / '92
Major Edward Gayle

Dearest Eddy,

How thrilled I am to receive your wedding invitation & how kind of you to include me. Please extend my congratulations to your fiancée, & tell her from someone who has known you for many years that she is fortunate to have captured such a fine young man as you. As you well know, I mean this from the bottom of my heart. I would like nothing more than to be in attendance & to see West Point for the first time—a military wedding in that setting would be a sight to behold. I think, however, that I must decline. I do not venture far from home these days, &, though I hope to someday see you again, it may require you to travel to Lowell. Please, if your travels bring you this way, don't forget your friend Annie.

You cannot know how often I think of our long conversations &

letters on the subject of Edgar Poe & the effect upon me to tell my story to someone whom I feel possesses the requisite sympathetic understanding. I believe I told you once that there are many kinds of love & that one word alone is insufficient. From all you have told me about your intended, I perceive a love on your part for her that comes in many shades. Perhaps the greatest love is that which encompasses every one imaginable, &, therefore, in your case I believe that one word—*Love*—does indeed suffice.

Know that you have *my* love & best wishes for a long & joyous marriage, & may God be with you & with your bride to be.

Yours ever,
Annie

...
...
...

(ITEM 82: *Charlotte Ayers*)
...

May 18, 1888
Mrs. Canady's School

My dear Major Gayle,

Quite out of the blue, an old and perhaps mutual friend, Walter Brown—I suppose you might consider him a friend—but do you even remember him?—sent me a clipping from the *Providence Journal*, the headline reading, "New England's First Indian Uprising in Over 50 Years," detailing a violent clash between Penobscot Indian log-drivers and mercenaries hired by American timber companies on the upper reaches of the Penobscot River near Fort Pownall, Maine. As I read— wondering as I did why Walter sent it to me—I saw that a battalion of the United States Army was ordered in to quell the violence and uphold the Indian's rights to their lands, logging jobs, and wages equal to whites. You can imagine my amazement when I read who commanded the battalion—"Major Edward E. Gayle" could only be you, and your name was mentioned with highest praise.

I am so proud of you, Eddy. Forgive me for calling you by your nickname, Major Gayle. Though it has been years, I cannot help but remember you as "Eddy." I always admired your heartfelt concern for the horrible plight of the American Indian. You are, indeed, a fine man, and I congratulate you on your marvelous and humane accomplishment. I wonder if you continue to pursue your interest in Edgar Allan Poe? I always thought that if I ever heard of you again, it would be in that regard.

Most cordially,
Charlotte Ayers

(ITEM 84: *Charlotte Ayers*)

...

June 20, 1888
Aboard Ilyra
Upon the High Seas!

Dear Major Gayle,

Your wonderful letter arrived just one day before I set sail. I am traveling with the Grays from Bridgeport, and we are bound for the Mediterranean to visit Spain, France, Italy, and Greece. It is a dream come true for me. Mr. Gray's daughter, Priscilla, is one of my students at Mrs. Canady's School, and two other students—Priscilla's two best girlfriends—are with us also. I am their chaperone so that Mr. Gray is at leisure to enjoy himself. We will be gone ten weeks. Being aboard ship in the middle of the Atlantic—I suppose we are not quite yet precisely in the middle—is a thrill I never expected. I am not in the least seasick; in fact, I've never felt happier nor more alive. We dined at the captain's table last night, and he invited the girls and I to join him on the bridge this afternoon to help with sighting Bermuda where we are expected to arrive before nightfall, and I will post this letter there.

How shall I begin? My mother died three years ago. In all the years after that disastrous night in Providence, we never spoke of it again. I think she thought me hopelessly insane; in fact, I think she was fearful of me, and I found it quite convenient to do nothing to dispel that. Perhaps I *was* insane. At any rate, I cannot explain what happened. In time I decided that I had been so fearful that she would ruin things between us that when I sensed it happening, I had to make her stop, and the only way I could stop her was to scream. I can only imagine what you must have thought. As your visit approached, I became more and more apprehensive. No doubt you sensed my agitation in the letters I wrote just before your arrival. What else can I say, Eddy? I lost control. And in so doing, I lost you. Later, I was so mortified by what I'd done that I couldn't bring myself to answer your letters. I lost confidence; I questioned my own sanity, and perhaps I decided you were better off without me or that it would never work, not with me still somewhat dependent upon my mother. Nothing was said to anyone—my mother refused to even call a doctor—so no one in Providence knew, and I soon returned to work, throwing myself into that and trying to forget everything, including you. I think of that winter now as my hiatus from life. I shut myself away, avoiding friends, entertainments, even family meals. My work with Mrs. Whitman's papers enabled me to keep to myself even while working. I think I must have gone weeks without uttering a word.

The following summer, with the help of Mrs. Caroline Ticknor, Mrs. Whitman's biographer, I secured the teaching position at Mrs. Canady's School in Bridgeport for the fall semester of 1879. I have been there ever since. No, as you correctly guessed, I never married (nor can I help but wonder how the girls escaped someone as fine and handsome as you, *Major* Gayle!). I live in a house on the school grounds with the eight girls who board at Mrs. Canady's; the rest are day-students who live in Bridgeport. I love my girls; they are my joy. I am their old-maid schoolteacher, and I cherish my role. I teach literature, art, and (would you believe?) deportment. Mrs. Canady allows me some latitude with the syllabus; therefore—with a loving nod to Helen Whitman—I see to it that the girls read as many women writers as men. Do you think me subversive? Well, I suppose I am and proud of it. I think I'm much too independent-minded to ever marry.

I am glad to read that your interest in Poe continues, though sad to hear you say that your intensity for that pursuit has abated. I find it fascinating that you continue to occasionally correspond with people who knew him. I would have thought them all dead by now. Mrs. Weiss sounds fascinating. I would love to meet her. Your description of her reminds me so much of Helen. I thank God every day that I knew and worked with Helen Whitman. When I return, I will see what I can find of Mrs. Weiss's poetry. Did you ever find an answer to your question regarding Griswold? All that was so fascinating—Cato the cat, men gambling with black coins, Griswold in a minister's robe that turned into a black dress, and Longfellow. Wasn't he involved somehow? I've forgotten. I brag to my students that I once met Longfellow, though I suppose that's an exaggeration. I was one of many who were introduced to him the afternoon of Helen's funeral. Everyone was so in awe of him and rightly so, I suppose. He seemed very kind.

Well, the whistle has sounded for lunch, so I'll close. Thank you for your letter, Eddy. You will always be special to me.

With enduring affection,
Charlotte

(ITEM 85: *Charlotte Ayers*)
...

September 14, 1888
Mrs. Canady's
Bridgeport, Connecticut

Dear Eddy,

I was surprised to find not one, but four letters from you awaiting my return. I have read them all, and I thank you. Yes, I would like to see you too, but I don't think I can handle that just yet. Perhaps in time. You must understand that I am shocked to learn that my mother sent a note to your hotel, telling you that I was "indisposed" and could not receive you. She did not ask my permission, Eddy, nor did she ever tell me that she sent you a note. I was upset, but in no way indisposed. I waited lunch for you, and when you did not come, I walked to your hotel, refusing to let my mother accompany me. I wanted to talk to you privately, to try to explain what happened. When I was told you had checked out, I assumed you had taken the ferry to New York, so shocked by what happened that you had left of your own accord.

I beg time. I find the implications of this too depressing to consider right now, and I have so much to do in preparation for the new semester which begins tomorrow. I cannot think about this now, Eddy.

Forgive me, Charlotte

8

MYRA SHELTON

::

(ITEM 16: *Sarah Elmira Royster Shelton*)

...

414 North 10th Street
Richmond, Virginia
May 22, 1877

Dear Sir:

Yours of the 5th not recd. until yesterday owing to my absence from the city. I knew the gentleman, but, as regards the particulars of your inquiry, I have no knowledge. It is true that, as I had been widowed for five years prior to his visit to Richmond in the summer of 1848 when we renewed our acquaintance, we were considering marriage at the time of his death. The letters he wrote to me, however, vanished long ago; therefore, I am in possession of no autographs. More than this I cannot say, & I beg to be excused from any communication that might bring my name before the public.

 Yours very truly,
 Sarah E. Shelton

(ITEM 73: *Elmira Shelton*)

...

414 North 10th Street
Richmond, Virginia
June 14, 1884

Dear Captain Gayle:

I am in receipt of your note of the 4th along with the newspaper notice of Mrs. Nichols's death which you kindly enclosed. I did not know the lady, nor did I recall her name in reference to Edgar. On consulting my library, however, I found her accounts of visits to Fordham in the year preceding Virginia Poe's death. They were told with such vivid detail & compassion that I felt myself wishing I had known her. I must say that your description of your long & enjoyable correspondence with Mrs. Nichols left me feeling envious & rather regretful of my long & strict silence on a subject that has garnered far more attention than I would ever have dreamed—namely, Edgar Allan Poe.

You have been generous & dutiful during the years since our first exchange in sending articles & clippings pertaining to Edgar. I am almost ashamed to admit that you have had nothing in return but the occasional acknowledgment. You could not have known, of course, that after reading Mr. Ingram's biography, I did not wish to be informed on the subject.

I am, nevertheless, impressed by your perseverance. On Sunday last, I had occasion to speak to Mrs. Susan Weiss at St. John's Episcopal Church, &, knowing from one of your past letters that you correspond with her also, I made mention of having heard from you. You cannot imagine how her face lit up when I called your name. She is exceedingly fond of you, Captain, in addition to having great admiration for you. Susan is almost closer in age to my son than to me; therefore, I do not know her well, but we had an enjoyable conversation, speaking primarily of you.

Among other things, Susan informed me that you come through Richmond once or twice each year, on your way home to North Carolina to visit family. If you have previously told me this, forgive my having forgotten. If quite convenient on your next trip through, I invite you to call on me, & we can have that talk about Edgar Poe that you have so patiently awaited.

Truly, I am your friend,
Elmira Shelton

:: I SUPPOSE THE YEARS HAVE HARDENED MY HEART. Women are so easily brought to tears, but for the longest time, though I have much to regret in my long life, I found little about which to cry. Generally, I am not a sentimental person, though neither do I consider myself in the least unfeeling. I am rather more practical in my opinions and arrangements, that by way of disappointments, by the burden of overseeing property, and by having survived a devastating war that threatened the destruction of everything I owned and held dear, even including my very existence. By necessity, I developed a hard crust, but it is not so hard as it appears.

I shall give you a for instance: A Dr. Moran—the very same Dr. Moran who ministered to Edgar on his deathbed in Baltimore thirty-five years ago—recently gave a lecture here in Richmond on the subject. I attended and, after he spoke, I introduced myself. As we talked I was amazed to find tears streaming down my cheeks such that I even caused Dr. Moran, himself, to commence crying. Before that night I would have thought I had lost all capacity for sentiment, particularly regarding Edgar Poe. This may surprise you. Suffice it to say, there is much as yet untold, and I suppose the time has come to tell it.

To begin, I must return to the Richmond of a very different era—that of 1823—the year I saw Edgar for the first time. I was twelve; he was fourteen and had recently returned from England. I think of that Richmond as a bustling town full of industry and energy. Ships packed the river; the wharves were crammed with bales of golden tobacco, the air scented with its pungent sweetness. The streets were dirt and thickly trafficked with horse-drawn drays and carriages. I recall ever-present stacks of lumber and the sound of hammers driving nails. Indians were still a common sight in those days, their mute expressions as fearsome as their savage past. The markets were filled with every commodity imaginable, including slaves, and I never tired of watching the auctions, so fascinated was I by the exotic faces of the Negroes.

My family lived on 2nd Street with a clear view across gardens of the Allan house. Edgar had been abroad with his parents for six years which explains why I had not seen him before. I don't remember how we met. I suppose it was as children inevitably meet who run and play in the same neighborhood—a game of hide-and-seek or capture the flag on summer nights after supper, before the sun goes down. Being a typically shy girl just entering her teens, I took notice of everything while thinking no one took the least notice of me. Then one night, our parents called us in, and, because of where Edgar and I were on that particular evening, our paths led home in the same direction. We walked along, alone together for the first time, and Edgar said to me, "I have never been so close to a girl before."

I was thrilled by his words, too young to suspect that he was merely repeating something he'd read or heard older boys say. Truthfully, we weren't all that close to each other; we were just walking home side-by-side. There was not a suggestion of holding hands or anything like that, and when I peeled off to go into the house, Edgar broke into a run, heading toward his own home, and ducking under clotheslines and hopping a fence, he disappeared. But that was the first night I remember thinking about him. Before then he'd just been another boy in the neighborhood, except in the way he talked. He still had something of an English accent which would soon disappear, though he always spoke in a singular way. After that night I became aware of him staring at me, and doubtless I stared at him, but for months neither of us said a word, not wanting to be teased by the other kids who always enjoy ragging sweethearts.

Edgar took to appearing when I least expected. I would be walking home from school, and he would suddenly be walking along beside me. He never offered to carry my books, or anything so old-hat as that. He would shuffle along beside me, almost as if I were pestering him. I knew his pride was at stake, and I played my role as best I could. I accepted his many expressions of boredom, there for the other kids to see, as the price I had to pay for his being there, and every time I could feel the swelling in my chest and the blood rushing to my head. I longed for the least little kindness. The most infinitesimal straw of affection would have pricked a galaxy of thrills. I waited patiently, certain I could take no lead, praying he would work up the courage to make some inviting comment to which, of course, I would immediately agree. For almost a year I was all nerves in his presence. I never left the classroom without a prayer in my mind as I descended the steps, "God—*please!*—let him be there."

At that time there was a large vacant lot at the corner of 2nd and Main that is now called Linden Square. Edgar referred to it as the "Enchanted Garden." I never wondered why it was not overgrown with weeds, since it was, indeed, a well-tended garden shaded by lindens and redbuds. I suppose I had imagined that a house once stood on the lot, since it was surrounded by a brick wall covered in areas of shade with English ivy and in sunnier spots with climbing pink and white roses. The entrance was protected by a heavy wooden gate, but the boards were old and rotting and the metal latch, rusted and beyond serviceability. The whole of it seemed old to my girlish imagination, as old as the ruins of a bygone time. The garden stood opposite the home of Charles Ellis, John Allan's partner in Ellis & Allan, the same John Allan who was Edgar's foster father. I didn't know at the time that Mr. Ellis's wife enjoyed the view of the garden from her front windows, and, therefore, Mr. Ellis's gardener kept it up, despite it being owned by a relative of Mr. Allan. Within the brick wall were neat beds of lilacs and tea roses, well-pruned for cuttings for the dining table. Close up to the front wall in the westernmost corner, one could sit or even stand, hidden from view of even the upstairs windows of the surrounding houses, and it was to this spot that Edgar lured me one afternoon with nothing more than, "Let's go in."

After strolling all around and in between each dark-soil, well-weeded bed, admiring as we went, we ended up in that unseen corner, and there Edgar talked about his plans—his plans for going to university, for returning to Europe thereafter, for achieving greatness in some field of endeavor. Richmond could not hold him, he explained; it was far too provincial for someone like him. I did not know what "provincial" meant, but I was with him all the way. I would be his wife, travel the world with him, stop at nothing to assist his endeavors in whatever way a wife does those sorts of things. He talked nonstop; I said nothing. When he finished talking, we stood for a long time. I stared at him, expecting and hoping that, what with our plans made, the time had come for us to kiss. "You'd best go on home," was all he said. I nodded and went on home.

One day, not long thereafter, in precisely the same spot, he called me by my name for the first time ever. He called me Myra. "Myra," he asked, "do you like your father?"

"Yes, of course," I replied, not knowing why he would ask such a question. But it seemed so personal, and I had been waiting for over a year to hear him call my name or ask me a question to which I could reply in the affirmative that it felt as if I had accepted nothing less than a proposal of marriage. I had just turned fourteen, and I was now spoken for. I considered myself betrothed, not hesitating for an instant. He was the most beautiful boy I'd ever imagined, so unlike all the others. He had dark gray eyes that penetrated my soul. He had a thin, swimmer's body with shoulders out to here, a classic face, patrician nose, and a forehead that told of brains other boys could only dream of. He was quiet and serious, and more compelling than anything else, there was a profound sadness about him that revealed unimaginable depth and cried out for consolation—*my* consolation.

Soon after this incident, on one of our many walks in the autumn of that year and burying once-and-for-all any doubts remaining in my mind, Edgar led me to Shockoe Hill Cemetery. I knew Robert Stanard; he was one of the neighborhood boys who ran in our circle, and I had met his mother. I had no idea, however, the depth of Edgar's love for Robert's mother. She had died only a few months before, in April, I recall. As we stood over her grave, Edgar confessed to me that he often came here at night to be with her, that he was neither ashamed nor afraid to lie on her grave. I could see by his grief the depth of his love for her, but it was not the kind of love that would have elicited jealousy on my part, and I felt none. Edgar's mother was still alive at this time, or at least the woman I presumed was his mother. I knew his name was Poe, not Allan, but I did not know the particulars—that he was a foster child, not an adopted child, or perhaps I thought that he was Fanny Allan's child by a previous marriage, that his father was dead and that his mother had remarried John Allan. Truth be known, I don't remember what I thought, but it never occurred to me that his attachment to Robert Stanard's mother might have resulted from a feeling of alienation from his father. Had I understood this better, I might have been better prepared for what later happened. All I thought at the time was that the boy I loved cared deeply for those he loved and that his affections were abiding, and what could have been more reassuring to a fourteen-year-old girl than to comprehend at a profound level that the love of the love-of-her-life was so durable as to persist beyond the grave? For the secrets he shared, I could not have loved him more. I was virtually his.

Our love was not without passion. In our enchanted garden he kissed me, tentatively at first, but our kisses lingered and in time we learned to part our lips, open our mouths, and touch our tongues together. Though this act scared me at first and felt sinful, it became an irresistible thing to do. The playfulness with which our tongues touched made me long for more. I desperately wanted Edgar to touch my breasts. I could feel my nipples stiffen when he kissed me, and I dreamed of his fingertips. During such wide-awake dreams, I could not resist imagining that my own fingers were his. It was at such a time that I had my first orgasm. I was not prepared; I knew not what was happening inside me, but whatever it was, I wanted to feel it again. I recall one day watching Edgar put the tip of his thumb in his mouth, there to trifle it with his tongue and teeth, and I thought if he did not stop, I would go crazy. It was then I realized I was spinning out of control. Honestly I don't believe I cared.

We became inseparable. We took our teasing from the other kids, unfazed by it. Edgar became a fixture in my home. I played the piano, and Edgar played the flute or sang in a fine tenor voice. Or he would read to me in the window seat on the stair landing from which we could look out the casement window at the back of his house. Sometimes we would walk up to Church Hill, and on rare occasions on out into the country, once or twice to Duncan's Lodge to see his sister, Rosalie, and the Mackenzie boys. Edgar was kind to Rosalie, though she pestered and clung, a bit too needy for Edgar. Still he tolerated her.

In bits and pieces I came to know more of Edgar's precarious situation in the Allan household. Though his foster mother and his "Aunt Nancy" Valentine, who lived with the family, appeared to dote on Edgar, there was apparent friction in his relationship with his foster father. John Allan was a demanding man, and Edgar seemed always to be in hot water. Looking back on it now, I think John Allan resented the fact that Edgar did not manifest greater appreciation for having been "taken in," but considering that he had been only three at the time, how could he? Mr. Allan's subtle reminders told Edgar that he was not a son, and his understandable sense of alienation served to further confound the relationship.

In February of 1826, Edgar enrolled at the new university in Charlottesville. He desperately wanted a good education and to be out from under his foster father's roof. On the other hand, leaving meant leaving me. By then we had declared our love for each other. I was approaching my fifteenth birthday; Edgar had just turned seventeen. He never asked, in so many words, if I would marry him, but such was our intention, and we talked about our futures in terms of "we"—one future sufficed for the both of us.

My father, John Royster, was a friend of Mr. Allan. He tolerated Edgar, though I sensed he disapproved of our being sweethearts. He was strict in limiting our time together, particularly in the evenings, and it seemed the older I became, the stricter he became, forever reminding me that I was too young to have a serious boyfriend. When he learned that Edgar was to go to university, he was enthusiastic and suddenly very kind to Edgar. I failed to perceive that Edgar and my separation was the source of his enthusiasm; I took it to be approval of Edgar's ambition, and I made the mistake of confiding in my mother that Edgar and I intended to someday marry. My father said nothing about this until Edgar left, but immediately thereafter he came down hard on me, insisting that I was much too young to entertain such ideas. I was to banish such thoughts and instructed not to write to Edgar. I resolved to write anyway, secretly if I must; I was not about to obey my father on this score.

The morning Edgar left, since it was a school day, I went early to tell him goodbye. James Hill, the Allan's Negro coachman, had already drawn the carriage up in front of the house and was loading trunks on top when I arrived. I waited, chatting with James, then Mrs. Allan came out, wearing coat and hat, an indication that she intended to make the trip to Charlottesville also. I greeted her, and she said some kind things about my appearance and that Edgar was sure to miss me. Then Edgar and Mr. Allan came out onto the porch, and they had words, something to do with money, and Mrs. Allan looked away, her expression tense. Edgar came down the steps, his lips pressed tight. There were tears in his eyes, and he brushed past me and into the carriage, embarrassed, I suppose. James helped Mrs. Allan up and in, then he climbed up on the seat and gave the horses rein. I waved and Edgar waved back, but not a word was exchanged.

Two days later James Hill brought over a letter that Edgar had given him to bring back for me, and he left it with my mother. She said, as she handed it to me when I got home from school, "Remember what your father said."

In the letter Edgar explained that his father had given him so little money that he couldn't hope to pay all his expenses, that his father didn't seem to understand the amounts necessary for room and board plus furniture, clothes, laundry, etc., not to mention books. He left Richmond with $110 dollars, but after paying tuition and board immediately upon arrival, he was left owing almost $50 more for room and furniture. He was in debt before the end of his first day. He railed about these troubles for all but enough space at the end of his letter to lament that he had been unable to kiss me goodbye due to his mother's presence and to add that he loved me and would write soon and often.

He didn't write.

I wrote and posted letter after letter, but received nothing in return.

Once a week my father played whist with Mr. Allan and other men, and he returned home from one of those sessions to relate the shocking news that John Allan had heard regarding the goings-on at the university—fist fights, cowhiding, bottles and bricks thrown at professors, nightly drinking and gambling, not to mention other, thoroughly dissolute acts of depravity and corruption. It was shameful, and if Thomas Jefferson didn't take drastic measures and soon, the new University of Virginia would soon be defunct.

I ceased writing him, persuaded by his not writing me and mindful of what my father reported that his head had been turned by other, more manly pursuits. I did not see him for over a year. Though I believe he came home on occasion, I was either away or our paths didn't cross. I was heartbroken at first, but this gave way to resentment and anger and too much pride. The following winter, I began receiving calls from Barrett Shelton, a man my parents eagerly promoted. Barrett was exacting in his pursuit of me. It seems he had just recently decided that his situation was sufficiently well established to allow him to take a wife, and, with that decision made, as if the matter was one of simple domestication, he perused the Richmond stables for a suitable mare. He was a dozen years older than I, from a wealthy and prominent Richmond family, and I cannot say that I disliked him, though there was nothing between us of the intimacy and passion I had known with Edgar. Barrett was all about material things. He wanted a fine house on Church Hill with all the amenities dictated by a prosperous situation.

Little did I suspect that I was one of them. My parents and, indeed, all their friends promoted the match with a sort of presumption that I could not possibly be anything other than enthusiastic, and I found myself swept along in a tide of certainty that such a match would surely bring me happiness. I had just turned sixteen when Barrett asked my father's permission to propose, and my father gladly gave his consent. A year earlier I had been too young to have a serious boyfriend; now I was old enough to marry. My parents planned an engagement party for late in May, and half of Richmond was invited.

For the occasion, a tent was erected in our back yard to cover a platform built to accommodate an ensemble of musicians and to serve as a dance floor. This tent was connected to the house by a trellis constructed of wood, whitewashed, and the uprights were painted to resemble climbing vines and plump bunches of purple grapes and all was lit by standing wrought iron candelabras placed at intervals around the perimeter holding candles inside hurricane lanterns. Inside the house, all rooms were decorated with hothouse flowers—all that Richmond could provide for a gala so early in the season, and the dining room table and two sideboards provided fare from our own kitchen and half a dozen local purveyors. One would have thought my father a millionaire.

I was not unaware of an element of haste in the preparations, but I marked it down to my parents' eager enthusiasm for a favorable match for their daughter, and I became caught up in the excitement of new clothes, wedding gifts, and being quite suddenly the center of attention. And I was impressed by Barrett to the point that I felt confident that my favorable impression would tip over into love when all was said and done. It was sure to happen any time now, perhaps even this evening when we would be called on to dance for the applause of all.

I wore a pale blue gown of luminous satin, cut low and off my shoulders—*décolleté* as I learned to call it—crinolines galore, and my mother and our maid spent an hour with the curling iron so that by the time our guests arrived, I would have perfect ringlets drooling around my ears. Admiring myself in the mirror, I decided I was quite beautiful. My dark hair, which I had always thought boring, was suddenly rich with luster; my figure, in the past so girlishly skinny, now appeared womanly thanks to the miracle of corseting. I waited impatiently for

Barrett to arrive, as I could not go down until he did. After greeting my father and just as he turned to look up toward the landing, I appeared on cue and descended to accept his outstretched hand and the applause of those gathered there. I suppose I was never more beautiful nor Barrett more *gallant*. With all eyes on me, I imagined dreams coming true.

I have no words—alas!—to tell
The loveliness of loving well!

I danced every dance. No gentleman worth his salt would allow a bride-to-be to languish for a second without attention. The line to break on whomever I was dancing with was never less than three or four. They came in an endless stream—dressed in their finery, all gushing with the same sugary compliments—some I knew, some I didn't, until I almost ceased paying attention to them. What with all the fuss over me, I became heady with my own success. Sometime after midnight, having danced for hours, I saw yet another hand reach out to tap my partner on the shoulder, and I turned to find myself in the arms of Edgar Poe.

My first impulse was to run, but Edgar's grip refused my attempt, forcing me to face him. "Is it true what they say, Myra?" he demanded, "That you're engaged?"

The muscles in his jaw clinched, and remembering what my father said about the goings-on at the university, I wondered if he had been drinking and might pick a fight. Worried that he would ruin the night, I became indignant. "Yes, it is true, *Mr. Poe*," I said, "but surely that's of no concern to you?"

"You've changed, Myra," he said, loosening his grip slightly. "You weren't like this. Or did I misjudge you all those years?"

"You're the one who changed. I trusted you. I trusted you like a stupid fool."

Someone tapped Edgar on the shoulder, and when he refused to let me go, he found himself surrounded by a handful of Barrett's male friends. Giving way, he released me and raised his left hand to signal his surrender, though he never once took his gaze off me. "So this is how it is?" he asked, turned, and walked away followed by two or three of the men. He walked around where the musicians played and toward the back of the yard where the Allans' garden met ours. I assumed he was leaving the party, going home.

I excused myself and almost ran through the house and up to my bedroom. I had to be alone just then, to compose myself if nothing else. I was shaking like a leaf. I sat on the edge of the bed, my head in my hands. I imagined him being muscled away by Barrett's friends, and the thought crushed me. He seemed so defenseless by comparison to them, and I prayed they didn't hurt him. Then I remembered his changed expression when I had said that about trusting him. It was not the expression I would have expected. At first it had been anger and hurt pride, but that then vanished into something else, something I could not quite discern. Bewilderment?

There was a knock at the door. "He's gone, lambkin," my father said. "The coast is clear. You can come back down now. Don't disappoint your guests, sweet pea."

What did he think I was thinking?

I made myself return, but unable to dance anymore, I politely refused the invitations. I wanted the party over. Seeing Edgar had undermined all my certainty; the engagement was a horrible mistake. I avoided Barrett, fixed myself a plate of breakfast which was now being served. It must be three, I realized, the hour appointed for serving breakfast to our guests. I latched on to Mary Winfree, my cousin from Chesterfield, and we carried our plates outside. I needed fresh air, I wanted cold, fresh air. To not be noticed, Mary and I wandered into the side yard, concealing ourselves among the boxwoods at the edge of the yard. I could feel goose bumps rising on my bare shoulders, and I took a bite of cold scrambled eggs.

"Why did you say that?" a voice came from the darkness,—"About trusting me."

Mary looked up at me, her eyes wide, a forkful of scrambled egg poised above her plate. Behind her in the darkness, I perceived his dark silhouette, though I could not see details of his face.

"Go away, Edgar," I said. I didn't want to be unkind, but nor did I want another scene or to have him hurt.

"Tell me why first. I demand to know."

Mary froze, not moving a muscle.

"You never wrote to me like you promised. That's what I meant."

"I *did* write. What are you talking about? It was you who stopped writing."

"I stopped because I never heard from you."

"I must have written you a dozen letters—maybe more." I heard him laugh, then stop, then let go a sigh. "Oh, Myra. I wondered why your letters never acknowledged mine or answered any of my questions—you never got them. The first one I gave to James Hill to hand deliver to you. Did you not even get that one?"

"I did get that one," I said, grasping his implication, "but no more. Not even *one* more."

"If you don't believe me, I will swear to you on Jane Stanard's grave that I wrote you at least a dozen letters." For a moment he said nothing. Mary Winfree stood, still frozen between us, still staring at me as I stared beyond her at Edgar. "I'd wager," he continued, "that *your father* knows what happened, and if you won't ask him, I will."

I waited, confused, incredulous, but also afraid suddenly that he meant to go in and confront my father then and there. Instead, his dark silhouette seemed to vaporize like smoke. I heard a rustling of bushes and tree limbs then nothing. Without moving, I focused on Mary. She read my mind. "Not a word. I swear."

> Halo of Hell! And with a pain
> Hell shall make me fear again—
> O craving heart, for the lost flowers
> And sunshine of my summer hours!

I did ask my father. I asked him the following morning, confronting him in his study as soon as I came downstairs. Though it was nearly noon, he was reading his newspaper, his coffee cup on the table beside his chair. "Have a seat, Myra," he said. He put his paper down and went to close the study door.

I don't recall how I had put the question. "What happened to Edgar's letters," or some such. I had been unable to sleep. I kept thinking of all the tables that my mother planned to set up in our parlor now that my engagement party was over, tables to be filled with wedding gifts. I had been so excited by the prospect of so many presents, and now it all seemed a burlesque, a parlor drama in which I was the unsuspecting victim of a heroine.

My father cleared his throat. He seemed nervous. No doubt he'd hoped this moment would never come, and I found that so infuriating, I wanted to scream.

"Lambkin," he said, "I thought you were long over Edgar Poe." He spoke softly, forcing a sympathetic smile.

I searched his eyes, trying to understand how my own father could have done such a thing. It was too unbelievable. I recalled then what he'd said about my being too young for a boyfriend. That hadn't been it at all. "Did you steal his letters?"

"Steal!" He was irritated now, but he kept his voice down. "That's a trifle unfair, *young lady.* There are some things you need to understand—things that I had hoped you would have the good sense to figure out for yourself."

"Did you *take* them?"

"Listen to me, Myra. Barrett Shelton is a fine man. He's handsome, kind, honorable. He comes from a fine family. And he adores you. You'll have a fine life—children who will grow up with advantages most children never have. Look on the bright side." With this he turned and reached for his coffee cup. "There are things about Edgar that I can't tell you. Things told to me in confidence. Things about which, I daresay, he has not yet come to realize, but that can't be denied or ignored. Understand that it was the hardest thing I ever did, but I didn't want you to get hurt, and I knew you would be. I know in my heart that I did the right thing. I did it for you."

"Do you still have them? His letters? I want them."

He shook his head as if such a notion was ridiculous. "No. Of course not."

"Did you read them?"

"Of course not, lambkin!"

"Did you let Barrett read them too?"

He did not deign to answer. My interview was at an end. I stood, walked to the door, opened it, and turned back to my father. "Tell Barrett the wedding is off."

I was sent away to boarding school. When my parents learned that Edgar did not intend to return to Charlottesville to continue his studies, they worried that his presence in Richmond presented too great an opportunity for a chance meeting, and, since I had discovered the theft of the letters, the chance was too great for a reconciliation that would confound my parents' plans for me to marry Barrett. To placate Barrett, my father resorted to his old excuse of my being too young. What harm will it do, putting it off a year, I suppose he said. I know they talked—plotted more likely. And I know that my father talked to John Allan, and I could only imagine what transpired. He refused to even acknowledge such goings-on, but I was certain they were conspiring sub rosa. I was forbidden to see Edgar, and I imagined he had been forbidden to see me. I heard through friends that he had moved out of the Allan house into a boarding house but that he could be reached by mail at the Courthouse Tavern. I thought of writing, but then, quite mysteriously he was gone. That was mid-summer. I left for school in the fall. A year and a half later, on December 6, 1828, I became Mrs. Alexander Barrett Shelton. I was seventeen.

> And childhood is a summer sun
> Whose waning is the dreariest one—
> For all we live to know is known
> And all we seek to keep hath flown—

Edgar's letters to me had not been destroyed, at least not all. I found one. Almost on the eve of my wedding I found it quite accidently while going through the drawers of my father's desk, looking for something. It had been opened. I suppose my father had saved it for showing to Barrett and forgot to destroy it afterward. When I confronted Barrett with this suspicion, he admitted that my father had shown it to him. The letter professed Edgar's desire to marry me as soon as he took his degree at which time he expected to be taken into John Allan's business when he would be able to support us. I supposed also that my father wanted to prove to Barrett that if he wished to marry me, he'd best press his suit. Again I considered calling off the wedding. Not for any hope of being courted by Edgar again; he had been gone from Richmond for a year and a half, and no one seemed to know where he was. He had totally disappeared. I considered calling it off because the whole thing seemed to implicate Barrett. Were it not for my son, I would wish now that I had called it off.

Mary Winfree knew all. After the night of our engagement party when she had overheard the exchange between Edgar and me, we became closer than we had ever been before. She kept her promise not to breathe a word, and I loved her for it. I confided everything, and so sad did she think the story that I do believe she almost fell in love with Edgar herself. It appeared he fascinated her, and I didn't discourage her. I needed her sympathy.

About three years after my marriage, we learned that Edgar was then living with his aunt in Baltimore. It so happened that summer Mary planned to go there to visit friends. She wrote from Chesterfield to say that she intended to look him up, that she would happily convey any messages, and that she would provide a full report when she returned. I could not resist sending her a gift book to take to him, a book entitled *Bijou*. It contained a story I had written to which I refrained from signing my name, but I told Mary that it was mine. It must be remembered that, to that time, I had never told Edgar what I had learned about his letters, and for all I knew, he still harbored resentment toward me. Once while I had been away at school, before my marriage to Barrett, he had returned to Richmond and had come around to see me. He ended up confronting my father, and they argued. I guessed the argument arose, because Edgar accused him of stealing his letters, and I suspected my father had threatened him in some way. I had never wanted him to think badly of me, but nor had the opportunity presented itself for me to explain, so, since my little story in *Bijou* was a veiled telling of everything, I decided it was a suitably indirect way of conveying my regret. It might seem daring of me, but I didn't care. I was not happy in my marriage. My father's deception and Barrett's complicity in that deception had given birth to a strain that seemed a pall on our marriage from the very first, and in all our fifteen years together it never lifted. It hasn't lifted to this day, forty years after Barrett was thrown from his horse and trampled to death. Ours was a professional marriage; there is no other way to describe it.

Mary did find Edgar. She gave him the gift book and, I gathered, told him everything. When she returned, she wrote to tell me that he was well but very poor, that he lived in a cramped three rooms with his aunt and her daughter, and his brother, William Henry, who was a sailor and a writer, and who had resolved, after hearing Mary, to write a story about Edgar and me. I never suspected that he would actually do it, but he did. He called it "The Pirate," though he never got it published.

Mary's visit served to put a final chapter on our affair, or so it seemed to me. In my first five years of marriage, I gave birth to two daughters, both named for me and who both died before their first birthday. I had great difficulty during my second pregnancy and was told by the doctor that if I risked more children, I might not survive. This was a blow to Barrett as well; he wanted an heir more than anything in the world. These tragedies served to supplant my feelings of resentment for past wrongs with an abject hopelessness for the future. I became quite discouraged. In desperation I started reading the Bible, searching for something—anything to give life purpose. I joined St. John's Episcopal Church and was baptized there on my twenty-second birthday. But this did little to allay my depression.

In August of 1835 I read an announcement in the *Southern Literary Messenger* that its new editor was Edgar A. Poe. I had heard not a word about him for over three years. I did not know that he had gone into magazine work, but I had known something when we were young about his aspirations to become a writer through his long recitations of Lord Byron and other poets. In the September issue of the magazine, there appeared an unsigned poem, "To Sarah," and I was certain Edgar had written it.

The silvery streamlet gurgling on,
The mock-bird chirping on the thorn,
Remind me, love, of thee.
They seem to whisper thoughts of love,
As thou didst when the stars above
Witnessed thy vows to me.

I fancied it an obvious reference to the promises we'd made before he left for university. I was certain the day would come when our paths would cross. I found excuses to be in the vicinity of the *Messenger* office and even Mrs. Yarrington's, the boarding house where I understood Edgar was living, but I didn't so much as catch a glimpse of him.

Early one Saturday morning in September, Barrett and I, in company with others, took a yacht down the James for a picnic at Beverly, one of the more imposing of the James River Plantations. Located on a sharp bend in the river, we were disgorged at the dock at about noon, and, as ladies were accustomed to doing in those days when invited for an all-day affair, upon entering the house we adjourned upstairs, there to strip down to our underclothes for tea or lemonade, a sponge bath, and a short nap before the picnic began. The staircase at Beverly was grand. It curved up from both sides of the spacious front hall to meet at a landing two-thirds of the way up where a huge bay window gave view to gardens and the river beyond. On either side of the bay window was a small niche partially hidden by floor to ceiling chintz curtains. The bay window faced south and the sun shone through and into my eyes as I ascended the stairs, removing my hat as I went. I was more or less alone. Others had gone on ahead or were gathering at the bottom. I paused at the landing to stick my hatpin back into my hat so I wouldn't lose it, and when I looked up, Edgar was staring at me, having parted the curtain that had concealed him. For more than a moment we stood, staring at each other. Not four feet separated us. Then, from nowhere it seemed, Barrett was beside me, his arm around my waist, leading me back down the stairs and outside where he demanded a carriage to return us to Richmond at once.

Most of the way back, I leaned my head against the cushion, my eyes closed. I wonder if I was recovering from what had seemed to be a cessation of my heartbeat. I loved that he had planted himself there and waited for me. How in the world had he wrangled an invitation and then made it to the landing without being noticed? How long had he been waiting? The more I thought about it, the more thrilled I was. Then I remembered that Barrett was beside me and probably furious with me, and I wondered if I had been smiling as we drove, jostled and bumped as we were, thinking of Edgar. I then remembered that Barrett claimed to be a crack shot, though I didn't know if this was true or idle boasting. Barrett wasn't particularly devoted to the truth. I turned to see him looking out the carriage window, his jaw pushed forward, murder in his expression. "Promise you won't do anything, Barrett."

"I'll promise nothing."

"He wouldn't have come without an invitation. He had a right to be there."

"Not on the landing, he didn't."

"I'll bear you another child," I said.

He turned to look at me suddenly, a look of puzzlement and surprise on his face. I meant it, and he must have seen that I meant it. Was I saving Edgar from a duel? I don't think so. It was convenient; that's all. I had decided to bear another child anyway, despite the doctor's warnings. At that point in my life I didn't really care if I lived or died.

By the following summer Edgar had become somewhat well known in Richmond. His stories in the *Messenger* drew much attention—"Berenice," "Morella," "Hans Phaall"—all Gothic and immensely popular. It seemed he was making his way. His foster parents were both dead by then, most recently his foster father, John Allan, who was reputedly the richest man in Virginia, but when the contents of Mr. Allan's will became known, it was apparent that Edgar had been disinherited. I could have cried for such heartlessness, but I had ceased crying by then.

Edgar's marriage was announced in the spring after our encounter at Beverly. Mary Winfree wrote to inform me that his bride was also his first cousin whom Mary had met on her trip to Baltimore four years earlier. "And did you know," Mary confided, "that she is only thirteen."

It wasn't long after that I encountered the newly married couple, having a Sunday afternoon stroll on Broad Street in Church Hill. Edgar introduced me to Virginia, and she was truly lovely. Yes, she was quite young, but her complexion was flawless, and her face possessed a remarkable softness that needed touching to be believed. I could not resist caressing her cheek, complimenting her beauty and congratulating her as I did so. Most arresting of all was her pitch-black hair, so black as to be almost startling. I did not linger but moved on as if Edgar and I were mere acquaintances, though at that same instant memories of our walks together in that very spot, expressing our affection in our awkward adolescent way, fueled a feeling of agony. I tried to shake it from my mind, reminding myself that I was a married woman. It had only been a dozen years, but it felt like another lifetime.

> O human love! thou spirit given
> On earth of all we hope in Heaven!
> Which fallest into the soul like rain
> Upon the Syroc-wither'd plain,

And failing of thy power to bless,
But leavest the heart a wilderness!

Twelve years went by. Partway, I gave birth to a healthy son, thus
providing Barrett with an heir. He was thrilled, and I survived it, but
not without excruciating pain and four months flat on my back. I
vowed never again. Then, midway, in 1843 while foxhunting, Barrett
was thrown from his horse taking a downhill jump over a split rail
fence into rutted cow pasture, leading a dozen or more riders unable
to rein in their horses in time. Half of them were already in midair, so
I was told, and Barrett was trampled to death. His horse survived, but
with a foreleg so broken that his hoof swung at the end of sinew like
a pocket watch at the end of a chain. Despite this he ran four miles
before he could be caught and put down. I cried. I cried for the poor
horse. I was thirty-two years old, the mother of a five-year-old boy and
a widow. And very soon thereafter I learned that I was a wealthy widow
and now the proprietress of a thriving dry goods business.

My parents were still alive then. My father rushed in to offer his
experience and managerial expertise in helping run the business, but
I declined his help. I declined politely in the interest of family harmony, but I was of a mind to be an independent woman, and—not to
trumpet my own achievements—I exacted profits that put Barrett to
shame. I found I had a knack for saying no, and came to learn that this
simple, two-letter word was the secret to making "money-plenty"—to
borrow a phrase from Benjamin Franklin. I came to enjoy the challenge and was emboldened to learn that, so long as I tithed, the Bible
held nothing against such enterprising activity.

On a Sunday morning in August of 1848, as I was dressing for
church, a maidservant knocked on my bedroom door to announce a
visitor. I was rather aggravated that any right-thinking person would
pay a call at ten-thirty o'clock on a Sunday morning, and I called to
her to say that I was coming down, but that I was on my way to church
and would not be delayed. When I entered the parlor, I saw Edgar Poe
standing at the far end in front of the mantle.

"Myra! Is it really you?"

I have said that I developed a hard crust. I suppose I had become
harder than hardwood. Perhaps better said, I had become an iron

horse, a locomotive. I was a slave to habitude, rigidly refusing to stray. Such was my makeup.

"I would be happy to see you, Edgar," I said, "but not just now. I'm on my way to church."

I could see he was hurt at first, but he recovered quickly and politely asked if he could come that afternoon to pay a call. I agreed and moved aside to permit him to leave.

As the congregation sang "Onward Christian Soldiers," I almost regretted having been so abrupt and ungracious, but I beat back such thoughts with not-so-gentle admonition. I marvel that I possessed so little toleration. Why was Edgar not in church, I wondered, then answered my own question with recollections of infamous reports of his intemperance. Sadly his reputation preceded him, and I wondered if I should have anything at all to do with him. Yes, he had become a famous writer, but where was the moral fortitude, I asked? In my mind I found it lacking, and I wondered if he was beyond redemption. Still, I could not dismiss a feeling of compassion. I knew of Virginia's death. How could I not welcome him in the aftermath of that? On the other hand, why was he here? Men had been after my money for years. I would not be fooled or softened by the likes of "Myra, is it really you?"

He paid his visit that afternoon. I rebuffed every effort on his part to draw me back into the past. I refused to go down memory lane with him, and his disappointment was evident. As our interview drew to a close, I recalled something he'd said to me in the garden, in the dark, the night of my engagement party—"You've changed, Myra." I had changed, indeed. I was an upright, respectable, and devout Christian woman, and for the first time in years—perhaps ever—I wondered if that related in any way to happiness. That, in turn, led to a question that had not occurred at all, or at least in living memory—was I unhappy? Suddenly it seemed an odd word. An almost alien word. And I beat it down with the stick of iron resolve that then ruled my life, just as I had beat down my ungraciousness as I sang a battle-hymn in church that very morning. Suddenly Edgar's presence was unnerving, and I wished he would leave and told him so in so many words.

He stood, seeming to sense a discomfort that I preferred he not perceive. "May I come again?" he asked.

"For what purpose, Edgar?"

He gave my question thought. I could see he was hurt by its apathy, but I didn't have the heart to soften it. I think I had no heart at all. I perceived that he would leave without another word, and again I recalled our exchange in my father's garden the night of my engagement party, and, worried that I might lose forever the chance to say it, so without premeditation I blurted: "You didn't misjudge me, Edgar—all those years ago, I mean. Time and circumstances change us. You can't know—about me, that is. You have no way of knowing. I hardly know myself."

He stared at me, questions in his eyes. "May I come again?"

I smiled at him. Was it the first time I had smiled in years? "Yes," I said. "You may."

My breast her shield in wintry weather,
And when the friendly sunshine smil'd,
And she would mark the opening skies,
I saw no Heaven but in her eyes.

He came often, always in the mornings. I came to expect his visits. On occasion he would bring his sister, Rosalie, apologizing to me with his eyes, for Rosalie was difficult and needy, but I admired him greatly for his tolerating her. His kindness and consideration for her signaled nobility on his part in my way of thinking, elevating him in my esteem. His feelings for her were genuine; anyone could see that. One morning I asked him to read "The Raven" for me. He recited it instead, and as he finished, tears welled in his eyes. When he had regained his composure, I asked, "What is it about it that makes you cry. Is it Virginia? Your wife, I mean?"

He thought for a moment. "You don't understand, Myra." He smiled, sadly, and looked away, down at his hands clasped and resting on one knee crossed over his other leg. "I wonder if I should even tell you. It almost embarrasses me. Do you remember Jane Stanard?" he asked, looking back up at me. "I wrote a poem to Jane that I entitled 'To Helen.' I was comparing her to Helen of Troy. I wrote it when I was young; I don't recall when exactly. The name sort of evolved in my work from Helen to Lenore. Don't ask me how; I don't know why. It just happened. I wrote a poem called 'Lenore.' Then, later, I used the name again in 'The Raven' because it had always been in my mind and because it served to rhyme with 'nevermore.' It was a convenient device, so to speak. Something a poet leans on, you might say. But in my mind, Lenore was always you. Or, at least, my memory of you."

He would not look at me just then, and I was grateful for that kindness, though I stared at him, his downcast eyes. I believed him. I believed every word and still do. It all rang true. I became lost in thoughts of the history of my life, each disappointing turn, and of how it might have been different—different for both of us. Were we too far gone? Was it not possible to go back to that particular instant when things took the wrong turn and somehow right it? Though I realized just then that circumstances had engendered in me a pessimism so great as to seem impossible to overrule, I considered for the first time in over twenty years the prospect of a different outcome. May there really be, after all—I entertained, marveled, and embraced—Hope?

Edgar left soon after this revelation that served to reduce me to putty. He promised to return soon and renew his addresses. I believed him. I had come to think that nothing he'd ever said was to be disbelieved. I thought back, searching diligently my memory, even of our earliest pledges, and found nothing inconsistent with what he now said. He promised to write and he did, not often, and his letters were never long. He was busy. His writing was going well, and he was besieged with demands for stories, poems, and reviews. He lamented the delays in being paid for his work, citing the ploys and deceptions of editors employed in a market overrun with cheap competition. His answer was his own literary magazine, and he had a plan, one that would free him from the caprices of the marketplace. All he needed was the seed-money, and he listed his prospects, seeming to be certain of success. He named names.

His letters became more desperate the following spring. It seemed the *Southern Literary Messenger* owed him a lot of money, and he may have to come to collect. Did I know the new owner? Was he to be depended upon? I didn't know. Could he raise subscriptions for his new magazine in Richmond? Was a trip worth his time? I didn't know. Was *I* worth his time? My putty hardened again. Or had Edgar and I traveled the same road? Had he become as steeped in business as I? And did it matter?

I decided that I wasn't waiting. If he came, he came. If he didn't, so be it. He did come. He came every morning, just as he had the previous summer. He had taken rooms at the Swan Tavern. He had been engaged to lecture in Richmond and Norfolk, and he had plans to stay the summer with trips farther south in order to raise money for *The Stylus*—his magazine now had a name—and there were interested investors as far afield as the Carolinas, Georgia, and Tennessee. It was sure to succeed, and he was thinking of headquartering the venture right here in Richmond. He laid it all out for me on his first visit, and, before the night was over, hinted at a proposal of marriage.

I said no, but begged time for further consideration.

He said—laughing as he did so—"A love that hesitates is not a love for me."

This was not the Edgar I had known—not years ago, not even the previous year—and in a roundabout way I said so.

He retreated, sat up in his chair, swelled his chest, and agreed with me. "You read me like a book, Myra. I shouldn't be surprised. No one knows me better. I will tell you that I'm done with magazine work. You can't imagine the pressure. If I can't have my own journal, I'll retire to the country to write and hope to be paid for it. I've been through hell. I'm done with New York and Boston *and* Philadelphia. Richmond is home." He closed his eyes and dropped his head to his hands as if he might cry. "I'm spent, Myra. Coleridge burned out at an early age. Perhaps I'm no different."

"You're a great writer, Edgar."

He shrugged me off. "At best I *was*—*Was*! *Was* a great writer. But I can't bring myself to call myself a *writer*. It seems somehow presumptuous to call myself by that name. I'd rather be forgotten than be called a writer. I hate the name."

He grasped his forehead with the fingers of his right hand and squeezed hard, as if he would rip out his brain if he could.

"Yes. I'll marry you," I said. It seemed the only way to save him.

My acceptance, no sooner out of my mouth, gave rise to a myriad of problems. Before nightfall, all of Richmond knew of our engagement. Edgar had left my house and gone straight to Duncan's Lodge to make the announcement to the Mackenzies. It seems Mrs. Mackenzie had first put the idea of marrying me in Edgar's head. She was excited for him and for her own role in the arrangement and could not wait to spread the word. My son heard about it before I had the opportunity to tell him. He was ten at the time and did not like Edgar. He would roll his eyes when Edgar wasn't looking. He had been only five when he lost his father, and his father had doted on him, so thrilled was Barrett to have a son and heir. Therefore, my son idolized him, and I had fiercely protected these feelings as a way to help him cope with the loss. Edgar, for his part, was very ill at ease in the presence of a ten-year-old boy. Unable to relate, he avoided addressing my son at all, even avoided his presence. This concerned me greatly.

More and more frequently now, during his regular morning visits, Edgar spoke of *The Stylus*. His purpose seemed too thinly veiled, and it irked me no end. It made his proposal suspect in my mind, so very soon after my compulsive acceptance, I informed him of the terms of my husband's will. So as to guard his estate for his son and heir, Barrett's will included a provision that, in the event I remarried, I gave up all right to principal—it then going into the hands of a trustee for our son—and my income was to be reduced by three-fourths. I could continue living in the house as could my new husband, but the house itself became the property of my son and control of it to his guardian. Needless to say this would leave me with little to invest in a literary magazine even if I had the desire to do so which I did not. I had heard Edgar's tales about the precarious financial condition of most magazines, including their inability to pay writers. The venture had no appeal to my business sense or to my better judgment regarding Edgar's welfare. I believed that he should write, not run a business. It seemed an unwise use of his talents.

I was very frank in expressing all of this. It was my nature to be candid. As I have said, I was not in the least shy about saying no. The discomfort caused by this was immediate. Edgar made excuses to leave, and I did not see him for a week. I had a note from him one morning to say that he'd been gravely ill and had been taken from the Swan to Duncan's Lodge where he could be cared for around the clock. I suspected and soon confirmed the cause of his illness—drunkenness. Upon arrival that summer and resumption of his courting me, Edgar had taken the Temperance Pledge. He had done so without any prompting from me, and he saw to it that notice of his pledge was mentioned in the newspapers. This had served to remove that objection before it was ever raised. Now, of course, it was on the table again. Edgar had backed me against the wall. I drove out to Duncan's Lodge and demanded the return of my letters. Though there was nothing in my letters that would in any way embarrass me, by demanding their return, I was making it quite clear that the engagement was off.

The month of August went by with no word from Edgar. He remained at Duncan's Lodge. One of the Mackenzie children was getting married during that time, and, though I was invited to attend, I declined. Then in September he showed up as if nothing had happened, again pressing his suit. There was not mention of my husband's will or of Edgar's intemperance. He gave a lecture one evening, and I attended. The crowd was not large, but the next day the newspapers had nothing but high praise for his performance. He came every morning and stayed until after lunch. He begged me to play the piano, and we sang together, and soon that became an almost daily part of our routine. I began to soften again. As September drew to a close, his entreaties became more pressing, and when time approached for his departure, I found it distressing how he begged me. I never agreed, but when he left, we had an understanding of sorts. He would bring Mrs. Clemm to Richmond to meet me, and, if all went well, we would go from there. The night before he left, the 26th, he came to bid me goodbye and complained of not feeling well. I took his pulse and realized he had a fever. I advised him not to travel if he didn't feel up to it, thinking forty-eight hours on the steamboat might make him even sicker. I went to the Swan the following morning to find that he had already gone.

On a morning in early October, I was casually reading the newspaper when my eye hit on the notice of his death. It almost didn't register at first. Baltimore? He would have been in New York by now. In fact I was expecting a letter postmarked New York. There must be some mistake. Then the horrible truth became undeniable. Not an hour later John Thompson, owner of the *Messenger*, brought to the house an extract from the *Baltimore Sun*. It said that Edgar had died on Sunday, the 7th, after a seven day illness, of congestion of the brain. I went immediately to write to Mrs. Clemm. How I managed that, I don't know. I sent the letter with Mr. Thompson to post and went to bed.

Thine eyes, in Heaven of heart enshrined
Then desolately fall,
Oh God! On my funereal mind
Like starlight on a pall—

I was never more shocked than by the revelations of Griswold's memoir. As I read, I cannot describe the dread with which I approached the end of that section that chronicled Edgar's life for fear there would be some mention of me. And there was. The fact that Griswold refrained from naming me did nothing to avert the notoriety of being associated with such slander. I was the proprietress of a dry goods store that bore the name Shelton. It was common knowledge in Richmond that I was the person referred to. I prayed that Edgar's friends would discount the more lurid and atrocious accusations, but I assumed that those who had not known him would accept the whole of it as fact. I was so embarrassed by it that for years afterward, I refused to even speak of him or hear his name spoken. Such was my mortification. I grieved for the second Mrs. Allan, more than for myself, for she was named and associated with the most disgusting of Griswold's accusations. I imagined with horror the rumors that must have been going the rounds. I withdrew from all activity to the degree that I could. I refused all invitations and solicitations of which, particularly in the case of the latter, were many and pressing—journalists, editors, autograph seekers, mere curiosity seekers. It was not unusual to look out my front windows and see people standing in the street, pointing to the house. I was a circus freak-show.

Writers sent letters, imploring me to assist them in telling the truth, citing Griswold's memoir as a slanderous fiction. I refused even them. Ten or so years ago, a young Richmond friend, Virginius Valentine, a cousin of the Allans, appealed to me to communicate with John Henry Ingram of London who was preparing a definitive biography. It would do Edgar honor, so he said. I refused. Virginius then pressed his appeal in other ways, imploring me to give him something to report to Mr. Ingram to help with exposing the inaccuracies of Griswold's memoir. He appealed to my sense of justice. I agreed to a few short interviews, knowing that Virginius was reporting all I said to Mr. Ingram. But I kept them brief and factual. Two years ago a package came from Ingram himself, the two volumes of his new biography. I read them with interest, hoping they would serve to undo the harm done by Griswold.

In the main, I suppose Ingram's work did bring clarity and restore a sense of fairness to Edgar's life. But in one respect, its impact on me personally was more disturbing than anything Griswold had said. In fact I found it disheartening at first. Before reading it, I had not known that when Edgar left Richmond in the summer of 1848, having come very close to asking me to marry him, that he then traveled to Providence, Rhode Island, to propose to someone else. I recalled the haste with which he left that late July. A letter had come. I had assumed it was some pressing business matter. Now I learned that he left me for someone else, someone, I can only presume, he desired more. And not just that, when he returned to Richmond the following summer and resumed courting me, he did so because not one but two women in the North had rejected him. I was not even second on his list.

Naturally, I felt resentful. I think I even hated him for a time. For over thirty years I had believed that Edgar loved me, that I was his lost Lenore, that I had been his first love and was to be his last—that I was the one greatest love of his life. That belief had governed *my* life. It had been the cause of my near-reclusiveness. It had provided the certainty upon which was built the high dudgeon of my feelings toward Griswold, and it collapsed like a house of cards. I found myself yelling at Edgar as if he were here to listen, and what I said to him, I suddenly realized that I had said already—nearly sixty years ago, in a garden, not ten blocks from where I sit at this moment—"I trusted you. I trusted you like a silly fool."

When it occurred to me that I was repeating myself, I laughed right out loud—a belly laugh! Had I laughed in years? I laughed until the maid peeked in the door to the parlor, certain I had lost my mind. I think I must have scared her to death.

Why, I ask you, do we women turn into silly fools for the sake of men's love? And when disappointed, spend the rest of our lives pining for them. Like martyrs, we become. Thirty years of martyrdom. Isn't it rich? Isn't it richly ironic that all these women have spent so much time and energy trying to redeem this man's character? And why? In order not to have been mere silly fools. Don't you think that's it? How many "Lenores" and "Annabel Lees" did Edgar leave? There may be dozens of us.

I don't mean to condemn the whole of the male of the specie. Or female, for that matter. I should speak only for myself.

I am devoutly religious. I believe in forgiveness. I would like to be able to say that I have forgiven Edgar, but I can't say that I have. Though I searched my soul, I honestly do not know. But whether I forgive him or not is unimportant in one respect—that I, at least, face up to what happened. I think I have come to some understanding. I can't be certain of what motivated Edgar, but toward the end, I am quite certain it was money and not much else. Mrs. Whitman was a wealthy widow. I was a wealthy widow. He was a desperate man. In the end, both Mrs. Whitman and I were spared what would probably have been a horrible marriage. I should be thankful.

Had John Henry Ingram wanted to—or had he been the least bit sensitive or perceptive—he would have drawn from Edgar's duplicity the same conclusion I did, but such would have worked against his goal of redeeming Edgar's character from Griswold's condemnation. So he refused, and by his refusal, he ruined his biography. I can't be sorry for him. It matters little to me. What matters to me now is not spending my remaining years like I have these past thirty—but to live a life, not a myth. That's where you come in, for I realized that one way to achieve this is to let go the myth—set it free—let it out of its cage. Let it fly away.

...

...

...

September 26, 1888
Mrs. Canady's School
Bridgeport, Connecticut

My Dear Eddy,

Thank you for your forbearance. You are a kind and generous man—so true. Don't blame yourself. I *never* blamed you. Don't think that—*ever*! That summer—can it really be ten years ago?—when you were to come to Providence and after Helen died, Miss Power was put into a sanatorium. I could not handle her. Even Helen had struggled with her. I so wanted to remain in Helen's house, but my mother wouldn't hear of it—a young unmarried girl, living alone there when her own home was just a few short blocks away. How would it look?—that was all my mother cared about. Why did I give in? I'll never know. We argued bitterly about it, and it was during that time that I had to tell her of your coming. She blamed Helen for having brought us together, and she spoke of Helen with such invective that we argued about that too. I could not tolerate her criticizing Helen. It seemed we argued about everything, and one night at the supper table my younger brother who was still living at home started yelling at my mother and me. He was enraged; he'd had enough; he told us to shut up, then, turning to me, he said he hated me for coming back home and wished I'd get out and never come back. He was fifteen and desperately needed a father. Our arguments and his supper-table tantrums became an almost nightly occurrence. The situation was poisonous. Instead of writing to warn you, I should have told you not to come. I made my brother promise not to yell at the dinner table while you were there, so what happened? I yelled.

I tell you this, hoping it might make what I did seem a little less insane. We were no longer a family. If ever we had been, it had long since been blown apart by my mother's relentless social-climbing and my father's running away. My brother no longer speaks to me. He lives in Portland; I've never met his wife or children, and I am deeply troubled by that. My sister escaped. Thank God! She married young and well—while I was still living with Helen—and her marriage pleased my mother, a thing that ultimately became a burden to my sister, but thankfully, she handled it well. We are close, though perhaps not intimate; I visit her annually for the Christmas holidays, the only times I ever return to Providence. I adore her son, Jake. He is twelve and calls me "Auntie-Lottie"—or, at least, that's the way it sounds. Now that I see the words, I realize I've never seen it written. I used to hate the nickname, Lottie, and refused to allow anyone to call me that, but from Jake it is music to my ears. I adore him.

That's my story.

Do you recall that you gave me your carte de visite for my twenty-first birthday? I have it still. It is in a frame and sits on my dresser with my mirror and brushes. I even took it to Europe with me. In ten years, not a morning has passed that I haven't glanced at you while brushing my hair. Eddy, the time has come to tell you that you are the love of my life. I have always believed that you loved me too, only I thought it was past love until I received your beautiful note of the 20th.

Do write to me and tell me all that has happened to you in these last ten years—where all you've been and the things you've seen. Leave nothing out. I want to know everything about you if you will tell me. You once said you loved letter writing and that you would overwhelm me. Overwhelm me, Eddy.

I adore you,
Charlotte

(ITEM 87: *Charlotte Ayers*)

...

October 10, 1888
Mrs. Canady's School
Bridgeport, Connecticut

Dearest,

Thank you for your long, long letter. I am fascinated by all you say, but in particular I want to respond to what you said about the letters you have collected, relating to Edgar Allan Poe. Until now I never realized the extent of your correspondence in that regard. I thought perhaps it was confined to Helen and perhaps two or three others, including Mrs. Lewis of England whose address I remember copying out for you for insertion in one of Helen's letters to you. I recall Helen being quite amused by your request for Mrs. Lewis's address; she did not think very highly of Mrs. Lewis for reasons I vividly recall from her correspondence with John Ingram. But Helen was quite willing to let your inquiries lead wherever you wished. Forgive me for saying this, but I believe her willingness to do so gives evidence of her veracity. She had nothing to hide insofar as Poe was concerned with one, single, and apparently important exception—Fanny Osgood! Helen was fiercely loyal to Fanny. She never told me what happened that needed hiding from Ingram, but it was easy enough to guess—Fanny bore Poe's child. But you know this! How do you know? I confess I am impressed, Major Gayle. I was going to tell you. Remember that I told you that I knew much and that I would tell you all I knew after Helen died. That was one of the things I wanted to tell you—perhaps the most important thing. And I also guessed that it had something to do with Griswold's awful memoir of Poe. The portraits. I knew about the portraits too. Helen never confided any secrets to me, but I copied all her letters to Ingram, and I knew Helen well. I could sense when she was holding back or pointing him away from some path she preferred he not venture down.

My point is, Eddy, that Ingram didn't tell the whole story. No one has. It's been eight years since his biography of Poe was published. Those who might have been compromised by a full telling of the story are dead, including, most importantly, Fanny's husband, Samuel Stillman Osgood. He died three years ago. I think Helen might have been protecting him, among others, by not giving Ingram all the facts.

It seems you have corresponded with many of the most important people who knew about this "hidden" story. There is no one more qualified than you to tell it. Why not consider it? You tell me that your remaining correspondence includes only Mrs. Richmond and Mrs. Weiss, that all the others are dead now. Furthermore, you tell me that this correspondence has devolved to the level of friendship only. I think, while there is still time, you should renew your pursuit of the question that brought you to Helen Whitman (and by way of her to me also)—why did Griswold so mistreat Poe? You know the truth about Fanny, and that truth has not been told, but is it not still possible to learn the truth about this question regarding Griswold? Helen was convinced that it was never fully explained, and were it not important, why would she have held a séance for the sole purpose of learning the answer? And we still don't understand what happened that night. I will tell you that it was of such significance that it changed Helen, and I don't think the change in her was related to Cato alone. Something else happened that night that was a revelation to her. Don't you recall that when she left the room, it wasn't Cato she warned you about— Cato's message was for her alone—the message she warned you not to attach significance to was what she termed "blackmail." What did she mean by that? Do you know? Black coins. Griswold in a black minister's robe that was transformed into a black dress. There was something there, Eddy. I am certain of it. Something important. But perhaps time is running out. I don't want you to abandon this, because I know in my soul that it's important. I lived with Helen for the final two years of her life, and I can assure you that she was a changed person as a result of that séance. Something important happened, and you must find out what it was before it's too late. I think this is your life's work. Perhaps we have been brought back together for this purpose. Has this occurred to you? I believe that things happen for a reason. I cannot credit Darwin, nor do I dismiss him. I don't believe everything I read in the Bible either, but don't tell Mrs. Canady that. Do I shock you? I imagine you are a strict Christian, though you have not told me.

I believe in Truth. Do you recall that I told you that ten years ago? I believe passionately in it. And I believe that we are placed on this earth to pursue truth, placed here for that purpose by some mysterious entity we cannot comprehend. And that we are somehow guided by this entity to seek out Truth. I believe—with all my heart—that you and I were brought back together for some reason larger even than our love for each other. In fact, I believe our love for each other was the means by which we were brought back together in order to pursue something important. I don't know what it is or even if it is very significant in the great scheme of things. Perhaps it is merely some small Truth, but like the Parthenon, great Truths are built stone-upon-stone.

I thought of you when I stood on the Acropolis. I recalled how I had envied you when I read your descriptions of Montana. I knew you would envy me, standing among the ruins of Ancient Greece. In the midst of such historical magnificence, natural or manmade, one cannot but know that we are here for a reason, not for mere survival. What could be more trivial than mere survival—air to breathe, a full stomach, warm fire, soft mattress, someone to comfort us—is that all we should aspire to? And given that, what of those who are mistreated? You have gone out of your way to right wrongs. I have loved that about you since first I met you.

Something drew you to Providence twelve years ago. Think of that, Eddy. Providence! Purpose motivated you. I don't think you've finished that work, nor do I think anyone else in this world is more capable.

Eddy, I must tell you that I am not a virgin. I will say no more about this, and I thank you not to ask. If you still wish to see me, I would prefer you not visit while school is in session. You must understand that I have had men callers in my time here—though none who could hold a candle to you. And each time it caused such a stir that I had a devil of a time living it down. Girls will be girls! Would it be possible for you to come during Thanksgiving or to Providence during Christmas? How far is Portland? Surely you wish to also spend your leave with family in North Carolina. I don't know what to suggest. Come when you can. I'll deal with the girls if I must; I couldn't bear to wait until Easter—that's far too distant.

I love you,
Charlotte

(ITEM 88: *Charlotte Ayers*)

...

October 24, 1888
Mrs. Canada's
Bridgeport, Connecticut

Dearest,

Thanksgiving it is then! I don't remember being this eager ten years ago, awaiting your arrival in Providence. I will be waiting at the train station, having reserved a room for you at a nearby boarding house that is clean and respectable.

I am heartened to hear your response to my long and preachy letter. Forgive me that. Honestly, I wasn't trying to tell you what to do. Now

I learn from you that after the disaster of Providence, your interest in Poe waned. I cannot help but feel guilty about that. I remember that we were going to talk about the letters Helen had received from Wilmot Griswold. Do you still have them?—the copies I made for you? Was there anything there that gave you a clue?

Eddy, would you bring all you letters when you come? Would that be possible? Don't forget, darling, that for two and a half years I assisted Helen who assisted John Ingram with his biography. Sometimes I think I must know more details about Poe's life than anyone in America. Perhaps if I read the letters you've received, I could supply additional details about what your correspondents told you that would help unlock the mystery we sought answers to in Providence the night of the séance. Assisting you with a biography of Poe would be a labor of love for me. You could not ask for someone more qualified. You can't imagine how intensely I feel that we have been brought back together for this purpose, but not for this purpose alone, my darling—we have other, more delicious reasons to be together, but when I think about that I become positively dizzy and weak-kneed. Yes, my dear, you may have that kiss you were denied ten years ago—that one and all the more you want. I will bathe you in kisses.

But back to Poe (otherwise, I will become incoherent): there are other people you could interview who might help. James Russell Lowell is still alive. Did you ever write to him? He must have known Griswold, and he certainly knew Poe. He and Helen corresponded. I could obtain his address for you; he lives in Cambridge. Perhaps there are others. I recall from Mrs. Whitman's correspondence with Ingram that an important source of information was a Mrs. Botta of New York (her maiden name was Anne Lynch), but she was firmly resolved to remain silent. She was a particular friend of Fanny Osgood. I also remember that Poe brought a lawsuit against the *New York Mirror* that involved T. D. English. He, too, is alive, and is a member of the U.S. Congress. He would have been hostile to Poe, but even so, he might be helpful. There may be other avenues to pursue.

Darling, you tell me that you are no writer, but I beg to differ, my dear. I have had the immense pleasure of reading your letters. And I have taught literature for ten years. I can say with no small authority that you are a marvelous writer—every bit the writer John Ingram was. Such a work as you imagine is *not* beyond your ability. If you can imagine it, it is possible.

In one month I shall see you. That prospect elicits so many emotions that I cannot begin to list them, but I have to tell you that fear is among them—fear for how you will view me. I am not a girl anymore. Don't come expecting to find that eighteen-year-old girl who fell in love with you that first night in Providence. You told me that at that meeting you thought I was shocked by how short you are. You are wrong. True, I was paralyzed by you—but not by your stature—I was paralyzed by emotions inside me that I did not understand, that I had never felt for another human being. I was so frozen by them that all I could do was guard my feelings for fear of making a fool of myself staring at you. I have loved you from that instant, and I have never—before or since—felt such emotion for another human being. But I am no longer young, Eddy. I don't have the figure I had then, though I have tried to maintain it and though I have been told that I'm pretty. But I am no judge of me, and I don't want to disappoint you. I can only hope that you will love me, knowing not why.

Yours ever, my dearest,
Charlotte

9

SUSAN TALLEY

::

(ITEM 12: *Susan Archer Talley Weiss*)

...

January 4, 1877
Talavera
Richmond, Virginia

Dear Lieutenant Gayle,

I so enjoyed your letter. I was thrilled by the story of your mother's valiant confrontation with the Union cavalry officer during the war. I wonder if you told me that story because of something you were told at the *Messenger* office about my own experience during the war. Women like your mother and me were forced to feats that surprised even us. I would like to write to her, if I may, and send her your letter, for she should have it. I think it would mean very much to her to hear you speak of her with such pride.

And please tell me more about your father, particularly anything you know about his experiences during the siege of Richmond. Do you recall the name of his unit and can you tell me where he was wounded and how he managed to survive with such a serious wound? Was he ever captured or imprisoned? I correspond with many soldiers on both sides, including several general officers, and it may be my destiny to write a book on this subject someday. I would value knowing more about your father.

Of course I share your appreciation for the work of Edgar Poe. I believe that I do not exaggerate when I say that we were good friends; in fact, I had the pleasure of discussing with him his great poem, "The Raven," on a rainy morning in September of 1849, just a few weeks before his death. I assure you that he was a man of perfect courtesy and of indescribable charm with a magnetism about the eyes that was more alluring than any person I have ever known. He was a man of warmth and compassion, truly a Southern gentleman, and, needless to say, the possessor of an incredibly remarkable intellect.

Regarding your inquiry, there are many in Richmond alive today who were close personal friends of Edgar—especially the Cabells and the Sullys. Of Mrs. Allan, you must understand that she is advanced in years, and, being a woman of wealth and social standing, she is subject to strong opinions. She is not apt to forget the least slight or insult. Mr. Griswold's memoir made her the topic of gossip and speculation to the effect, unfortunately, of embittering her toward Edgar. Her friends would not dream of mentioning his name in her presence. I must say that I am astonished you heard from her in the first instance, so don't be disappointed if you have no further response.

Hoping that this information is helpful to you and wishing you a happy New Year.

I am very truly yours,
Susan Weiss

:: ALL ROADS SOUTH OF THE CAPITAL were especially dangerous during the summer of 1865, much too dangerous for me to travel. Horrible stories were reported of marauding bands of freed slaves and renegade soldiers bent on robbery and other unspeakable acts of mayhem. But the main reasons I delayed my return to Richmond were that my husband was dying of camp-fever—dysentery, I suppose—most likely the result of bad food—plus I was seven months pregnant when the war finally ended. The commandant at Fort McHenry, a cultured man and a gentleman, kindly permitted us to remain where we had been imprisoned for nearly four years, even providing food, albeit sometimes tainted and inedible. I think he admired and took pity on me, though he had rather heartlessly evicted all the other Confederate prisoners regardless of their physical condition. The prison was converted into a hospital, and we ended up housed in a barracks crammed with sick and wounded Union soldiers brought up from prison camps in the South. Our privacy depended on quilts and blankets hung from clotheslines surrounding a cramped corner of the second story. I was the only woman among hundreds of men. The noise was awful; the heat, oppressive, but worst of all was the smell—a mix of urine, ether, and the coppery odor of blood. I would have assisted the doctors to the degree I was able, but it seemed I was an unwelcome sight to dying Union soldiers who had learned by way of rumor that I had been a spy for the Confederacy. And perhaps my swollen belly was also a bitter reminder of a life they might never know. I ached for fresh air, but on most days I was too scared to leave our little concealed corner, waiting until after dark to visit the facilities. My husband agonized with terrible cramps and diarrhea, and nothing seemed to help. I did for him what I could, and, though the doctors attended to him on occasion, his being a Confederate prisoner of war made him every bit the pariah I was myself. In the end I think he starved to death. He died on Independence Day, a month and a day before our son, Stuart, was born. I delivered with the help of one of the doctors while half the ward crowded around to watch. It was a mid-afternoon in August, stifling hot, and Stuart's birth-screams were greeted with laughter—"a Rebel yell," they called it. I could hear neither my son nor the soldier's laughter, but I could see Stuart's cries in his pinched, purple little face just as I could see derision on the faces of gawking soldiers. I was in such pain that I unknowingly pulled hanks of hair from my scalp; my sweat-soaked nightgown was knotted and bunched up around my neck and failed to cover my breasts; I lay on bare, blood-soaked ticking with no sheet, feeling like someone had cleaved me open. I was disoriented, exhausted, forty-three years old, and deaf as a stone.

In mid-September, on a solemn promise to repay, I begged the commandant to arrange for deck passage for Stuart and me on a skipjack carrying cargo from Baltimore to Newport News. I had no money, but had written several letters, saying we were coming and hoping someone was there to receive them and come to meet us. We set sail at sunset, and I was seasick throughout the night, not a wink of sleep. The deck was crammed with barrels stacked and tied down so that wherever I tried to lie down, I seemed to be inevitably in the way of the sailors. Asking several times what all the barrels contained, I was repeatedly told "horseshoes—nails." This fascinated me. I couldn't imagine there were enough horses and mules left in the South to yield profit from a cargo of horseshoes. I had heard that Sherman had either stolen or killed them all. We reached the mouth of the Potomac just at daybreak, and on the western shore, from the deck of the ship, I could see no evidence of the destruction I expected. The shore appeared green and lush, mostly forest and pasture, but a few times I could see fields of crops—corn, soybeans, even tobacco. It was as if there had been no war at all, and I grew more optimistic, thinking things might not be as bad as had been reported. Cheered by this, I imagined the old days and started humming a song to my infant whom I nursed as I sat among the barrels stacked on the deckhouse. The song was one of the darkies' spirituals that I remembered from my childhood. Though I cannot hear, music plays inside me in a way that is difficult to explain. It's almost as if I can hear it, but I suppose it's more accurate to say that I feel it—feel vibrations in my head and chest. I hum and sing constantly. Watching the south shore of the Potomac just then, I sang aloud a song I had learned before losing my hearing, the voices of the slaves coming up on summer nights from the quarters while we sat on the porch after supper—"Oh, Lordy, I got happy down in my heart / And so I told my Lord I'd never depart / I shouted 'Hallelujah, Glory to God' . . ."—the words failed me as I remembered marauding bands of those same slaves, menacing the roads. Why, I wondered? For the most part, they had been happy in their place. They won't know what to do with freedom, I thought; it's beyond their ken. What a tragedy, this war. What a cruel fate for innocents like them and, indeed, for all of us. The roads will never be safe again; anarchy will reign in the South. And thinking this, I turned from my nursing son's anxious eyes and looked again at the shore, again hoping the destruction wasn't so bad. Richmond had been burned. I'd been told that and had read about it in the few newspapers we'd gotten our hands on. But per- haps the burning wasn't so widespread, and I hoped Talavera had been spared. Was the avenue still there, the cedar-lined avenue that ran up to the house? It seemed to me at that moment that we could survive somehow so long as we had a roof over our head. And I thought how good it will feel to be home again. Talavera was my rock, and I hadn't seen it for four long years.

Both my parents had died before the war, but being unmarried I had naturally stayed home even after that. All during my childhood I had suffered with earaches, and losing my hearing when I was nine years old had been tantamount to losing my balance. I came to learn this about myself. I knew that I'd spent timeless years waiting to hear something. It's as if I had slept for seven years to be awaken when I was sixteen, though I was really still nine. Those seven years were lost. I think I must have been in such shock that I lost all memory of them except for an ever-present fear. I left school and seldom, if ever, ventured beyond the limits of Talavera. My father took me from one doctor to another, but the answer was always the same perplexed shaking of the head. No one could explain; no one could do anything. My mother tried to compensate, but even she was at a loss as to what to do. Books—that was her answer for my education. Read! I suppose I did. I hardly remember. But somewhere in that time I started reading poetry, and writing verse became the thing that brought me out from under. It saved me.

I came to believe that those were not truly lived years, and that, therefore, I wasn't really forty-three when Stuart was born; I was really thirty-six. How else to explain conceiving at such an advanced age? It seemed a miracle, but almost an unwanted miracle, considering our imprisonment. No one would believe me, of course, when I say that I did not age in those seven years, but I am certain of it. God gave me seven years grace in which to adjust. He held those years in abeyance as His way of compensating me for giving my hearing to someone in greater need of it. And that's not all He gave me. He gave me song which in my unhearing state became poetry, and through poetry I was awakened. I often wondered who He gave my hearing to, and I decided it was a child my age who had lost her sight and needed more acute hearing. And so it goes—a gift from one to another, one to another—small gifts; big gifts. That's how God does His work. My compensating gift—my poetry—became more precious to me than hearing or any of my other senses, and, though deafness seemed so cruel at first—cruel for seven years—I came to understand that I had been repaid many fold. It was thus that I learned to live without hearing, but at that moment, on the deck of the skipjack bearing south on the Chesapeake Bay, as we rounded Stingray Point, announcing the Rappahannock River, I felt I could not endure losing my home—losing Talavera.

My brother, Sam, was waiting for us at the wharf late that afternoon. It had been only four years since I'd seen him, but he seemed to have aged decades. His hair was gray, and, though his eyes gladdened at the sight of me, they were ringed dark—tired eyes—as if he hadn't slept for days. He had with him a gig drawn by a skin-and-bones nag, and at once I recognized her. She was Sassy Lady, a large, once-spirited, dappled gray pony I had ridden hundreds of times from Talavera down into town or to Duncan's Lodge for a house party or out into the countryside for a romp or a picnic. I wept to see her so listless, her eyes cloudy, mossed over, void of recognition. "It's me, Sassy. You remember your Suzie, don't you?" I asked, rubbing her nose, then turning to my brother, "Have you no feed?"

"Have we no feed?" He chuckled, half-heartedly, shaking his head and mouthing his words so I could read his lips. "No feed, Suzie. No feed. No nothing."

"And Talavera? Did it survive?"

He breathed a disconsolate sigh. "It survived. But not like you remember it."

We spent the night in a hotel in Newport News and left for Richmond the following morning. It was slow-going and bleak. Ruin was everywhere. Sometimes it seemed there was not a living thing but for the men we saw. Traveling bands of men like dummies—black and white—walked in ranks with picks and shovels thrown over their shoulders such that they might have been prisoners. "Where are they going; what are they doing?" I asked repeatedly. Sam said nothing, only shook his head. Other men lay beside the road or in ditches—emaciated, languid, in tatters, and mute, as if awaiting death. The scene was a mix of lethargy or mindless marching-about on some useless errand as if some unseen madman had commanded the total destruction of all vegetation, of anything green, leaving only clay. The road—when something like a road was discernable—was rutted and pockmarked. Wheels came off wagons; men struggled to fix them. Dead animals lay where they had fallen. One stinking mule I saw whose stiff leg stuck straight up in the air seemed to point at us with his shoeless hoof as if to mock the cargo of horseshoes, a thing as ludicrously mad as everything else seemed to be. I almost laughed at the sight of it—the utter futility. All was scraped bare. Hope abandoned me.

:: I HAD GIVEN UP WRITING DURING my imprisonment. Poetry seemed a trivial and senseless pursuit, though I often found myself reciting verses I knew by heart that seemed to fit some mood or small task. It is difficult from the perspective of today to imagine the tenor of those years—the war years and those just after. It was not a time for creativity, but rather of destruction—and a time for spending every waking moment endeavoring to survive. We had no money and little to eat. Talavera had survived, but just the house. Nothing else. There was not a tree standing; not a shrub, not a blade of grass or even weeds, save broom-straw. The outbuildings had been leveled, so completely wiped away that I could find no trace of their ever having been there. I knew where the kitchen had stood; I knew the exact spot, but found not a clue that it had ever existed, not a brick, not a recognizable foundation stone, not even ashes to prove that once meals had been cooked there. Only trenches. The house had been headquarters for a Confederate artillery battery during the siege of Richmond, the grounds a firing range. Rotting and charred remains of gun carriages were scattered about, some of them upturned like the carcasses of dead animals. Rusting bayonets littered the ground. Furniture remained, but only the larger pieces. Everything the size of a trunk or smaller had disappeared, including all my books, papers, notebooks, keepsakes, curios that I had carelessly left behind. What had I been thinking in carrying information through battle lines to General McGruder without securing my things in the event I might be caught? Capture had not even occurred to me; I had thought that my being a woman—and a deaf woman at that—protected me. Now I let go of any nobility I may still have felt for that and other acts in the service of my country. Suddenly they seemed as senseless and dumb as a load of horseshoes. The effect of this was the same palpable fear that had gripped me when I became deaf—a loss of balance as if my legs had been knocked out from under me. I recall telling Sam what had happened to me, my capture and transport north to Fort McHenry, my meeting and marriage to fellow-prisoner, Louis Weiss, the miracle of my pregnancy, Stuart's awful birth. Sam listened with a dazed disinterest as if I were reading aloud an article in the newspaper while his mind was already jumping ahead to something he had to do. I cannot recall his ever asking questions. I remember looking at my reflection in a broken mirror that first night home and reading my own lips—"You stupid fool."

Of our family's slaves only one elderly couple remained, Sampson and Minnie, and they now lived in the house with us—me, my brother, Sam, and his wife who was bedridden and consumptive and would not survive the coming winter. The arrangement shocked me at first—Negroes living in the house!—my mother would roll over in her grave if she knew darkies were living in her guest room. Sam, sitting at his desk when I quizzed him about the propriety of it, laughed me off with a disgusted and sarcastic roll of his eyes. What was I thinking?—that the world would revert to the way it had been? He ignored me. My son and I were just more mouths to feed. Sam spent his days at his desk, leafing through newspapers or lying on the bed in his room, staring up at the ceiling. He would leave for days at a time, riding out for various reasons having to do with our survival or with seeking information about friends or other members of our scattered family. In particular he sought information about his son, my nephew, who was last heard of that spring in the battle at Shyler's Creek. We never learned his fate. Sam was so changed, so helpless and dispirited. I imagined he wanted to run away and be rid of us *and* Talavera—everything. I even imagined he wanted to die.

Wild bands of freed slaves still roamed the countryside, looking for anything they could get their hands on, so at night Sampson, Minnie, and I barricaded the doors and downstairs windows with furniture and mattresses. One such night in early October, a thunderstorm having come through, adding to the disquiet, while I put on my nightgown I heard a woman's voice calling from outside the house. I grabbed the candle and ran downstairs, calling for Sampson to come too. He pushed away the breakfront with which we'd blocked the front door, and, upon opening the door, I perceived the dark figure of Rosalie Poe. I had known Rose all my life and recognized her immediately by her stooped posture and the vacant way in which her mouth lolled open. She was dressed in black and carried a suitcase. She crossed the trench that had been dug to protect the front of the house, and I brought her in as Sampson stoked the living room fire back to life. Rose had walked from Duncan's Lodge, the Mackenzie place, which I had not yet had a chance to visit, and I still did not know what had become of that family with whom I had been so close before the war and all during my growing-up years. Sitting across from me in the light of the fire, Rosalie reported with tears in her eyes that Mrs. Mackenzie was dead as was her son, "Dr. Tom," and that Richard was in wretched health, not expected to survive, and that Jane Mackenzie had died in England and "Mattie"—my dear childhood friend, Martha—had lost her husband and had taken her beautiful daughter and a cow to a place in the country to live. "They have to work for a living now," Rosalie said, "but I'm not strong enough to work." Of John Mackenzie, fun-loving "Jack"—Edgar's best boyhood friend whom everyone loved—they had no news. Rosalie spent the night in the bed with me and left the next morning with plans to somehow make her way to Baltimore in hopes of being taken in by relatives. As I watched her leave—such a strange, eccentric woman—I remembered how her brother had humored and endured her peculiar and somewhat demented temperament. I recalled one time when he'd been asked to recite "The Raven," which he did, sitting in a chair, there in our living room at Talavera, when, as he neared the end of the poem, Rosalie entered the room and plopped herself down on his lap. It ruined the ending, and giggles were heard among the youngsters when it was over, but Edgar took it in stride and swore that, henceforth, he would always have Rose present when he recited, so she could play the part of the raven. Not seeing the jest, she smiled proudly, kissed his cheek, and buried her head in his shoulder. She idolized him. Watching her leave now, a confused, sixty-four-year-old woman about to brave the treacherous roads between Richmond and Baltimore, I wondered if I would ever see her again. She had been such an ever-present fixture of life at Duncan's Lodge where I had spent so much time that her going saddened me more than I would have expected. She was so strange, had been such a bother in some ways, but the vision of her leaving, suitcase in hand, together with the sad news she brought of the Mackenzie family and the sad state of affairs at Talavera, was yet another symptom that all of that was gone, never to return.

October 30, 1888
6 North Park Street
Richmond, Virginia

Dear Major Gayle,

What an unexpected and pleasurable surprise to hear from you after all these years. There was a time when I felt certain you were assembling information for a biography of Edgar Allan Poe, and I was glad to assist in that effort. Then after the biographies by Gill, Didier, and Ingram were all published in such short order, I concluded by your less frequent letters and by what you said in them that you had abandoned that crowded field. Now it seems your interest is revived, and I am heartedly glad, for the whole story has not been told, and the merit of at least one of these works—namely that by Gill—is decidedly inferior. And neither Ingram nor Didier gave sufficient attention to Edgar's Richmond years, so that I think they missed perhaps the most important portions of his life.

What these men failed to recognize was that Edgar Poe was a product of the South, and I think it is very important to view his life in that light. I believe, Major Gayle, that only a Southerner can approach the subject with the unique understanding necessary to portray the man accurately. I myself have considered such a work, but my resources being meager and considering my age and handicap and the travel necessary to do a proper job of research, I decided the task was excessively ambitious. Nevertheless, I am eager and able to help.

Do you still have my article from *Scribner's Monthly*, "The Last Days of Edgar A. Poe"? I recall that when you wrote to me after reading that article, you expressed a wish to visit the "Hermitage" with me. The old house has fallen in, sad to say—a flattened ruin now, but it is still there, and, if, indeed, you come through Richmond on your next trip home, then we should go there, and I can tell you things that the limitations of space prevented me from saying in my *Scribner's* article. None of the above-mentioned biographers ever contacted me or any of numerous friends of Edgar's who were still living and who possessed valuable information. Only Mrs. Shelton was contacted, and the information she provided was, I assure you, polished to a smoothness that had burnished away much of the truth. And now, whatever truth she might have told is gone. Elmira Shelton passed away earlier this year. So many are gone that it seems time is quickly running out.

I would welcome your visit. I remain in good health, thank you. Do you recall my telling you that my actual age is seven years short of my chronological age, owing to the seven years I was forced to learn to live with deafness? I am, therefore, not sixty-six, but a mere fifty-nine, hale and hardy, and with my first grandchild due in two months, a thing that has brought me more excitement than I would have imagined possible.

I am eager to hear from you again and hopeful of seeing you soon.

Yours most earnestly,

Susan Talley Weiss

:: SOME YEARS BACK I HAD A LETTER from Rosalie Poe, enclosing a number of photographs of Edgar and asking me to dispose of them on her behalf for a dollar apiece. I endeavored to do so, since the tone of her note indicated her need; I suspected she was in a desperate way financially. I sent some of the photographs to a relative in Boston, a Mrs. M. A. Kidder, asking her to help, and later she wrote back to say that she had no success, even at the reduced price of twenty-five cents, explaining that no one had sufficient respect for Edgar's character to care to possess a likeness of him. I suppose this opinion largely persists, even now, twenty years later, despite recent biographies. The damage to Edgar done by Griswold seems irreparable, and it may be that Edgar's true character will never be known. I wish you to understand something of that character that may surprise you.

In August of that summer—1849—Edgar's last summer, while he was in Richmond, Martha Mackenzie got married. Mattie or Mat, as we all called her, was exactly my age and one of my best friends, and I was thrilled when she asked me to be one of her bridesmaids. All our other friends were married and had children, but Mat had always been a rebellious and independent girl, and it was claimed that no man in Richmond could tame her. She was the youngest of the Mackenzie children and as careless of opinion as she was the dictates of society. It seemed she much preferred her horse and her dog, Dean, to any human being. Dean slept in the bed with her, and Mat spent hours every day in the stables, wearing boots, jodhpurs, and one of her brother's shirts, pitchfork in hand, shoveling manure, toting oats, bales of hay, buckets of water. Her hands were calloused, her arms muscled, and she paid no attention to her hair, covering it with a straw hat when working in the stables or a top hat when out riding. She was rather more handsome than pretty, such a tomboy. She cussed like a sailor, and I am certain I never saw her flirt in my entire life. She had dark hair and a round face, untouched by makeup and unfashionably suntanned in summer, brown eyes, and everyone wondered what she wore beneath her outfit, for no one could imagine her in anything as feminine as a slip or lacy chemise. She inevitably wore a grin, a rather crooked, sarcastic grin. She treated me with a sort of offhand, friendly indifference which I loved, so unlike the solicitousness and condescension with which others treated "poor, plain, deaf Suzie Talley." The Mackenzie family was large, attractive, and very popular. Duncan's Lodge, where they lived, was owned by Mat's widowed Aunt Jane, her father's sister-in-law, and Mat had three older brothers, Tom, Richard, and Jack who was Edgar Poe's best friend growing up, and, of course, Rosalie Poe lived with them also, having been taken in and raised by the Mackenzies from the age of four. To everyone's astonishment, Mat became engaged that spring to Harry Byrd who was four years younger, and just as independent-minded. Harry was handsome, respectable, and it was said of him that he "sat a fine saddle." It was the perfect match. Mat's Aunt Jane sailed for England in June, but she left Mat enough money for the wedding and a week's worth of festivities.

Edgar had arrived in July and initially took room and board at Swan's Tavern on Broad Street which was cheap but clean, a place popular with traveling businessmen. He arrived with the intention of courting Elmira Shelton, and immediately upon his arrival word had it they were engaged. Mrs. Shelton was a widow, very religious, wealthy and frugal (one might say parsimonious to a fault), and of rather dour character. Perhaps she had once been pretty. His habit from the start was to pay a visit each morning at her house in Church Hill, lunch with her, then walk to the western suburbs to Duncan's Lodge to spend the afternoon with the Mackenzies. There were no streetcars in those days, and the walk was long and hot, and, as often as not, Edgar would break his trip with a visit to Dr. John Carter, a young physician whom he had met shortly after arriving. It is my stated opinion (and I hold to it) that Edgar's courtship of Mrs. Shelton was motivated by money. It's true they had been sweethearts during adolescence, but that had been many years earlier. I say this about her money, because of things Edgar later told me about Fanny Osgood and also, in part, because of his attentions to me and other eligible Richmond women. This is not to say that Edgar ever made advances that might have been construed as indicative of serious intent, but flirt he did in such a way that I knew that he was not in love with Mrs. Shelton. I didn't fault him then, and I don't fault him now. A marriage of convenience for people their age and circumstance is not only respectable in my opinion, it is infinitely practical and in the best interest of society as a whole—a thing to be honored, flirting with others notwithstanding.

The main purpose of Edgar's visit to Richmond was to raise funds for a literary journal which he intended to found—*The Stylus*, it was to be called—and all his Richmond friends, the Mackenzies, Cabells, and Sullys, were enthusiastic in their promise of support. Mrs. Shelton proved less so; in fact, I am certain she refused him her financial support, and such was the cause of the rupture of their engagement, though Edgar's biographers have insisted that he left Richmond on his ill-fated return trip to Fordham for the purpose of bringing his mother-in-law, Mrs. Clemm, to Richmond for his wedding. Had those biographers bothered to visit Richmond to interview Edgar's surviving friends, they would not have erred to the degree they did. From things he said to me, I became convinced that the only woman Edgar Poe ever really loved was Mrs. Osgood, a thing that throws a dark shadow over his marriage to his cousin.

Shortly after his arrival, Edgar, succumbing to the temptation of men wishing nothing more than to befriend and fete the author of "The Raven," had what we came to call a "bout." By some peculiarity from birth in his chemical makeup or his fragile temperament or emotional vulnerability, Edgar could not imbibe spirits without becoming seriously ill. But neither could he, on occasion, due to his congenial nature and sensitivity to the generosity of friends, refuse it when offered. Through long experience, he had learned this about himself, still the problem persisted. His first bout left him prostrate at the Swan for a week, often visited there by Mrs. Shelton and the Mackenzies and his new friend, Dr. Carter. His second bout caused his removal to Duncan's Lodge where he could be cared for round the clock. He was at death's door during this time, and I suspect the second bout was in part caused by the developing rupture with Mrs. Shelton. By this time Edgar and I had met and become friends, and as Mat later told me, he was particularly concerned that I not hear of the cause of his illness. He sent affectionate notes and, on one occasion, flowers and an anonymous poem clipped from a newspaper that had caught his eye and that he admired. Among all his Richmond friends, I was the only poet; therefore, he considered us colleagues, workers in the same field. But there seemed to be a reason beyond our shared craft: I think he felt that my deafness rendered me a safe and secure confidante. He had dear friends in Richmond, close friends, but perhaps there was no one with whom he could speak so easily from the heart. A poet must have that outlet; otherwise, he or she suffocates.

By the time festivities began leading up to Mat's wedding, Edgar had fully recovered and was feeling quite himself, and he threw himself into the celebrations with cheeriness and enthusiasm. He adored Mat—the little tomboy sister of his friend, Jack. He had known her since childhood and loved to rag her.

"Will you wear a dress, Mat?" he asked her one afternoon as the group of us squatted on the lawn watching the darkies whitewashing the trellis beneath which Mat was to be married. "Or do you intend to wear serge knickers and one of Jack's dress shirts?"

"Go to hell, Edgar Poe," Mat said. "If you say one word about my dress, so help me, you'll get cake in your face—in your hair, up your nose. You'll reek of sponge cake. And don't think for a minute I won't do it."

Rosalie looked suddenly grave, taking Mat seriously and seeming much discomforted by the vision. For the life of her, she couldn't tell the difference between a ragging and serious conversation.

"Don't fret, Rose," Mat said. "I'm not going to hurt him so long as he promises not to lure all the men into a game of ghost or leapfrog while I'm walking down the aisle."

"By God, let's do it, Jack," Edgar said, smiling. "Let's have a game of leapfrog. Where's Richard? There must be three of us, or it's not a real contest."

Before long, Richard was called out and pressed into the game. Their shirts and shoes came off, and barefoot, in pants held up by suspenders over bare torsos, the men leaped until, breathless, sweating, and laughing, they collapsed in a huddle. Then Jack and Edgar wrestled on the lawn until their strength gave out, after which we all just lay there in the grass, looking up at the cloudless July blue sky, careless of what the darkies must have thought.

"I could lie here forever," Edgar said, staring skyward.

I turned to look at him and watched contentment fade from his face, and I imagined all the cares that beset him had returned suddenly. That was as close as I ever came to thinking him handsome, as he stared up into the sunshine, his thin bare chest glistening with sweat, expanding and contracting, but care had come into his eyes and mouth.

Don't marry *her*, I wanted to say, thinking of Mrs. Shelton, knowing he didn't love her. *Marry me*!

The thought came without premeditation or even a hint that such a notion was in my brain, and I was shocked by it. I turned away hurriedly, stared at the sky, my eyes wide with surprise. Perhaps the others talked; I couldn't hear and didn't look to see. I had thought of marriage, of course, but not to Edgar, but suddenly it seemed like such the perfect thing, such the perfect solution for both of us. My father was still alive; we were comfortably situated. Edgar could write without worrying about starting a new journal and making a living from it, a thing that seemed so futile. We could find a place for Sissy's mother to live. I could learn to love him; it might even be easy. Perhaps I loved him already and hadn't realized it, and perhaps he felt the same about me, but hadn't expressed it or acted on it, because of his commitment to Mrs. Shelton. Ah, but that was over now! It must be; I'd heard the rumors and had listened between the lines of what he'd said. I was seized suddenly by a gush of desire to care for him, to guard him from temptation and make him happy.

Mat shook my arm. "Are you coming?" she asked, then she perceived my alarm. "What's wrong, Suzie?"

The men were already walking up toward the house, carrying their shirts in their hands, and Rose followed close behind, dogging Edgar as always. Mat stood up and extended her hand to help me up. I tried to smile at her but couldn't. The expression on her face relaxed as if she suddenly perceived the source of my mood, and she knelt down beside where I lay. She rubbed my arm in a way that made me aware that in my whole life I don't think Mat had ever touched me. The uncharacteristic tenderness made me cry, alarming Mat even more. I tried to laugh through my tears, knowing Mat hated displays of emotion.

"It'll happen," she said. "Don't worry, Suzie. It'll happen to you too."

I knew what she implied, and without thinking I shook my head as if to tell her that *that* was not what I was crying about, but she took it the wrong way.

"It *will*. It *will*. I promise it will. You'll see."

"Edgar!" I blurted as if to convey to her that I was concerned for him, but not to betray any affection for him, but I couldn't finish my sentence.

"*No*, Suzie!" Mat said, seriously alarmed. "Not Edgar. Never. I love him too, but you mustn't in that way. Don't even think it. I won't let you. Don't you understand?"

I gave in and turned away from her, still unable to speak. In the end she had perceived everything as accurately as if I'd told her. Never mind that the idea had only just popped into my head moments before. That didn't matter. She took her hand away and lay down beside me, and for a time nothing was said. Mat knew that I must look at her to read her lips, so she waited patiently until I turned to her again, and she smiled sympathetically before speaking.

"I would never allow you to do that." She appeared to be whispering or merely mouthing her words. "I care too much for you. I care too much for both of you. You don't know that I worry about him, but I do, and I know deep down that *it is hopeless*. Don't ask me how I know; I just know. You would be lost and miserable. Put it out of your mind, Suzie. Promise me before we leave this spot that you will put it out of your mind."

I stared at Mat for the longest time, trying to read in her eyes why she said what she'd said about *it* being hopeless. I knew she was talking, not about a romance between Edger and me, but that *he* was hopeless, and I wanted to know why, but something told me that I really didn't want to know. It was as if Mat knew his fate, as if she could foretell the future. Of course she did and could. It explained why she never talked seriously, never went beneath the surface of things, was always joking and laughing, making light of everything, never the dreamy girl, all frills and hope. That wasn't Mat, and I understood this for the first time that noonday in the grass, lying beside her, just days before her wedding, just months before Edgar died. She could sense the future; she possessed a kind of wisdom that she spurned because it wasn't worth having, wasn't something to be wished for, and I knew that she was right; I never doubted it for an instant. How could it be that I had never known this about my own best friend? It was more of a surprise to me than had been my sudden gush of desire for Edgar.

How long had all that taken? Maybe five minutes. No more. Still Mat stared at me. She would have her answer before she let me up. I could see that. Nor would she relent for the rest of the week, through all the celebration. I caught her staring at me time and again. Even during the wedding ceremony, she turned to look at me, always the same admonishment in her eyes, and I acceded to her demand and forced myself to smile and seem happy when, in fact, I think my life had changed, and I don't overstate it. Life turns on ripples of small discovery, not crashing waves.

(ITEM 115: *Susan Archer Talley Weiss*)
...

October 13, 1895
6 North Park Street
Richmond, Virginia

Dear Eddy,

You ask about Virginia Poe. How I know what I know? My source was Jack Mackenzie who, better than anyone, would know. Edgar had been back in Richmond for several months after years away—then working for Mr. White at the *Southern Literary Messenger*. This was in the mid-1830s; Edgar was twenty-five or twenty-six. He and Jack picked up right where they had left off. They were both young bachelors—mischievous, fun-loving, often up to no good. Edgar's foster father, Mr. Allan, was dead by then, and I suppose Edgar felt somewhat liberated and comfortably home again. Jack told me that one afternoon he stopped by the *Messenger* office to see if Edgar wanted to go carousing that night. Edgar seemed distracted, but went anyway. After a few drinks, he confessed to Jack that he wasn't seeing Eliza White anymore, that he had broken the news to her that he intended to marry someone else. Jack was shocked. "Who?" he asked, and Edgar told him. Jack had never met Virginia, but he knew who she was and that she was his first cousin and only thirteen years of age. When he asked why repeatedly, Edgar replied repeatedly—"I have to!" Jack would not relent and badgered Edgar with reasons why he should not enter into such a marriage until finally Edgar blurted, "Jack, it's done already, that by a promise made before I left Baltimore. There's no going back."

Edgar had been courting Eliza White for months. She was the daughter of his employer, a lovely and loving girl of eighteen whose father had lost a son and had come to think of Edgar as that son. It would have been a wonderful match for all of them. But it appears a letter had come from Mrs. Clemm, saying that Virginia had become inconsolable by Edgar's departure from Baltimore and that she feared for Virginia's health. Edgar was devoted to his little cousin as he would have been to a younger sister, and his soft heart would not let him hurt her in any way. The promise may or may not have been in earnest. One can imagine such a promise to help wipe away tears on the eve of departure. I don't mean to say this is what happened, only that something as trivial as this may have constituted the "promise made" that Edgar felt bound by. I am quite certain that his promise was no more substantial than this. He couldn't bear Virginia's pain, so he did what he considered his duty, but in so doing, he became linked for life to someone who could not hope to be his intellectual equal or even care for him in the way in which a wife should care for a husband. Mrs. Clemm would provide much of that. In a perverse sense, Edgar married the both of them, knowing it was a grave mistake, and one can't help but think that his weak giving-in to life's inevitable temptations became his way of drowning the depression that quite naturally resulted from such a match. I recall, after Edgar's death, the Mackenzies lamenting his weakness—referring in particular to his weakness for spirits—when Jack intoned that Edgar's greatest weakness was his giving into Mrs. Clemm's persistent entreaties regarding Virginia, that Edgar's marriage was the greatest misfortune of his life, and that his little cousin had been a "millstone around his neck." Cruel as this may sound, I am certain it is the truth. This is not to say that he did not love Virginia, on the contrary, perhaps he cared too much for her, even for *her* own good, for by his own admission to Jack during his last visit to Richmond, his marriage "had not been a congenial one." Such a thing cuts both ways, I should think.

These things aside, I read in the tone of your letter of the 28th great enthusiasm for the information you have collected over the years pertaining to Edgar's life, but it seems this is coupled with a feeling of inadequacy regarding your writing skill. I believe I can offer you a bit of advice in this regard, for I had a marvelous writing lesson one morning from that selfsame individual—Edgar Poe. Who better to learn from? It was late in September of that summer when we became friends. He came over to Talavera for a visit as he often did. He'd resisted temptation for more than a month and appeared healthy and happy if somewhat preoccupied. I am quite certain that he had neither seen nor heard from Mrs. Shelton for more than a month at which time she had appeared at Duncan's Lodge with intentions of securing her letters to him. The exchange of letters was ultimately accomplished, ending for good the engagement that had linked them. It was raining that morning. I sat with my back to my desk on which were some magazines and a vase of tea roses. Edgar sat opposite, a table between us on which sat a bowl of grapes, his favorite fruit, and we picked them, popping them into our mouths, chatting amiably. He brushed back his hair with his hand, becoming more relaxed as time went by, when presently he asked about my method of composing poetry. Having no particular method, I told him that my compositions arose from inspiration as I assumed was the case with all poets. He smiled at this and told me that I reminded him of Fanny Osgood, a comparison that I accepted as high praise, knowing his great regard for her work. "She scribbles and scribbles, never with a plan and never with an intention of polishing a work. She has no patience for revision, though I tried to persuade her to do so, even showing her how she might improve a poem, using one of my own as an example. I've never truly finished a poem in my life. There's not one I've ever written that I wouldn't like to revise even now. Everything I've ever written can be improved upon, including 'The Raven'—most *especially* 'The Raven.'"

This surprised me. I couldn't imagine improving upon "The Raven" and told him so. "Do you have a copy," he asked, and I did, a copy I had written out for a friend, so I fetched it, and, at his request, read it to him. He closed his eyes and listened without expression until I got to the line: "Bird or beast upon the sculptured bust above my chamber door" to which I noticed a perceptible wince in his expression. I stopped reading, wishing for some explanation. "I must get rid of that line," he said, "for how can a beast occupy such a position?" I thought for a moment, then laughed out loud. "It could have been a mouse," I said at which he leaned back in his chair and laughed out loud. Edgar seldom laughed; he seldom even smiled such that he showed his teeth; therefore, I could not help but laugh also. "Suzie," he said at last, "how is it you are so easy to talk to? It seems you understand me. I think only Fanny understands me as well as you. And I have always believed that Fanny understands me better than anyone I've ever known. But you, too, and it is for this reason that I so value your company."

There followed an awkward moment, and I couldn't help but be reminded of that day in July when, for an instant, I had wished him to marry me. I had promised Mattie. What in the world would I do now if, in fact, he did propose marriage? So, to preclude that possibility, I resumed reading "The Raven," and Edgar continued to demonstrate the process of revision, making pencil notes on the manuscript at numerous points until we came to the one line that he declared hopeless—"And the lamplight o'er him streaming casts his shadow on the floor." He shook his head, genuinely dejected, and declared it a hopeless "tangle,"—a "knot"—apparent to all the world, a blunder that destroyed the whole poem, for how could there be a light "*above* the raven—*above* the bust of Pallas—*above* the chamber door?" He shook his head, disgust on his face, until he perceived the smile on mine.

"I know how," I replied—"The light came from the hall through a transom above the door."

Edgar's eyes grew large, and again he threw back his head and laughed. Then, spreading his arms as if in surrender or astonishment, he said, "Miss Talley, you *are extraordinary*! All the editors in New York City pale beside you. Henceforth and forevermore, I will not publish another poem until and unless you have undone all the knots and tangles. Will you consider yourself henceforth my editor-in-chief?"

A proposal of marriage it was not, but in our case, I suppose, it seemed at the time a far, far wiser engagement. I graciously and happily accepted, knowing full well that he was not really serious, but—serious or not—I would never have suspected that Edgar Allan Poe had already written his last poem.

On one of his last nights, we had a party at Talavera for Mat and Harry who had just returned from their honeymoon. Edgar was the last to leave. I was standing on the portico to wish him a goodnight. He walked a few paces then turned and lifted his hat to bid me adieu. Just at that moment, a brilliant meteor appeared in the sky directly above him then vanished in the east. I remembered that afterward with great sadness.

My still-young friend, I will wait to tell you more of my last day with Edgar when I see you here in Richmond. By so doing, I insure your coming soon, and I want to see you once more before I lose my memory altogether. Don't delay long, Eddy. I need not remind you that I am your sole surviving Poe correspondent, and despite seven years grace, I won't live forever. We still have much to talk about, and *you*—you!—have much work yet to do.

As always, with my sincerest affection,
Susan

Just after five in the morning the train arrived in Richmond, wrenching
to a halt with air brakes gasping exhaustion. The morning was overcast
and unseasonably cool for early June. I stepped down from the car, one
hand gripping my brown leather suitcase, the other fingering the top
button of my uniform jacket, searching for the buttonhole. The task
proved impossible, so I stopped, put down my suitcase, and buttoned
my jacket properly. Should I, I wondered, stop to ask directions for
a suitable place to bathe and shave or just make my way uptown and
find one to my liking? I decided on the latter. I could have used more
hours of sleep after the herky-jerky overnight from Raleigh. The train
seats were too cramped for lying down, and it was cold with all the
windows open. I had another such night in store, the price to pay for
a full day in Richmond, and momentarily I regretted leaving Charlotte
and our new baby a night earlier than was absolutely necessary. We
had christened her Sarah, a name chosen in part to honor Sarah Helen
Whitman. She was our second child, our second daughter.

Much as I had wanted for some years to have this day, I still wondered why I bothered going to the trouble. I was quite confident,
however, that when it was over I'd be glad I had. It might be the last
time I'd see Susan Weiss, and as I exited the station, I smiled thinking
this, an expression that belied the sorrow of it. How old was she? I
did the math, knowing well all the dates of birth—same as Virginia
Poe—1822. That meant Susan was seventy-four.

The morning air was damp; the gray cobbles still wet; only the birds
seemed to have the streets; then from off to my right I heard the plod-
ding hooves of a horse. Two bits for a bath, I was thinking; two more
for breakfast, another for a tip for guarding my suitcase until I got

back, and another for the streetcar out and back. That's all it should take. Susan would provide lunch. That would leave me four dollars and change. I already had my train ticket, so that would be enough to get me back to the Point. I spied a likely place across the street and halfway down a side street, but decided to go a bit farther, thinking this a seedy part of town.

I'd been home nearly a month, a leave long-planned. We had sold the farm and bought a frame house on Pinkney Street in downtown Whiteville, one block north of the courthouse square. I'd hired a team of workmen to add a second story, and that work had started before I left. My mother seemed quite happy with the arrangement, having grown weary of keeping up the farm, and she and Charlotte got along famously. Times were tough; there was a depression on, but I figured we could make it, what with my promotion to lieutenant colonel last fall and the money we got for the farm. We'd been lucky to find a buyer. In fact, finding a buyer had precipitated moving from West Point, but that had been our plan all along, albeit not so soon. I'd miss them, but they'd be okay. It was only for a few years. I had my twenty years in, and I was still a young man, but I figured I'd re-up for another tour or two then retire and live on my pension, fill the back yard up with kids, and maybe take up banking or write a book. The vision made me quite content. Charlotte would be a marvelous mother and teacher, no doubt about that. My only concern was how she would take to living in the South and how Whiteville would take to her, being, as she was, a tad independent-minded for a woman. I couldn't stifle a chuckle, thinking this. Charlotte's rebellious pluck was one of the things I loved most about her, but it was for certain it would get me in hot water one of these days—with the neighbors or the school board or the town council or the Masons or the Klan. There was no telling which, but it was sure to happen. I almost looked forward to it, thinking, as I did, that the time had come for the South to emerge from her torpor—a new century was approaching.

I found a respectable-looking boarding house and took a long nap-ping, soaking bath. No need to hurry; Susan didn't expect me until noon. After my bath I shaved, guiding my razor over still-rosy cheeks nearly devoid of whiskers. Only my chin and neck required care. I dried my face with a towel and brushed waxed fingertips into my mustache. Then I put on a clean shirt and my dress blues, having planned to look my best for Susan in the event this would, in fact, be our last encounter.

I took the streetcar out. Other patrons nodded, respecting the uniform, but one older man eyed me suspiciously as if he found the bluecoat offensive, so I asked him—addressing him as "Sir" and in an accent more Southern than my usual—which stop I should take for North Park Street. I knew already, but I didn't like being taken for a Yankee—not in Richmond, I didn't—or perhaps that wasn't it. Perhaps it was merely a friendly reminder that the old war was over. My question served the purpose, and the two of us chatted amiably all the way to my stop.

"Be brave," he said as I stepped down from the car.

I turned and smiled, snapping a salute as the streetcar pulled away, and I could see him look away, his mouth betraying what might have been remorse mixed with painful memories. I held my salute until the streetcar had gone a block or two. As I did, I couldn't help but wonder how many such men there must be in Richmond and all over the South, still guarding bitter memories. I recalled the bitterness on my own father's face, a bitterness that never went away. How many generations does it take to end a war?

I turned to a street lined with fine houses, shade trees, and neat gardens where bloomed magnolias and hydrangeas, white and blue, and a few late azaleas. The day had warmed, but I didn't want to remove my coat until Susan had seen me in it. I found number six, a yellow frame house, climbed the steps, and turned the bell. A black woman came to open the door, smiled, and led me to the living room.

"Mizz Weiss'll be right down," she said and left me there alone.

The room smelled of old books and mildew. Covering the floor was a faded green carpet of good quality, and in one corner was a round table covered with lace cloth and filled with framed photographs and a vase of white roses, their edges turning brown. I had just bent down to study one of the photographs when Susan entered. I turned to see her standing straight, her eyes glad and eager. It had been years, but she didn't appear as old as I'd expected.

"Mrs. Weiss," I said, coming to near-attention.

"Susan," she corrected, smiling. "How long has it been, Colonel Gayle—Eddy? Sixteen years?" She motioned me to a chair then took one herself but sat just on the edge as if she didn't intend to sit there long. "I'd wager," she continued, "that you've passed through Richmond at least sixteen times in sixteen years, not once stopping to see *an old friend*. I should be angry with you, but I'm not. How is your family?"

I told her all that had happened since my last letter—Sarah's birth, closing up housekeeping in West Point, the move to Whiteville. "My mother sends her regards," I said. "She always remembers your kindness."

"How good of her. I'll always remember your story about her and the Yankee captain. I think she and I would have a lot to talk about. I'll write to her and tell her about our great adventure together—our great, long-awaited adventure. Ella has packed a picnic for us, and James is harnessing the horse, so let's be off. No time to waste. We can chat on the way."

Susan did not seem her age at all, a marvel I thought. Perhaps she was right about those seven years. She required no assistance climbing aboard the gig. I asked permission to remove my coat, tossed it behind the seat with the picnic basket, and took the reins.

Susan wore a wide-brimmed straw hat and a blue printed dress. She was slender, still a fine figure of a woman, and with her gray hair up and covered, the two of us could have been a couple despite our thirty-two-year age difference. As we drove, I rolled the sleeves of the white shirt I wore under my wide, military suspenders. My navy uniform pants with wide red stripes covering the side seams were well pressed, and my black boots wore a high gloss. I had wanted Susan to be proud of me. The sun came out, and I pulled the bill of my cap lower to shade my eyes. From time to time Susan pointed, indicating a turn, and soon we were beyond town limits and on a road that paralleled the James River above the falls and ran west at first then northwest toward Charlottesville. Our destination was a place known as the Hermitage.

Along the way Susan explained that the plantation had been owned by a friend of her grandfather, Captain Archer, her mother's father, and that the two men had soldiered together in the War of 1812. She did not name the man, and I didn't interrupt to ask. Communication with Susan was best when face-to-face. The friend of her grandfather had died in 1830 and left the Hermitage to his son who professed to be a writer (though no one could ever remember anything he wrote) and who preferred to spend his time and money in Richmond, drinking and gambling and frequenting the brothels in an area along the wharfs known as the Rocketts. The story went that the young man was hijacked there one night by an English press gang and, wearing only his skivvies, was secreted aboard a ship, appropriately named *Ambuscade*. The ship set sail for the Falkland Islands before he could buy his freedom or effect his escape. Quite unexpectedly he took to the sea and traveled much of the world before returning to Richmond four years later only to find his affairs in such a ruinous state that he sold off his lands and returned to sea—this time as an officer aboard an American merchant ship—never to be heard from again. Legend had it, however, that he had made a fortune in blackbirding—kidnaping South Sea islanders and shipping them to work on plantations in Australia and South America, a cruel and vicious slave trade. With his fortune made, he settled on an island in Polynesia, surrounded by a lagoon and where vanilla trees grew wild and in such abundance that the air, so scented by the vanilla bean, acted as an aphrodisiac on the natives who thereby had become peaceful, lazy, and promiscuous. There this erstwhile, wayward Virginia planter with his ill-gotten fortune lived like a king, filling his grass bungalow with a harem of Polynesian slave-girls, purchased one-by-one for the price of a pig or machete.

I turned to see considerable amusement in Susan's expression as she told this last part. She was near to laughing at the tall tale.

"But more than one Richmond lad," she continued, "has been seduced by this legend and lured to sea." She explained that the Hermitage had gained a certain notoriety as a result. "Perhaps it's true. Perhaps it's pure nonsense. At any rate Edgar Poe never heard that story. I don't recall hearing it before the war, or maybe I did. I can't remember. But I am certain Edgar visited the Hermitage before its decline, because I recall how sad he was to see it in such a state of disrepair. I remember him talking about fun times there, though I don't imagine he visited it more than once or twice. I expect Jack Mackenzie took him there when they were boys or young men in their twenties. But I never knew the place to be anything but a ruin. I was too young. Edgar knew it in its heyday, but not me. We're coming up on it now. Here. Pull over here. We'll have to walk the rest of the way."

I did as Susan bade. South of us were woods that I guessed ran down to the river and to our right was a broad swale of tan clay ground, perhaps fifty acres, recently plowed but not yet planted. In its midst, on a rise a couple of hundred yards off the road, was a circular island of tall trees and thick undergrowth, littered with boulders, perhaps a hundred yards in diameter. Susan pointed to it.

"That's the Hermitage. Or what's left of it."

On impulse I looked down at Susan's feet, wondering if she wore boots under her skirt; it would be a muddy hike. She smiled and lifted her skirts to reveal well-worn riding boots.

"I came prepared," she said.

I laughed, marveling at her. She was better prepared than I. I'd be cleaning and polishing boots on the train that very night, but perhaps that's the price I had to pay for walking in legendary footsteps.

I fetched the picnic basket, handed it to Susan, and then unharnessed the horse, deciding we shouldn't leave him in the traces for as long as we might be. I pulled the bit out of his mouth, leaving the bridal as a halter, and, giving him plenty of scope to graze, tied him to the right rear wheel.

Grabbing my uniform coat and throwing it over my shoulder, I followed Susan up one of the ruts. The soil was clayey but not as wet as it appeared. Susan held her skirts above the ground until the land sloped up, and we entered upon a floor of leaves and pine straw. There she turned to face me.

"The day I came here with Edgar," she began, "we were on horseback, and we stopped about here before dismounting. The house was still standing then, so we walked our horses up to the porch." With this said, she turned and studied the circle of trees and brush. I could clearly discern the rubble of the fallen-in house—roof shingles, warped and rotting boards heaped on top of foundation bricks mostly covered with vines of Virginia Creeper.

Susan pointed to a dead tree. "That oak must have been alive then. Think, Eddy. How many years ago was it—1849?"

"It would be forty-seven," I said.

Susan smiled. "Forty-seven years come September—hard to believe—I stood on this very spot with Edgar Allan Poe."

There was nothing sad or sentimental in her voice, no hint of pride or bragging. It was a fact stated. Susan was so totally without guile that I felt a certain thrill for her just then. I shouldn't have waited so long to make this trip. She had been wanting to bring me here for years, and now I sensed how special that day forty-seven years ago must have been.

"Tell me everything, Susan. Every detail."

She smiled, savoring the opportunity, and took my arm to lead me up to the mound of rubble, all that remained of the grand old house that had once stood there. "I wish you could have seen it as it was then, not as grand as Duncan's Lodge, but imposing—a wide porch, two stories—inside, a small foyer with covered stairs on either side leading to a sort of great room above with a second-story porch from which the river must have been visible at one time. We didn't venture upstairs—Edgar and I—though we could have easily enough. The structure was still quite sound. Instead we went through the foyer into what might have been a small parlor or maybe a downstairs bedroom. I remember there was still a carpet on the floor—threadbare and mildewed—and wallpaper flaking off the walls, and a window seat but no window. I recall louvered shutters that pushed open into a recess beside the sill and thinking how well constructed the house had been. Edgar sat down on the window seat, and I remember that he pulled one of the shutters to see if it was still on its hinges. It worked despite ivy climbing through its louvers. The movement of the shutter pleased him but also made him sad, and he talked about the old days. I can also remember what he said—something about a place such as this being haunted—not by ghosts, but by sorrow. Yes, that's very clear to me. He was very sad that day. I think the leaves were beginning to turn, at least the dogwood leaves. It was early fall. We wandered through empty rooms then came back to that spot and again he sat on the window seat.

"What am I going to do, Suzie?" he asked. "I don't want to leave, but there's no reason to stay. I've thought of going to Baltimore and Philadelphia to raise money for *The Stylus*, but the truth is I've lost my energy for the thing. Perhaps I should just write, but I confess that, like you, I depend on inspiration, and I seem to have lost it. I couldn't be less inspired."

"They will publish whatever you write," I told him. "Your name sells magazines."

He laughed derisively. "I've heard that before," he said. "You don't understand, Suzie. My name is mud in the publishing world, and it's partially my own fault."

"What do you mean?" I asked.

"I was too critical of certain people. I should have stuck to stories and poems and left the reviews to others. I should have kept my opinions to myself. But at the time I didn't know how the game was played or that I was being used to fuel a controversy the purpose of which was to sell magazines. I was too naive to see the bigger picture. You don't understand, Suzie. How could you? Let me tell you something. In the publishing world one man stands above all the rest, and he has reason to hate me."

"Who?" I asked. "Griswold?"

Edgar laughed out loud and kept laughing, much amused. "Griswold," he said, "—him I owe fifty bucks. No, not Griswold, but that reminds me, I have debts all over New York City—Greeley, Halleck, Duyckinck, even Colton, and it was to him I sold the greatest poem I ever wrote for a mere fifteen dollars. Thank God there are no more debtors' prisons."

"Stop, Susan," I said, interrupting her. "Wait. What was it he said?" I grabbed her by her arm to make her face me squarely to read my lips. "What was it he said?"

Susan studied me, perplexed, her eyes darting back and forth, trying to think of what part I might be referring to.

"About 'one man,'" I reminded her.

"One man?" She thought back. "Do you mean 'one man stands above all the rest?' Was that it?"

"Is that exactly what he said?" I did not wait for an answer. I knew what she meant even if she didn't. I laughed out loud, and Susan smiled at my amusement but did not follow my train of thought. "Is that *precisely* what he said? Try and remember."

"I think so. Yes. 'In the publishing world one man stands above all the rest.' It was something like that. Why?"

"Longfellow!"

Susan stared at me, still perplexed. "Do you think he meant Longfellow?"

I turned from her to view the ruin of the once-proud house—rubbish, rotting in the sun in the middle of a field that would be knee-high in tobacco come July. Longfellow! Of course. That was the answer to the question that had brought me to this place. It had taken so long to get here—over twenty years—that I had almost forgotten my reason for starting this journey—the question that had led me to Helen Whitman's parlor the day I met Charlotte—*Why did Griswold crucify Poe?* I remembered now that Loui Shew had as much as told me, but at the time I didn't make the connection. Even Charlotte had sensed it, but in all those years, in all those letters, in all that had happened, I had almost forgotten the question. Now it came back, prompted by something Edgar Allan Poe said forty-seven years ago. How could I have been so stupid as to miss it?

Still Susan stared at me, not following my revelation.

"Don't you see, Susan? The man who stood above all the rest was Longfellow. Not Griswold. Of course not Griswold. Griswold was just doing what he was expected to do. Longfellow pulled the strings. I never told you this, because I never attached much significance to it, but Loui Shew told me that on Broadway one day she confronted Griswold about the tenor of his memoir, and he told her that 'it was done and that Longfellow had given his approval.' Do you see now? Poe was Longfellow's only rival for America's greatest poet, so upon his death, what better way for Longfellow to win than to destroy Poe's character. Not directly. It wasn't Longfellow's doing, not by his own pen that is. *That* was unnecessary; *that* would have been beneath him. And he probably never said a word to Griswold—probably gave no order. It wasn't necessary. He was the general. There were majors and captains who could give the orders. Probably Lowell was one of them. He and Griswold were friends, so I was told. Griswold was just carrying out orders, and he died of remorse for having done so—with Poe's portrait—and Fanny's—hanging on his bedroom wall."

The thing was clear to me, but perhaps not so clear to Susan.

"You miss the point, Eddy."

"What do you mean?" I asked.

"He was maligned because he was Southern. That's why he didn't fit the mold. That's why he never gained respect. That's why he was crucified by Griswold. He was Southern! He was one of us. That's why they all hated him—Griswold, Longfellow, the whole lot of them. You didn't live then. You can't know what it was like. We've always been looked down upon—the way we speak, our put-on manners. We're seen as inferior, weak-minded. It's always been that way."

I considered what Susan said. I didn't respond. She suggested that we have our picnic, and we ate in near silence. I was thankful then for Susan's deafness; I didn't want to argue with her. When the silence became awkward, I asked questions about the Hermitage, and for the remainder of the day avoided the subject of Edgar Poe. There were no longer any truths to learn there, only slants.

On the train north, I tried to give Susan the benefit of the doubt. But for the life of me I couldn't. Whatever led to the assassination of the character of Edgar Allan Poe—his being Southern, his drinking, his debts, his affair with Fanny Osgood, his vicious reviews of the work of Henry Wadsworth Longfellow—the defamation of his character had been a fait accompli—the work of some individual or some conspiracy. I imagined no concerted plan. Events had conveniently fallen into the hands of like-minded individuals. There had been no need to plot it, for by Poe's own carelessness, weakness, vulnerability, and death, he had played into their hands. If such was the case, of course, there would be no evidence. It wasn't exactly getting away with murder. Perhaps there were letters back and forth between New York and Boston, but surely they would have been destroyed. Perhaps others were involved—Lowell, I suspected, but he too was dead now—they were all dead. And, though Susan had unwittingly supplied the clue, it had turned out not to be the issue most dear to her. She wants Poe for Richmond and the South.

Enough of Poe. I think I'm Poed-out.

The motion of the train makes writing difficult, so with this written I will put away my pencil. The regular rhythm of the train wheels crossing ties makes me sleepy, and, though it isn't yet late, I think I'll try to get some shut-eye.

The night before the night I left Whiteville, Charlotte and I made love—the first time in our new home—and as I head north toward

Washington—away from her—I can't help but recall the smile on her face as I entered her. At first I feared I was hurting her and her smile, not a smile but a grimace. I asked, but she smiled more broadly and shook her head. How good it felt, how loved I felt, to bring her such pleasure. It will be Christmas before I see her again.

E. E. Gayle

(ITEM 120: *Charlotte Ayers*)

...

June 12, 1896
600 Pinkney Street
Whiteville, North Carolina

Dearest,

I have made a startling discovery. I cannot prove I'm right, but never have I been more certain. Do you recall Poe's poem, "To Helen"? Not the first one, but the one written to Helen Whitman—the one she wrote out and read to us the night of the séance in Providence—the one Cato scratched to pieces? I read it again tonight. As you know, I have been reading Eugene Didier's biography of Poe, and again I came across a fact that we have discussed—that Poe made two trips to Providence in 1845, in July and October, for the purpose of visiting Fanny Osgood. We both concluded that on the second visit he made love to her, leaving her with child.

There is *no record* of Poe having visited Providence again until 1848 when he went there to court Helen. I have checked Didier, Gill, and Ingram on this and find no record whatsoever of a trip to Providence between those years—'45 and '48. His whereabouts during this time are well documented. For most of '46 and the first half of '47 he never left Fordham except for brief, mostly day trips into New York City or to Brooklyn to visit Stella Lewis. What's more, there was no reason for him to go to Providence.

The poem, "To Helen," begins with these lines: "I saw thee once— once only—years ago: / I must <u>not</u> say how many—but <u>not</u> many. / It was a July midnight ..." The underlinings are Poe's, not mine. When could he have seen her on a *July* midnight before 1848, if not on his trip to visit Fanny there in July of 1845. And why "must" he *not* say "*how* many" years? Because saying would tell the tale? Certainly three years qualifies as "*not* many," wouldn't you agree?

Does it make any sense that he would have traveled to Providence for a clandestine rendezvous with one woman and fall in love with another on the same night, seeing her only indistinctly through "silvery-silken, sultry and slumbering" moonlight? I rather think not. It's quite clear that Fanny was the love of Poe's life; the evidence is all through the letters you've received and Mary Gove makes no bones about it. How could it be that just as his affair with Fanny was approaching crescendo that his head would be turned by such a midnight vision? He stayed at the City Hotel—the same place you stayed the night of the séance. It's highly unlikely that he would have spent the entire night with Fanny. For the sake of propriety she would have forbidden it, even if she were also staying at the hotel. Isn't it more likely that she was staying with her brother's family? Her daughters would have been with her. If their tryst occurred at night (and with young children how could it have been otherwise), it would have occurred relatively early—before midnight, and she would have returned to her children wherever they were staying. This is the only scenario that makes sense.

If the incident Poe writes of in "To Helen" really happened, he must have been wandering the streets of Providence by himself late that same night. Perhaps he couldn't sleep. Perhaps he was love-struck, or he might have been filled with remorse for his infidelity. I rather think love-struck in light of the sentiments expressed in the poem.

At any rate, my point is this: if, indeed, he *did* see Helen wandering in her rose garden in a white dress on a moonlit midnight, he wasn't thinking of her. Rather he was being reminded by the *vision* of her of the woman who had just left his bed—*Fanny*!

I think this must have been what happened, even if he didn't write the poem until 1848 when he was courting Helen. He was conveniently transferring the yearning he had earlier felt for Fanny to Helen, and she bought it. It was calculated to help win her—surely you understand the effect of love poems on women, Eddy Gayle, despite the fact that you have never written one to me! And you and I both know that Poe was not above taking an old love poem, dusting it off, changing the title, and sending it forth to a new love. He did just that with the poem "To Mary" which he wrote to Mary Starr then later renamed,

"To F——," for Fanny. Perhaps "To Helen" was not even a new poem but one he hadn't published—one he had earlier sent to Fanny. You men are incorrigible!

Reading "To Helen" the night of the séance in order to invite the spirit of Edgar Allan Poe was tantamount to inviting the truth of the poem, and Cato's disdainful treatment of it was tantamount to Poe revealing to Helen that the sentiments of the poem were meant for someone else. Poor Helen! I think this is what she inferred; she might even have deduced the hidden fallacy of the poem—that it had been conceived in Providence while under the spell of Fanny. I think this is what put her to bed for days afterward, not the blackmail, and you're probably right that Griswold was being blackmailed by someone who knew him to be a . . . a what?—a Nancy-boy! I know another word for it but cannot bring myself to say it. The word is awful, cruel, and intolerant. Could it possibly be that Stella Lewis was right, that Griswold was in love with Poe? No!—makes no sense—never did. Or does it? Yes, it could explain Poe's portrait hanging in his bedroom, but that seems so absurd to me. I suppose stranger things have happened. But Poe could not have been the blackmailer, unless he tried and failed, and I think such a thing as blackmail was beneath him. Certainly there is no evidence of his ever being the beneficiary of an ill-gotten windfall—cash or otherwise. So who was blackmailing Griswold and what did they gain from him?

I have to tell you, my darling, just to unburden myself, that I cannot bring myself to label "sinful" such affinities as Griswold may have borne in terms of his affections. I have long struggled with this; react as you will; call me "radical" if you must. Why would a man (or a woman) *elect* such a thing *voluntarily*; it makes no sense. I think they do it for reasons over which they have no power to rule, and, if this is the case, how can it be sinful? Think about it. I ask you, are there people perverse enough to murder for no reason whatsoever? The answer is,— only those who suffer hopeless insanity. Even the most contemptible of murderers has some reason for his crime, albeit unjustified—a reason that can be deduced—jealousy, envy, anger, avarice, revenge, starvation, survival, lust—lust for any number of things. But why would someone elect to love someone of his or her own sex. Where is the gain? Are they all hopelessly insane? And if so, is insanity a sin? There is no Commandment against it, though we know from the story of Sodom and Gomorrah that such a thing existed in biblical times, so why did God not command: "Thou shalt neither covet thy neighbor's wife nor thy neighbor, himself?" I am quite certain you will respond to this diatribe by quoting scriptural verses of which I'm unaware. I am forever amazed at the facility with which you Southerners quote the Bible. Sometimes I think Southern children who failed to memorize it cover to cover must have had their heads pinched off. I can only be thankful that at least *you* are not "*religious*" about it; I can't say that for your mother, though I love her nonetheless. This much I promise you, Edward Edgerly Gayle, our daughters will have liberal educations— they will have minds of their own and not be ventriloquists' dummies.

But to return,—when the séance was over, Helen pointed you to the blackmail to point you *away* from the message that was more significant to her—devastating to her, in fact! Don't you see? Cato's abominable treatment of the poem had nothing to do with the dreams or visions that visited Walter and me. There were two messages conveyed that night: one, in answer to the question that you and Helen wished to pose regarding what was between Griswold and Poe that led to Griswold's awful memoir, and the other—uninvited (and cruel I might add)—to tell Helen that he had never loved her, that it was Fanny he loved. But perhaps also, to be *overly* generous, Poe's spirit would not have revealed the second message had Helen not read "To Helen." Could it be that spirits *must* tell the truth? This, at any rate, is the *only* reason I would forgive him for such a dastardly act. And poor Cato; I hope the constable didn't drown him.

The answer to the first question remains a mystery, but I can't help but think that we are close.

Have you ever wondered why and don't you think it strange that Helen never revealed her own experience during the séance? Of course we'll never know, but I can tell you this—she was never the same after that night. She all but abandoned her correspondence with Ingram; she wanted nothing more to do with Edgar Allan Poe. When I asked her if she planned to write to Ingram again, she remarked that she was "already ankle-deep in asphodels" and had not time left in her life to argue with John Ingram again.

Oh, Eddy, I am certain I'm right. I've written out a copy of "To

Helen" for you in the event that your books don't contain the poem, and I must know at once what you think? I can't believe that it has taken more than twenty years to get to the bottom of this. Of course, implicit in all, is that the spirit of Edgar Poe really did—what is the word?—"possess" the body of Cato. That in itself defies belief. I'm so excited. Please write me at once and don't say I'm daft, because you know I'm not.

Your loving, devoted, and remarkably clever wife,
Charlotte

P.S. Grace is an angel—most of the time—but she hasn't yet decided if she's happy having a younger sister. Sarah is still not sleeping through the night, and if the carpenters don't hurry up and finish, I'm certain I'll go mad. Were it not for your mother, I could never survive mother-hood. She is well. We send our love. Please give Phyllis and Hugh my best. Tell Phyllis that I'm aware I owe her a letter and that I'll write soon. Kisses.

(ITEM 122: *Charlotte Ayers*)
...

June 25, 1896
600 Pinkney Street
Whiteville, North Carolina

Dearest,

What could have possibly happened with Susan to discourage you? I am very distressed to hear you say this. You haven't told me a thing about your visit, and I was eager for a full report. This is so unlike you. Nor did your letter say one word about my revelation regarding "To Helen," and I'm left to think that you've either concluded that it holds no water or that you're just not interested. What happened? Please tell me. I'm certain it could not have been as bad as all that.

I wish you had not left your mother and me in charge of this con-struction. Every day there are scores of little details that require a decision, and I have no idea if we are making the right ones or not. The staircase must cut in front of the transom above your mother's bedroom door—either that or the bottom step is too close to the entrance to the front hall. This is only the most frustrating one. Since her transom opens into the bedroom, she will still be able to open it, but the question remains, will it provide any ventilation? We've considered every alternative, but there just isn't one that's acceptable. Your mother said we should go ahead and block the transom, but I know she's not happy about it. I suggested she take one of the new bedrooms upstairs, but she won't hear of it. She's being a trooper, Eddy, but this is wearing us both down. The pitch of the roof was too flat, so we raised it. I know it will cost a pretty penny, but at least it gives more height to the attic and much improves the appearance of the house from the street. I can only hope that your bonus for re-enlisting comes through quickly, or we'll have to go to the bank to increase the amount of the mortgage. What else can we do?

Did Hugh make colonel? You haven't told me. And what are your new quarters like? What view do you have? I miss West Point. I miss New England summers. It's hot as the blazes here, and it seems nothing ever completely dries out. I put sheets out to dry and hours later they're still as damp as they were when I hung them. I'm coming to know what it's like to live in a swamp. I'm not complaining; I'm merely stating fact.

Now please write to me at once and tell me everything that happened in Richmond with Susan. It's mean of you to hold out on me like this. And tell me what you make of my letter about "To Helen." The girls are fine as is your mother. The Highs are back in town, returning from two months visiting their daughter in Raleigh, and they are very nice. Your mother is thrilled to have them next door, and Mr. High has kindly offered to consult on all our construction issues. I'll write more in a day or two. Sarah slept through the night last night— bless her precious little heart. We all send kisses.

All my love,
Charlotte

Afterword

::

The journal of Edward Edgerly Gayle does not end with the entry made on June 9, 1896, the day he visited the Hermitage with Susan Weiss. He kept it up, more or less faithfully, until his retirement from the army in 1909, but, fascinating though it is, never again—in entries made for another thirteen years—is there mention of the name, Edgar Allan Poe.

At four foot eight inches tall, Edward Edgerly Gayle was the shortest man ever to attend the United States Military Academy at West Point, New York. He served at a time when advancement in rank was painfully slow, and in one letter to Susan Weiss he laments the fact that he never saw action. She responded that he should not regret such a thing, but one suspects he did. He served a dozen years out west during the Indian Wars followed by ten years back at the Point as an artillery instructor and wrestling coach, then five years in Cuba, but not until just after the Spanish American war ended, then three years in the Philippines, along with stints at posts in California, Wyoming, Montana, Kansas, Vermont, and Maine. In his memoir, General John J. Pershing affectionately recalls that at his graduation he received a warm smile and a wink from "Little Eddy Gayle."

In his thirty-seventh year he married Charlotte Bartlett Ayers whom he had met fifteen years earlier in Providence, Rhode Island, the night of the séance at Sarah Helen Whitman's. After the wedding the couple resided for a time at West Point where Charlotte gave birth to their first daughter, Grace. In the summer of 1896 he moved his family to Whiteville, North Carolina. A second daughter, Sarah, was born in 1898, and in 1901 Charlotte died giving birth to the Gayle's third daughter, Kate. At the time Colonel Gayle was stationed in Havana. He returned home for a belated memorial service and after thirty days leave, left his daughters in his mother's care, though she was now in her seventies. When Mary Jane Gayle, whose good looks and defiant spirit had so charmed a Yankee cavalry officer during the Civil War, died in 1907, Colonel Gayle prevailed upon his sister, Dixie, now a widow, to move in with her six children, one of whom had been named for him, Edward Gayle Burkhead. Thereafter, Dixie Gayle Burkhead raised nine children, including the colonel's three daughters with the help of Annie Mae, who had been born a slave on the Gayle farm. Assisting her also were letters from Colonel Gayle filled with lists of books to be read by the children, instructions for their music and art lessons, household chores, hours to be set aside for schoolwork, hours to be set aside for singing and poetry recitation, horseback riding instruction, proper maintenance of tools, harness, the gig, and the necessary care and feeding of the family horse, strict accounting for weekly allowance, regular Sunday school and church attendance, instructions on how to make a bed properly, and in what order nightshirts and nightgowns should be hung on the pegs in the boys' and girls' bedrooms.

Needless to say, the Gayle sisters grew up seeing little of their father until his retirement from the army in 1909, having served thirty-seven years from the day of his appointment to the Academy. By that time his oldest, Grace, was fifteen, Sarah, thirteen, and Kate, eleven, and remaining in the household was their Aunt Dixie whose own children were now grown and gone. Nine years later, on a trip to Washington D.C., on a matter regarding his pension, Eddy Gayle died of pneumonia at the Ebbitt House Hotel at the age of sixty-four. He was buried with full military honors in Arlington National Cemetery.

Grace married an attorney from nearby Elizabethtown where she lived until her death in 1982, and Sarah remained in Whiteville, married an insurance agent, and lived until 1986. Kate never married. She taught school at Whiteville Elementary for fifty years and survived to age ninety-six, having lived all her life in the same house on Pinkney Street.

The Gayle sisters (as, in Whiteville, they are still remembered) were small women, though all three were taller than their father. There survives a sepia-tinted photograph of them taken in June of 1916, the month of Grace's marriage to Clarke Chatham. In age, the sisters were each exactly three years apart, and when the photograph was taken, Grace had just turned twenty-two, Sarah was eighteen, going on nineteen, and Kate was sixteen. The background, a studio backdrop, is an indistinct landscape looking more English than Carolina Bay country. Taken from the waist up, all three wear white organza blouses trimmed with tucks or lace and buttoned to the neck. Their postures are erect; their hair which looks to be light brown is done up in Gibson-girl fashion; and they are all beautiful. Their eyes are eager, their lips are narrow, but their mouths are pleasantly formed. They are not smiling, but one senses all three will break out laughing as soon as the flash powder ignites. None are looking at the camera. All three are looking at someone standing beside the photographer. Was it their father? None of them are wearing earrings; the only jewel is a small pin worn by Sarah. It had been a gift to Charlotte Ayers from Sarah Helen Whitman. Grace was the tallest and was always considered the most beautiful. Kate was the shortest, and Sarah was said to be the brightest by her sisters, but they were all bright, well educated, proper, and quite remarkable.

Such are the broad strokes of the life of a boy who became a soldier and of his wife and daughters and of the journal and letters he spent nearly a lifetime collecting. Perhaps his daughters had noticed the item numbers carefully written in the lower left hand corner of each envelop, the key to the colonel's system of organization, but if they did, they made no mention of it. Only Kate had read more than a few of the letters, and even she read only a small fraction of the one hundred and forty-one letters in the collection. Did illegible handwriting stop her or tedium or her own pursuits? Or did Kate fail to share her father's fascination?

The rest of what we know of Colonel Edward Edgerly Gayle comes in dribs and drabs from comments made about things he wrote in letters that are lost, written to people of little consequence but for one singular thing: they had all known Edgar Allan Poe. And in their telling of what they knew of him, they told their own stories just as Eddy Gayle must have told them his. He must have had the gift of gab, for he apparently had a knack for befriending even the most reluctant correspondent. The letters he received give ample evidence of this. Often the subject of the letters wanders away from the track and into day-to-day inquiry and concern for this little soldier whom they all admired, perhaps even loved. For his part, he sought to know about one life, instead he came to know nine others which were in many ways more interesting than the one he sought, and the apparent pleasure he took in these friendships must have been richly rewarding.

It is impossible to know precisely why Colonel Gayle abandoned his intention to write a book about Edgar Allan Poe. One can only speculate. Perhaps his daughters were right, that other writers "stole a march" on him. In 1902 George Woodberry published a thorough and extensively researched life of Poe that remained the definitive biography for forty years. It is probable that Eddy Gayle read it, and, if he did, he would have found it riddled with small inaccuracies. One can't help but suspect, however, that he had abandoned the project years earlier, perhaps the day he visited the Hermitage with Susan Weiss in 1896. He and Mrs. Weiss continued to correspond, though rarely. Those letters survive. They are newsy and cordial, but they contain nothing of consequence regarding Poe. The last one—the last mention of the name Edgar Allan Poe in all of Eddy Gayle's letters and papers—was received just a year before his death.

(ITEM 141: *Stuart Archer Weiss*)

...

3216 West Marshall Street
Richmond, Virginia
June 14, 1917

Dear Col. Gayle,

In response to your letter of April 5th to Mrs. Louis Weiss, I regret to inform you that my mother died on April 7th. Forgive me for not writing sooner, as I infer from your letter that you and Mother were old friends. Had I known of this, of course, I would have written sooner. Despite her ninety-six years, Mother's death was quite sudden and unexpected, and only recently have I had an opportunity to begin going through her papers and letters (the volume of which would overwhelm the Library of Congress). Only yesterday did I find your letter. It was unopened.

I confess to being curious regarding your correspondence with my mother, inferring from your letter that it had something to do with Edgar Allan Poe. I wonder if you know that in this city for more years than most of us can count, Susan Archer Talley Weiss was the foremost authority on Richmond's two most notable titles—namely, the Capital of the Confederacy and the childhood home of Edgar Allan Poe. As you are from nearby North Carolina, I need not tell you that resentments die hard, particularly regarding the struggles our region has endured for the past fifty years, but insofar as this is concerned, Mother remained above the fray. With humor in her voice, she inevitably referred to the War Between the States—even after all these years—as "the recent unpleasantness." She was above petty resentments and utterly without bitterness for all that befell her in her long lifetime, from her total loss of hearing at the age of nine to her imprisonment in Fort McHenry in Baltimore during the Civil War—the only woman among thousands of Confederate soldiers. Even to this day, I hear men who were incarcerated with her extol her remarkable courage, indomitable spirit, and unshakable self-assurance. She became the "grand old lady" of Richmond, and her death was universally mourned, but now I think I begin to sound like a too-boastful son, so forgive me this also.

Be aware that your long friendship with my mother makes you special to me as well, and if I may serve you in any capacity, such would be my honor and pleasure. I look forward to that opportunity should it arise.

Yours most sincerely,
Stuart A. Weiss, Esq.

:: DID EDDY GAYLE LOSE HIS TASTE FOR A BOOK about Poe as a result of revelations uncovered on his visit to the Hermitage with Susan Weiss, namely that Henry Wadsworth Longfellow had been ultimately responsible for the defamation of Edgar Allan Poe? Did he recoil from the notion of besmirching the name of America's most beloved poet? Or did he think the thread of evidence too tenuous and impossible to prove? Or did he think the whole thing too implausible? Or was he just too busy, first with his career and later with raising teenage girls and finding the means for their education on a rather meager military pension? Or did all these things and an early death preclude what might have been the work of a lifetime? It is more likely that he had promises to honor, promises to friends willing to share in confidence their memories of Poe.

Treasures often come in the most unexpected packages, like a blue-and-white checked pillowcase. When it arrived at Special Collections in the Jackson Library on the campus of the University of North Carolina at Greensboro in July 1996, it drew curious attention. When the archivist read the first letter, the oldest postdate, to a casual assembly of librarians and graduate assistants, eyes widened, jaws dropped. Here, indeed, was treasure.

Acknowledgments

::

The Poe Letters is a work of fiction. Everything herein—letters, journal entries, and narratives—are my own creation. They are, however, based closely on the records left by the nine women who make up the nine chapters of this book. These women were very real. Though they may have been controversial or given to self-serving exaggeration, I accepted their versions of events at face value, filling in the gaps using my own imagination based on extensive reading of original documents and the vast historical and biographical record of Edgar Allan Poe.

The journal entry entitled "March 1865" was inspired by the odyssey of Corporal James Pike. Accompanied by two fellow soldiers and dressed in the uniform of a Union cavalry officer, Pike was entrusted with a dispatch from General William Tecumseh Sherman to General John Schofield. At the time, Sherman's army was encamped four miles west of Laurinburg, North Carolina. Schofield was in Wilmington, a hundred miles away. The dispatch ordered Schofield to move his army by train to Goldsboro, there to join forces with Sherman for a final confrontation with the army of Confederate General Joseph Johnston. A direct route from Laurinburg to Wilmington would have taken Corporal Pike near Whiteville as described.

The séance at Sarah Helen Whitman's house was my own invention, but Whitman was, indeed, a spiritualist who engaged in séances with such enthusiasm that she arranged for a photograph of herself conducting a séance. The cover photograph of her is genuine.

In one critical instance, I quoted Marie Louise Shew Houghton verbatim, as I deemed it necessary in light of the book's contention that Henry Wadsworth Longfellow was involved in a plot to destroy Poe's character by way of the biography written by Rufus Wilmot Griswold. In a letter to John Henry Ingram, Poe's biographer, Mrs. Houghton wrote that she met Griswold on Broadway in New York City one day, and, knowing he was preparing the biography, asked him to be kind to Poe. She goes on to state that he responded by saying the work was finished and that Longfellow had given his approval.

To think that Longfellow had read Griswold's biography before it was published and gave it his approval is nothing less than stunning. There was certainly no love in Boston for Poe, and Poe must bear responsibility for that. In reviews he had often been unkind to Longfellow's poetry. He had belittled the "Frogpondians"—his term for all Bostonian intellectuals. And he had ridiculed Boston by delivering a nonsensical, juvenile poem to an august assembly there after which he proceeded to get drunk. This notwithstanding, if Longfellow did conspire to slander Poe after his death, what else can we conclude but that his lust for the honor of being called American's greatest poet would tolerate no rival, living or dead.

I have no evidence of this charge against Longfellow other than the word of Loui Shew. Ingram decided she was unreliable, but I found her refreshingly honest. She was a strong-willed, intelligent, and generous woman who had nothing whatsoever to gain by coming forward with her story. She had experienced no romantic attachment to Poe, hence no vanity to be soothed by the redemption of his reputation. She did not even read his stories and poems. Furthermore, it is known that Griswold had a close working relationship with many in Boston, including Longfellow and James Russell Lowell. Griswold and Longfellow exchanged letters, and some survive. The charge is entirely plausible.

On the other hand, the implication that Griswold was being blackmailed into doing the deed was my own invention in order to provide him with a reason for doing Boston's bidding. I have come across no evidence that he was gay; although, several close relationships, including his marriages, suggest some sexual peccadillo. He was a prolific anthologist and well respected by many. He was very kind to poet Frances Osgood in her last year. Osgood's husband, Samuel, could not bring himself to tell his wife that she was dying and asked Griswold to do it in his place. It is true that Griswold died in his bedroom in his New York City apartment on the walls of which hung portraits of Poe and Osgood, both painted by her husband. Today both portraits are in the collection of the New-York Historical Society.

In order to present these narratives, I required some device to bind them together. This came in the form of my great-great uncle, Edward E. Gayle and the correspondence I imagined. He was, indeed, the shortest man to ever attend West Point and other things stated about him are true. A wonderful sense of humor is apparent from the few letters and documents of his that have come down to me. In the Poe context presented here, however, he is purely fictional, as are Grace, Sarah, and Kate. They were his nieces, the daughters of his sister, Dixie Gayle Burkhead. Kate Burkhead was my grandmother, and as a child, I often visited her home on Pinkney Street in Whiteville, and my memories of it are vivid. The house still stands. Eddy Gayle's wife was not "Charlotte," but "Mary" Bartlett Ayers. I wrote this book several years ago, and I cannot recall why I changed her name. Lastly, I am not, nor have I ever been, a college professor.

John May
Santlache
Chapel Hill, NC
Saturday, June 14, 2014

www.ingramcontent.com/pod-product-compliance
Lightning Source LLC
Chambersburg PA
CBHW070043030726
47506CB00002B/318